By the Author

Business of the Heart

We Met in a Bar

Visit us at www.boldstrokesbooks.com

WE MET IN A BAR

by

Claire Forsythe

2023

WE MET IN A BAR

ISBN 13: 978-1-63679-521-8

THIS TRADE PAPERBACK ORIGINAL IS PUBLISHED BY
BOLD STROKES BOOKS, INC.
P.O. BOX 249
VALLEY FALLS, NY 12185

FIRST EDITION: OCTOBER 2023

CREDITS
EDITOR: JENNY HARMON
PRODUCTION DESIGN: STACIA SEAMAN
COVER DESIGN BY INKSPIRAL DESIGN

Acknowledgments

My second book. Yay! I had always wanted to write a book, but after I did that, I realized that I wanted to write more. So I'm very happy to be getting my second novel out into the world—I really hope you enjoy reading it as much as I enjoyed writing it.

When I wrote my first book, it was during lockdown, so I had a lot of free time on my hands. This time round was very different, mainly because of the arrival of my baby boy. Free time? What is that? Yeah, life is different now, but in the very best way. I have the sweetest son, who I love to the moon and back.

I did, however, need some help to get the time to write this, so I have a few people to thank.

My partner, Mary. There's so much, where do I start? I'll just say thank you for everything. I'm very lucky to have you, and your constant support means more than you know. That sleep deprivation was fun, huh?

My mum (who, thankfully, is nothing like the mother in this book). I can't even begin to thank you for all that you do for me. From babysitting so I could write, to feeding me when I forgot to eat. You already know how much I appreciate you, but I still like to remind you that you're the best.

Dad, don't worry, I haven't forgotten that you put the shifts in too. What would I do without you? I'm blessed to have such an amazing family. I love you all.

Next, a big extra special thanks to my friend Paula, who went above and beyond to help me do this. I couldn't have got this book written without everything you did. You have no idea how much I appreciate it. And my friend Geraldine, for all your help too—and for lending me your wife so often.

My friend Becks. For your daily check-ins to make sure I was both working and okay. And for understanding when I forgot to reply for hours.

Shout-outs to all the people whose support and encouragement I am so grateful for. My sister Kerry. Auntie Nicola. My good friends. Ellie. Jenna. Jenny. Alyson. Thank you.

Thank you to everyone at BSB who has made my dream of writing become a reality. Everyone's so lovely and helpful, and I feel so lucky to be a part of the BSB family. My editor, Jenny Harmon, a huge thank you for all your help, guidance, and patience. For teaching me so much about writing, and for putting up with all my local idioms.

And finally, to you, reader. The fact that you are taking the time to read my book means everything to me. I really hope you like it.

For my partner, Mary, whose support is endless.
I'm very lucky. Thank you.
All my love x

CHAPTER ONE

The arrival of the appetisers allowed Erica to sneak a quick glance at her watch. She wished she hadn't bothered. Only forty minutes had passed during what was turning out to be one of the most boring dates she had ever been on in her life—and that was saying something. With the snoozers she had been on lately, the competition was fierce for that top spot of monotony. Her current date was shaping up to be a serious contender.

Erica smiled politely and thanked the waiter, then dragged her attention back to Victoria Barrett, who didn't seem to stop for breath from atop her soapbox, nor did she stop to utter a simple *thank you* to the waiter herself.

So far, Victoria hadn't bothered to ask Erica anything about herself, and Erica's only contribution to the conversation had been to give a few *hmms* and *ahs* in the right places. She wasn't going to fight to speak, and that would have been the only way possible for her to get a word in. At least her lack of actual involvement in the conversation gave Erica a chance to appraise the woman in front of her.

She estimated that Victoria was ten years older than her—putting Victoria around forty-five—and it was clear that she spent a lot of time, effort, and most likely money, looking after her appearance. She looked fantastic, which, let's face it, was what had led Erica to agree to the date in the first place, shallow as that might be. Victoria's long, dark hair was perfectly blown out, likely by a stylist that day. Her skin looked seamless, as if she had also managed to fit in a facial as well as a trip to the hairdresser. Probably Botox. Her fingernails were perfectly manicured, Erica also noted, as she watched Victoria reach for her glass of champagne with long, dainty fingers, while she was still harping on about some gossip that Erica wasn't giving much attention to. Erica hoped she at least looked like she was listening. It wasn't that she was being rude on purpose—but there was only so much ego Erica could take being thrown in her face at one time, and Victoria was all ego. Erica was used to women like Victoria. She was surrounded by them. Hell, most people would probably put her in the same category, especially if they didn't know her.

Erica got a flash of perfectly straight, white teeth as Victoria laughed at her own comment—not for the first time—before politely sipping from her glass. Yes, Victoria was utterly self-involved, but she was also very easy on the eye. She was exactly Erica's type. Distinguished, successful, well-groomed, and gorgeous. It was the type she had always gone for. The type that her mother had drilled into her to date. Unfortunately, as much as she appreciated all those redeeming qualities—because she absolutely did—her type also usually tended to be, well, dull company. Victoria, for instance, was incredibly full of her own self-importance and only wanted to talk about things like money, social standing, her high-powered job as a barrister, and tedious gossip about the other women in the same social circles. Social circles which Erica found herself to be a part of, by choice or not, she wasn't even sure herself. It was just the world she lived in. What she'd always known. And she was fine with that. Erica had a good life, and she was thankful.

Victoria was also the daughter of one of her mother's friends, therefore she already had the stamp of approval from the formidable Gloria Frost. That mattered to Erica, and she hated that it did.

"And that's when I said, Audrey, darling, you pick the woman who can provide you with the best things in life. Wouldn't you agree, Erica?" Victoria asked, finally looking for her opinion on something. No, opinion wasn't the right word. Women like Victoria only looked for agreement and the knowledge that whoever was in their company was hanging on their every word. Erica had dated enough of these kinds of women to know what they wanted from her, and she was fluent in agreeable.

She blinked a few times to try and regain her focus on the conversation after she had become distracted while giving Victoria the once-over. She forced a smile, which she knew made it appear like she had been listening to Victoria the whole time. She had that look well-rehearsed. Something about Audrey and who she was dating. She'd caught bits.

"Absolutely," she said enthusiastically with a nod of her head. That seemed to appease Victoria.

Erica hadn't been surprised to learn that Audrey was a mutual acquaintance of theirs, nor was she surprised that Victoria seemed to be unashamedly interested in Audrey's personal life. In their social circle, everyone seemed to know one another, or at least know *of* one another, and they liked to talk about things that were almost always none of their business. Tedious gossip. Audrey was clearly the latest victim of the unnecessary but inevitable scrutiny. She wondered how Audrey was holding up, no doubt aware that she was this week's hot topic. Erica·had been there herself and she personally hated the whispers and unwanted focus, but she had grown a thick skin. Audrey had never struck her as someone who craved the limelight either. Any time Erica had been in her company she had been reasonably quiet and inconspicuous, and well, nice. Erica wouldn't class her as one of the gossips anyway. She hoped she was okay. A breakup was never easy, let alone when everyone felt like they had the right to offer up their opinions on it, like Victoria here.

"I'm so glad you get it, Erica. I simply would have died if she had decided to pursue the waitress. I'm sure they had their fun, which is fine for a short time, if you're discreet about it, but Lydia is a much better fit for Audrey. Lydia runs her own law firm for crying out loud. She must make thirty times the amount of money that waitress does, at the very least. Audrey should be grateful that she's interested. And it's not like Audrey could ever have brought the waitress along to any of our events, could you imagine how outrageous that would have been?" Victoria said, laughing bitterly. "She would have stood out like a sore thumb. She probably would have been on the catering staff anyway."

Erica watched as Victoria lifted a tiny forkful of salad to her mouth, making her re-evaluate what she considered to be her own normal-sized mouthfuls, which were already small just as her mother had taught her from the moment that she was old enough to hold a fork. Etiquette was everything after all. She discreetly let half of a cherry tomato drop from her fork back onto her plate before taking another, humbler mouthful that she barely even had to chew. She hummed her agreement to Victoria after she swallowed her miniscule bite.

Did Erica really agree with what Victoria was saying? She knew her mother certainly would. Most of her friends would. But did she? If this waitress, who apparently Victoria didn't think was important enough to mention by name, was the one who made Audrey truly happy, did it matter what she did for a living? Or how much money she had? Of course, Erica never dared to pose such questions out loud. Just because she didn't think the pairing was the end of the world, not ideal perhaps, but not taboo either, she knew that she was in the minority with that opinion in most company she kept.

On the other hand, she knew that she could never become involved in such a union, as snobbish as that sounded. She almost laughed out loud when she pictured what her mother's face would look like. It would probably equate to the face she had made when Erica told her that she was a lesbian. Now, that information had gone down like a lead balloon. Erica was surprised that she hadn't been shunned from the family when she dropped that bombshell. Thankfully, it had gone in her favour that her mother knew a few successful and wealthy lesbians. So, despite some initial distaste, she had slowly managed to begrudgingly come to terms with it. Distaste being a nice way of saying monumental meltdown. Surprisingly, the other ladies in Gloria's inner circle didn't seem to have an issue with it, and that had also helped Erica secure her mother's reluctant acceptance. However, along with acceptance came opinions. And Erica's mother made her opinions very clear on the type of women that Erica should date. And Erica complied. Did that make her seem a little bit under the thumb? Perhaps. But it made life so much easier when she did what her mother expected of her. After all, Gloria Frost had given her a lifestyle many women could only dream of. The least Erica could do was find a suitable partner whom her mother approved of. Victoria was a prime example of that.

"And how is business going for you?" Victoria asked. Finally, a question about Erica. Even if it was only to pry about the important things. Money.

She dabbed the corner of her mouth with the linen serviette. "Things are running along nicely," Erica replied with a fleeting smile.

"You're in the bar business?" Victoria asked to confirm what Erica was sure she already knew. Victoria was the type of woman who would have done ample research before deciding whether or not Erica was worthy of dating. The fact that they were sitting in one of the finest restaurants on the south coast of England told Erica that she had already passed that particular test. Still, Erica had expected that she would be asked for specifics.

"Well, my father was," Erica said. "My brother, Zachary, and I inherited the string of businesses from him when he passed away. Zachary takes charge of the running of things, while I prefer to remain a silent partner."

"And rightly so. No need to get your hands dirty in that business." Victoria made a show of shuddering, as though Erica was running a bunch of seedy brothels rather than bars. "Better that you can sit back and enjoy the profits." Victoria didn't mention Erica's father's death or offer condolences—instead she stuck to the juicy part. "I imagine it is lucrative, the bar business?" She lifted her eyebrows as if she was waiting to give her approval.

Erica was sure that Victoria would have been happy for her to offer up the details of her yearly income there and then. However, she never had been in the same league of bragging as these women. She decided to remain vague.

"It can be. It allows me to focus on organising my fundraisers for my mother's foundation, and of course taking a back seat to the day-to-day running of things means I don't have to travel to London. And it also means that I have the time to enjoy this excellent meal with you." Erica gave what she hoped was a flirtatious smile, simply because she felt that she had to do *something* to try and salvage the date, which from where she was sitting, was going from bad to worse—especially after the Audrey story, although she was sure that Victoria was oblivious to that.

Victoria's raised eyebrow told Erica that she approved of the comment. "Successful, gorgeous, and a smooth-talker, Miss Frost," Victoria replied before raising a finger like she had just remembered something. "Speaking of meals, this salad reminds me of this divine little restaurant I stumbled upon when I spent last summer in the south of France…"

And as easy as that, Erica's flirtatious efforts resulted in teeing Victoria up for another long-winded story all about Victoria and only Victoria. She painted an interested smile on her face as she listened about all the five-star experiences that Victoria had had in France. Again, Victoria didn't even take the waiter who came to take their plates under her notice. A lack of manners was a common trait of the type of women that Erica spent time with, though not a trait that Erica shared. Even though she was used to that kind of behaviour it still niggled at her each and every time she witnessed it. She found herself being extra polite to compensate, saying her please-and-thank-yous with a little extra oomph.

As Victoria continued her boast-fest, Erica started to wonder if her jaw and cheek muscles could handle the prolonged period of forced smiling that they would have to endure during the remainder of the evening. There was still the main course and dessert to go. She hoped Victoria didn't want a nightcap.

Erica should have felt like the luckiest woman in the world to be sitting across the table from Victoria Barrett. She didn't know anyone who wouldn't envy her in her position. Victoria was sought after. A catch. This should really be the date of all dates. The pinnacle. The date all previous dates had led up to. Yet it fell very short of any of those expectations. Erica felt as though she was simply going through the motions that she had gone through so many times before. Dating was always portrayed as some big romantic experience, full of sparks and butterflies. Who made that nonsense up? Dating was simply a fact-finding mission to determine whether two people were a match for one another, and if it was a success, then each carried the other around on their arm like a trophy. At least, that's what dating was like in Erica's world. She herself made an excellent trophy. A big in-your-face golden cup. She came from money, and a lot of it. Her mother was like royalty in the circles they belonged to, as was her grandmother. The family ties alone made Erica a catch. Not to mention that she wasn't exactly hard on the eye herself—so she was told. She had long, wavy, dark brown hair with a natural highlight that most women had to pay for. Her eyes were a distinct emerald-green colour that seemed unique to her. She had also inherited her mother's tall, slim, but curvaceous build, meaning she could pretty much wear any dress and it would cling to all the right places. Yes—Erica had lucked out in the looks and wealth department. She had almost been given it all, but so far, her luck hadn't stretched to her love life. That didn't seem to be about to change.

❖

It was after eleven p.m. when Erica finally sat down alone on her deck with a glass of Sauvignon Blanc, overlooking the Celtic Sea. She closed her eyes as she sipped from her oversized wineglass, taking in the sounds of the gently lapping waves below her. There was nothing quite like the soothing sounds of the water, and Erica instantly relaxed as she breathed in the fresh sea air. Whether the waves were calm like tonight, or rough and choppy, crashing against the side of the cliff, it didn't matter. Erica loved the water. This was her own little piece of paradise. Her clifftop cottage near St Ives was just far enough outside of the seaside town to ensure that her peaceful existence was never interrupted by the sounds of passing traffic, dogs barking, or people chattering. She was only a few minutes' drive away from the town, which was convenient, but she cherished the privacy and seclusion that her cottage offered her the rest of the time. For an introvert, it was the perfect spot—because Erica was *that*. Not that anyone ever would have guessed, given that she was constantly surrounded by people and regularly attended social events, but appearances could be deceiving. Erica was an introvert in disguise. Was there such a thing as an extroverted introvert? There had to be.

The May weather was still cool enough that she needed a jacket some of the time, and especially at this time of night, but Erica happily bundled herself up to grab a few moments of blissful quiet outside. It had become her nightly ritual, regardless of the weather. She had an awning she could wind out if it was raining, but she didn't need to use it tonight. She opened her eyes and gazed up at the sky, pleased that the night was clear enough that she could see the array of twinkling stars that were scattered across the dark canvas. The full moon reflected off the water. The scene was idyllic, and one that Erica never tired of, day or night. A soft brush against her legs told her that Hera, her British Shorthair kitty, had finished her treats and was ready to be showered with affection. Erica happily obliged, lightly scratching behind Hera's ears, who in turn raised her head to ensure the spot under her chin wasn't missed—not that Erica would dare forget. She knew the drill.

"It's our favourite kind of night out here," Erica said quietly as she continued to fuss over the feline. Hera responded by purring while headbutting Erica's hand over and over, determined to drag out petting-time for as long as possible. Eventually, when Hera decided she had received a sufficient amount of affection—it was on her terms, after all—she jumped onto Erica's lap, curling herself up into a ball, her favourite position. Rub demands aside, Hera was actually pretty low maintenance for a cat. She never wandered far, preferring to laze around the cottage or relax on the deck, much to Erica's relief. She liked that Hera always stayed close and was glad that she didn't have to worry about her setting off on adventures, not knowing when she was going to return.

Erica quickly slipped back into relaxation mode, stroking Hera absent-mindedly on her lap, enjoying the peace and quiet. She had hoped she would be sitting there giddily going over every aspect of her date, swooning even, but her date had not succeeded in bringing her longed-for giddiness, and the only cause of swooning would be if her wine sent her on her way to Tipsyland. No, instead of swooning, she switched off. Enjoyed the nature around her. The moment was short-lived, as she was disturbed by the more unnatural sound of her phone buzzing beside her.

She sighed as she reached for the offending object, bracing herself for a conversation with her mother, who was no doubt itching for a rundown on her date with Victoria. She knew it was coming. She would of course tell her what she wanted to hear, that the date went well, and she was flattered by Victoria's attention. Her mother would be delighted. She would ring Victoria's mother. Start planning centrepieces for the wedding. Everyone would be happy. Almost everyone. In reality, she would eagerly anticipate her next check-up at the dentist more than she would look forward to a second date with Victoria, which she had already grudgingly agreed to. And if there was one thing Erica dreaded in life, it was the dentist. A sadistic career choice, in her opinion. A shiver ran down her spine even thinking about it.

Without looking down to check who was calling she blew out a breath and swiped the screen to answer. "Hello, Mother," she said. She tried to muster up a slight tone of enthusiasm, though she wasn't too sure about her success levels on that one. She could always blame the wine.

"Not your mother, you'll be glad to know," replied an amused voice on the other end of the call that instantly brought a genuine smile to Erica's face. Tess. Her best friend.

"Thank goodness for that. Hi," Erica said. She breathed out a sigh of relief. "I know you're calling for the same reason, though."

"But of course—however, unlike your mother, you can give me the real version containing all the dirty deets," Tess said.

Erica could picture her friend, head in hand, eager to hear all about her latest dating debacle. Tess had been happily married to Scott for ten years, so she enjoyed living vicariously through Erica.

"If only there were dirty details to share. A kiss on the cheek before we went our separate ways was as hot as it got."

"I assumed as much seeing as you answered my call. I was half-hoping it would go to voicemail so I could finally do the happy dance I've been practicing for whenever one of these dates is finally a success," Tess said. "It's like salsa meets the robot. You'd love it."

"I don't quite know how to picture that." Erica tried to imagine it. "Is that even possible?"

"It's in the hips." A pause. "You have to see it to appreciate it."

"You just did it, didn't you?"

"Maybe."

Erica laughed. "Anyway, as for giving you a reason to do your strange robotic salsa, chance would be a fine thing. It turned out to be yet another boring evening with yet another egotistical woman."

"It amazes me that you continue to act surprised by this every single time."

"What do you mean?"

"I mean that that's just the kind of women you're attracted to, Erica. It's like you don't actually like them, but you date them because that's what you know, that's what you're drawn to. You don't do down to earth."

Erica blinked a few times as she absorbed this information. Rolled it around in her head a bit. She enjoyed the *no shit* approach that Tess took with her. It was a welcome change from her other friends, who always made sure to say the right thing whether it was the truth or not. To her face anyway. Behind her back was a different story, she was sure.

Erica had been friends with Tess for almost five years, and Tess, thankfully, wasn't a member of the *elite crowd*, as they liked to think of themselves. She had hired Tess to be her interior designer when she had purchased her cottage a few years prior. Not only had Tess designed her the home of her dreams, but they had ended up hitting it off and they became friends. Maybe not immediately, but quickly. In actual fact, Tess had told Erica that she had found her to be a complete snob initially—a fact that they both laughed about now—even though Erica could sometimes be, admittedly, a little stuck up. It was something she was working on. Tess on the other hand wasn't at all stuck up, and Erica hadn't realized how badly she needed someone grounded like Tess in her life until she had met her.

"So, I have a thing for strong, high-powered women," Erica said in her own defence. "That doesn't mean that I have a thing for self-centred women."

"The two seem to go hand in hand, though, don't they?" Tess said.

She had a point. "In my experience, I guess so."

"Tell me everything about your dreadfully boring evening with the infamous Victoria Barrett, then, I'm simply dying to know, darling," Tess said in an uppity tone. Tess often liked to mock Erica's polished way of speaking. It was annoyingly accurate, and it always made Erica laugh.

Erica was able to tell Tess all about the latest company Victoria had been hired to sue, who was having affairs with whom, Audrey ending her supposedly scandalous relationship with the waitress, whose fashion disaster was the worst, and how much Victoria had spent on her most recent kitchen remodel—after getting tired of her previous kitchen which she had installed eight months earlier.

"Fascinating," Tess deadpanned. "Did Victoria learn anything about you on this date? Or was it all about her?"

Erica let out a humourless laugh. "Mainly that I earn a pleasing amount of money and I do an excellent impression of a nodding dog." Erica found herself nodding again to emphasize her own point, even though Tess couldn't see her. "Oh, and she also told me that my cottage was *adorable*—her word, her tone—as her car dropped me off," Erica added. She mimicked the patronising way Victoria had said it.

Erica could hear Tess scoff. "Your cottage is stylish, cosy, and elegant, with a perfect kitchen that requires no remodelling, I beg your pardon."

"Which is exactly why I love it. You already know I'm a big fan of your work and I refuse to massage your ego any further. Besides, Victoria only saw outside. I didn't give her an invitation inside, so she didn't get the opportunity to marvel at your decorating skills."

"Maybe you can show off my excellent taste in bedroom decor on date two," Tess said.

"I can feel a headache coming on already," Erica said.

"I thought you said you found her attractive?"

"I did. I do. She's gorgeous. But what's the point if I have no intentions of getting into a relationship with her?" Erica asked.

"Um, getting laid? Meaningless sex? Scratching the itch? Take your pick," Tess said, like it was the most obvious thing in the world.

"You know how I feel about one-night stands."

"Which is why you were the perfect lady on date one, therefore not a one-night stand."

"Fine, a fling then. Whatever you want to call it."

"How about casual dating? Has a better ring to it," Tess said.

"Ugh, when have you ever known me to do casual anything. I'm pretty much the least casual person in the world," Erica said.

"Oh yes, I forgot you're a stuffy snob."

"And I forgot you're a bitch." They both burst out laughing.

"Well, I refuse to endure this childish name-calling of yours any longer," Tess said, feigning offence.

"Until tomorrow. Don't forget brunch."

"See you then," Tess said before she clicked off the call abruptly like she always did, not wasting time having long drawn-out good-byes on the phone like so many people did.

Erica pulled the phone from her ear and quickly held the button to switch it off. Tomorrow was time enough to undergo the inevitable interrogation from her mother.

Erica knew that she allowed her mother to have way too much influence over her life decisions. It was one of her weak points—she knew it and it bugged her—but she had let it happen for so long she was used to it. It wasn't like Erica had a bad life. She was lucky in so many ways.

Her mother only wanted the best for her, that being for Erica to be the best and have the best of everything. Could her mother be overbearing? For sure. Opinionated? Absolutely. Manipulative? Unfortunately. And Erica constantly asked herself why she allowed herself to be manipulated and controlled by her mother when she would never let anyone else walk over her. For a quiet life? That was part of it. Maybe it was a touch of guilt too. A sense of responsibility. With her brother moved away living his own life, Erica was really all her mother had. And as much as Erica envied her brother, she didn't feel like she had the freedom to follow in his footsteps, which meant that she remained at home bearing the brunt of her mother's difficult behaviour. Trying to impress a woman who seemed near impossible to impress seemed futile, yet Erica had never been able to shake her desperation for her mother's approval. Maybe securing a future with someone like Victoria would finally do it.

Still, she could wait for the lecture on how the clock was ticking and she was well overdue in settling down. To her mother, being single at thirty-five practically made her a spinster. She had heard the speech so many times now, she could recite it in her sleep. And, of course, her mother would go on and on about how Victoria Barrett was the perfect fit.

And on paper, Victoria was perfect for Erica. She knew that. Victoria ticked a lot of Erica's boxes. She should be smitten right now. But how Erica *should* feel and how she *did* feel were two very different things. There was attraction, of course, as well as admiration, but there was no excitement there for Erica. No desire to see her again. She didn't feel the ever-elusive butterflies or feel warm and fuzzy inside. Still, maybe she would grow to fall in love with Victoria if she gave her a chance. After all, she was everything Erica wanted, wasn't she?

Chapter Two

This wasn't her bedroom. That was the first thought that Charlie had when she opened her eyes to unfamiliar surroundings. And she wasn't alone, she realized. There was an arm slung across her waist and a warm body pressed against hers. She lifted the covers gently to confirm her suspicion that, yes, she was also naked. On further inspection, she saw a trail of her clothes from the night before leading from the bedroom door right up to the strange bed she found herself in. She cast a glance at the sleeping woman beside her as she started to recall the night before.

She had met the owner of the slung arm—*Hannah was it?*—at Oasis, the bar around the corner from her apartment and her regular go-to spot for a night out. Oasis wasn't a gay bar, but it had become more and more popular with the queer community. She had spotted Hannah with a group of friends beside the bar and couldn't resist offering to buy her a drink. Hannah had gladly accepted her offer and asked her to dance shortly after. They had flirted throughout the night, much to her best friend Val's delight, as it meant she was free to chat up the redhead she'd had her eye on, without having to worry about Charlie. Not that that usually stopped Val. Charlie wondered if that redhead had ended up back in the apartment that she and Val shared. Probably.

Hannah had asked Charlie if she wanted to come back to her place, and Charlie had been more than happy to accept her offer. The rest of the night had involved very few clothes, and very little sleep. In fact, a quick look at her watch told her that she'd probably only had around three hours' sleep, for which she was going to suffer at work for the rest of the day. Luckily Charlie wasn't a big drinker, so at least she didn't have a hangover to contend with as well.

She hadn't meant to fall asleep at Hannah's place. She didn't make a habit of sleeping over as she didn't like to blur the lines between *fun between two consenting adults* and *this is going somewhere between two consenting adults.*

Charlie had never been in a serious relationship, or anything remotely close to it. Throughout her twenties she had never felt the urge to commit. In fact, she actively avoided it. She enjoyed her care-free life, with no ties, and no responsibilities.

She was about to hit thirty in a few weeks. She could admit that there was a little voice inside her head sometimes telling her that maybe there was more to life than one-night stands and short-term flings. But she ignored it. Pushed those thoughts away. It was only because she was approaching the big three-oh. The truth was that Charlie liked her life the way it was. And in her defence, it wasn't like she had ever met anyone who grabbed her attention enough to make her consider settling down. The opportunity had never arisen, and Charlie had never gone looking for it. Was there anything wrong with that? Charlie didn't think so.

If sneaking out before Hannah woke up had been an option, it was gone now as the sleeping woman stirred and shifted against her.

"Morning," Hannah mumbled. "Surprised you're still here," she added in a sleepy voice.

Charlie couldn't gauge if it was a good surprise or bad surprise, but she was relieved at the surprise in general. It showed that Hannah understood what their night had been. Charlie was always clear about her intentions and very careful to make sure anyone that she got involved with was on the same page. She wasn't out to hurt anyone. She was just having fun with like-minded women.

"You completely tired me out, I fell asleep." Charlie gave her a wink.

Hannah gave her a sleepy smile before she stretched her arms above her head. The duvet gave way enough to show that Hannah was also naked, top half anyway, probably fully. Hannah caught Charlie looking, but she didn't bother to cover herself back up.

"It's fine. Rumour has it that you don't hang about is all. I thought you'd have left."

"I mean, I don't usually want to confuse things or complicate things." She felt like she needed to explain herself, especially given the current situation. Waking up naked on Hannah's turf made her feel a little vulnerable.

"Trust me, Charlie, if a relationship was what I was looking for, you would be the last woman I'd ask into my bed."

Ouch. Did she have to put it quite as bluntly as that? That stung more than Charlie expected. The look on her face must have shown it too.

Hannah continued, "I don't mean any offense. I only mean that you're a hookup kind of girl, and that was exactly what I needed last night. Everyone knows you can't do serious."

It wasn't anything Charlie hadn't heard before. Usually, she wouldn't even blink an eye. Maybe the looming thirtieth was playing with her head more than she cared to admit. Charlie was aware that she and Hannah had several mutual friends, and she knew that they liked to talk—but she wasn't thrilled at being the subject of their conversation. "Everyone knows, do they?"

"Oh, come on. You're fun, Charlie. It's a good thing. You don't let yourself get tied down or involved in the serious stuff. I admire it," Hannah said.

"It's not that I *can't* do serious, I just choose not to," Charlie said. She didn't know why she felt the need to defend herself. But she did.

Hannah attempted an apologetic face that was entirely unconvincing. "Yeah, that's what I meant."

It wasn't at all what she meant but Charlie decided to let it go. The truth was, she didn't know whether it was a choice or not. She was terrified of something serious. The finality of forever. Besides, relationships could go horribly wrong. She'd seen that first-hand growing up.

Could she settle down? Possibly not. She hadn't tried, so how would she know? She certainly wasn't going to analyse that while she was in a strange bed with a woman who barely knew her.

"I'm sorry, Charlie. Have I offended you? I'm still half asleep—what I meant was that I had fun with you last night—and I'm happy with what it was." Hannah grinned. "Besides, everyone's talk is incredibly complimentary. I can see why, especially after that thing you did with your tongue."

Hannah was right. They had had fun and that's what they had both wanted last night. "No, you're right. I had a lot of fun with you too." Charlie attempted a smile.

"Good." Hannah's eyes dropped to Charlie's lips as she leaned in to kiss her. "I do have twenty minutes before I have to get up," she said, with a glint in her eye.

Charlie could dwell on her apparently well-known commitment issues another time. She probably deserved the reputation she had gained anyway. She couldn't think of a better way to avoid any further conversation. She leaned into Hannah's kiss. "I can work with that," she said, as she rolled herself on top of Hannah's naked body and eased herself down. "Was this the tongue thing you meant?"

❖

"You need to put one of these in Toby's food every morning for the next fourteen days, Mrs Hunter. You should see an improvement over the next few days, but if you're worried about him at all or think he's getting any worse, you can give us a call or bring him back in, okay?" Charlie smiled as she passed the Labrador's dog lead and the box of pills over to his owner, before leaning down and ruffling the dog's short fur, much to his delight.

"Thank you, Charlie, you're such a dear," Mrs Hunter replied as she patted Charlie's cheek in that sweet way a doting grandmother would. She waved as she left the clinic.

Charlie couldn't stifle a yawn and stretched her arms out as she walked back behind the reception desk of the veterinary practice, Little Paws Clinic, where she worked as a vet's assistant. The receptionist, Hilary, was on a break, so Charlie was covering for her. She tilted her head from side to side, cracking her neck to loosen it up.

"Late night?" Dr Ashbourne asked with a raised eyebrow and knowing smile as she glanced at Charlie over the files she was holding.

Charlie groaned as she rolled her shoulders. "You could say that."

Even though Dr Ashbourne—Liz—was Charlie's boss, she was her friend too. She had got to know Liz over the years they had worked closely together—Charlie as Liz's assistant—and she received regular invites to join her and her wife, Nancy, for dinner. She always took them up on the invites, because Nancy was a chef, and a very good one, and there was no way that Charlie would miss out on sampling her cooking skills whenever Liz offered. It beat instant noodles or ready-made pasta, which was really the extent of Charlie's own culinary repertoire. Basically, if it could go in the microwave, Charlie could cook it. Anything more complicated than that was beyond her.

Lucky for Charlie, dinner at Liz and Nancy's had become at least a monthly occasion, and Charlie enjoyed a heavenly meal, and their company. Liz and Nancy were so settled and content. While a relationship like theirs had never been Charlie's aspiration, even she knew that they were couple goals.

Fine, maybe there was the odd time that Charlie was envious of the pair's happiness, but that was normal, right? It was more like admiration than envy. Like *aw, look at them, that's nice.*

The downside to being such good friends with her boss was that it also meant that Liz could read her like a book, and she couldn't get away with hiding things from her. Like right now, highlighted by the hand gesture that Liz was making, that meant *elaborate, Charlie.* Charlie knew that until Liz had details, she wasn't going to stop. She was like a dog with a bone—vet pun intended.

"I met a woman called Hannah last night. We had fun," Charlie said, shrugging her shoulders because it wasn't a big deal. It wasn't like Hannah was the first woman Charlie had told her boss-friend about. She'd lost count now of how many times this same conversation had occurred.

"When are you seeing her again?" Liz asked, with an innocent look on her face that was entirely put on. She already knew the answer to that question.

Charlie threw Liz back a look of her own that said she knew that Liz was toying with her. Then after a few beats, "Do you think I'm undatable?"

Liz thought about it. "No. I don't think you want to be datable. That's different. Why?"

"Just something Hannah said this morning. Apparently, *everyone* thinks that I can't handle a relationship or anything remotely serious. It's a thing. People talk about it."

"People should worry more about themselves," Liz said.

"Yet they prefer to focus on everyone else. Me in this instance."

"And it's annoyed you?"

"A little, I guess. It's made me question things some. Like, am I incapable of the type of relationship you and Nancy have? Would I even want something like that? Or did watching my parents scream and throw things at each other every day throughout my entire childhood fuck me up beyond repair?"

Liz reached out to pat Charlie's arm. "For starters, you're not fucked up at all, and you know it. You just started life with the worst example of what love should look like. You know that I think a relationship would be good for you, I've been telling you that for years, but you never listen."

"I know that it seems like something I should be doing at my age, you know? But take my scarred experience out of it—last night, for instance, I had a good time. A lot of fun. We got along well. Yet I have no desire to see her again. I never do with any of them," Charlie admitted, before grimacing. "Is that bad?"

Liz took a minute to mull her response over in her head, making a show of tilting her head from one side to another. "It's not *bad*," she said slowly. "Don't get me wrong—it's not great either." Another look. "But I think it just means you haven't met the right woman yet."

"I don't think there is only one right woman," Charlie said with a frown.

"There is. Trust me. And when you meet her, you'll know. Like I did with Nancy," Liz said. She smiled at the mere mention of her wife's name.

"Love that. Love you guys—but I don't think that's on the cards for me. But hey, I love my life. I'm definitely not complaining," Charlie said, with a cheeky grin that felt a little more forced than normal.

Liz didn't seem to buy it. "You'll surprise me someday, and yourself. And when you do, I have no doubt you'll not only be capable of it, but great at it."

"But there are so many women out there and so little time," Charlie said.

Liz threw her hands in the air and audibly growled, walking back into the exam room behind her as the front door opened. "That's all bravado, and you know it," she tossed back over her shoulder.

"Yeah, yeah, yeah," Charlie muttered under her breath, before slipping back into her professional persona as their next patient approached the counter. "Mrs Frank, what can we do for Daisy today?"

❖

Another thing Charlie noticed as thirty approached was that all-nighters on a work night were not as easy to recover from as they used to be. When she entered the door to her apartment, she kicked it shut behind her and let her bag slip from her shoulder to the floor before slumping herself onto the sofa, headfirst, with a loud groan. Her shoes landed with a thud beside her on the floor as she kicked them off.

"Hello to you too." Val's voice came from somewhere to her right, though exactly where she wasn't sure, as she didn't have the energy to open her eyes to look. She gave a half-assed wave in the general direction which was really more like a hand flop.

Charlie heard Val give a laugh through her nose before being further disturbed by a cushion landing on her head. She groaned again for good measure as she reluctantly moved Val's weapon of choice. She cranked her eyes open and rolled onto her back. "I'm so tired."

"Oh my God, you're twenty-nine, not seventy-nine." Val stood with her hands on her hips observing her.

"I don't know if there would be many seventy-nine-year-olds doing the things I was doing last night," Charlie said. "Though I hope there are. Never lose passion and all that."

"And this morning too, I heard."

"It never ceases to amaze me how quickly word spreads around here. I'm quickly learning just how impossible privacy is." Charlie dragged herself into a sitting position.

"I heard before lunch," Val said, taking the opportunity to grab the seat beside her.

"Great," Charlie said with a shake of her head. The whole thing was so ridiculous. "Heard what exactly?"

"Just that you stayed over. It's not like you."

"Therefore, it must be *big news*." Charlie threw her hands in the air. The drama.

Val chuckled. "You know what it's like around here. Anything out of the ordinary becomes news. Apparently, that Hannah girl is very smug about getting you to stay the night. Please tell me you're not about to go all lovey-dovey and mushy on me?"

"No danger of that, my friend," Charlie said, holding her fist out for Val to bump, which she wasted no time in doing. "Now can you please let me sleep?"

"Fine, you grump." Val got up which allowed Charlie to sprawl out.

"Wait," Charlie said, "how did it go with the redhead?"

Val gave her a wide grin. "She got a taxi home from here at around four this morning. No sleepovers here. I'm more sensible than you."

"I'd guessed as much—do they talk about you too?"

"All the bloody time. I couldn't care less. Don't be going soft on me," Val called as she walked toward her bedroom.

"I wasn't going soft," Charlie called back.

"We don't sleep over for a reason, Charlie, don't forget the rules," Val shouted from the other room before her door clicked shut.

She knew the rules. She and Val had come up with a strict set of rules years ago to help avoid clinginess or complications. When she had met Val, they quickly learned that they had the same outlook on love and relationships. Val had just got out of a terrible relationship with a serial cheater and vowed never to be in that position again. Charlie's own views on relationships were jaded because of the hell she had witnessed growing up. Why her parents had stayed together was beyond her. They made each other miserable, but it was like they were addicted to the drama. Maybe neither of them knew any different and they had got used to *their normal*. Whatever the reason, Charlie refused to let anything like that become *her* normal. Unattachment worked for her. It wasn't like she was alone—she had Val, she had friends, her job, and she enjoyed many a night of intimacy.

The rules worked. They kept her life easy and simple. She had fun. And that was exactly what she wanted, thirty be damned.

CHAPTER THREE

Erica managed to wait until nine o'clock the morning after her date with Victoria before switching her phone back on, or more accurately, before allowing herself to become a sitting target for her mother through open lines of communication. She held in the power button and threw the phone on the bed before she went into the bathroom to brush her teeth. She chuckled as she scrubbed, listening to the alerts from her phone sounding from the conjoining room. Ding, ding, ding, ding. My, my, she was popular. She lost count of the dings. Erica was sure her mother would be having a fit after being made to wait for an update from her. Oh well. Not rushing herself, she finished her brushing, swirled some mouthwash round her mouth for longer than necessary before spitting it down the sink, rinsed said sink, flashed her teeth in the mirror in a way that was neither a smile nor a grimace, then finally, slowly dragged herself back to her bedroom to assess the damage.

Seven missed calls from her mother—*no surprise there*. A text message from Victoria thanking her for a lovely evening and expressing her excitement for seeing her again—*can hardly wait*. Some message from a bank she didn't use which was clearly fraud—*idiots*. And a more unexpected two missed calls from her brother Zachary. She smiled at that and immediately hit the call button. Her brother lived in London, and she didn't get to see him nearly as much as she would like to, but they were close despite the distance.

"You know, I would love to say that my sister must have been up to all sorts of mischief seeing as I couldn't get her on the phone, but I know you far too well for that to be true," Zachary said in a way of greeting. He never did settle for a simple hello.

Erica snorted her amusement. "You mean to say that there's no chance that I've been in bed with a vivacious woman all night?"

He gasped. "Have you?"

"No," Erica replied. She laughed when her brother's own laughter sounded down the phone.

"You break my heart, darling older sis. A little rumpy-pumpy would do you the world of good," Zachary said.

"Okay firstly, I'm only older sis by six minutes. Meaning calling me older sis is basically ridiculous. Secondly, rumpy-pumpy, Zachary? Really?"

"What's wrong with rumpy-pumpy? I have plenty of rumpy-pumpy myself."

"Who would want to sleep with someone who says ridiculous things like rumpy-pumpy?" Erica said. "That's a mood killer all on its own."

She and her brother always did thrive on teasing one another, even when they were little. Their banter just bounced off each other perfectly. Maybe it was a sibling thing, or more likely that very in-tune twin thing. Whatever it was, they had it down.

"Plenty of beautiful men wish to have rumpy-pumpy with me, I'll have you know. Alas, I have chosen a rumpy-pumpy partner for life. Hearts all over London are breaking right now. If you're quiet enough, you may hear them shatter." Zachary sighed.

Erica laughed as she could picture him saying his exaggerated statement in full earnest, clutching his hand to his chest. He was always one for dramatics. Of course, when *he* had come out to their mother, not an eyelid had been batted. Not that it was a revelation to anyone. It had been obvious from the moment Zachary left the womb. Her mother was delighted at the information when he finally came out officially at the age of seventeen. Apparently having a gay son was a lot more on trend than having a gay daughter by Gloria Frost's standards. Then again, Zachary never could do anything wrong. Erica found that entertaining rather than annoying and got to tease her brother endlessly for being the golden child.

She pinched the bridge of her nose trying to remember Zachary's latest conquest's name. It wasn't her fault she was struggling. The list was everchanging.

"Ah, yes. The swimming instructor? Right?"

"Oh please, dear Erica, he was *so* last March. Olly works in fashion."

As it happened, Erica had not heard of Olly who worked in fashion, meaning he had been on the scene for a maximum of three weeks, unless her brother had been keeping him a secret the last time they spoke. As Zachary couldn't keep a secret to save his life, that was highly unlikely. "I see. And what does Olly do in the fashion world and where did we meet him?" Erica imagined that dreamy look on Zachary's face, the one he got when he fell smitten. She didn't need to see him to know it was there.

"He's a design assistant, thank you very much, and we fought over the last pair of shoes in a store. It was all very serendipity-esque."

Erica refrained from rolling her eyes because although Zachary fell in love quickly and often, it all felt real to him—every single time—and she prided herself on playing the role of the ever-supportive sister. "How wonderfully romantic."

She hoped her response didn't sound as dry as it had in her head. She was always happy for her brother no matter how ridiculous or unbelievable the situation. But the whole *our eyes met in a crowded room* thing made her nauseous. She refused to believe that things like that happened in real life. Sparks came from fires, not people.

"It was incredibly romantic, you cynic," Zachary replied.

Apparently, her tone was obvious after all.

"I'm sure it was." Erica wasn't sure how sincere that sounded either but pressed on with the conversation. "So, are you calling to rub it in with your tale of romantic bliss?"

"As much as I do enjoy listening to you dry heave over the soppy stuff, my call was actually business related."

That piqued Erica's interest. Zachary normally left her out of most of the business dealings. They had made this agreement when they had unexpectedly inherited the string of bars from their father when he had passed away. The inheritance had come as a shock to both of them. They were estranged from their father, and Erica could barely picture him by that point in her life, and their mother had nothing but bad things to say about the man. To say Erica wanted nothing to do with the bars was an understatement. It had been her intention to sell the lot, or at least her half, but Zachary had convinced her to remain a silent partner and allow him to take charge of running things. Reluctantly she had agreed, and honestly, she couldn't pretend that she didn't enjoy the income that came her way every month. The only good that had come from a father who had walked out on them when they were little.

"Everything okay?" she asked. The fact that they rarely discussed the business made her a little concerned about what Zachary was going to tell her.

"Well," Zachary started with a sigh. Nothing good ever came from that intro.

"Are we having financial troubles?" she asked.

"No, not exactly. The bars are doing well, better than ever. Duh, I'm in charge."

Erica realized she had been pacing up and down her bedroom and sat on the edge of the bed. "Okay, then what's the issue?"

"There's money going missing in one of the busiest clubs, Oasis. And I'm not talking pocket change here, I'm talking major pounds."

"*Okay...*" Erica said, dragging the word out. "So, find the thief and have them prosecuted." She felt her shoulders shrugging. It seemed like an easy fix to her.

"Yeah, finding them has proved to be extremely tricky, the slippery little shit. They're careful. Very careful. There's nothing on CCTV, no witnesses. We've been trying to nail the son of a bitch for weeks now, and it's really starting to get on my tits."

Erica drummed her fingernails on the cabinet beside her. It's not that she minded her brother talking to her about the business, but it was surprising as he normally didn't bother. She couldn't help but wonder why he was coming to her now. Maybe he needed a sisterly sounding board.

"Can you not question the staff one by one?"

Zachary chuckled. "No. For starters, there's like forty staff. You can't accuse a bunch of innocent people of stealing. Besides, the culprit will hardly come out and admit it, Erica, will they?"

"What about the manager? Surely if he or she was keeping an eye on things properly, they could catch them in the act. Unless it is the manager?" she suggested.

"No, it's not Brandon. I know it isn't him," Zachary said quickly. Too quickly. "Though I agree with you that I had hoped he would have seen something by now."

"He'll have to keep a closer eye. I'm sure they'll mess up eventually."

"You see, darling sister, this is what I was phoning to talk to you about."

So, Zachary wasn't just phoning so they could play Columbo together, he wanted something. He had that voice on, the one that meant he was going to ask for something that he knew he wasn't likely to get. "Uh huh," Erica said. "Spit it out, Zachary. What do you want?"

"Well, they obviously won't do anything in front of Brandon, and they definitely won't do anything in front of me. What I was thinking of…was sort of…an undercover kind of thingy."

Erica laughed. "Dramatic, but not surprising coming from you. What's that got to do with me?"

There was a pause on the other end of the call, Zachary's breathing the only sound, and it only took a few seconds until Erica realized exactly what he was asking.

"Absolutely not, Zachary. No!"

"But you're the only person I can trust," he said in a whiny voice.

"I don't care, find someone else. I'm not doing it." Erica stood up from her spot on the bed and began pacing the room again. "Why can't you go and put the pressure on this Brandon fellow to get the job done? How are you so sure he isn't the one doing it anyway? Surely, he should have caught them in the act by now."

"I trust that Brandon has tried his best."

"Fire him, then. He's clearly not up the job. Get someone more competent who can do what needs to be done. Someone who can keep the staff in line." She knew that she was raising her voice, but the prospect of *her* going to work in a *nightclub* was beyond preposterous. She couldn't believe that Zachary would ever make such an astounding suggestion. She had made her feelings about their father's businesses very clear from the moment they learned of them. Her father had abandoned them, and she didn't want to be involved in anything to do with him, especially not his grotty bars. Not that she had never stepped foot in one, but she never had any intention of finding out what they were like. She was happy with her preconceived ideas. Plus, Erica Frost did not pull pints. The entire concept was unimaginable.

"I can't just fire him. He hasn't done anything wrong." Another pause. "Besides, we kind of have a bit of a history."

Erica pursed her lips as realization dawned on her about Zachary's sheepishness regarding this Brandon fellow. "A history as in…?" She let the end of the sentence hang. She knew the answer, but she wasn't about to go easy on Zachary. He would have to come right out and say it.

"As in we had rum…"

"Zachary!"

"Sex. We slept together. A few times."

Erica closed her eyes and slowly shook her head. "With an employee? Seriously, Zachary?"

"I know, I know. It was stupid and it shouldn't have happened.

And I will never do anything like that again. But I do know him well enough to know that it wasn't him." He did sound ashamed of it, which was something.

"Really stupid."

"I know. I promise I know it was stupid. I've learned my lesson."

"Fine." Erica shook her head but didn't push the subject. Zachary already knew that she disapproved. Back to the reason for Zachary's call. "Why don't you just go undercover yourself? Go in disguise or something."

"What? Glue on a moustache, dye my hair blond, and hope no one will recognize me?" Zachary laughed. "You've been watching too much TV, Sis."

"Yeah, well, you'll still have to find someone else. I'm not doing it."

The whiny voice was back. "But I had it all worked out. You would work behind the bar, keeping an eye on things. You'd be one of them. They would trust you. Hopefully then you would catch them in the act. Plus, Olly lives literally around the corner from Oasis, so you would stay in his apartment, and he would stay with me. Bonus. You'd have your own space because I know you like that. It would be like a holiday for you. You love London. Plus—big plus—I'd get to see you."

"You seem to have thought this whole thing through."

"I have, I've thought of everything. And it will work, I know it will."

"I can literally hear you pouting," Erica said.

"Is it working? What if I say pretty, pretty please?" Zachary asked in a hopeful voice.

"Definitely not, but nice try," she answered quickly. "Do keep me updated on the manhunt for the Oasis bandit, though."

The sigh on the other end of the phone was almost comical. Followed by a several moments of silence before Zachary admitted defeat. "Fine. I knew it was a long shot."

Erica felt bad. She didn't like to let her brother down. But she didn't feel bad enough to change her mind. They chatted for a bit longer. She filled him in on her anticlimactic date with Victoria, as well as their mother's latest antics. He told her a little bit more about Olly, who sounded like a pretty decent guy, thankfully. Her brother tended to have questionable taste in men at times, but she had slightly higher hopes for this one. Her suspicions had been correct, though. Zachary had only known Olly for two weeks.

She promised to call her brother with updates on Victoria, and he in turn promised to keep her up to date on his latest romance and developments on their kleptomaniac.

When they ended the call, she dropped back down onto the edge of the bed and shook her head. Zachary truly did come up with some ridiculous ideas at times, but she, Erica Frost, working undercover in a London nightclub—that took the biscuit.

❖

Erica waved over to Tess, who was sitting at a table by the window waiting for her. There were two glasses of white wine in front of her, bless her heart. They met for Sunday brunch as regularly as they could. Erica zigzagged between the tables toward Tess and smiled as she sat down.

"Thank you for this," she said. She lifted the glass to take a sip. A large sip. She moaned her appreciation as she swallowed it down.

"Whoa, okay, mid-morning drinking much needed today, I see." Tess's eyes held a glint of amusement.

"I just had the most ludicrous request from Zachary." Erica fidgeted with the stem of the glass in front of her. She explained her brother's idea, laughing at how absurd the whole thing was. "I know that I'm half owner too and doing accounts or something would be fair enough if Zachary needed me to. I'd be a team player. But posing as a bartender? What is he thinking?" She shook her head.

She looked at Tess's face, expecting her to see shock, hilarity, horror, surprise. Any of those things. But Tess's face looked more... intrigued. Her eyebrows were lifted, and her expression was posed. "Why are you looking at me like that?"

Tess rolled her lips in for a second. "I think it sounds kind of fun."

"Oh, not you as well." Erica frowned. She took another large gulp from her glass.

"What? A few weeks away to London. Pretending to be someone you're not. An exciting undercover op. In a nightclub. Like I said, fun. Hell, I'd almost offer myself, only Scott would kill me."

"There's no way I'm doing it, Tess. It's not my sort of thing at all. Could you imagine me bartending?"

Tess waved off Erica's comment. "That's just your bred-into-you snobbishness rearing its ugly head. Where's your sense of adventure? Live a little, Erica. You might even enjoy it."

The waiter chose the perfect time to come round to take their order. Eggs Benedict for Tess and a vegetarian omelette for Erica. Although Erica wasn't a sworn veggie, she tried to avoid eating meat when she could. Nothing to do with diet or anything, Erica just loved animals. So, if there was a veggie option, Erica took it. Okay, she caved the odd time and ate chicken or fish, but that was it. Nothing else. Lamb, for example? Nope. Those little lambs frolicking around the fields? She couldn't knowingly eat them. No way. Her *mostly*-vegetarianism had earned her quite a few eye rolls in her time, but she didn't care. It made her feel good.

Live a little, Erica. Tess's words. Was she seriously that uptight? She concluded that maybe she was, because there was no way in hell that she was doing it. If that made her snobby or boring, or unadventurous, then so be it. She would not back down.

"There is nothing about working in a club that I would enjoy," she said to Tess when the waiter left.

"You've never done it, so how do you know? I had a bar gig at uni, and I had a great time," Tess said.

"Tess, I love you. I love who you are. But you know that you and I are very different people. This particular adventure isn't going to happen."

Tess shrugged and leaned back in her chair. "Fine. I'll drop it. No adventures for you."

"I'll go camping or something if you truly insist on this adventurous streak."

"No, you won't," Tess said.

"No, I won't." Erica grinned. Camping? No luxuries. Not her style at all. But that was fine. She could live with the fact that she enjoyed her home comforts and wasn't all that audacious. At least she always had a hairdryer nearby. "Enough about my unexciting existence. What's new with you?"

"Firstly, you are not unexciting. Set in your ways, maybe. But not unexciting. And for the record, I love who you are too. And me—okay, well in actual fact, I do have news." The corners of Tess's mouth turned slightly upward as she looked at Erica almost nervously.

"Tell me," Erica said.

"Scott and I are trying for a baby," Tess said softly. Her grin got bigger. "As in properly trying. Doing the ovulation stick thingies, and the whole tracking on the calendar thing. Really, actively, putting everything into trying."

Erica smiled. "That *is* big. I'm so happy for you two."

"The timing's right. Scott has been ready for a while now, but I've kept putting it off. I think it's because I'm scared of the unknown. But now I'm ready, Erica. I'm ready to try." There was a slight glistening in Tess's eyes and Erica couldn't help tearing up a little herself. Tess and Scott deserved every happiness.

Erica reached over and covered Tess's hand with her own. "I think it's brilliant. It's brave, and huge, and exciting."

Tess took a deep breath. "It's also terrifying."

"It is. But in the best way." Erica gave her a reassuring smile. "I am so signing up for babysitting duties."

"Babysitting duties? I was more thinking godmother duties," Tess said with an expectant look on her face.

Erica held her hand up to her heart. "Really?"

"Of course. You're my best friend. Who else is going to teach them which fork is used for salad? It's not like Scott or I would have a bloody clue."

Erica laughed. "In that case it's a must. You need me."

"You have no idea how much," Tess said with a warm smile, which Erica returned.

"So, potentially, this is the last boozy brunch for a while, then?"

"Oh, my word, you're right. We need to make the most of it. Champagne?" Tess said.

"My thoughts exactly. My treat. We're celebrating," Erica replied. She gestured to the waiter.

Erica ordered the most expensive bottle of champagne on the menu, ignoring any and all protests from Tess. What was the point in having money if you couldn't treat your best friend to champagne to celebrate great news?

Tess shot Erica a look which she instantly waved off. "Celebrating," Erica repeated.

Tess opened her mouth to argue but went still when something behind Erica grabbed her attention. She lowered her voice. "Speaking of motherhood, isn't that your dear old mum over there?"

Erica's head turned round so fast she was at risk of getting whiplash. Had she returned her mother's calls yet? No. Would that make unexpectedly running into her mother even worse? Yes, it would. Erica had specifically chosen that particular restaurant because it was somewhere that her mother and her friends did not frequent. Yet there was her mother. Laughing and joking with…was that Victoria's mother? Erica squinted to make sure. She really needed to stop putting off that eye test. Yes, squinting confirmed that her mother and Victoria's mother were brunching. *How fucking lovely*. And she didn't need three guesses to know what that conversation would be about.

Erica quickly turned back to Tess. "Fabulous."

"If it helps, I don't think she's clocked us yet. I could sneak you out behind my coat."

"If only," Erica said, taking another drink of wine. "Mother's laser vision would probably see straight through it."

"It never fails to amuse me to hear you refer to *mother*."

"Don't start," Erica said with a smile.

"That and your perfectly poker-straight posture straightens even more if that's possible," Tess added.

"So, I have mummy issues," Erica said. "That's not news to either of us."

"Posh girl problems," Tess said with a wave of her hand. After a few seconds she let out a low whistle. "Who is the hottie that's joined them?" she asked, looking over Erica's shoulder again.

Erica glanced round, a little more subtly this time, and let out a sigh. She turned back toward Tess and closed her eyes, rubbing her temples. This was going from bad to worse. "That would be Victoria." When Erica glanced back again, she saw that Victoria had noticed her too and gave a little wave before proceeding to point her out to the two mothers.

"Brace yourself," Tess whispered from behind her fist, which covered her mouth. Tess's posture straightened too, which could only mean that her mother was on the move. Erica noted to tease her about it later.

"Darling!" Gloria Frost strode purposefully toward their table, her hands held out in front of her. Erica stood to be taken in the embrace. "You haven't called me back," Gloria whispered in her ear with a sharp tone, her smile never faltering as she leaned back, hands still on Erica's shoulders. Appearances really were everything. Gloria was an expert at saying one thing and ensuring her face was telling a different story.

"Sorry, Mother, I haven't had a chance. I was going to visit you later today." That was a lie, but her mother didn't need to know that.

"Why wait? You must join us for brunch. Hello…Tess," Erica's mother said as an afterthought. She glanced briefly in Tess's direction with a smile that didn't reach her eyes. She turned back to Erica and whispered, "Victoria is with us."

"I saw that," Erica whispered back. Clearing her throat, she added, "I'm with Tess, and we have a lot to discuss. I'll come over and say hello afterward." She knew that her mother wouldn't like her refusal to join them, but she also knew that she would never make a scene.

"Very well," Gloria replied with the same fake smile. She stared at Erica for a few beats, clearly unhappy that Erica didn't come running when she clicked her fingers. "Make sure that you do."

Gloria glided back across to their table, where Victoria and her mother watched on. Victoria gave a nod in her direction, which Erica returned with a forced smile before sitting back down.

Tess waited until Gloria was out of earshot before quietly saying, "Your mum hates me."

Erica snorted. "She doesn't hate you. You just don't suck up to her and she doesn't know how to handle that."

"Well, I feel like hugging you for not dragging me over to join them."

"Oh please, don't pretend you wouldn't have found it hilarious watching me having to make small talk with those three."

Tess held up her finger and thumb a little bit apart. "Might have been a tiny bit funny. It would have been the only silver lining if you had forced me over there."

"You're terrible." She leaned her head on her hand. "Mother is clearly very keen on mine and Victoria's union."

Tess shook her head. "You're your own woman. You don't need me to tell you that. If you aren't feeling it, I wish you would come out and say so. So what if your mum's pissed off."

"You say that like it's simple."

"Because it is simple."

"Not in my family." She sighed. "Who knows. Maybe she'll grow on me after a few dates." She wasn't looking forward to spending more time with Victoria, though.

"Just say no," Tess said again.

"I can't." Their champagne arrived, and the waiter poured each of them a flute and set the rest of the bottle in an ice bucket in the middle of the table. Erica held up her glass. "Anyway, let's forget about my tragic dating life and my reluctance to disappoint my mother. There are much more important things. To trying," she toasted. Her mood immediately lightened as she refocused on her best friend's news.

Tess clinked her glass against Erica's. "To trying."

They spent the rest of brunch catching up. Tess was in the middle of a huge design project for a new apartment building. Her boss had trusted her to design the lot, which wasn't at all a surprise, because Erica knew first-hand how good she was. Erica was starting to plan yet another fundraiser for a charity her mother was supporting that year. Not one that would have been her own choice, but at least there was a cause helped.

Erica tried not to let her mother and Victoria's presence behind her affect her, but she felt eyes burning into the back of her skull regularly. It made her squirm, but she refused to look round in their direction. She knew she had to face them eventually. She could only ignore them and stall for so long.

"Let's get this over with," she murmured to Tess as they stood and put their coats on to leave.

"Good luck," Tess whispered. "I'll be right there with you."

Erica appreciated the moral support.

Victoria stood from the table as they approached and leaned in to kiss Erica's cheek. Out of the corner of her eye she could see her mother conspiratorially smile at Victoria's mother.

"So good to see you again, Erica." Victoria beamed.

"And you, Victoria. And lovely to see you, Mrs Barrett," Erica added. Mrs Barrett simply nodded at her in response with a prim smile on her face. Erica continued, "This is my good friend, Tess. Tess, this is Victoria, who I was telling you about, and her mother. And you already know my mother, of course."

"Nice to see you all," Tess said with a polite smile.

"And you," Victoria said. To her credit she leaned over to shake Tess's hand. They were a formal crowd.

"Sorry we couldn't join you today, we have kind of a standing Sunday brunch date," Erica said, with an apologetic look that was entirely put on. She was not even slightly sorry.

Victoria waved her off. "No problem. Though you missed out on the table over by that window," she said, subtly nodding her head in that direction without ever looking round. "Anthony Donaldson is here with a woman. One who is not his wife and definitely not his daughter." Victoria lowered her voice even more. "Though more similar in age to his daughter than to his wife."

"She's about twenty. Quite a scandal," Victoria's mother added. "Though not surprising from him."

Erica's mother laughed. "Indeed."

Erica supressed an eye roll. These people lived for gossip and finding out everyone else's business. Instead, she played along and replied, "How outrageous."

That seemed to appease the women at the table. She glanced round at Tess who, clear to Erica, was supressing an eyeroll of her own.

"We were also discussing a spa weekend. The four of us." Her mother said, gesturing to Erica and herself, then to Victoria and her mother. "Victoria told us you had such a lovely evening last night, so we thought it would be a splendid way for you to get to know each other better. And for me to get to know Victoria better." She gave her a smile that Erica knew implied *you're going, young lady.*

"She would love to go, wouldn't you, Erica?" Victoria said, putting a possessive arm around Erica's waist. *Wow.* Was Victoria answering for her now? They'd been on one date. Who the hell did she think she was?

Erica held back everything she really wanted to say, and instead went with, "When?"

"Everyone free this weekend?" Victoria said with another massive smile. "Why wait?"

Both mothers nodded enthusiastically.

"As it happens, I can't do this weekend, I'm going to be out of town," Erica said without thinking. It was the first thing that came into her head. She quickly needed a way out of this horrendous weekend that was being forced upon her.

"Oh? And where might you be going?" her mother asked with a frown. "I didn't know you were going anywhere."

"Urgent business in London. Zachary needs me to help out with an issue in one of the bars. I promised I'd be there tomorrow," Erica blurted out. Where had that come from? Of all the things she could have said. *Shit.*

"He didn't say anything to me," Gloria said. She pursed her lips. A sure sign of her annoyance.

"It was only arranged this morning, Mother."

"And how long are you going to be gone?" Victoria this time.

"A few weeks," Erica said. What had she done? Was she really going to do this? Would she have to go now? It wasn't like she could just disappear—hide away in her cottage and hope no one would know she was there. Someone would find her.

Victoria's smile dropped off her face, morphing into that of a petulant child not getting her own way. Her arm also dropped from Erica's waist, much to Erica's relief. They weren't on those terms after a single date. And an unsuccessful date, as far as Erica was concerned. Victoria's mother simply looked at Erica's mother for her reaction. Erica braced herself for that one. Her mother's face was blank. Probably unreadable for Mrs Barrett. But Erica was experienced enough and could read it. She was *not* happy.

"We will schedule it for whenever you get back from your business trip, then," Victoria said slowly. She didn't sound pleased, but she would want to save face. It wasn't in her best interests to come right out and show her annoyance.

"Absolutely." *Not.* A few weeks away would give Erica a chance to work out how she was going to handle this Victoria situation.

Erica said her good-byes to Victoria and Mrs Barrett and promised her mother she would visit later. She could expect an earful from her mother. That her time should be devoted to securing her courtship with Victoria, and that a woman shouldn't be in the bar business. *Highly un-ladylike* she heard her mother's voice say in her head. They quickly exited the restaurant leaving three women gaping at them in their wake.

"London, huh?" Tess said as they walked out.

"Not a word," Erica said.

Tess laughed hysterically and threw her arm around Erica as they walked.

And that was how Erica found herself stepping off the train at Paddington Station the very next day, suitcase in one hand, and Hera in her cat carrier in the other.

What the hell was she doing?

CHAPTER FOUR

Dua Lipa's "Physical" was blasting from the speakers when Charlie walked into Oasis to meet Val. She scanned the bar area and spotted Val chatting to a group of their friends. She quickly made her way over to them, weaving her way through the bodies blocking her path.

"There she is," Val said with a smile. "We were literally just talking about you."

Charlie hesitated. More talking. The realization that she was gossiped about had left her a little guarded.

"Nothing bad," Val added quickly. She explained that one of the girls had rescued a pup, and Val had suggested that she take him to Little Paws to get checked out.

That kind of talking about her was totally fine. "Absolutely, I'll set you up an appointment tomorrow," she said. She felt her wariness soften. She should have known her friends wouldn't be saying anything bad. "Drinks, anyone?"

"I'll get them," Val said. "Pretty sure it's been my round for weeks." She took note of what everyone wanted and made her way to the bar. It was cocktail night and Charlie decided on a Bramble.

While the conversation switched to some sci-fi show that she didn't watch, Charlie scanned the room. She clocked several of the usual suspects. She waved at a few people she knew, smiled at a few she didn't. She stopped scanning when she caught the eye of a woman she hadn't seen before. The woman gave a shy grin and looked down at the table she was sitting at with her friends for a few seconds, before lifting her eyes back up to look at Charlie again. She smiled fully then, obviously pleased by the fact that Charlie was still looking. Her gaze roamed up and down Charlie's body. She was checking Charlie out and making no secret of it. Charlie grinned back at her and gave her a once over of her own. She was cute. Blond hair, not quite as light as Charlie's, but a similar long, wavy style, draping down past her shoulders. She was pretty, nice smile. Charlie broke the eye contact but vowed to herself to look for her again in a little while.

Before she knew it there was a cocktail in her hand, and she had fallen into easy chitchat with her friends.

"Incoming," Val muttered a few minutes later. She looked down at her shoes but gestured her head to the left. Sure enough, the blonde with the sexy eye contact was approaching. Even sooner than Charlie had expected. She wasn't wasting any time.

"Hey," Blondie said as she tucked her hair behind her ear.

"Hey yourself." Charlie flashed her a grin. She saw her friends shift away slightly in her peripheral vision but kept eye contact with Blondie. She also realized she needed to amend the Blondie part. "I'm Charlie," she said.

"Steph."

"And what brings you over here to my part of the bar, Steph?" Charlie asked.

Steph bit her lip. "I was wondering if I could buy you a drink?"

Charlie held up her still almost-full glass. "I've got one, but how about I buy you a drink?"

Steph tilted her head. "How's that fair?"

"Well," Charlie said, going into full charm mode, "if I buy you a drink, then you owe me a dance. And I really, really want to dance with you." She closed the gap between them slightly and gave another smile.

Steph laughed and raised her eyebrow. It was cute. "That's your move then, a dance for a drink?"

"If it is a move, do you think it will work?"

Steph nodded a silent agreement and Charlie made her way to the bar. All right, so it seemed that Steph wasn't the biggest conversationalist. But that was fine. She didn't need an in-depth conversation or even witty banter. She seemed fun. Interested. And she was attractive.

As she stood and waited to be served, she looked around. She recognized most of the bar staff, which wasn't surprising. She went to Oasis almost every week. There was a guy in a suit she had seen before. He was clearly in charge. But what sparked Charlie's interest was who he was talking to. She could only see the back of the woman. It wasn't a back she recognized, but it was one she wouldn't forget in a hurry.

She was tall—Charlie loved a woman that was taller than her.

God, that body. Curvaceous in all the right places. Legs for days and a bum that was so good it should be illegal, showcased by black, form-fitting trousers. She had a white dress-shirt tucked in that contrasted with long, dark hair that had a lightness to it as well. Highlights? They blended so well she couldn't be sure. Her hair fell down her back in waves. If Charlie were a cartoon character, her little cartoon eyes would be literally popping out of her head right now. Maybe her human ones were, she couldn't be sure at that moment. There was something else about the woman. The way she stood. Carried herself. Like she was a woman who was sure of herself. Charlie could tell even from behind.

Ash, one of the bartenders she recognized, signalled her and she was forced to look away from the mystery woman. She felt regret immediately. What was she here for? Beer. For Steph. Steph who was waiting to dance with her. That's who she needed to focus on. She ordered the beer and waited. She looked for the woman again, just to look, but she was too late. The boss man and the perfectly sculpted woman were disappearing from the bar into another room, and Charlie only caught another momentary glimpse before the door closed behind them.

"New hire?" she asked, nodding her head toward the door.

"Yeah." Ash gave Charlie a knowing look as she poured the pint. "Haven't met her properly yet, though. First night."

Charlie nodded and paid for the drink. At least she knew the woman worked here so the chances of Charlie seeing her again were extremely high. She looked forward to putting a face to the mystery woman.

She turned her attention back to Steph. That's who it was about tonight. Charlie walked purposefully toward her and handed her the beer.

As she had suspected, the conversation didn't get much better. She learned that Steph was a hairdresser, had recently split up from her girlfriend, and was looking for a rebound. Steph was in luck. Charlie was an excellent rebound girl. Charlie told her about her job, which Steph screwed her face up at, because quote, "Animals freak me out." *Who the hell doesn't like animals*? Charlie tried to push that nugget of information to the back of her mind, even though Steph had lost serious points for the admission. She didn't need to date the woman. Charlie was just there to be the rebound girl. Animals needn't be involved. But yuck.

Steph excused herself to go back to speak with her friends quickly, and Charlie took the breather to look for her own friends. She had a look around for Val, but she couldn't spot her. Eventually, her eyes settled on the bar.

The woman was back. She was still turned away from Charlie, being shown around by Ash the bartender.

Turn around, turn around. Then she did. It felt like it happened in slow motion. The woman turned around, flicking her long hair back behind her as she did.

Charlie was staring, knew it, couldn't look away. She was the type of woman who would walk into a room and every head in the place would turn to look at her, because how could you not? She was beautiful. That didn't do her justice. Stunning? Exquisite? Delectable? None of them seemed quite good enough. This woman needed a word of her own. Charlie was only human for staring. She felt powerless not to.

She watched as the woman nodded at a customer at the bar. Ash was beside her pointing at things and talking a lot with her hands. Maybe she was training her. She watched as the woman walked to the end of the bar and pointed at a bottle. Ash nodded. Charlie was right with her initial assessment, there was something about how the woman carried herself. She was elegant and poised. She walked like she owned the place. Full of confidence and self-assuredness.

Then the woman looked up—directly at Charlie. Even from across the room Charlie could see that the woman's eyes were dark—a green maybe—made even darker by long, black lashes. And those eyes had caught Charlie looking. Her lips were red—not an in your face red, more of a red wine colour. The colour suited the woman's almost olive skin. She looked amused that she had caught Charlie in the act.

That was Charlie's moment to give her *the look.* Charlie was good at *the look.* She had it down. A direct stare, a bit of smoulder, and the receiver was putty in her hands. But instead, Charlie froze. She snapped her head away. Her mouth had gone dry. She felt these tingles all over her body. And her stomach, whoa. What was doing somersaults in there? It felt like there was an army of little green men doing flip-flops all over it. Green—because that's how she imagined stomach men to be, like toy soldiers. It felt like nervousness, but how could it be? Charlie had never been nervous around a woman in her entire life.

"Snap out of it," she muttered to herself.

When she looked back toward the bar the woman had busied

herself again, and it gave Charlie a chance to notice the woman's shirt. A damn tease of a white shirt with just enough buttons left open to give a flash of a sexy collarbone that Charlie immediately wanted to run her tongue over.

She zoned out for a few seconds thinking about doing just that. When she zoned back in those eyes met hers again. Charlie tried to hold the eye contact this time, ignoring the weird feelings she was having. Charlie Bradshaw did not do nervous.

Steph came bounding back to her with a "Hey you."

That broke the spell. Charlie was forced this time to look away and give her attention to Steph. "Hey. Were your friends okay?"

"Yeah, I told them I probably wouldn't see them again tonight," Steph said with a suggestive look in her eyes, all the while running her hand down Charlie's arm before interlacing their fingers. "Dance?"

Focus on Steph. Charlie nodded and allowed herself to be dragged onto the dance floor, some sort of dance song playing that she couldn't remember the name of. Steph wasted no time in pulling their bodies together, grinding her hips tightly against Charlie. Usually, Charlie would be in her element with an attractive woman practically throwing herself at her. She made all the right moves, grabbing hold of Steph's hips and pushing into her grind, matching her rhythm, but for some reason she wasn't feeling it. She didn't have time to consider why before Steph's tongue was in her mouth. Yep, Steph had put her hands around Charlie's neck, pulled her face to hers and kissed her with immediate tongue in one swift movement. The next thing Charlie knew was that Steph's hands were grasping her bum, pulling their bodies even closer together if that was possible. The kiss was sloppy, hurried. Steph tasted of beer, and was that cigarettes? Maybe that's where she had disappeared to with her friends. Not that she minded people smoking, it just wasn't her thing. It wasn't the best kiss she'd ever had. She tried to take control of it, lighten up on the tongue a little because Steph's was currently pounding repeatedly in and out of her mouth and it wasn't doing it for Charlie. Thankfully after a few more seconds Steph pulled back, looking at her with hooded eyes.

"Your place or mine?" Steph said to her breathlessly.

Charlie had expected the invitation. She'd initially hoped for it. So why did she find herself saying, "I'm not feeling all that well, Steph, I think I might be coming down with something. Maybe we could take a rain check?"

Steph froze and stared at her, her eyes narrowing. "I thought we were having a good time?"

"We definitely were, we are, I just can't tonight." Charlie gave an apologetic smile.

Steph's eyebrows went up as if she was in disbelief at what she was hearing. She shifted from one foot to the other, then snorted an unpleasant laugh. "Your loss, then."

Steph turned on her heel and walked away and Charlie was left standing alone in the middle of the dance floor. Charlie sighed and risked a glance back in the direction of the bar. Sure enough, those warm eyes were on her again, only this time the warm eyes held an ice-cold glare laced with judgement, maybe? Annoyance? She didn't have much time to decide which because as quickly as their eyes met, the woman's eyes darted away, and she walked out of sight to the other side of the bar.

What was that about?

❖

One thing that always made Charlie feel better was ice cream. She swore it had medicinal qualities. Therefore, her freezer was always stocked with all of her favourite flavours. There were a few, because how could you only choose one? Honeycomb, mint chocolate chip, cherry, Chunky Monkey, salted caramel. They were all freezer requirements. She opted for a full tub of mint as she lay on the sofa watching reruns of *Friends*, which let's face it, never ever got old. Who needed therapy when *Friends* and ice cream made her mood turn instantly better?

Okay, so her night had been a bust. She wasn't herself. Steph had basically offered herself up on a plate and Charlie had turned her down. No big deal. That wasn't what she was dwelling on. What was really bothering Charlie was the new bartender. Or more so, how the new bartender had affected her. She had never looked at a woman and felt so completely off-kilter before. It was as though everyone else around her had disappeared, the pumping music had faded away, and there was nothing else but this woman and the way she was making her feel. Charlie was used to being flirted with, she enjoyed having admiring eyes on her. But this was different. It had felt like every part of her body had reacted all at once, her heart, her brain, her skin, her legs, and other parts of her body too—they had all definitely jumped to attention.

She could still feel the pulsing between her legs. Talk about an instant attraction. She could never remember her body ever feeling so alert from a single look.

But then there was that other look. The glare the woman had given her. It was understandable, she could admit. One minute Charlie had been looking into the new bartender's eyes showing obvious interest, and the next she had another woman's tongue down her throat. She knew it wasn't her finest moment. She had even felt the urge to go over to the bar and explain herself. That was a first for Charlie. She didn't explain herself to anyone. She didn't have to. She wasn't doing anything wrong. She was a single girl, out and enjoying herself. But still, the obvious judgement in the bartender's eyes had got to her.

Instead, she had decided to call it a night at Oasis. Hence her lying on the sofa at two in the morning, halfway through a decent sized tub of ice cream, and in the middle of watching that episode of *Friends* where they throw the ball to each other again and again.

Keys rattled in the door and Val came into the living room. Alone, thankfully.

"Okay. I thought you flaked out without saying bye to anyone because you pulled that blond girl. What I didn't expect was you, frozen treats, and episodes of *Friends* that you've watched a gazillion times already—what gives?" Val asked, as she made her way from the front door to the space on the sofa beside Charlie.

Charlie shrugged her shoulders. "I wasn't feeling it."

Val looked confused. "When are you ever not *feeling it*?"

Charlie shrugged again without answering and continued eating her ice cream. She tilted the tub toward Val, who got up to grab a spoon and joined her again on the sofa.

"What happened?" Val asked as she dipped her own spoon into the tub.

"Nothing happened. Steph was fine, and fun, but I wasn't in the mood. No biggie."

"Okay." Val dragged the word out. "So why the ice cream? As great as it is." She plopped a spoonful in her mouth.

"I'm just consoling myself that my mojo wasn't there tonight." Technically it wasn't a lie. She hadn't been her usual confident self with either woman she had encountered that night.

"We all have off nights. Maybe this Steph girl will be there another night and you can make it up to her."

Charlie didn't really care about making it up to Steph. They sat in comfortable silence for a few minutes watching the TV, taking turns to dip their spoons into the ice cream tub.

Charlie broke the silence. "Have you ever been, like, instantly interested in someone?"

Val nodded. "Like an instant attraction. Sure."

"Yeah, like that. But like someone grabs your attention more than usual. Like attraction on steroids." Charlie was doing a bad job of explaining. But how could she explain a feeling she didn't understand herself?

Val sat and thought for a few moments. "There was that girl at the gym that time. Remember? I was a mess for weeks. Thought I was in love."

"Didn't she turn out to be straight?" Charlie squinted as she tried to remember.

"There was one night she wasn't. Two actually."

Charlie laughed and swatted Val on the arm. "You are terrible."

Val snickered. "Also turned out that I wasn't in love. I was just smitten for a few weeks, and I got over it quick. I don't believe in all that connection shit. We're attracted to some people more than others, I think. But you know, you and me are the same. It never sticks."

Charlie nodded in agreement. It never did stick. They did everything to make sure it didn't stick, hence their rules. She and Val were like two peas in a pod, especially in that regard. "Did you see the new bartender?" If Charlie had noticed her, surely Val had as well.

"She is Fine with a capital F," Val said. "Wait. Is that who the feels are all about? Because I'm pretty sure half of the folk who were at Oasis tonight are at home right now, feeling the exact same way about her."

"I'm betting half of Oasis didn't have the sexy eye contact that I had with her." Charlie took another mouthful of ice cream. "Before I fucked it up," she mumbled with her mouth full, a bit of melted ice cream running down her chin.

"If only she could see you now."

Charlie wiped her mouth and gave Val a playful glare. She went on to explain about Steph and the dance floor activities. "If there was even a chance of her being interested, she didn't look too impressed after that."

"Nothing Charlie Bradshaw can't come back from."

Charlie grinned. "That's true."

"You'll need to bring your A-game though. I heard her talking, all posh and shit. She was walking around like she was on a catwalk. What a woman like that is doing tending bar at Oasis, I do not know."

"She's sophisticated. What's wrong with that?"

"Nothing. She seems a bit out of place is all."

"She definitely stands out."

"Ugh, you do have a crush." Val stood up from the sofa and stretched. "I'm going to bed. Stop worrying—next time you see her you can turn on the Charlie charm, and you can get your little crush out of your system before you turn into a tub of mint choc chip."

Charlie looked down at the empty carton and looked back at Val. "You helped."

CHAPTER FIVE

It was almost four in the morning by the time Erica got back to her temporary apartment. She leaned against the door as it shut and let out a long groan of exhaustion. Hera wasted no time in showing her delight at her arrival by meowing and rubbing against her ankles.

"You must be hungry, little lady."

She peeled her body from the door and walked slowly to the kitchen. Heels had not been the brightest idea for her first night of sheer manual labour, but she didn't own anything else. She felt instant relief as she stepped out of them, leaving them in the middle of the floor. She was too tired to pick them up. She walked to the food bowl she had set out for Hera before she'd left for Oasis, but the cat food she had left her was untouched. She frowned as she lifted the bowl to discard the old food and replace it with a fresh pack. Hera never usually missed a meal. In fact, Erica could never remember her missing a meal.

She laid down the fresh food bowl and watched as Hera walked over and sniffed at it. Then Hera ran off across the living room and jumped on top of the sofa.

"That's not like you." She followed her to the sofa and gave her a few scratches behind her ears which Hera obviously appreciated if her purrs were anything to go by. When she had had enough, she hopped down and curled up in her bed, which Erica had put beside the radiator. She seemed okay apart from the lack of appetite. Erica would keep an eye on it.

Climbing into bed had never felt so good. Usually, she hated sleeping in beds that weren't her own. Even in the plushest of hotels, nothing felt as good as her own bed. But at that point a wooden bench would have felt like luxury.

Work was *hard*. Erica was well out of her depth. She was slightly ashamed to admit that she'd never had to work hard for anything. It wasn't that she was without skills. She was a fantastic organizer, and a great problem solver. She could network with all kinds of people. She arranged events for her mother's foundation regularly. But organising fundraisers and planning soirees had not prepared her for serving drinks to a multitude of party goers. It was a hard graft, and she had a newfound respect for those who did it. For starters, all the bottles looked the same to her. She was used to having drinks given to her already poured into a glass. She couldn't tell one bottle from another. Ash, who had been tasked with training Erica, thankfully had the patience of a saint, telling her where and what everything was repeatedly. And always with a smile on her face, like she wasn't bothered that Erica had to ask her which gin was which about ten times over. She would have to remember to tell Zachary that Ash deserved a raise. Of course, as far as Ash was concerned, Erica was just a new colleague. Only Brandon knew the truth, and Zachary, of course. Zachary had decided to stay away from Oasis while she was working there, though. They weren't identical twins, of course. But put them side by side and it was possible to notice the similarity. So, she was left to deal with Brandon, who didn't seem too thrilled about her presence—hopefully she wouldn't have to deal with him often. She gathered from the rest of the staff that he tended to keep himself to himself.

Then there were the customers. Every time Erica had turned around there were at least ten people trying to get her attention, hands in the air, waving money at her, shouting to be heard over the music. She couldn't serve them all at once, and she found it difficult to know who was there first. The demand was endless. She hadn't stopped working all night and her entire body was paying the price. Her aching muscles hated her for not opting for that spa weekend instead. She was starting to question her decision herself.

One thing she did enjoy was the people watching. Groups of friends having a good time. People with dance moves that belonged on the stage, and others that should have kept them hidden in the living room. The chat-ups gone right, and the ones that were clearly going horribly wrong.

Then there was *her.* The woman with the blond hair who had been looking at her. She was gorgeous. Erica would be lying if she said she hadn't enjoyed the attention. Even the little flustered look when Erica had caught her watching her was endearing.

That hadn't lasted long. Only seconds later she was grinding against another woman, playing tonsil tennis in the middle of the dance floor. Talk about an immediate turn off. Whether it had been her girlfriend, and she had taken the time to eye up Erica while the girlfriend wasn't there, or it was just a hookup on a night out, Erica was not impressed. She hated cheaters, and she hated players, so Erica's interest had been very short-lived.

Not that it mattered. Erica wasn't in London for romance. She had a job to do. Help Zachary by finding the thief, and then she could get back to her seaside cottage where she belonged. She would have to face her mother and Victoria. But that was a problem for another day.

❖

Erica was relieved to be working with Ash again the following night. She hadn't had time to really get to know anyone else, but she got a quick introduction to Kelly-Ann, who spent more time making eyes at the guy who worked on the door than doing any actual real work. He was called Tom, she was told. He had arms that rivalled The Rock's. No one would ever dare mess with Tom.

She would try to make it round to everyone so she could start gauging what they were like. The quicker she got to know them, the quicker she could finish her secret mission, as Zachary liked to call it.

Oasis was much nicer than she had pictured in her head so many times. Classier. There was nothing dark and dingy about it, for starters. There was a cosy looking seating area, with its own smaller bar. There were all types of tables and chairs scattered around it and it led to an outdoor seating area as well, with awnings and patio heaters. In the main bar area, there was a large dance floor, with glittering disco balls hanging from the ceiling. There were booths with plush black and grey leather seats surrounding the area. Although the insides of bars were characteristically dark, Oasis felt bright and colourful with the walls and bar areas lit up in pinks and purples. The main bar had two sides to it. One side served right onto the dance floor, and the other was lined with stools, and had a more spacious area for people to hang out. Because it was obviously the busier bar, there was a small, conjoined stock room that made it easier to refill stock quickly—one of the only jobs Erica could do so far. She was working on the main bar again that night.

The next few hours flew by, with Ash taking the time to show her the ropes. Erica couldn't pull a decent pint to save her life, unless half a glass of foam was the new thing—the Oasis clientele didn't think so. Nor was she able to pull off a good cocktail. Lucky for her, everyone wanted their cocktail to be made by Ash anyway. Ash did plenty of showboating, throwing the shaker around and catching behind her back, and doing all kinds of tricks. Erica was, however, getting better at passing bottles out of the fridges, and her measures were improving. Small victories.

How the hell had Tess got the impression that she would find any of it fun? She was having the total opposite of fun.

At least Erica didn't *need* to be the best bartender in the world. All she needed to do was keep her eyes open and look for clues. She didn't know what she was looking for exactly, but she was sure she would know when she saw something suspicious. At one point, Brandon lifted a wad of cash from the till, and Erica watched out of the corner of her eye. It was a sizable amount. What would he do with it? But he bagged the money and went to his office to put in the safe. Nothing out of the ordinary about that. She wished he had stuck it in his pocket and her job would have been done. She could get the hell out of there and back to where she belonged.

She watched to see if anyone else did anything remotely suspicious. Ash was too busy showing off her skills to adoring fans at the bar to do anything else. Erica really hoped it wasn't her. She had been the most welcoming and down to earth out of everyone. She didn't think it could be her, but she had to keep all of her options open. As for Kelly-Ann, she looked like she wanted to rip Tom the bouncer's clothes off there and then. Sultry looks across the bar were all she was guilty of. Nothing out of the ordinary. Still, she kept a surreptitious eye on them all.

"Can I order a glass of white wine please?"

The voice must have been talking to her because Ash was at the other end of the bar. She was sure that she could handle a glass of white wine solo. When she looked up, she saw it was none other than the blond from the night before.

Erica didn't let her recognition show. "What kind?"

"Pinot Grigio?" The woman gave Erica a smile that bordered on flirty rather than friendly.

Erica turned and poured the measure of wine into a glass. Ash was giving her a thumbs up from a few feet away. Probably glad that Erica was finally able to do something by herself. She set the glass on the bar and took the money without speaking. She wasn't going to encourage any flirtation. Erica had already decided that was a hard no from her after what she had witnessed the night before.

"How's your second day going?" the woman asked as Erica passed her change over. There was that smile again too.

"What?" Erica asked. She tried for a bored tone of voice.

"Your second day? Last night was your first, and today is your second. How's it going?"

"Fine." Erica looked around for her next customer to serve, but for once there was no one waiting. Figured.

"Glad to hear it. I'm Charlie." She held out a hand for Erica to shake.

Erica looked down at the outstretched hand but didn't take it. "Okay. Can I get you anything else?"

"Just your name," Charlie said, pulling her hand back undeterred. *Forward.*

"You've got your drink. You don't need to know my name." She knew that she was being rude, but she had seen everything she had needed to see the previous night to know that this woman—Charlie— was trouble. Even if Erica had momentarily found her attractive, she knew what women like Charlie were like. And she wasn't going to entertain her attentions.

"That's where you're wrong. I really need to know your name. It's the whole reason that I'm here tonight."

Charlie had game. Erica had to give her that. If she were younger or more naïve, she would probably be feeling flattered at the attention Charlie was showing her. Flattered that she was here for her, or so she said. But Erica was not younger, nor naïve. And she refused to be flattered by the likes of Charlie. She wasn't going to tell Charlie a thing about herself. Deflection was the best course of action. Erica had never met a woman who didn't want the opportunity to talk about themselves. "Is Charlie short for Charlotte then?" Hopefully if she kept the spotlight on Charlie, she could avoid being asked any more questions about herself.

Charlie winced. "It is, but nobody calls me that. I hate it. I've been Charlie ever since I had a say."

"I don't understand why people shorten their names, especially when they have perfectly acceptable given names."

"Do you have an acceptable name?" Charlie grinned.

Deflection clearly wasn't going to work with this woman. "I do."

"But you aren't going to tell me what it is?"

"No."

"And I take it that means you aren't going to tell me where you're from, either?" Charlie asked. "You aren't a Londoner. Your accent is too nice. Fancy."

"I'm sure there are many well-spoken people in London."

"Are you from London, then?"

"No."

"Aha! Now we're getting somewhere." Charlie looked triumphant.

Erica cursed herself for slipping up, but she played it off. "I'm still not telling you where."

"Is this about last night?" Charlie asked. "Is that why you won't talk to me?"

"Last night?" Erica hoped her face conveyed her disinterest to Charlie. An image of Charlie lip-locked with that other girl flashed through her mind, but unless Charlie was a mind reader, she wouldn't know that.

"Come on, you know what I mean. The dancing. The kissing."

Erica shook her head. "Doesn't ring a bell. You're talking about your girlfriend or something, I assume?" She posed the question casually, but the truth was she was interested in the answer. She wanted to know whether Charlie was a cheater or a player. The answer wouldn't change anything, but it would satisfy her own curiosity.

"She wasn't my girlfriend. I don't have a girlfriend. She was just a girl. It was nothing."

A player, then. "Good for you."

Charlie narrowed her eyes. "You did see me last night. I know you did."

"I saw a lot of people last night. It mustn't have been that memorable."

Charlie put her hand over her heart. "I'd say I was offended, but I know you're lying."

"Why do you think I'm lying?"

"You asked me if it was my girlfriend. I never said it was a woman." Charlie looked smug.

She was good, Erica could admit that. She did everything in her power to hold back the smile that was threatening. "From your attempt to chat me up, I'd say it was a fairly obvious assumption."

"Do you like me chatting you up?"

"No." Being blunt was the only way to put a stop to it.

"Are you seriously not going to tell me your name?" She wasn't backing down.

Neither was Erica. "I have to get back to work now, Charlotte. Thanks for the…talk."

Charlie shook her head but laughed. "It's Charlie."

"Whatever," Erica shouted over her shoulder as she walked away. She went to rejoin Ash further down the bar.

"I see you've caught Charlie's eye," Ash said as she replenished some clean glasses on the shelf.

"You know her?" Erica asked, as she reached for some glasses herself to help.

"Yeah, she comes in here quite a bit. She's harmless, don't worry."

Erica fought the urge to glance back in Charlie's direction, where she was sure Charlie would still be watching. "I'm not looking to get involved with anyone." And she definitely wasn't looking to get involved with someone like Charlie. Even Charlie's persistence and brazen attitude bothered Erica. Erica had made it clear that she wasn't interested and still Charlie had pushed and pushed. That was not the type of woman she went for. Erica could admit that for a few moments she had thought Charlie was attractive, but her actions were not. The conversation had solidified Erica's conclusion from the night before. Charlie couldn't be further from her type.

"Girlfriend waiting at home? Or boyfriend?" Ash asked. She was probably just trying to get to know Erica.

"It would be girlfriend if there was one, but there isn't. I'm not looking right now." Technically true. Victoria was not her girlfriend, and she wasn't looking to date anyone while she was staying in London.

"Well, you're probably right. Not getting involved with Charlie. She's hot and a lot of fun and all, but she isn't relationship material. I don't think she often goes back for seconds, if you know what I mean." Ash shook her head and chuckled.

"Are you speaking from experience?" For some reason, Erica couldn't help being a touch curious about Charlie. Ash clearly had insight. It was good to get to know the people she was working with too. It would give her a better chance of finding the thief.

"Not myself, no. I'm with someone. But I don't miss much that goes on in here."

"Have you worked here long?" Erica flipped into investigator mode.

Ash nodded. "Over two years now. I was hired when Zach took it over. He was left this bar and a few others from his dad, Rick, from what I heard. Did the place up and hired a bunch of new staff. It looked a bit shabby and dated before that apparently, but he made it into a really cool place. I like working here. Did you get to meet Zach, or was it just Brandon who interviewed you?"

Zachary, Erica corrected in her head. She hadn't lied about not being a fan of shortened names, though she had only called Charlie her given name to mess with her.

"It was just Brandon." She needed to keep herself and Zachary separate. She didn't want to spout too many lies and trip herself up. "Would you say you're close with all of the staff, then? Seeing as you've worked here for a while."

Ash put her head from side to side. "I'd say I *know* everyone, but I'm not close to them all. I do get along with most of them."

"Is there anyone I should watch out for?" Maybe Ash and her insider knowledge would be the key to cracking the case.

Ash thought about it for a moment and then lowered her voice. "I always feel like there's something shady about Tom. The doorman. Maybe it's that whole intimidating look thing he has going on, but I can't help but feel like there's something off about him. Of course, that could all be my imagination."

Erica found herself glancing over at scowling Tom, who was keeping his eye on Kelly-Ann. Maybe Erica would keep an extra close eye on him. "Good to know," was all she said in reply to Ash.

"What brings you to work here? I hope you don't mind me saying, but you aren't the usual type of bar staff we get in here."

"I fancied a change of scenery." Partly true.

"But you haven't done bar work before? That's obvious. No offense." Ash smiled and Erica knew she didn't mean it badly. She had to agree, it was kind of obvious. "What did you do before this?"

"Office work mostly. I got fed up sitting behind a desk all the time. Hence, the job change." Erica and Zachary had rehearsed a small back story for her in case anyone asked for details. They decided no one would be likely to delve further into *office work*. Judging by Ash's simple head nod, they were right.

There wasn't much more time for small talk for the rest of the night. There was a steady stream of people. Luckily that meant that Charlie hadn't been able to hound her again either. She had noticed that

Charlie had joined a group of friends, but apart from that, Erica ignored her existence. After last orders had been called, she did have a final look around, just so that she could be prepared if Charlie did try to talk to her again, but she was nowhere to be seen.

Erica wasn't disappointed at all.

CHAPTER SIX

L et me get this straight," Liz said, as she dropped the extracted tooth into the metal tray beside her with a clink. "You were attracted to her, but you had already turned the moves on someone else?"

Charlie took the instrument from Liz and put it back on the trolley beside the small operating table where a poor Yorkshire terrier called Murphy was getting some dental treatment. "You make me sound terrible, but yes."

"Then she saw you kissing this other woman and she didn't fall at your feet when you went to chat her up the next night? Wow, what the hell is wrong with her?"

"Okay, I get it. I do. But she was so rude. She didn't have to be rude." Charlie stroked the dog's brown and black fur. He was under anaesthesia, but there was nothing wrong with a little extra comforting.

Liz threw her head back and laughed. Outright laughed. Like she had just heard the funniest joke in the world.

"You're laughing at me? I tell you I get turned down and you laugh?"

"You deserve it. The serial rejector gets rejected. You've got to love the irony." Liz was still chuckling as she injected Murphy with a painkiller before starting to remove her surgical gear.

Charlie gently lifted Murphy into the little dog bed where he would sleep off the rest of the drugs and hopefully wake up feeling much better. Good-bye nasty abscess. She removed her own surgical clothes too when she had Murphy all safe and comfy. "It was more than a rejection. It was like she couldn't even stand to speak to me."

"So, go and move on to the next one. Isn't that your thing? Why are you so bothered?"

But Charlie was still going. "And she called me Charlotte. You know I *hate* being called Charlotte."

Liz tried again. "As you always say, plenty more fish in the sea."

"And then she walked away. Just ended the conversation, turned her back and left me standing there." Charlie threw her hands out at her sides and then dramatically flopped them back down. "The whole night, she didn't look in my direction. Not once." She noticed Liz's quizzical look. "What?"

"Nothing."

Charlie pointed at Liz's face. Drew an air circle around it. "What's this all about?"

"I was just thinking that in all the years I've known you, I've never seen you so affected by a woman."

Charlie scoffed. "I am not affected. I think she was rude, is all." She scoffed again in case the first one hadn't already proved Liz's ridiculous statement to be wrong.

Liz nodded, which was contradictory to the face she was making, which said she didn't believe a word of Charlie's argument. "You talked about her the whole way through Murphy's surgery."

"Yes. Because she was *rude*." She was raising her voice. She dropped it back down again. "Very, very hot. But horrible."

"Maybe you should try and talk to her again. You know, without all the Charlieness."

"Charlieness? What do you mean?"

"You know. The cockiness. The presumptuousness. All of that. Turn off the Charlie charm and talk to her like a normal human being."

Charlie's jaw dropped open. "I am not cocky or presumptuous."

"If you say so," Liz said.

Charlie gathered her and Liz's disposable gowns and gloves and threw them in the wastebasket. "Anyway, I'm not going to try to talk to her again."

"No?"

"Nope. She had her chance."

Liz threw her hands in the air as she walked past Charlie to leave the small operating room. "I could shake you sometimes."

"What does that mean?" Charlie called after her, but she was already away to her office.

Why would Charlie try and talk to someone who clearly didn't want to talk to her when there were so many other women out there who did? It wasn't like she struggled.

She continued to tidy and then sat down to write up the chart. She tapped the pen against her lip. She was not affected. She didn't get affected. Not ever. Yes, she had been thinking about it all night, and all day. That was only because she was so annoyed about the whole thing. She wasn't used to being rejected. Of course, it had happened before, but never like that. The woman, whose name she still didn't know, had no right to speak to Charlie like that. Charlie was a nice person. She was friendly. But it was clear that she thought she was better than Charlie. Better than most people, judging from her posh voice and abrupt manner. And Liz thought Charlie would try and talk to her again? No chance.

But the woman was attractive. Even more so when Charlie had got up close. Full lips waiting to be kissed. Green eyes that were bright and shiny like emeralds.

Nope. Not going there.

❖

Charlie was ready for a night of doing nothing. She had the place to herself. Val was visiting her parents. Liz had let her slip away thirty minutes early, with Little Paws quietening down for the day. She had grabbed herself some Chinese food on her way home—vegetable spring rolls, a mixed vegetable chow mein, and egg fried rice, *yum*. And she could feel her pyjamas calling to her from her apartment a few floors above when she arrived at her building. She started her climb up the stairs to the fourth floor. There only were five floors, but at least she didn't have to go all the way to the top.

Charlie never got in the lift. She hated them. They weren't all sexy and angsty and drama-filled like *Grey's Anatomy* led folks to believe. Nope. It was a metal box, sometimes a very rickety one, that got stuck way more often than it should, leaving its helpless passengers dangling in mid-air by some cables, which could snap and cause them to plunge to their deaths at any given moment. Best-case scenario, they'd be stuck in said metal box for an unpredictable amount of time until rescued. Why would she put herself at risk like that? So up the stairs she climbed.

"Son of a bitch."

Charlie heard her before she saw her. A woman was crouched down fiddling with the lock on the door of the apartment next to hers. Olly's place. If she was trying to break in, she was doing a terrible job, but Charlie didn't think that was likely. It looked like she was trying to get the key to shift, and surely a robber wouldn't have a key. Nor attempt to get in through the front door in the middle of the afternoon, or early evening, as it was now.

She couldn't remember ever seeing a woman coming and going from Olly's place. She knew it couldn't be a romantic interest. Not Olly's type. Charlie tried to think if she could ever remember Olly mentioning a sister.

The woman growled out loud. Then she slumped against the door, as if that would miraculously budge it. It didn't and she slid down to the ground. It seemed she had given up. Charlie realized she was frozen to the spot, watching these events unfold.

She gave herself a shake and walked over to the woman. "Do you need some help? These doors are old, and the locks can get a little—" The woman turned round to face her. She had not expected to come face-to-face with the new bartender from Oasis in the middle of her hallway, but here she was. What the hell was she doing here?

"You." The woman looked skyward and shook her head. She must have thought some higher being was messing with her. Like Charlie's presence made her day go from bad to worse. "Wait. Are you following me?"

"No," Charlie said, astounded. Why did this woman have such an issue with her? She indicated her own front door with her head. "I live here. I can't believe you even thought that."

At least the woman had the decency to look slightly embarrassed. "Right, well." An apology was apparently too much to expect. She proceeded to get up from her spot on the ground and dust herself off. Charlie guessed that no one was supposed to witness her moment of self-pity on the floor.

"Do you want my help or not?" Charlie tapped her foot on the tiled floor and the woman looked down at it before lifting her gaze to meet Charlie's. She really was gorgeous. Charlie couldn't deny that.

"I'm perfectly capable of unlocking a door by myself." She folded her arms. Could she have made herself seem any more stubborn?

"It doesn't look like it." Charlie held her hand out toward the door that remained shut as evidence.

Her lips moved but no sound came out. Eventually, she stuck her nose in the air. "I don't need your help."

"Okay, fine. You know what, forget I offered." Charlie turned to her own front door and unlocked it with ease. She couldn't resist throwing a smug look over her shoulder. She stepped in and closed the door behind her. She felt like slamming it, but she didn't. She wouldn't want to give her the satisfaction.

Oh, but that woman made Charlie's blood boil. She marched over to the kitchen and grabbed herself a plate. Charlie wouldn't let her ruin her quiet night in. She didn't like Charlie, that was clear. Crystal. *Whatever.*

Charlie untied the bag containing her food.

The woman was probably stubborn enough to stand out there all night. She deserved to be locked out, with that kind of attitude. Why was she trying to get into Olly's place anyway? And how did she know him? Olly was such a lovely person. She would have to ask him how he knew Miss Snooty Pants.

She started to dish the food onto her plate when there was a tapping at the door. Three quick taps. Abrupt. Leaving Charlie in no doubt who it was.

What does she want now? Charlie sighed and quickly put the cover back on her food to keep it warm. She swung the door open and leaned against it. "Yes?"

The woman cleared her throat and spoke quietly. "Fine. You can help me to open the door."

"Sorry, was that you *asking* me for help?" Charlie laughed. "Unbelievable." This woman had some nerve.

The woman narrowed her eyes. "Can you help me open the door?" she asked a bit louder.

"I'm sure I can, but I'm not sure I want to, now."

The woman set her jaw. "Look, will you help me or not?" she asked impatiently.

Charlie stood and regarded her for a few moments. She should close the door in her face. She wouldn't, but she should. "Can I help you open the *door*...?" There was no way Charlie was letting her off that easily. Charlie tapped her lip. "I'm sure there's more to that sentence."

"Please. Can you help me open the door, please?" she asked, defeated.

Charlie gave her a wide smile. "Why, of course I can," she said, purposely with too much enthusiasm. The woman looked unamused.

She stepped out and walked over to the door. "Do you have the key?"

The woman wordlessly handed Charlie the key.

"These locks, they need a gentle touch. Like a woman, really. If you push too hard, or move too quick, it might not have the desired effect. You can't go in full force. You need to put a little bit of work in first. But if you know exactly what you're doing—which lucky for you, I do, with a little finesse…" She put the key in the door and softly moved it from side to side, all the while holding the other woman's gaze, "Nice and slow, just enough pressure, in just the right spot…" She turned the key with a click. "Works every time." Charlie grinned.

The woman shook her head with the same unamused look on her face she had when she had been asking Charlie for help. "Very smooth."

Was Charlie imagining it or was the woman's chest rising and falling a little faster? Maybe her charms were not completely wasted after all. No, Charlie had to be imagining it. Ice didn't thaw so quickly.

The woman walked toward the door and pushed it slightly, as if she was making sure that Charlie had opened it properly. When it budged, she gave Charlie a quick nod. Was that supposed to be thanks? She went to walk inside.

"Wow. Okay. You're welcome."

The woman paused in the doorway but didn't turn back around. "Thank you, Charlotte." The door clicked shut.

God, that woman was infuriating.

❖

Tess answered the phone to Erica on the second ring.

"Anyone would think you were sitting by the phone awaiting my call." Erica stuck her phone onto speaker while she went about Olly's kitchen making her dinner. She got some red onion and a green pepper out of the fridge and began chopping.

After not getting to bed until the wee hours of the morning again, she had slept in until mid-morning. She had a day off from working at Oasis. She didn't really want one. The more she was there doing her fake work, the more likely she was to get to the bottom of the missing money, and the whole charade would be over. But she had to blend in as one of the staff, which meant she had two days off per week. She hoped it wouldn't be for too many weeks. On the upside, a day off gave her a little bit of time to do things she needed to do. She had gone grocery shopping and stocked up on enough food to last her the week. She bought six different types of food for Hera, who still hadn't touched her food since their arrival in London. Erica hoped that at least one of them would entice her to find her appetite again.

"I've been sitting by the phone for days now, and all I've had are three measly text messages. Three!" Tess said. "And they told me nothing. I know nothing, other than the fact that you are, thankfully, still alive."

Erica chuckled. "What is it that you want to know? I've pretty much only arrived. There isn't a lot to tell."

"I need details. I want to know everything. You, Erica Frost, are working in a bar, for crying out loud. That in itself should be made into a reality TV show."

"Sometimes I wonder why I remain friends with you. It's dreadful for my self-esteem."

"Shut up. You love me. And you know I love you. Now spill. How is your big London adventure?"

"First of all, this is not an adventure. There is nothing adventurous about my sore feet, aching arms, and eyes with black rings around them. It is exhausting. People really work like this all the time. They deserve a medal." She stretched her arms out. *Yep, still sore.*

"Spoken like a true privileged brat. At least you appreciate us underlings now."

Erica knew Tess was teasing. "You may laugh, but you're right. I do appreciate these hard-working people an awful lot more than I did before."

"Apart from your newfound appreciation of servers, how's it going? Are you any further on with your manhunt?"

Erica shook her head. She lifted the chopping board with her chopped vegetables, and they sizzled as she pushed them into her already heated pan. She added some shredded carrot, beansprouts, and sliced mushrooms. She had no idea what she was making yet, some kind of vegetable stir-fry. She made it up as she went along. "No suspects yet. There's a doorman who's a possibility, but that's more of a feeling. I have zero evidence."

"Feelings can be right sometimes."

"Maybe." So far Tom hadn't done anything but scowl at everyone around him. That didn't give him grounds to be her number one suspect, but she had nothing else.

"And the bar, Oasis, is it? Is working there really all that bad?"

Erica sighed. "It's tiring. I don't get to sleep until the morning. And I'm the worst bartender ever. The woman who I've been working with has been nice, though, so that's something. I don't know how she hasn't murdered me by now, with the amount of drink orders I've mixed up."

Tess giggled. "And there's no way she could be your thief?"

"I don't think so, but who knows? I hope she isn't. I'd be worried if I turned out to be such a terrible judge of character." Erica stirred her vegetables around in the pan. She lifted it and gave them a toss before throwing a few bits of seasoning in. She got another pan out and added some noodles and boiling water.

"What about the apartment you're staying in? Is it okay? Would my obsessive interior designing brain be having a meltdown?"

Erica poured herself a half glass of Shiraz and looked around her. The open plan apartment was nice. The kitchen was modern. Olly had kept the walls and floors pretty neutral. Mostly whites and greys. He'd added colour with his accessories—rugs, bright paintings, stylish vases, and cushions scattered around the large corner sofa. There was a large bookcase carefully decorated with a mixture of books and ornaments. It all went well together. Then again, Olly was in fashion, so he knew how to put colours together. "No, you'd cope. It's a really nice place. Modern. Spacious." Erica took a sip from her glass before muttering, "It's a shame about the neighbours."

"Why? What's wrong with the neighbours?"

She shouldn't have said that. "Nothing really."

"Obviously something."

"It's just this woman. She chatted me up at Oasis and it turns out that she lives in the apartment next door. Which is inconvenient to say the least." She held up two sachets of sauce to look at them. "Do you think Vietnamese plum sauce or sweet chilli and ginger would be nicer?"

"The plum. Now go back?"

"To what?" Erica asked. She knew, but she enjoyed playing with Tess too much. She should have known better than to say anything. Tess wouldn't drop the subject until she knew everything. Not that there was much to tell.

Tess tutted. "To your neighbour who chatted you up. Why you didn't lead with that I don't know. The rest of this phone call has clearly been a waste of time."

"That's nearly all there is to it. She came on to me in the bar. I made it clear I wasn't interested. Then I had an embarrassing experience where I had to ask her to help me unlock the door to the apartment because the lock got stuck. That's it."

"Rewind again. She came onto you in the bar…"

"Right. Well, it kind of started the night before that. There were a few looks shared, but then the next thing, she was kissing some other girl. She's one of those types that jumps from one woman to another, you know the kind I mean. The type I don't have time for. No, thank you."

"Right. Because you don't do casual." Tess mimicked their conversation from a few days ago.

"Exactly."

"And the looks. The looks must have been totally one-sided then?"

Erica added the sauce to the pan and stirred it in. "What do you mean?"

"You said there were looks. Was she just staring you out? Stalker style?"

Damn Tess and her attention to detail. It made her a fantastic interior designer and probably would make her an even better detective if she ever decided on a career change. "I suppose I was looking too. At first. If you want to get all specific about the whole thing."

"So, you found her attractive?"

"I never said that she was unattractive. I said she was a player. And that is unattractive to me."

"And let me guess—when she tried to talk to you, you treated her like shit? Then you almost had a heart attack when you realized that she was your neighbour, so you treated her like shit some more. Then you had to swallow some humble pie and ask her for help. Which you absolutely hated, hence it being embarrassing, as you put it. And now you're in a mood about it. Tell me I'm close."

Erica looked around the apartment. Was Tess behind the curtains? Under the table? Surely, she wasn't *that* predictable.

"I'll take your silence as a big fat yes. That poor girl," Tess said.

"How the hell do you know all of that? And what do you mean *poor girl*?"

Tess chuckled on the other end of the line. "Because I know you. And when you're attracted to someone you think you shouldn't be, you're mean to them. Which totally scares them off. It's like some kind of defence mechanism. You should really speak to your therapist about it."

"Thanks, I'll bring it up somewhere between my daddy abandonment issues and strained mother-daughter relationship."

Tess's laugh sounded through the phone and Erica couldn't help but join in.

"Seriously, though, this is what you do, Erica. You have a clear picture in your head about the type of woman you should be with, and the way they should act, and you won't deviate from that. Anyone who's outside of your norms doesn't stand a chance."

"Wow. Tell me how you truly feel there, Tess."

"Tell me I'm wrong?"

"In this case, you are. Yes, she's unbelievably good looking. Like, really, really good looking." Erica closed her eyes as she pictured the beauty that was Charlie. She shook her head. Dwelling on that would lead to nothing good. "But it's not only because she's outside of my norms. Even the girl I work with said she's only interested in one-night stands. She kissed that other girl, then told me the next night that it was nothing. Nothing! How disrespectful is that? Why the hell would I want to be the next *nothing*?" Her voice was getting higher and louder, but she was on a rant, so she kept going. "And she had this confidence, like I was going to jump into bed with her just because she asked. Like I should have been flattered by her mere attention." She beat the wooden spoon against the pan with more force than necessary. "No, she's just a player...like my deadbeat father was. Look how that turned out for my mother. On top of all of that, she calls herself Charlie instead of Charlotte. You know I despise when people do that with their names. Be called what you're called."

"You've never said anything about my name."

"That's because your name is Tess. That isn't short for anything."

"It's short for Theresa."

Erica was silent for a few moments. "Yeah, well. That's different."

"How?" Tess sounded amused.

"Because I didn't know that." They both laughed.

"Does this mean I can't call you Ri-Ri?"

"Don't even think about it."

Tess laughed again. "Look." She took a breath. "All I'm saying is, don't jump to conclusions. Don't rule anything out. And for fuck's sake don't go all mean-girl-Erica on some innocent girl whose only crime was trying to get into your pants. God knows you could do with it."

Erica snorted. "Thanks for that."

"Anytime. It's what I'm here for. Insults and reality checks. Speaking of getting into pants, I've got to go. Scott's just pulled into the driveway and I have to go and jump his bones and try and make a baby."

Erica smiled. "Now, good luck with *that*."

They signed off and Erica put the finishing touches on her dinner.

Once the noodles were stirred in, she put it into a bowl and decided to curl up on the sofa to eat it. Hera was lying sleeping beside her. She reached down and petted her, but she didn't get much of a reaction. She still hadn't eaten anything, but Erica had five more types of food to try. She was sure one of them would work. She pulled her phone out anyway and did a search for the veterinary practices in the area with the best reviews. She wanted to at least be prepared. Erica liked being prepared for whatever life threw at her.

CHAPTER SEVEN

Erica woke up the next day feeling energized and refreshed. An early night and a good sleep, through the night like a normal person, had been exactly what she needed. She opened the curtains, and the sunlight came beaming through the window. It was still early, a couple of hours before the hustle and bustle of folk making their way to work or wherever they were headed for the day. Erica decided to quickly get ready and go and enjoy the slower pace of the city for a little while. Maybe grab some coffee and breakfast while she was out. She had either been working or sleeping since she had arrived in London and hadn't a lot of time to wander.

Hera was curled up in her bed, still fast asleep, Erica's presence not disturbing her in the slightest. The previous night's food was still untouched—the first out of the six she bought. She threw it away and put out number two, as well as some fresh water. She had decided that she would try all of the different food she had bought, and if none of them worked, then she would bring Hera to the vet. A Google search had suggested that Hera might just be adjusting to new surroundings, and that she would find her appetite again in no time. Google also came up with some other horrible things that Erica refused to consider yet. The new surroundings thing made sense. She was sure that was all it was.

Erica made her way outside. She stopped for a few seconds to take in a few breaths of the cool fresh air. It wasn't cold as such, but she was glad she wore a jacket. Though it seemed like a day that would warm up quick. Spring was turning into summer. There were a few people out and about, but it was nowhere near as busy as she knew London would get in the next couple of hours. The perfect time for a leisurely walk. She could stroll without having to fight her way through the crowds or constantly having to zigzag between people to avoid crashing into them. She didn't have a plan of where she was headed, so she just walked. Olly didn't live far from Hyde Park and that's where she ended up. She wandered along the pathway surrounded by green trees and freshly cut grass. There were squirrels dancing around the green beside her, chasing each other up the branches of the trees that were swaying gently in the soft breeze.

She passed a few people out walking their dogs. A particularly friendly Collie ran over to greet her. She laughed as it rolled over, showing off to get petted. She leaned down and gave the attention it was looking for. Why wouldn't she? The Collie's human, an older lady, caught up with the dog and apologized to Erica for the intrusion. Which of course, it wasn't, at all, and Erica told her so. The dog's name was Cookie, and she was only two years old and a bundle of energy, according to her owner. After the normal small talk about Cookie and the weather, the lady told Erica to enjoy her day, and she and Cookie set off in the opposite direction.

Erica smiled as she continued along her walk. There was something nice about exchanging simple pleasantries with strangers. A friendliness. People should do it more often.

In the distance she could see a woman jogging toward her. As she got a bit closer, Erica couldn't help but admire the jogger's physique— clearly fit and toned, showcased by her tight-fitting running shorts and sports top. Her blond hair was in a ponytail swaying behind her. Erica squinted. As the jogger got closer, she started to look oddly familiar.

That's because she was.

"You've got to be kidding," Erica whispered under her breath, as Charlie ran toward her. Her recognition had obviously twigged too, because as she approached, she beamed and slowed her jog to a walk. Straight toward Erica.

"Good morning," Charlie said. The smile never left her face. Her breathing was slightly quicker than normal because of the exercise, and there were a couple of beads of sweat on her forehead. It made her look even hotter, if that were possible, and Erica silently cursed, because how was that fair?

"Morning, Charlotte," Erica muttered back. See, she had manners.

"It's Charlie."

It worked every time. "Yes. You've told me." She waved a hand. "Whatever." She started to step away, but Charlie's voice stopped her.

"It seems like you can't keep away from me." There was that cocky grin again. The one from Oasis, and from when Charlie had unlocked her door. The one that irked Erica, because it was attractive and irritating at the same time.

"Don't be ridiculous. I clearly just keep finding myself in the wrong place at the wrong time." She folded her arms.

Charlie's smile faltered slightly. "Relax, I was kidding. You're really quite rude, do you know that?"

Erica thought about what Tess had said to her about being mean to people she was attracted to. And there she was lusting after the blond jogger who turned out to be Charlie, who she had already previously lusted over, and Tess was right. Charlie was right. She *was* rude. Mean. Still, she couldn't back down. She couldn't show that she was embarrassed by her own behaviour—even though she was. "Well, you don't *have* to talk to me, you know? Then I wouldn't be rude to you. A win-win for both of us."

"But we're neighbours. I was brought up to be nice to my neighbours." Charlie cocked her head to the side. "Why are we neighbours, by the way? How do you know Olly?"

Erica couldn't tell Charlie the truth. She would blow her cover. "Again, you're asking things that are none of your business."

"Right. Like your name. I take it that's still none of my business, either? Even though we're neighbours now."

Charlie did *not* give up. "Exactly. None of your business. Why don't you stop asking me personal questions? Maybe you're the one who's rude."

Charlie held her hands up. "Okay, fine. I get the message. You aren't interested in me, and you aren't interested in talking to me."

"At least we have that clear," Erica said. Could she sound any more like her mother?

"Can I just ask…did I do something to you? Offend you in some way?"

Erica felt a pang in her chest at that. Charlie hadn't done anything wrong. Erica was the one with the problem here, not Charlie. But she didn't soften. "You're just always there. You must have something better to do than to keep constantly bothering me. Can you please just leave me alone?"

Charlie awkwardly shifted from one foot to another, looking down at them as she did so. She looked like she was about to say something, but then decided against it. Instead, she looked at Erica one last time, pressed her lips together, and gave a simple nod before she started off on her jog again.

Erica turned around to watch the woman literally run away from her. Well, technically, Erica had chased her. She let a breath out, deflated, and turned away. Her behaviour was uncalled for, and she knew it. She didn't like that she was the reason for the smile leaving Charlie's face. She didn't enjoy acting that way. But it was for the best. Charlie would get over it.

Erica's steps became brisker as she continued her walk. As if some extra exertion would help her to forget the whole encounter with Charlie. It kind of worked because she lost track of time. She must have walked for miles. Everywhere was starting to get busy and shops were starting to open up all around her. She looked up at a billboard that was pointing her toward a coffee shop called Haze and she followed it. Who was she to argue with directions to the best coffee around, if the sign was to be trusted. She wandered up a charming little cobbled street and found the coffee shop. It did look cosy. And there was a line, which was always a good sign. She joined it and waited. She got a whiff of fresh pastries and that was enough to entice her to grab breakfast there too. When she got to the front of the queue, she ordered both a cheese croissant and a chocolate twist—because she couldn't ever choose between sweet and savoury, so she had to have both—as well as an Americano.

"Have a great day," the friendly woman behind the counter said, as she passed Erica her order. Abby, according to her name badge. As she said it, another woman joined her behind the counter. Quite a professional looking woman. She tucked an arm around this Abby, and they smiled at each other. They were clearly a couple—an attractive looking couple too.

Erica was warmed by their display of obvious affection for one another. "You both have a great day too."

As she left the shop, she tried to imagine what it must be like, to have a relationship like that. She tried to picture herself and Victoria looking at one another with that kind of love and affection. She couldn't conjure up the image. Her brain wouldn't go there.

But when she replaced Victoria with Charlie, well, that was an image that stuck.

She shook her head to get rid of it and took a sip from her coffee. She was being ridiculous. It was only because she had run into Charlie that morning. And she was feeling guilty for the way she had spoken to her again. That was the only reason why such a silly thing would even pop into her head. Yet, she didn't think of much else during her long walk home.

❖

Erica almost called Brandon to say she couldn't make it into work. The last thing on her mind was playing detective and pouring drinks all night. There was something wrong with Hera. She had tried all the different types of food with no success. The one time Hera did attempt to eat something, she threw it straight back up again. Erica was now acknowledging all the terrible things that she had read online that could possibly be the matter.

Hera was lying asleep in her bed. She didn't seem distressed. Erica didn't want to leave her, but the sooner she could finish what she started and get herself and Hera home, the better. There were no vets open at that time anyway. She would take her first thing in the morning. She had already found a practice online that was only a short walk away and got excellent reviews.

Erica was extra focused on her task when she got to Oasis. Ash wasn't working that night, which meant she pretty much had to fend for herself as far as the work was concerned. She didn't care. She wasn't there to win an award for bartender of the year or employee of the month. She was there to watch. And that's what she did.

She was working with mostly different staff than she had met before that night. That wasn't a bad thing. More suspects to add to her list. Tom the doorman was there, however, trademark scowl ever present. Kelly-Ann was the only one of the bar staff with whom she had worked before. She was friendly enough. A bit gigglier and more girly than Erica was used to, but she was fine. Small, blond, and very bouncy was how Erica would describe Kelly-Ann. Then there was Damien. He was possibly even clumsier than Erica. She wasn't sure if that was a relief or a worry. She quickly learned not to stand too close to him after her legs got showered with beer because of his butterfingers. There were a couple of other guys who mostly kept to themselves. Students, Erica guessed.

Erica watched them all. Anytime one of them left the bar, Erica watched exactly where they went. She kept an extra close eye on Tom, her number one suspect. He still hadn't left the door area, and he was looking at Kelly-Ann half of the night—who was loving the attention.

"Are Tom and you together?" Erica asked her when they were serving beside one another.

"Why do you think that?"

"Just the way he keeps looking at you," Erica said.

Kelly-Ann giggled. "He does, doesn't he? He doesn't say much, but we've been eye-flirting for a few weeks now. I think he's pretty interested."

"He does seem like a man of few words."

"He wouldn't need to say too many words to me if you know what I mean." Kelly-Ann gave her a friendly nudge, then skipped off down the bar.

Too much information, Erica thought to herself. She served the next customers at the bar. Two hen parties had arrived at the same time and the bar was surrounded. Then she realized that Charlie was there. She wasn't at the bar, but Erica spotted her in the distance. She was with a girl she had noticed her with before. One of her friends. Erica wondered how long she had been there.

Charlie didn't try to speak to Erica. Come to think of it, Charlie didn't go anywhere near the bar at all. Erica was strangely disappointed by that. She found herself keeping tabs on where Charlie was throughout the night. Now and again. In between spying and serving. Then Charlie's friend left her side, and some woman with black hair and long legs swooped in. The woman leaned in and said something to Charlie. Judging by the way Charlie smiled at her, she liked whatever it was she said.

Erica scoffed. "Unbelievable," she said to no one in particular.

She turned her attention back to Tom, but he was nowhere to be seen. She looked all around Oasis, but there was no sign of him. She went to leave the bar to look for him when another large group of people arrived. *Dammit.* When she looked around, she saw that Damien was the only other bartender there. She couldn't leave him on his own. It was her own fault. If she hadn't been so busy watching Charlie, she would have seen Tom leave and maybe she could have followed him. It had been the moment she had been waiting for the whole night and she missed her chance. Within seconds there were about thirty hands waving to be served. She picked one. She still hadn't mastered how to gauge who was there first, so she picked a hand at random and went from there.

A few minutes later Kelly-Ann appeared beside her.

"Hey, did you see where Tom went?" Erica asked her. "It's getting busy." It sounded like a reasonable explanation for asking about Tom's whereabouts.

Kelly-Ann looked in the direction of the door. "Oh." She frowned. "No, I didn't see him leave."

Erica made a joke of it. "Surprising, when you two can't keep your eyes off each other."

"I know, right?" Kelly-Ann gave her usual little giggle, but Erica could see her eyes darting around the club, looking for Tom. She really was smitten. "Here he comes now," she said after a couple of minutes.

Surely enough, Tom was back in his usual spot, when Erica looked over. He glanced toward them and narrowed his eyes. She and Kelly-Ann were both staring, so she couldn't blame him for the look he was giving them. Erica left him and Kelly-Ann to do their weird eye-flirting. She had clearly missed her chance to spy on Tom. She wouldn't let herself get so distracted again the next time.

She glanced around the bar to see if there was anything else out of the ordinary, but everyone was where they should be.

She scanned the room again. She wasn't looking for Charlie—she wasn't—but she found her anyway. There was a remix of an Adele song on, which made it a little more upbeat, but still slow enough to slow-dance to, and Charlie was in the middle of the dance floor with Long-legs. *How cosy.*

Erica felt an unexpected and overwhelming feeling of jealousy. As much as she didn't want to entertain Charlie's attentions, she was now jealous that Charlie had moved on and aimed her attention elsewhere. Did she have any right to be annoyed? No. She had told Charlie to go away and leave her alone that very same day. Was she annoyed anyway? Damn right she was.

"It's for the best," she said to herself, despite how it felt.

❖

Charlie had danced for six or seven songs, both fast and slow, and she was exhausted. She had run into Hannah shortly after she had arrived at Oasis, and Hannah had quickly made her intentions clear to Charlie that she was interested in a repeat of their night together. Another hookup. Maybe Charlie had unintentionally opened the door to that possibility when she had accidentally stayed the night at Hannah's place before, but she had to admit that she wasn't totally against the idea. They'd had fun that night, and they were enjoying themselves tonight. "I'm just going to go and make sure my friend's okay," she shouted over the music. If she was going to consider breaking the rules again, she wanted to at least talk to Val first.

Hannah nodded and gestured that she was going to do the same.

Charlie's night had been fun. Easy. She was enjoying Hannah's company. Hannah was funny, pretty, and a great dancer. That was good enough for her.

Val found Charlie rather than the other way around.

"How's your night going?" Charlie asked her.

"Terrible. Remember the redhead from the other night? She's here. And she started a whole scene in the ladies' toilets because she had seen me chatting to someone else." She looked around as if she was going to appear beside them. "She completely went off on one, Char."

"I hate it when that happens." Sometimes people were more clingy than they first seemed.

"I think I'm going to call it a night. I don't need the drama," Val said.

"Of course, I'll come with you."

"Don't be silly. Stay. You look like you're having a good time. Hannah, right?"

"That girl knows where you live. What if she follows you?" Charlie shook her head. "No, I'm coming with you. There will be plenty of other nights. Give me ten minutes, I'll find Hannah and tell her I'm going. And I'm busting for the loo."

Val gave her a thumbs up. "I'll be over here." She pointed toward the booth they had been sitting at earlier in the night. "Thanks, Charlie."

Charlie headed toward the ladies' toilets first. She always used the ones at the back of Oasis, because not many people knew they were there. The two connected to the main floor were always queued. She pushed the door open, and the automatic light flickered on. An out of order sign had been on one of the stalls for weeks—they didn't seem to rush themselves to fix things at Oasis. Charlie went into the stall next to it.

There were footsteps as Charlie was about to exit the stall. Heels clip-clopping on the tiled floor of the corridor outside. She walked over to the sinks and started to wash her hands just as the heels reached their destination and the bathroom door opened.

If it wasn't her favourite bartender.

Charlie had stayed away. She hadn't gone near the bar the entire night. Hell, she had barely looked in the other woman's direction. Until then.

Their eyes met in the mirror and they both froze. The only sounds were from the water still running where Charlie had been washing her hands, and the faded beat of music coming from the club. Charlie looked away first. She turned the tap off and cleared her throat. She grabbed a handful of paper towels to dry her hands with. But she didn't say anything. She wouldn't *bother* the woman as she had so eloquently put it that morning. Their heels tapped on the tiled floor as they walked past each other in awkward silence.

Charlie went to pull the door open to leave when the woman's voice stopped her in her tracks.

"Looks like you're having a good night."

"I'm sorry?" Charlie turned to look at the woman, who was fixing her hair in the mirror.

"With that woman. The one you've had your arms wrapped around half the night. Seems like you're enjoying yourself."

She let go of the door then and took a small step back into the room. "What's it to you?"

"Nothing. I was just making an observation."

Charlie's annoyance flared. This woman had ignored her, brushed her off, spoken to her like shit, and basically told her to get lost. "Well, good for you. Your skills of observation are next to none. If there's nothing else, I'm going to go now." She turned to leave.

The voice continued. "I can't help wondering who it will be next."

Charlie stopped in her tracks again. "Excuse me?"

"Oh, come on. I met you a few days ago. There's already been the blonde. You tried your luck with me. And now there's this woman tonight."

"I thought you didn't see me that first night." Charlie tried not to look smug—because that's how she felt, albeit a little insulted too—but she wasn't sure how successful she was. She noticed the other woman's jaw clench. Point to Charlie.

The woman recovered quickly. "Yeah, well. That wasn't really the point I was making. Was it?"

"What was the point you were trying to make, then? Why don't you just come out and say what's on your mind." Charlie was getting tired of whatever game they were playing.

The woman turned from the mirror to face her. "I can see how you get your reputation. Once you've had one woman, you're straight onto the next. I know your type. You're hardly original."

Charlie was shocked by her audacity. *How dare she?* Her temper bubbled to the surface. "Don't act like you know me. You don't know me at all. And what I do is absolutely none of your business. None!"

They held eye contact, neither of them backing down. After a few beats the woman spoke calmly. "You're right. It's not. Thank God for that."

"I don't need to listen to this." Charlie turned to leave again, throwing the door open with force.

"If you bring your friend home, do try and keep the noise down. We share a wall and I have an early start in the morning."

"You are unbelievable," Charlie tossed back over her shoulder as she stormed out of the bathroom, letting the door slam behind her.

She marched back out toward the main floor. She quickly found Hannah with her group of friends and made her apologies for having to leave. Hannah took it well—told her they would maybe run into each other again, and they left it at that.

Charlie then went to the booth to find Val. Neither of them could get out of Oasis quick enough. Charlie was quiet on the walk home. Val didn't question her about it until they got back to their apartment.

"Did something happen?" she asked her.

"That woman fucking hates me," Charlie said. She didn't know if she was angry or hurt. A little of both maybe. Charlie hadn't done anything to deserve any of her harsh words or judgement.

Val scrunched her face up. "The woman you were dancing with? Hannah? Why would she hate you? Because you left?"

Charlie shook her head. "No, not her. The bartender."

Val made an *oh* shape with her mouth and nodded. "Her. Yeah, she gave you daggers the whole night."

"What do you mean?"

Val flung herself onto the sofa. "Make sure you put the chain on the door in case redhead comes to storm the place."

Charlie put the chain on and double checked the door was locked. "Done."

"Thanks." Val visibly relaxed. "Anyway. The whole time you were dancing, your bartender couldn't keep her eyes off you. I swear, at one point I thought she was going to jump across the bar to get at that girl you were dancing with."

"First, she's not *my* anything. Second, why would she do that?"

"For someone so smart, you really are seriously clueless sometimes." Val raised her eyebrows at her. "Do I have to spell it out?"

"Spell what out?" Charlie asked.

Val chuckled and looked skyward. "Charlie, she's jealous. J-E-A-L-O-U-S."

Charlie laughed it off. Because that wasn't true. It couldn't be. She wasn't even interested in Charlie. She had made that perfectly clear on several occasions. She told Val about what had happened in the bathroom. She still couldn't believe the way she had been spoken to. For no good reason at all.

"Looks like both of us had our own bathroom dramas tonight." Val snorted. "But yeah, all that behaviour there." She moved her finger in a circle and pointed at Charlie. "Sheer jealousy. She's into you."

"You think?" It seemed unlikely, but when Val said it, it did make sense.

"I'd still stay away, though," Val said. "I don't trust her at all."

"How come?"

"For starters, look at how she's treated you already," Val replied. "Why would you not want to stay away?"

Charlie shrugged.

Val shook her head. "Also, and you're not going to like this..." She gritted her teeth. "She's sort of right. It's not like you're interested in a relationship with this woman. You fancy her. You think she's hot. But you know it's never going to go anywhere. So why give her the chance to say *told you so* when it doesn't."

Charlie flinched but she couldn't argue. "I guess you're right."

"Although," Val went on.

"Yeah?"

"If this was any other woman you would have lost interest long before now." Val lifted her shoulder. "Maybe there's something in that."

It was too bad Charlie would never have the chance to find out.

CHAPTER EIGHT

Erica found Little Paws Clinic quite easily. It had said on her phone that it was only an eight-minute walk away, so she had put Hera and her favourite blanket into her carrier and headed in the direction her phone told her. She had only managed to get a couple of hours' sleep on the sofa after she got back from Oasis, but she didn't care. Hera was more important. She wanted to be at the clinic when it opened.

She had read in the reviews online that Dr Elizabeth Ashbourne was the best, so she already knew who to ask for. She found the clinic more easily than she had expected to, and she had arrived right on time for opening. One man walked in ahead of her with a dog on a lead. She stood at reception behind the man, who was also waiting to see Dr Ashbourne, she overheard. That was to be expected. She was happy to wait her turn. A line had quickly formed behind her, so she was glad she had made the decision to get there bright and early.

The man moved into the waiting area. It was Erica's turn. She approached the reception desk. "I would like to make an appointment with Dr Ashbourne to look at my cat this morning please."

The receptionist, an older lady, peered over her glasses at her. "Can I take your name, please?"

"Oh, I'm not in the system. I'm only in town for a while." She went on to explain Hera's symptoms and that she needed to get an emergency appointment. She hoped that the receptionist would take pity on her and wouldn't turn her away.

She did get a sympathetic smile, but that was all. "I'm sorry, but appointments with Dr Ashbourne are made weeks in advance. And if your cat isn't a patient here, there's no way I can fit her in at such short notice. There is, however, an emergency clinic at twelve o'clock. One of the other vets should be able to check her over then."

"But I read that Dr Ashbourne is the best." Erica smiled to keep things friendly. She knew she needed to stay on this woman's good side if she was to stand any chance.

"I assure you that all of our vets are very good. Your cat will be in safe hands."

The receptionist looked past Erica, to the person standing behind her. She was obviously finished with the conversation.

Erica, however, was not. She shifted across back into the receptionist's line of sight. She kept her voice low. She didn't want to make a scene. "Look, I'm really worried about her. Is there no chance that Dr Ashbourne could squeeze us in this morning? I don't care how much it costs."

A voice that sounded familiar to her came from somewhere behind the receptionist. "Mr Cooper, you can bring Barney through now."

Erica looked toward the voice. It was Charlie. Charlie worked there. Of course she did. Why wouldn't the attractive woman Erica wanted to avoid for the rest of her life not only live in the apartment next to where she was staying, not only frequent her bar, but also work in the local vet clinic where her cat needed treatment? Why wouldn't she? *Seriously, universe?*

Charlie smiled at the man who had entered the clinic ahead of Erica, before looking back down at the clipboard in her hand. When the man, Mr Cooper, walked past her leading the dog into the room behind the reception desk, Charlie glanced up from her clipboard and saw her.

"Hi." She seemed as surprised as Erica was.

Erica's cheeks started to heat up. She could feel it. She was beyond embarrassed at how she had acted the night before. Especially now that she was face to face with Charlie. Her plan had been to avoid her from that moment on as best she could until her stay in London was over. That didn't seem to be an option.

She cleared her throat. "Hey."

Charlie walked to the open door that Mr Cooper had walked through and said something to whoever was inside that Erica couldn't make out. She shut the door softly from the outside and walked back to the reception desk. She was still looking at Erica. "What are you doing here? Everything okay?" Her tone sounded like she was genuinely concerned. Charlie lowered her gaze to the cat carrier in Erica's hand. "Who's this?"

Erica held the cat carrier up a little bit and looked in. Hera was peering out at them. "This is Hera. She hasn't been eating and she's been being sick."

The receptionist spoke to Charlie then. "This lady is trying to make an emergency appointment with Dr Ashbourne, but I've told her it isn't possible." She looked from Charlie to Erica, back to Charlie again. "I've already told her about the emergency clinic."

Charlie squinted at the woman's screen. She pointed at something. The screen was facing the opposite direction, so Erica had no idea what Charlie was pointing at. "Can we not slot them in here, Hilary?"

Hilary, the receptionist, lowered her voice. As if that meant that Erica wouldn't be able to hear her when she was right across the counter. "That's Dr Ashbourne's morning break."

Charlie gave Hilary a smile and patted her shoulder. "Let me worry about Dr Ashbourne. I'll take full responsibility, don't worry. Pop an appointment in for them there."

Hilary didn't look too comfortable with the whole thing. She puffed out a breath. But she clicked her mouse on something on her screen anyway. "Okay."

Charlie looked back to Erica. "I have to get back to work here. You're going to have to wait a little while, but we'll get to you as quick as we can, okay?"

Erica nodded. Charlie seemed totally different in this environment. She wasn't cocky, confident Charlie. She wasn't flirty Charlie. She was calm, professional Charlie who helped animals. What the hell was she meant to do with that? "Thank you," she said. She meant it. If she were in Charlie's shoes, she wasn't sure she would be so helpful after the way Erica had acted.

"No problem." Charlie turned to walk back to the room she had come from.

"So, the cat's name is Hera, yes?" Hilary asked her and Erica nodded. "Can I take your name as well, please?"

Erica glanced at Charlie's retreating figure, which had slowed down. Erica smiled and rolled her eyes. "Erica Frost." *You win, Charlie.*

Charlie glanced back over her shoulder and grinned before she disappeared into the exam room again.

Erica took a seat in the waiting room. She didn't care how long she had to wait. She was just grateful that she had managed to nab an appointment with a reputable vet. She wondered what Charlie's role was. She had led that man into Dr Ashbourne's exam room. She must be her secretary. Assistant? She wasn't quite sure how veterinary practice hierarchy worked. One thing she *did* know was that she was going to have to apologize. She had taken it too far with some of the things she had said to Charlie the night before. When she got the chance, she would tell Charlie she was sorry. She owed her that.

Her phone buzzed in her pocket while she was waiting. She lifted it out and saw it was her mother calling. She put it back in her pocket again. She had dodged her mother's calls a few times since she had arrived in London. The one time she had answered, she had got an hour-long lecture about how what she was doing in London was unnecessary, and how she should be at home securing a future with Victoria. Erica doubted she had anything new to say on the matter and she wasn't in the mood for more of the same.

She had received a couple of text messages from Victoria since she had been away too. They were generic messages—she hoped she was keeping well, she looked forward to seeing her again, things like that. She had replied with what she knew Victoria wanted to hear. That she was sorry she had to work, and she couldn't wait to get home so that they could pick up where they left off. That seemed to be enough to keep her happy. If only her mother were as easy.

At least an hour had passed. Every time Charlie came out of the exam room with her clipboard to call another patient, Erica's pulse picked up. Just because she hoped it was her turn. It wasn't for any other reason. It certainly wasn't because Charlie looked so great in those scrubs. No, it wasn't that.

She watched the other people coming and going from the waiting room. She had witnessed Hilary the receptionist turning two other people away. At least it hadn't been personal.

She looked around at the other worried faces in the waiting room. Everyone had that in common—they all loved their animals. Erica was no different. She couldn't bear to think about something happening to Hera. It made the waiting easier too, seeing the other people and their clear love for their pets. Every dog, cat, rabbit, and there had even been some kind of tropical bird at one point—they were all important and loved. And they all needed help. Everybody's turn was important.

Probably close to thirty minutes later, Charlie emerged with her clipboard again. "Ms Frost and Hera," she called out into the waiting room. She was grinning.

Erica got up and carried Hera toward Charlie.

"Would you prefer Ms Frost or Erica?" Charlie whispered to her before they entered the exam room. She had a twinkle in her eye that told Erica she was teasing her.

"Erica's fine."

"Erica it is." Charlie held the door open for her. "After you, Erica."

She walked into a surprisingly large exam room. For some reason she had expected it to be smaller. It was spotless. That could only be a good thing. The white tiled floor was gleaming, and the walls were a bright, clean white as well. There was a large stainless steel exam table in the middle and a woman in scrubs and a long white coat was smiling at her from beside it.

Erica approached the woman who extended her hand to shake. "Ms Frost. I'm Dr Ashbourne."

Erica took her hand and shook it. "Please, call me Erica. Thank you so much for fitting Hera in today, Dr Ashbourne."

The vet glanced at Charlie with an amused look. "Not a problem. Charlie here owes me one now, and that's never a bad thing." She winked at Erica.

"Yeah, yeah, yeah," Charlie mumbled, as she continued writing something down on her clipboard. She didn't look up at them, but she smiled.

Dr Ashbourne unzipped the cover of the cat carrier that Erica had set on the exam table. "And this must be Hera. Hello, little lady." She put her hand slowly toward the cat carrier, but let Hera come to her first. Within a few seconds she did, pushing her head against Dr Ashbourne's hand. After a few pets she reached in and gently lifted Hera out and set her on the table. "Now. Let's get a look at you," she said softly.

Charlie stood up then and went over to join Dr Ashbourne. She gave Hera a few pets herself. Hera loved every second of the attention. She leaned into Charlie's touch, purring away. "She's gorgeous," Charlie said to Erica. "How old is she?"

Erica paused while she tried to work out what year she had got Hera. "She's four. No, five. Yes, she's five now."

Charlie nodded and kept petting Hera with one hand while jotting the number down on her clipboard with her other hand.

"She likes you," Erica said to Charlie, as Hera headbutted Charlie's hand.

Charlie smiled at that.

"They all do. Can you tell us a little bit about what's been happening with Hera? Charlie will write it down for our records. Then we will give Hera a quick examination and see if we can get to the bottom of what's wrong. Then we can make her feel all better and like herself again." Dr Ashbourne's smile was wide. She was very likeable, Erica thought. She could see why she got so many good reviews. Hopefully her skills as a vet were as good as her personality.

She told them about Hera's lack of appetite. The different foods she had tried. The sickness. "I read online that they can become unsettled by change, and I only came to London last week."

"Oh, yeah?" Dr Ashbourne said, while she felt around Hera's paws one by one. "Where from?"

"Cornwall direction. Near St Ives." She glanced at Charlie for a reaction, but to her credit she remained completely professional. She was jotting down things that Erica was saying and holding Hera in place for Dr Ashbourne to examine when she wasn't writing. Charlie kept petting Hera to keep her calm, whispering reassurances as she did so. It was sweet. "Do you think it's the change in location that's making her sick? I'd hate to think it was my fault."

Dr Ashbourne shook her head. "I don't think so. Even if she didn't particularly like the change, she would have got hungry enough to eat eventually. Cats are good to themselves, look after their own needs. And the move wouldn't account for the sickness." She felt around Hera's neck and head. Erica saw her frown while she focused behind one of her ears. "There," she said to Charlie. Charlie then felt the spot Dr Ashbourne had been touching.

"Yeah, I feel it." Charlie nodded at the vet. She looked toward Erica. "Here, give me your hand."

Erica did and she couldn't deny that it felt good. Charlie's touch was soft and warm. She tried to ignore that thought as Charlie guided her hand to the same spot they had both been touching.

Erica felt a lump. It wasn't even small. How had she missed that? Panic bubbled up inside her. "What is that?"

"It's an abscess," Dr Ashbourne said in a calm voice. "It's causing an infection, which will be why this little lady has lost her appetite."

"What does that mean? Is that serious?"

"It's only serious if it's left untreated." Dr Ashbourne parted Hera's black and white fur and looked closer. "It doesn't look like she's had it too long."

"Can you treat it?" Erica asked.

"Absolutely. Can we fit Hera into the schedule today, Charlie?" Dr Ashbourne asked.

Charlie flipped through the pages on her clipboard until she found whatever she was looking for. She ran her finger down the page. "If we put her in at the end? We might have to stay a little later, but that's okay. Right?"

Dr Ashbourne smiled at Charlie, who wouldn't meet her eye. Charlie was pulling strings for her, and Erica hadn't missed it.

"Yes. That's fine." Dr Ashbourne looked toward Erica. "Hera will have to be sedated. The abscess hasn't opened up by itself, so I'll have to lance it. That would be a bit uncomfortable without sedation. Is that okay?"

Erica nodded. "Whatever you need to do."

"I'll drain the abscess and dress it. Then I'll give her two injections. An antibiotic and a painkiller. I'll also give you a course of oral antibiotics to give her at home to make sure we get rid of that infection. She'll be good as new in no time. Sound good?"

"Yes. Thank you so much, Dr Ashbourne. When can I take her home?"

"It will only be a small sedation. The procedure doesn't take too long. She will probably wake up within a couple of hours afterward. She'll be groggy, but you can collect her this evening. We could keep her for the night, but I'm sure you will want to get her home again."

"Yes. I'll pick her up tonight." The sooner the better, Erica thought. She just wanted her home—well, temporary home—safe and better.

"The sedative usually lingers for a day or so. She might be a little woozy and disorientated in that time. Are you okay to stay with her? Or is there someone who can?"

"I can call work and take the night off. It's no problem," Erica said.

"Are you okay to do that? It's still your first week," Charlie said. It was a fair point. It wasn't like Charlie knew her situation. What Erica was really doing at Oasis. To Charlie she was just the new bartender who could lose her job if she didn't show.

"I'm sure they'll understand," Erica said. She couldn't explain that she didn't really work there. Not as such.

"You can leave Hera here overnight if you have to work. We have nurses on all night," Dr Ashbourne suggested. "Collect her in the morning."

"Or I can look after her until you get back," Charlie said quickly. "If you want. I'm only next door to you and it means you wouldn't have to miss work. Most places are pretty strict about that kind of thing, especially with new starts."

Erica and Dr Ashbourne both turned to look at Charlie. Erica could tell that Dr Ashbourne hadn't been surprised that she and Charlie seemed to know each other. She wondered what Charlie had told her. She also wondered why Charlie would offer to look after her cat. They hardly knew each other, and Erica had hardly been pleasant to her in the short interactions that they had had. "I couldn't ask you to do that."

"Why not? I'll be there anyway, and you already said that Hera likes me." Charlie reached over to pet Hera, who purred on cue. Point proven. "I can take her home with me when I finish here. Then you can pick her up when you finish work."

"I don't get home until late. Or early. Whatever way you want to look at it."

"That's okay. Me and Hera can snooze." She looked toward Dr Ashbourne for backup.

"She would be in safe hands with Charlie. She's great with animals. But it's completely up to you," Dr Ashbourne said.

Erica couldn't think of an argument, so she found herself agreeing. "Okay, then." What harm could it do? At least Hera would be looked after. By a professional. And maybe this would be the night she would crack the case at Oasis, and then she could bring Hera home to her own house and her own comforts. That's what Erica would want if she was sick.

"That's settled then. If you want to give Hera a quick cuddle now, Charlie will take her and get her settled in before her surgery later on," Dr Ashbourne said.

Erica did. Her heart felt heavy in her chest at having to leave her, but it all sounded very routine, and she knew that Hera was in good hands. There was something about Dr Ashbourne, her warmth and calmness, that put Erica at ease. And Charlie too, she had to admit.

"We'll look after her, don't worry," Charlie added, as if she could read Erica's mind. Erica gave her a final pet and Charlie gently scooped her up and carried her into an adjoining room.

"I have a couple more things for you to fill out, and then I can let you go," Dr Ashbourne said to her. She passed Erica a form and a pen so that she could fill in contact and pet insurance details. "You know, Charlie seems to be pretty taken with you," she said as Erica was completing the form.

Erica looked up at her and laughed it off. "I don't think so. Charlie seems to have a lot of women after her."

Dr Ashbourne seemed to give her next sentence some thought. "I've known Charlie for years now, so believe me, I know what she can be like." She chuckled. "But for what it's worth, she is clearly very much trying to get on your good side. Any other time she would have given up by now. She doesn't usually put herself out there like she has today." Dr Ashbourne shrugged. "It's none of my business, but I want you to know that if you can make it past all the bravado and bluster, Charlie's a really great person."

Erica mulled that over. Dr Ashbourne didn't seem like the sort of person who would say something like that if she didn't mean it or believe it herself. "I'll keep that in mind." She passed the completed forms to Dr Ashbourne just as Charlie came back into the room. "Thank you so much again, Dr Ashbourne."

"Please, call me Liz."

"Thank you, Liz. Is there anything else you need from me?"

"Not a thing. You go get on with your day and try not to worry. We've got this."

"I'll walk you out," Charlie said. She walked forward and held the door open for Erica like she had done on her way in.

"Liz is short for Elizabeth, you know."

"And?" Erica tried not to laugh at Charlie's face.

"Does that mean you'll start calling me Charlie?"

Erica tilted her head from one side to the other. "I'll think about it. Charlotte is such a pretty name."

Charlie laughed. "You're so annoying."

Erica found herself smiling. She stopped when they reached the door. "I wanted to say I'm sorry for the way I acted last night."

Charlie waved her off. "Forget about it."

"No, I feel terrible. And you've been so kind and helpful today and, well, I don't even feel like I deserve it." Erica looked down at her feet and back up again. She had never been great at apologies, but this one was necessary. "I really am sorry."

"Apology accepted." They stared at each other for a few beats. "Anyway. I'll see you later. Knock the door when you finish work. It doesn't matter what time it is, so don't worry about that," Charlie said.

"Okay, I will. Thank you so much, again. You have no idea how much I appreciate it." Erica reached out and touched Charlie's arm before she could stop herself. "I'll see you later."

"Looking forward to it," Charlie said.

The scary thing was, so was Erica.

CHAPTER NINE

*W*ell, that morning was...unexpected.

Charlie walked back into the exam room where Liz was waiting with her hands on her hips and an amused expression on her face. She was giving Charlie that look way too often these days. "What?"

"Don't you *what* me. What the hell just happened?" Liz asked.

Charlie blew out a breath and threw herself down on Liz's office chair. "I was asking myself the exact same thing. I'm clearly into the *treat them mean, keep them keen* treatment." After the way Erica had spoken to her the previous night, Charlie should have been all kinds of angry. But the moment she saw Erica standing at reception needing help, the anger and resentment she had been feeling immediately vanished. Quickly replaced with an overwhelming urge to speak to Erica, to help her in any way she could. Ugh, she really did have a crush.

Liz clicked her fingers a couple of times and motioned for Charlie to get up. "No, no. You don't have time to sit there. We now have an extra busy day thanks to you and all the wooing you've been doing."

Charlie groaned as she stood up. "I was hardly wooing. I was being helpful is all."

"Oh please. You were wooing. Giving her preferential treatment. All the little smiles and eye contact. You're bloody well staying at work for an extra two hours just so you can bring her cat home and look after her all night. If that isn't trying to get into someone's good books, then I don't know what is."

Charlie gritted her teeth. "Too much?"

"No! I love it. I love this Charlie." Liz clapped her hands together. "You are finally into someone. I'm so happy about it. I already texted Nancy and told her."

Charlie closed her eyes. "Of course you did."

"She wants to arrange a dinner to hear all about it." Liz's eyes widened. "Maybe you can invite Erica."

Charlie laughed. "One step at a time, Cupid. You know that isn't really my style."

"What part of today *was* your style?" Liz asked. "Admit it. This woman's different."

She sighed. "I do seem to have a hard time…not thinking about her. I don't know why, seeing as all she's done since I met her is tell me to back off and leave her alone, but yeah."

"I think you might have earned yourself some points today."

"Thanks, by the way," Charlie said. "I know I've made your day a hell of a lot busier too."

"Please. I'd work ten of these days in a row if it helped you get a girlfriend."

"Don't get ahead of yourself. Even if there's some small chance Erica is interested in me—you know what I'm like."

"Can I give you a little bit of advice?" Liz asked.

Charlie grabbed the cleaner and sprayed it over the exam table. She ripped off some paper towel and wiped it down. "You know you will anyway, so go on."

"Don't overthink things. She's already held your interest for longer than anyone else has. Maybe that means something."

Charlie didn't answer but she also didn't argue. Maybe it did mean something. But acknowledging that freaked her out, so she preferred not to think about it.

They spent the rest of the afternoon swamped with patients and surgeries. Hera's surgery was the last thing on their schedule, and it went well. Charlie knew it would. Liz was a fantastic vet. She overheard Liz calling Erica to tell her that everything had gone according to plan. Charlie wished she had been the one to share the good news, but she would have to wait until later to speak to her.

She waited at the clinic long after Liz went home for the day, until Hera woke up from her sedated sleep. She didn't want to move her before that in case she had any type of reaction to the drugs or treatment. Thankfully, she didn't. Charlie petted her as she started to come round and she seemed fine, just sleepy, as expected. When Charlie was happy that Hera was safe to go home, she put her into the carrier that Erica had left and brought her home.

Val had left a note saying that she had gone to stay with her family for a couple of days, which was a normal occurrence. Unlike Charlie, who didn't have the best relationship with her parents, Val was close to her family. Charlie was relieved she wasn't home. She wasn't ready to explain the new developments with Erica, nor why Erica's cat was visiting. Val would think Charlie had lost her mind. If Charlie couldn't really understand what was happening herself, she wouldn't be able to explain it to Val.

"Here we are now, Hera," Charlie said to the cat as she opened the cat carrier on top of the sofa. Hera took a tentative step out. Charlie pulled her blanket out from the carrier and laid it out for her. She curled up on it straight away and went back to sleep. Charlie filled a bowl with some water. She knew Hera probably wouldn't go near it, cats were funny like that, but she wanted her to have the option if she went looking.

She grabbed a microwave meal out of the fridge for herself and popped it on. When it dinged, she plated it and took a spot on the sofa beside Hera. They would have a night in front of the TV. Charlie could grab a bit of sleep on the sofa while the cat was sleeping, but she would stay with her the whole time. If Charlie said she was going to look after her, she was going to do it right.

She was nervous about seeing Erica. Even though they hadn't known each other for long, she had already become used to their dynamic. Charlie flirted and Erica hated it. Charlie was interested and Erica wasn't. Hell, she hadn't so much as known the other woman's name until that morning. Erica Frost. By name and by nature, Charlie thought. She had certainly been on the receiving end of Erica's frosty demeanour. Had that all changed now? And what were they? Acquaintances? Neighbours? Friends? Was there even potential for anything more? Charlie didn't know. She was in new, unfamiliar territory.

Charlie was lost in her own thoughts until she drifted off. Three sharp raps on the door startled her awake. She quickly glanced over to make sure Hera was okay. She was still lying sound asleep. Charlie got off the sofa gently so that she didn't disturb her. She crossed the room and pulled the door open to reveal a tired and worried looking Erica.

"Hey," Charlie said through a yawn that she couldn't stifle.

"Is she okay?" Erica looked past Charlie into the apartment. "Where is she?"

Charlie moved aside to show Erica. "She's fine. She's asleep," she said quietly.

Erica breathed out a sigh of relief. "Sorry. Hi."

"Nothing to be sorry for. I'm sure you've been worried sick. Do you want to come in and I'll get her ready to go home?" Charlie asked, pointing in the direction of her apartment.

Erica hesitated for a few seconds before she stepped inside. Charlie closed the door behind them, and they were both left standing in silence. Maybe Erica didn't know how to act around Charlie anymore either.

"Um…so…I'm sure Liz called you, but everything went well. And she hasn't been acting funny or anything so there shouldn't be any problems." Charlie led Erica to where Hera was sleeping.

Erica pouted. "She looks so peaceful," she whispered. "I feel bad for disturbing her." She sat down on the edge of the sofa and softly ran her hand through Hera's fur.

Charlie was used to seeing the affectionate looks when owners were reunited with their pets, but watching Erica made her heart swell more than usual. "She can stay here for the rest of the night if you want. I can drop her in to you in the morning before I go to work."

"I can't ask you to do that. You've already done so much," Erica said.

"It's no big deal. I'm pretty sure anyone else would have done the same thing," Charlie said.

"Not many people I know would have," Erica said quietly.

Charlie couldn't imagine what kind of people Erica had in her life if that was true. "Like I said. It's been no trouble. We've had a great time. We watched some crime shows. We snuggled. I beat her at *Who Wants to be a Millionaire?*, but to be fair she didn't even try to win, so it wasn't difficult. Then both of us fell asleep during the chick flick I put on, so it mustn't have been very good."

Erica laughed. Charlie had never seen Erica laugh before, but she already knew that she wanted to see it again. To be the cause of it. Even at silly o'clock after working all night, Erica was gorgeous, and even more so when she smiled. "It sounds like you've had quite the night together."

"How was your night?" Charlie wanted to keep the conversation going. She didn't care what time it was, if she could somehow grab a few extra minutes in Erica's company, she would.

"That place is so busy. It never seems to stop." Erica reached down and rubbed her ankle, as if Charlie asking about work had reminded her that it hurt.

Charlie looked down at Erica's heeled feet. She nodded toward them. "You must be the only person I've met who could tend bar all night in stilettos. I'm sure it's an unspoken rule that you should wear flats for that kind of thing."

Erica grimaced. "Believe me, if I owned flats, I would wear them. It's torture."

Charlie didn't try to hide her surprise. "You don't own a pair of flat shoes?" Who didn't own at least one pair of trainers?

"No. A fact that I now regret. I keep meaning to go out and get some, but I haven't got round to it yet. Besides, I might not need them for long."

"Oh?" Charlie asked. "Are you not planning on staying there?"

Erica focused on her ankle for several seconds before she answered. "I mean, who knows, right?" she replied without looking up.

There seemed to be more to it, but Charlie didn't push it. "Right." She chewed her lip. Maybe she could push it a little. "I hope you don't mind me saying…"

Erica interrupted. "I don't think it would stop you if I did mind." There was a ghost of a smile on her face.

Charlie chuckled. "True."

"Go ahead," Erica said.

"You don't seem like the type of person who tends bar at Oasis. Not that there's anything wrong with it. There isn't at all. But it just seems like a strange fit to me."

"Why? Because my accent is…" She thought about it. "Fancy? Wasn't that how you put it?" Erica raised her eyebrow with a half-smile.

"It was." Charlie smiled too. "It's not only the accent, though. I think the heels play a part too. And your clothes—I know you have a uniform now, but your clothes on that first night—they were fancy too. And well, you, really."

"So, I'm a fancy bartender?"

"Exactly." They both chuckled.

"And what about you? I didn't expect you to be working at the veterinary clinic when I got there this morning."

"No? Too fancy?" They both laughed again.

"Now that I have seen you there, though, that is one that fits. You're good at your job. And you clearly care. It shows." Erica looked down at Hera. "What exactly is it that you do there?"

"I'm a veterinary nurse. I'm assigned to Liz mostly, unless she's off, then I help whoever needs me. I'd like to go all the way and get my vet training at some point."

"Why don't you?"

"I've got comfortable, I guess. I like working with Liz."

Erica hummed her agreement. "I did notice that you worked well together."

"Yeah. We've worked together for years. She's always on at me to go on and get my vet qualifications. Maybe someday. For now, I like my job. Not everyone can say that."

"Well, I was very glad that you ended up being there today." Hera chose that moment to yawn and stretch out. "I think that's our cue to leave and let you get some sleep." Erica looked at the clock. "Gosh, it's after four. You're going to be exhausted."

"I'll be fine." Charlie bundled Hera up in her blanket and put her into her carrier. "Bye, sweet girl," she said softly. She lifted a box from the coffee table and passed it to Erica. "These are Hera's antibiotics. The instructions are printed on there. You'll probably have to hide them in her food to get her to take them, but her appetite should come back pretty quick now, so that shouldn't be a problem."

Erica stood and took the box. She glanced at the label. "Great. Thanks."

Charlie passed the carrier to Erica too. "So, um…" She swung her arms by her sides. "If you have any questions or you're worried about anything, you know where to find me."

They both walked toward the door. "I do. And thank you again for today."

"You have got to stop thanking me, woman."

"I can't help it. I still don't know why you did it, but I appreciate it. I owe you one."

"Well, in that case…"

Erica closed her eyes and raised her free hand. "Please don't ruin it with whatever you're about to say next."

Charlie laughed. "Okay, okay." She pretended to zip her lips closed.

Erica smiled again. "Goodnight, Charlie."

"Goodnight, Erica." Charlie opened the door. "Hey, you called me Charlie."

"I did." Erica stepped out into the hallway and walked the few steps toward her own front door.

Charlie leaned out into the hallway. "Does that mean we're friends now?"

"I'll think about it."

Chapter Ten

Erica wanted to throw her phone across the room and smash it into ten thousand pieces. Why was it blaring at her? She couldn't remember setting an alarm. She prised one eye open very much against her own will to find the offending object. When she did, she saw that Zachary's name was flashing up on the screen. Not her alarm then.

She swiped to answer it. "What?" It came out more like a groan.

"Good morning to you too, my lovely sister," Zachary said in a sing-song voice.

Erica pulled her phone away from her ear to check the time. She groaned again and put the phone back to her ear. She pulled the duvet over her head at the same time to block out the light. "It's not even nine a.m. I work until four, Zachary. You can't be ringing me at this time unless someone's died." She thought on that for a second. "They haven't, have they?"

"Not that I know of, but won't you feel bad if they have?"

"What do you want, Zachary?"

"I'm just calling to check on my favourite bartender. You've been at Oasis for nearly a week now. You're bound to have lots to tell."

"Ugh." Erica closed her eyes tighter. "How about I call you back at a decent hour, and I'll tell you everything you want to know."

"But I want to know now."

There was a knock at the front door. *Seriously?* Who wanted her now? "Tough, Zachary. I'm tired and now there's someone at the door. I'm going to check who it is, and then I'm going back to sleep. Hopefully for several hours. I'll call you back later." Erica hung up the phone before he could argue. She threw herself out of the bed just as whoever was at the door knocked again. *Give me a damn minute.* She padded barefoot through the open plan kitchen and living area, glancing at Hera's bed as she passed. She was still asleep—and definitely breathing, Erica could see. She was sure that was a normal thing to worry about after her cat had been to the vet. But she had been assured by both Liz and Charlie that Hera was fine, and to expect Hera to sleep on and off through most of the day.

She checked the chain was on the door before she cranked it open. She didn't know who was on the other side. It could be a serial killer for all she knew. Unlikely, but not impossible. But when she pulled the door open as far as the chain would allow, a coffee cup was thrust toward her, rather than a knife or a chainsaw. She doubted a serial killer would provide refreshments. Zachary poked his head through the gap.

"Will you tell me now?"

She grabbed the cup out of his hand and took a sip before she pushed the door and took the chain off. When she opened it again, Zachary smiled sheepishly at her.

"Surprise?"

"Get in here."

He came in and wrapped his arms around her in a hug. "I only got to see you for a few minutes when you first got here. I couldn't wait any longer. Don't be angry." He pouted as he stepped back.

Erica sipped from her cup. "The coffee has helped your case. Only slightly."

He held up a paper bag. "I brought breakfast too."

Erica narrowed her eyes. "What is it?"

"Bagels."

"You're still only half forgiven. I'm fucking shattered." She grabbed the bag from him and brought it to the kitchen. She filled the kettle and flicked it on. More coffee was going to be required if Zachary insisted on keeping her from sleeping.

Good thing she loved her brother. And although she wouldn't tell him right that second, she was always glad to see him. They didn't see nearly enough of each other with Zachary living in London. They always promised to visit each other more, but life seemed to get in the way.

Zachary took a seat at one of the stools at the breakfast bar. "Now that I'm here, how's work?" He burst out laughing. "I'm sorry. I can't stop picturing you behind the bar. It pains me so much that I can't go to Oasis and watch it for myself."

Erica glared at him. "Ha ha ha, laugh it up. Erica has to work, Erica has to serve drinks, it's so funny." She swatted him on the arm. "I'm doing it for you, shithead."

"I'm sorry. It's just because it's *you*. Remember that time you decided that you wanted to be a server at one of Mother's big charity balls? You poured more drinks over people's laps than you served." He thought about it. "Didn't you set something on fire with a candle?"

"My apron. And I was fifteen, Zachary."

"Yes, you were fifteen, and then you never worked again."

"Mother wouldn't let me," Erica said. "Do you not remember I begged her to let me get a part-time job and she refused. *Frosts don't need to be seen working part-time jobs.*" She mimicked their mother's high-pitched voice.

Zachary sighed. "It's true. We weren't brought up to be practical." He bit into the bagel that Erica had set in front of him. "I'm sure you're much better at that kind of thing now, though."

"Well, I haven't set anything on fire yet."

"A clear improvement." They both laughed.

They sat in comfortable silence for a few minutes eating their breakfast. Erica spoke first. "I wouldn't say I'm the best bartender in the world. I don't know what anything is, or where anything is. I give the wrong drinks to people. I forget who I'm serving. And there may have been a few spills. Thankfully, not over anyone's lap this time."

"And that is why you aren't *really* a bartender, dear sis. The world wouldn't be ready for that. However, please tell me your skills of observation are better than your Piña Coladas."

Erica leaned on the table and propped her chin in her hand. "Not much. I'm trying. It's not as easy as you would think."

"I knew it wouldn't be easy. I already told you—it could take weeks. Let's go through everyone you've met together. Would that help?"

It would probably be a good idea to use Zachary as a sounding board rather than trying to work everything out for herself. "Actually yeah, it would."

Zachary got up and wandered into the living room. He came back with a pen and something to write on. "I wish we had one of those big suspect boards with everyone's picture pinned on it. We could do little sticky notes and make webs with string. But this will have to do." He clicked the pen a couple of times. "Okay. List everyone you've worked with so far."

"Maybe for our next undercover op." She counted on her fingers while she talked. "So, there's Ash, Brandon, Kelly-Ann, Damien, and Tom. I think that's it. I've seen other people, but they've been working a different station than me, so we haven't met long enough to have a conversation."

"I'll tell Brandon to move you around a bit more. Get you working with everyone."

Erica agreed. "Brandon doesn't really speak. To me, or anyone else. He hides away in the office the whole time. I've hardly seen him." She squinted at the list. "Are you sure it couldn't be him?"

Zachary thought about it for a bit. "It's not impossible. But it was Brandon that told me there was money going missing in the first place. Why would he draw attention to it if it was him?"

Erica understood Zachary's logic. "All I'm saying is don't rule him out completely just because you couldn't keep it in your pants."

Zachary had the decency to look embarrassed. "Noted. Moving on."

Erica did. "I'm ninety-nine percent sure that it isn't Ash. She's been great."

Zachary was scribbling on the page. Erica could see that he'd sketched out some columns and put the headings *Could be, Maybe but meh,* and *Probs not.* He was adding Ash to the *Probs not* column. "I like Ash. She'd be next in line for Brandon's job. Isn't she supposed to be like the female equivalent of Tom Cruise in *Cocktail* or something?"

"Yeah, she constantly has a queue of thirsty customers waiting for her to make their drinks. I don't know where she would get the time to steal, to be honest."

"Who's next?"

"Damien. If it's him, I'll eat my own hand. He is the most careless, clumsy, awkward human being that I've ever met in my whole life. He's even worse than me. There's no way he has the capability of stealing thousands of pounds from under everyone's nose without anyone noticing. If he lifted a handful of spare change, he would drop the lot."

Zachary laughed as he wrote. "Maybe that's his cover."

Erica considered that. "I'll keep that in mind." She looked down at the page. "Then there's Kelly-Ann. Pop her into the *Probs not* column. She's too cute and sweet. Friends with everyone. She's like the popular girl from high school, but the likeable one that was nice to everyone. Her love interest, Tom, on the other hand…"

"The doorman?" Zachary asked.

"Yes. He's suspect number one, right now. If I was a gambler, I'd be putting all my money on him."

"Yeah? What makes you say that?"

"His whole vibe. I know it's kind of in his job description to have the whole tough guy thing going on, but he's like that with everyone. It's intimidating. He looks shifty. Even Ash thinks so and she's worked with him for a lot longer than I have. He spends too long staring possessively at Kelly-Ann, and they aren't together, by the way. I asked. But he's always watching her. And he disappears sometimes. I'm not sure where to, but I plan to find out."

Zachary was writing non-stop. "This is all great, Erica. I think you've learned more than you think you have. And this is only in the first week. You'll get more of a feeling about everyone the more time you spend with them."

"Hopefully it doesn't have to be too much time."

"Is it really bad? If you don't want to do it any more, you know you can tell me, right?" Zachary's eyebrows were drawn together. Erica knew that he wouldn't want her to be unhappy.

It had been a shock to the system for the first couple of days. Erica hadn't known how she was going to last the week. But she had. She couldn't help but feel a small sense of accomplishment at that. She wasn't ready to give up. Not yet anyway. "No. I'm just tired. Some annoying person has decided that I'm not allowed to sleep."

"Do you want me to go?"

"Of course not." She nudged her brother playfully. "We haven't got started on Mother's latest antics yet. You'll have to spend the day with me to get through all of them."

Zachary looked at Erica with a pained expression. "Have you heard the latest? She's going off on one because Aunt Diana has started doing Zumba. It's unbecoming, she says." They both laughed, because if they didn't, they'd cry.

The ridiculous things that their mother said and did were always hot topics of conversation when they got together. They loved their mother dearly. Truly. But Gloria Frost was a force, and only Zachary and Erica understood what she was really like. They needed each other to vent to sometimes. It was the only way they could survive her.

Later that morning, Olly popped in for a few minutes to pack a few more of his clothes. Zachary and Olly's relationship seemed to be staying strong. Erica even dared to believe that Zachary might have found a keeper this time. Olly staying with Zachary seemed to be making the relationship rather than breaking it, and he didn't seem in any rush to get home.

"I really appreciate you letting me stay here, Olly," Erica said to him before he left.

Olly put his arm around Zachary. "Stay as long as you need to, Erica. It's a great excuse for me to spend more time with this one." He smiled at Zachary. They really did make a striking couple. And her brother looked as happy as she could ever remember.

"You clearly haven't heard him singing in the shower yet," Erica joked.

"A game changer?" Olly asked.

Erica nodded. "If you survive that, you'll survive anything."

"Maybe keep the spare room prepped in case I do need to make a swift return. Don't worry, I'm an excellent roommate," Olly said.

"Hey, I'm not that bad," Zachary argued. They all laughed.

Erica said good-bye to Olly, and then she left him and Zachary alone to say their good-byes, and likely kiss in the hall a hundred times. They were that nauseating, but she had to admit it was kind of adorable. She hoped she would get to spend some time with Olly so she could get to know him better while she was in London. Zachary said they would all get together soon.

After a lazy morning, sitting around the apartment chatting, Zachary suggested going out for lunch, but Erica told him she would prefer to stay in. She explained what had happened with Hera. She didn't want to leave her if she didn't have to. Hera had curled herself up into a comfortable, fluffy ball on Zachary's knee, so she was clearly enjoying the company too.

Erica didn't have great cooking skills, but she got by. She ate out a lot when she was at home. But when she cooked, she was a *throw everything into the pan and hope for the best* type of girl. Sometimes it worked out and sometimes it didn't. She did know how to throw together a simple cheese and mushroom omelette, however, so she started to make that. She threw in some onions as well to use them up.

"Was Hera okay on her own last night, while you were at Oasis? You know you could have taken the night off? You do own the place," Zachary said.

"Yeah, I know," she called from the kitchen. "But Charlie who lives next door took her home and looked after her. Turns out she works in the vet clinic. Actually, it's thanks to her that Hera got seen to so quickly." She turned the heat down low so that it didn't burn and went back to join Zachary in the living room for a couple of minutes while the egg cooked through.

"The next-door neighbour?"

"Yes."

It felt like Zachary stared at her for a long time. He looked like one of those villains from the films, the way he was looking at her while stroking the cat.

"What are you looking at me like that for?"

"She randomly offered to look after your cat all night? A woman you barely know?" Zachary's tone was disbelieving, to say the least.

"Yes. She did. What's your point?" It was easy to forget that she didn't know Charlie all that well, because she already felt like she did. Since she arrived in London, had there been a day that she hadn't bumped into her somewhere? She didn't think so.

"I don't know yet. I'm still working that out."

She turned back to the kitchen. "When you do, you can let me know." She put the finishing touches on her omelettes. Sprinkled a little salt and ground some pepper on top. She wasn't completely useless at practical things. Lunch looked more than acceptable. She set them on the table and grabbed a couple of forks from the drawer.

"Did you sleep with her?" Zachary asked as he took the same spot at the breakfast bar he had occupied earlier.

Erica did the same. "Who?"

"The neighbour?"

"No."

"Do you want to?"

Erica swallowed. "No."

Zachary picked up on the tiny delay in her answer. He pointed at her with wide eyes. "You do want to. You hesitated."

"I don't." Erica's voice was getting higher.

"Do you find her attractive?"

"Oh. Eat your eggs," she said, stabbing her fork into her own.

Zachary grinned from ear to ear. "Erica has a crush."

"Do not."

"Do too."

"Do NOT." God, they were still twelve years old sometimes.

Zachary continued chuckling while he ate his food. He was clearly delighted that he had found something he could use to tease Erica.

"She's not my type, okay? She attracts *a lot* of women, and she seems to enjoy that—the whole casual thing. I couldn't deal with that. Plus, could you imagine Mother's reaction if I came home with the nurse from the local vet? She'd throw a fit."

"You worry far too much about what Mother thinks." Zachary gave her a sad smile. "I wish you'd stop doing that. That's what I love about living in London. I'm free to live my life the way I want to. I hate that you feel like you can't."

Erica hated it too, but what was she supposed to do? She couldn't move away too. Her mother would be left with no one. "Yeah, well. It is what it is, Zachary." Erica had already had this argument many times before with her brother. They would never agree.

"It doesn't have to be. She has too much of a hold over you," Zachary said.

"She just wants what's best for me. So she has high standards— big deal. Would it not be worse if she didn't care at all?"

"You don't think that her high standards are *too* high?" he asked.

She did think so. The sad thing was that even though Erica had allowed her mother to dictate her life for too long, she still craved her approval. So, she continued to try and meet those ridiculously high standards of hers, even to her own detriment. "At times," she admitted.

"Maybe you can have a little fun while you're here," he said.

"I'm here to help you. To help out with the business. Can we focus on that? Please?"

Zachary reached his arm out and put it round her shoulders. "Of course we can, Sis." They both went back to eating their lunch. When they were done, Zachary insisted on cleaning up so that Erica could relax. They spent the afternoon watching mindless TV, while Erica dozed on and off. It was nice to spend the day together even if it consisted of them doing nothing. Erica hated how little time she got with Zachary.

Erica was careful not to bring up Charlie's name again. She wasn't surprised it had slipped off her tongue so easily. Charlie had never been far from her mind since the day before. Since they'd met, if she was entirely honest with herself. But Erica had found that initial, charming Charlie a lot easier to resist. She could tell herself that Charlie was like that with everyone, and that Erica was nothing special.

Then yesterday she had met another Charlie—one that seemed to Erica to be the more genuine version. This Charlie was kind, sweet, compassionate. She'd gone out of her way for Erica. That wasn't the sort of thing that she took for granted. Even when she had gone to pick Hera up from Charlie's apartment, they had only had a short conversation, but it had been…nice. Nice was a good word for it. There hadn't been any games or come-ons. In one way Erica was glad she had seen this whole other side of Charlie, and in another she wished that Charlie had remained the same Charlie that she met in the bar. She was going to find this new Charlie a lot harder to stay away from.

When they had said goodnight—and Erica hadn't wanted to—Charlie had asked her if they were friends. The truth was that friends had never entered Erica's head when it came to Charlie. It had seemed to be all or nothing. She either wanted her or she didn't. They would either be enemies or lovers. However, now they seemed to be in some confusing middle ground that Erica hadn't considered to be an option. She felt like they were teetering on the edge of something—and Erica had to move very carefully to make sure she tipped the scales in the right direction. She still hadn't decided which direction that would be.

Maybe being friends with Charlie was the safest option. Erica could do that. She could be friendly. She had plenty of friends. Granted, she didn't fantasize about any of them pushing her against the sinks in the Oasis bathroom, kissing her senseless while pushing their hand down her pants—but she could work on getting rid of thoughts like that.

But was being *just friends* with Charlie what she truly wanted? She wasn't ready to answer that.

❖

Later that day, she and Zachary were dishing up some dinner, and there was a knock at the door.

"Expecting someone?" Zachary asked.

"Who would I be expecting? I wasn't even expecting you, remember?" Erica said, as she walked toward the door.

She swung it open to find Charlie standing there. The instant fluttering in her stomach at the sight of her felt much more than friendly, and she found herself completely tongue-tied as a result. That, and she was very aware of the fact that Zachary was only a few feet behind her, and Zachary loved to meddle.

"Um, hi," Charlie said. She looked uneasy, like she didn't know if she should be there. Erica gaping at her probably wasn't helping either.

Erica needed to snap out of it. She just hadn't been expecting to see her. "Hi," she managed. *So articulate.*

"I came over because, um..." Charlie shifted from one foot to the other. "I didn't know if you were working tonight, and I was going to offer to watch Hera for you if you were." Was Charlie blushing? It looked like it.

"Oh." Erica was sure she looked surprised. She felt it. Was she blinking too much? "I am working tonight."

"I'm home all night anyway. So, if you want me to—"

"Yes," Erica said quickly. "That would be really great if you could. If you're sure?"

"Great. Yes. Um. What time do you start?"

Why did things feel more awkward now? Surely it should have been easier now that they were supposedly friendly. "Seven. Can I drop her in to you on my way?"

Charlie was nodding. A lot. At least she seemed to be feeling as awkward as Erica was. "Sounds good." Charlie glanced down at her hands. Or at a box that she was holding in her hands, to be more precise. "Um, also, I was clearing out stuff in my wardrobe and I found these running shoes. They're brand new, I haven't worn them yet. I don't know what size you are, but these are a six." She held the box out to Erica. "If they fit, they might be better for work than the heels."

Erica took the box. "Wow. I don't know what to say."

"Is that weird? Me giving you them? I didn't know, but I thought about how much your feet were hurting, and I had these sitting in my wardrobe doing nothing."

Erica wondered if Charlie knew that *this* Charlie was so much more charming than flirty Charlie. She probably didn't, but Erica sure did. "It isn't weird at all. It's incredibly thoughtful and sweet. And now, I have to thank you, again. Twice."

"No, you don't. That's what friends do. We're friends now, right?"

Erica pretended to think. She tapped her finger against her lips. "I believe I said I would think about it. You're being very presumptuous again, Charlotte."

Charlie grinned.

"Erica, who's at the door?" Zachary asked as he appeared beside her. She should have guessed that he wouldn't stay out of the way. It wasn't his style. She was honestly surprised he had waited as long as he had before he interrupted. The restraint had probably nearly killed him. "Well, hello there. Who's this?" he asked with a big grin on his face.

Erica knew that Zachary wasn't stupid. He knew exactly who it was. She went along with it and made introductions anyway. "Charlie,

this is my brother, Zachary. Zachary, Charlie. Charlie lives next door."
She tried to be discreet about giving Zachary a look that said *behave.*
She hoped he got the message.

Zachary and Charlie shook hands. "Nice to meet you, Charlie.
I've already heard a bit about you."

Erica elbowed him in the ribs. She obviously needed to be clearer.

He winced. "Ignore my sister. She's the evil twin. And the one
with no manners, apparently. Aren't you going to invite Charlie in,
Erica?"

"Oh, that's okay," Charlie said, waving him off. "I'm sure you
guys are busy. I didn't mean to interrupt."

"Nonsense. You're not interrupting anything, is she, Erica? Come
on in. You hungry? We just ordered take out and we've got loads. We
need help to eat it." He elbowed Erica in the ribs this time. Harder than
she did it to him, she was sure.

She rubbed her ribs and threw her brother a glare. "You can come
in if you want."

Charlie was looking between the two of them with a mixture of
uncertainty and amusement. "Really?"

Erica smiled at her then. "Really. Come on. The least I can do is
feed you after everything you've done for me."

Zachary put his arm around Charlie and led her inside. He was
confident like that. He instantly became everyone's friend. Erica had
always been the more reserved sibling. "So, how long have you lived
next door to Olly?"

Charlie gave Hera a few pets on the way past and then followed
them to the table. Erica went to the cupboard and pulled out an extra
plate. "Help yourself to whatever you want. We were just about to dish
some out for ourselves."

Charlie took the plate from her. "Thank you." She looked at
Zachary. "I've lived here for longer than Olly. He moved in last year,
if I remember right. I've lived here for three or four years, now." She
looked around. "Where is Olly?"

Zachary laughed. "Yeah, it must seem a bit strange. Olly disappears
and Erica moves in."

"I mean, it's not exactly any of my business. But come to think of
it, yes. It is a bit. I'm sure Olly would have told me if he was moving
out."

"Olly's been staying with me, to let my antisocial sister have some
space while she's in town."

"Zachary's dating Olly," Erica added to clarify.

"Oh, you are?" Charlie beamed. "That's amazing. Olly is a sweetheart. Such a great guy."

Zachary got his dreamy look. "He really is."

Erica added some rice to her plate. "I don't know him that well yet. I've only met him briefly a couple of times, once when I first got here and then earlier today. We're hoping to all get together soon, though."

"You should join us," Zachary said.

Erica threw him a look.

"Oh. Maybe, yeah," Charlie said, but she looked uncertain. She seemed to have caught Erica's scowl and now Erica felt guilty. It wasn't that she didn't want to spend time with Charlie. It was more that she wanted to, too much. But whether she gave in to that or not, she wanted it to be on her terms. Not Zachary's. Erica knew that her brother meant well, but she didn't need him interfering. Not with this.

"While you're in town. Does that mean you aren't staying in London?" Charlie was studying a spring roll like it was the most interesting thing she'd ever seen. She didn't look at Erica.

Erica and Zachary glanced at one another. "Um. I don't really know what I'm doing yet." She wasn't prepared for those kinds of questions. She couldn't say that she was staying—that was a lie. But she couldn't confirm she wasn't, because then what was she doing there, working at Oasis?

"I'm trying to get her to stay as long as I can." Zachary winked at Charlie.

Charlie seemed to accept that answer. If she was curious or suspicious at the vagueness of it, she didn't show it.

Zachary and Charlie did most of the talking through dinner. Erica still wasn't sure how to act around Charlie, and she didn't feel comfortable trying to find her feet in front of Zachary. Instead, she stayed quiet and took everything in. Charlie and Zachary seemed to hit it off, like fast friends. They shared some Olly stories. Zachary told her the romantic tale of how he and Olly met. Charlie told him that it sounded beautiful and touched her heart. She clearly wasn't a romance cynic like Erica was. Erica was surprised by that.

"He did mention a Zach, come to think of it," Charlie said. "I ran into him a couple of weeks ago in the hall and your name came up. Said he was meeting you for dinner or something."

Erica rolled her eyes and Zachary caught it. "Ignore my grumpy sister. She hates it when anyone calls me Zach."

"Is that right?" Charlie grinned. "Funny—she struggles to call me Charlie."

Zachary laughed. "Of course she does. Erica has such a thing about that. She can be utterly obnoxious."

"I've noticed."

"I am here, you know." Erica waved her hand to prove it.

Zachary bumped her with his shoulder. "You definitely get that from our dear mother." He looked at Charlie. "She's exactly the same way. We come from a very formal background, Erica and I. I've managed to shake some of it off, but Erica here is like a poster child for finishing school. But we love her in spite of that."

"I could disown you sometimes," Erica mumbled.

Charlie nudged her with her foot under the table. "Told you, you were fancy." When Erica looked up, Charlie was smiling at her. Erica couldn't help but smile back. She could handle a little teasing. "So, did you say you two are twins? I wouldn't have known," Charlie said. "Who's the oldest?"

"I'm the baby, by six minutes," Zachary announced proudly.

"And hasn't he milked it for his entire life?" Erica said. Two could play the teasing game.

Zachary pretended to huff, and Charlie laughed. She seemed to enjoy their banter. It all felt very natural and comfortable.

When Charlie and Zachary started to talk about their favourite London spots, Charlie stopped and studied him.

"You know, your face looks sort of familiar." Charlie cocked her head to the side. "Have you ever been to Oasis? Where Erica works?"

Uh-oh.

There was silence. It probably lasted for too long. Eventually Zachary said, "Maybe a while ago. I can't remember." It wasn't his worst attempt at lying. He had always been terrible at it. When they were younger and their mother had smelt smoke off Zachary's clothes, he had told her that he was helping the local fire brigade to put out a fire. When their mother had caught him dressing up in one of her finest evening gowns, he had told her that he was checking it for threads. This wasn't quite as bad, but Charlie looked unconvinced. She was still looking at Zachary like she was trying to place him.

Erica decided to put an end to the dinner party before she could. "Well, I hope you both don't mind. I have to go and get ready for work."

"Oh, of course." Charlie got up from her stool. "I'll get out of your hair. Thank you so much for dinner. Both of you."

Zachary jumped up and wrapped his arms around Charlie. "It was so good to meet you. I hope we get to hang out again soon." He looked toward Erica like it was up to her to say they could, but she busied herself gathering the plates and putting rubbish in the bin.

"I hope so too. I had a great time. Tell Olly I said hi and I hope to see him soon," Charlie said to him.

Erica let Zachary show Charlie to the door.

"You'll drop Hera round before you leave, then?" Charlie called back toward her.

"Yes. I will," she called back without turning round. She knew she was being rude by not showing Charlie out. She didn't mean to be. She knew that her face had guilt written all over it after Charlie could have rumbled her and Zachary for their little ruse.

Zachary practically skipped back into the kitchen once Charlie was gone. "Marry her."

Erica snorted. "You are an eejit sometimes, Zachary."

"I have never seen you have chemistry with someone before, but it was there in spades. It was all blushes and shy little looks at each other. It's *so* obvious that she likes you too." He clapped his hands together. He lifted the box that Charlie had given to Erica. "And she brought you shoes. How cute is that? Please, marry her."

"She recognized you. She even suspected that it was from Oasis. She could have busted us."

"So?" He put his palms out. "I doubt she would tell anyone. It's not like you're a super spy or anything. Who cares if she knows?"

He had a point. But Erica felt like she needed to keep her cards close to her chest. Just because recent circumstances meant that things had changed between her and Charlie, it didn't mean that Erica had to completely let her guard down. She could tell Charlie when *she* wanted to, *if* she wanted to.

"I already told you, Zachary, I'm here to focus on what I'm doing. I'd rather keep myself to myself. I don't need the next-door neighbour knowing my business."

"Oh, Sis. You know you want to be completely up in that girl's business." He wiggled his eyebrows.

She snatched the shoebox from him and stomped toward the bathroom to shower and change. "No, I don't," she tossed back over her shoulder.

"Keep telling yourself that," Zachary shouted after her.

Who was she kidding?

CHAPTER ELEVEN

W hy is there a cat here?" Val was home.
Charlie came out of her bedroom where she had been folding clothes. "I'm looking after her for a friend."

Val narrowed her eyes at Charlie. "What friend?"

"Erica."

"Who the hell is Erica? I've been gone for two days and there's a cat and an Erica I know nothing about." Val dumped the gym bag she had been carrying on her shoulder on the ground.

"You do know Erica," Charlie said. "The bartender from Oasis? She's staying in Olly's. That's her name."

Val lifted her eyebrows. "You slept with her?"

Charlie glared at her. "No, I didn't. It's nothing like that."

"Hold up." Val walked toward Charlie. "Last I knew, she had basically called you a womanizer and told you to piss off."

"Things changed," Charlie said, as she leaned against the door frame.

Hera hopped off the sofa and rubbed herself around Val's feet.

"That's Hera. Say hi."

Val pursed her lips, but leaned down and gave Hera the attention she was looking for. "She's kind of cute."

"She is." Charlie pushed off the doorframe and headed toward the kitchen. "How was your family?"

"Fine, but stop changing the subject." Val followed her. "What changed?"

"Erica and I, we've become friends. Or we're on the way to becoming friends at least."

"Right." Val frowned. "So, you don't fancy her anymore?"

Charlie lifted a glass and filled it with water from the tap. "I never said that." She took a long sip.

"I'm confused."

"I think I like her. Like, really like her." It felt good to say those words out loud.

"Oh." Val's eyes went wide. "Oh!" She sat down at their kitchen table. "Well, shit. You've got feels."

Charlie sat down too. "I think I do. I told you that it felt different that first night that I saw her. That I felt it more than usual."

"I know, but I thought that was because of how hot she is. A little crush. I didn't think it would last. We never get feels."

"Nope."

"Are you not freaking out right now? I'd be freaking out."

Charlie considered that. She'd thought she would be. She'd kept waiting for it to happen, but it never had. "Strangely, no."

"Does she have feels for you too?" Val asked her. "She *did* have that whole jealous thing going on the other night, don't forget."

"I have no idea. Nothing's happened between us or anything." Charlie explained what had happened the past couple of days, and how the ice between the two of them seemed to have thawed.

"So, Hera here is a matchmaker." The cat had jumped onto the chair beside Val, letting her pet her.

"It seems that way, yes." Charlie reached over to pet Hera herself. She was becoming fond of the furry little feline. "Her brother is so much fun too. It did get a little bit weird at the end though. I kept thinking the whole time, where do I recognize his face from? And then when I asked about it, they both seemed a bit uncomfortable."

"Why would that make them uncomfortable?"

"I don't know. But I know I have seen the guy's face before."

"Didn't you say he's dating Olly? Maybe you've passed him in the hall or something when he's been coming or going from Olly's place?"

Charlie guessed that was a possibility. "Yeah, maybe." It still didn't explain why they both looked so uncomfortable when she brought it up, though. Maybe she would ask Erica about it. "Anyway. You're home earlier than I thought you would be. I wasn't expecting you until at least tomorrow."

"The girls texted about going out, so I thought I would go. I was going to ask if you're coming, but I take it you aren't, now that you're cat-sitting?"

"Yeah, I'll stay home tonight. I already texted them to say I was busy."

Val walked over and grabbed her gym bag again, before heading in the direction of her room. "Suit yourself. We aren't going to Oasis, so you probably wouldn't want to come anyway. No hot bartenders for you to drool over." She gave Charlie a grin before she closed the door.

It wasn't like Charlie to miss out. If she were to ask her group of friends who was the life and soul of every party, they would all pick her. Closely followed by Val.

Charlie had received the invite to go out before she had offered to take care of Hera. So, it wasn't like that was the reason. She didn't fancy it. The thought of curling up on the sofa, with Hera, sounded so much better to her. Waiting to grab those precious few minutes again in the middle of the night with Erica. Just the two of them.

So, Charlie waited. She knew that it would be at least four, so when she and Hera had finished their movie-fest, they'd lain down for a few hours. Charlie had set an alarm for a few minutes before four so that she could wake up a little bit before Erica arrived. She didn't want to be groggy and talking rubbish when she did. Charlie knew she needed to be always on her A-game with Erica. Erica wasn't easy to impress. And yeah, she might have got up early to fix her hair and add a little lip gloss and mascara. She was only human.

Her heart picked up when she heard Erica's three raps on the door. It had become her signature knock as far as Charlie was concerned. She hurried over to open it. "Hey." She stood aside to let Erica in.

"Hi." Erica didn't hesitate before she entered this time. That was progress.

"How are you?" they both asked at the same time. They laughed.

"You go first," Charlie said.

"I'm fine. I might drop dead, right on this very spot, because I'm so exhausted. But apart from that I'm good."

Charlie had to stop herself from telling Erica how good she looked, despite her exhaustion. "I hope you don't leave a mark. That rug's new."

"I'll try not to."

"What? Drop dead or leave a mark?" Charlie asked.

"Both." They laughed again.

"How are you?" Erica asked. "I hope Hera has been behaving herself." She took the same seat on the sofa as the night before, beside Hera.

Charlie leaned against the arm of the chair opposite them. "I'm good. And doesn't she always? She's one of the most affectionate cats I've ever met. And that's saying something because I see a lot of them."

"Does that mean Hera's your favourite patient?"

"Oh, by far. I was wondering, though. About her name? I've never known a cat called Hera before."

Erica chuckled. "It is quite original, I suppose. I don't know how much you know about Greek mythology?"

Charlie wrinkled her nose. "Not a lot."

"Hera was the queen of the gods and the goddess of women. She was the one they all worshipped. And most accounts say she was very majestic." Erica looked lovingly toward Hera. "Anyway, when I brought this little ball of fluff home, I still had no name for her. While I was trying to think of a name that suited her, she had climbed on top of the bookcase and knocked over a book I had on Greek mythology. When I went to pick it up, she was sitting on the top shelf with her nose in the air. So, I took my inspiration from that. And it fits—she certainly thinks she is the queen in our house." Erica stroked Hera's fur.

"I can totally see that—she definitely has majestic qualities."

Erica lifted her shoulder. "Maybe it's silly, but I like it."

"I think it's a great name. As for the goddess of women part— she has me wrapped around her little finger. I may have bought some cat treats, and I may have spoiled her with them slightly. I apologize, but she skipped a few days of food so I figured she could afford the calories."

"Hey, you're the animal expert. If you say it's okay, then I say it's okay." Erica sat stroking Hera's fur. Charlie had already seen how much Erica adored Hera that day in the clinic, but it was sweet to watch again.

Charlie let out a mock sigh. "And there I was thinking that I was the goddess of women."

Erica laughed. "I don't think it was in quite the same way as you see yourself."

"Oh yeah? And how do you think I see myself?"

Erica pursed her lips while she thought, moving her mouth to the side. "Charming and irresistible, I would say."

Charlie was amused. "I do not think I'm irresistible. Charming, maybe. Sometimes. But it seems to me like my charms are wasted on some women." She said it light-heartedly. She wasn't flirting, exactly. Perhaps she was pushing the boundaries a little bit, but if there was any chance that there could be any more than friendship with Erica, then she wanted to know where she stood.

Erica looked away. "Not often, I'm sure."

"They were wasted on you, were they not?"

"Not completely. You charmed me into being your friend, didn't you?" Erica still wasn't looking at her.

There was that word again. Friend. Maybe that really was all that they ever would be. She had dared to hope that there was something more happening with Erica. For the first time in her whole life, she had real, can't-escape-from, all-consuming feelings for someone. For Erica. That didn't mean that Erica felt the same way. And that was fine. Disappointing, sure. But Charlie would get over it.

She hoped the disappointment didn't show on her face. "Friends it is, then."

"Well, I better get some sleep," Erica said. "Thank you so much again for looking after Hera for me."

"I enjoy it every bit as much as she does. Honestly, she can hang out here anytime."

Erica lifted Hera and her stuff and walked to the door. "Oh, and thank you for the shoes." She held her foot up and gave it a little shake. "Game changer."

"They fit!" Charlie said. "I'm glad they helped you."

"They did. However, I'm not used to being this short." Erica winced. "Though it's a small price to pay for feet that don't throb."

Charlie laughed. "You're still tall. I didn't even notice. But now that you say it, I can see your eyes better. They're even prettier closer up." The compliment just slipped out. She wasn't trying to flirt, or charm, or be too, well, Charlie. But she couldn't not say it. In that moment they were both standing at the door, inches apart, and Erica's eyes were twinkling like shiny emeralds. Charlie had never seen anything as beautiful.

They both froze in that moment. Erica looked down at Charlie's lips. She wasn't even subtle about it. She licked her own lips. But then she frowned and snapped her gaze back up again. She cleared her throat. "We're friends, Charlie. Don't go and ruin it."

And just like that, the moment was gone. Erica was gone. And Charlie was left wondering what the fuck had just happened.

Had she seriously thought that Erica was going to lean in and kiss her? Of course she wasn't. Charlie was being stupid. Whatever Erica's reasons were, she had told Charlie that she wasn't interested in her. Multiple times. Charlie needed to get over this crush she had developed—and fast.

It was a good thing, in a way. Charlie was free to get on with her life the way she had been before Erica had come into it. She could do that. Couldn't she?

❖

"I can't believe you're dragging me out again. You know I was out last night," Val said to Charlie, as they walked into Oasis.

"Oh, come on, you were home by midnight. I heard you go to bed," Charlie said. "And it's the weekend. When do you ever complain about going out at the weekend?"

"You've changed your tune from last night."

One of the staff asked if they had any coats or jackets to check in. Charlie didn't, but Val handed over her jacket and waited for her coupon. They were only in the hall, but they already had to raise their voices to hear each other over the thumping bass of the music inside.

"Erica isn't interested in me like that. So, I need to move on. Not necessarily tonight—but I'd rather go out and enjoy myself than sit around moping, you know."

Val nodded. "Distraction technique."

"Exactly."

"Then why did we come to Oasis, the one place where you know you're going to see Erica?"

It was a fair question, but Charlie didn't really have an answer. She was working on getting over her Erica crush. That didn't mean she *was* over it. It wasn't a switch that she could turn on and off. "I'm allowed to look, aren't I?"

Val shook her head. "You're unbelievable. You can't move on if you can't keep away from her."

"I can. I will," Charlie said. "Nothing wrong with admiring the view while I do."

Val was harping on about all the reasons that she should stay away from Erica as they entered the main bar. It was especially busy. It always was at the weekends. The music was thumping even louder. Charlie pointed in the air and then to her ear. "I can't hear you," she shouted.

Val narrowed her eyes at her, and Charlie grinned. She walked backward toward the dance floor. "I love this song. Come and dance with me," she shouted. She reached out and dragged Val by the arm.

Charlie just wanted to let loose and have a good time. The DJ was playing throwback songs and it made her feel like a teenager again. She and Val were swinging their arms in the air, jumping up and down, and doing all kinds of silly dance moves. They were laughing non-stop and basically just having fun—it was exactly what Charlie needed. She had lost count of how many songs that they'd danced to before they both decided they were exhausted and needed a break.

They grabbed a booth over by the side of the bar. "I'm sweating," Val said. "I need a drink. Do you want one?"

"I'll go," Charlie said quickly.

Val gave her a look, but she didn't argue. "Get me a beer, then." She went to get money out and Charlie waved her off.

"Back in a minute." She headed toward the bar. There were a couple of different bar areas at Oasis. Erica was working at the one closest to the dance floor. Charlie had already spotted her about thirty seconds after they had arrived. She slipped onto one of the stools and waited.

She had hoped Erica would be free to serve her, but the bar was super busy. Unfortunately, Ash spotted her first. "What can I get you?"

"Soda water and lime and a beer. Bottled. Please." Before Ash walked away, she added, "Would you mind telling Erica that I'm here?"

Ash raised a brow and nodded.

Charlie was so obvious. But it worked, because it was Erica who returned with the drinks.

"Hi," Erica said loudly to be heard over the music. She gave Charlie a wide smile.

Charlie had been a little bit nervous about seeing Erica after how they'd left things the night before. She feared it would go back to what it was like before, when Erica had wanted nothing to do with her. Erica's smile put her mind at rest. "Hey. How's your night going?" Charlie had to lean in so that they could hear each other. It was a lot harder trying to have a conversation when Ariana Grande was blasting in her ears.

"It's been busy." She indicated the dance floor with her head. "You had some good moves out there."

Erica had been watching her. Charlie had to remind herself that it didn't mean anything. Erica probably watched a lot of people throughout the night. "Val and I were reliving our younger days." She paid Erica for the drinks and waited for her to come back with the change. She sipped her soda water and lime from her straw.

"Hello again," a voice said from her right.

Charlie turned around. It was Hannah. "Oh. Hi."

"I was hoping to run into you here again." Hannah leaned on

the bar beside where Charlie was sitting and gave her a look that told Charlie exactly why Hannah was glad to run into her. She put her hand on Charlie's knee. Hannah wasn't wasting any time.

"Here's your change." Erica was back—because Charlie was the unluckiest person in the entire world, she was sure of it. Erica set the change on top of the bar, ignoring Charlie's outstretched hand.

Charlie jerked her knee to shake off Hannah's hand, but it was too late.

Erica had been staring right at the touch. She lifted her gaze to meet Charlie's. She stared for several seconds before she gave a slow nod. "Have a good night, ladies." And with that, Erica disappeared back up the bar.

Charlie wanted to call after her. To tell her that it wasn't what it looked like, but what good would that have done? What was the point? Erica didn't want her. And clearly Hannah did. The whole idea of coming out that night was so that Charlie could move on from her attraction to Erica. Besides, she had had a good time with Hannah. Another night with her could be the perfect remedy for her crush. "I'm with my friend. Do you want to join us for a drink?"

Hannah nodded and followed Charlie over to the booth. Val gave Charlie a funny look—a non-verbal what-the-fuck—but she didn't say anything. Hannah had waved her two friends over who joined them too.

They all chatted together for a while. It turned out that Val already knew one of Hannah's friends, so they enjoyed catching up. Charlie was quieter than usual. She couldn't seem to help it. It probably had something to do with the fact that she couldn't stop looking in the direction of the bar to see if Erica was watching. She caught her looking once, but never again after that.

Erica clearly wasn't bothered, so when Hannah shuffled closer to Charlie, Charlie let her. When Hannah led Charlie up to dance, Charlie let her. And when Hannah pressed her lips to Charlie's, Charlie let her. It was quick. There was nothing spectacular about it. It didn't give Charlie flutters or feelings. She tried to remember if she had felt any differently the last time. She'd ended up back at Hannah's place, after all. Judging by Hannah's hooded eyes when she leaned back from it, it had affected her a lot more than it had Charlie this time. Hannah was fun, though—Charlie could give her that. And she was interested in Charlie and didn't make any attempt to hide it. The fact that she wasn't looking for anything serious was perfect for Charlie.

Still, she wavered. She was at a crossroads, and she didn't know which road to go down. Her next move seemed significant, and she needed to think it through. She excused herself to go to the bathroom. She didn't dare look toward the bar as she passed, especially not after the kiss. She wasn't ready for Erica's judgement—or worse, if Erica didn't care at all. Charlie didn't want to see that either. Maybe Erica hadn't seen the kiss. That would be the best-case scenario.

She walked round to the bathroom in the back of Oasis like she always did. The automatic light was already on when she pushed the door open. She obviously wasn't the only one in the know about the secret bathroom.

She put her two hands on the edge of the sink and looked in the mirror. She stared at her own familiar reflection, but she felt like an unfamiliar version of the person staring back at her. The truth was, she barely recognized herself at all lately. Her head was all over the place. In a little over a week, it was like she had completely changed. She really felt like a different person. Before, Charlie would have been loving all the attention she was getting from Hannah. The flirting and the sneaky touches. The anticipation of where it would all lead. Tonight, she just felt uneasy.

Admittedly, even before she had met Erica, she had been questioning her life. Wondering when it was time to grow up and settle down. There had to be more to life than parties and one-night stands, she knew that. Then, after Erica had come into her life, she had been questioning things more than ever. She started to dream about what it might be like to share her life with someone else. Yes, it was surprising and scary, and Charlie didn't know if she was even capable of a relationship, but at least she had thought about trying. That had to count for something.

The toilet flushed in one of the cubicles and Charlie turned the tap on and washed her hands. She didn't want anyone to witness the fact that she had only come to the bathroom to re-evaluate everything she ever knew about herself. That was a little deep for bathroom chitchat on a night out.

The cubicle door opened, and Erica walked out.

Charlie wasn't even surprised. That seemed to be her life now—a series of coincidences, unexpected encounters, bad timing, and a complete lack of control.

Erica paused for a few seconds before she walked over to the sink beside Charlie and turned the tap on. "Hi," she said quietly.

At least she wasn't ignoring her, but she wasn't looking anywhere near her either. The smile from earlier had gone, replaced with a frown. Worry lines creased Erica's forehead.

"Fancy seeing you here." Charlie's attempt to lighten the mood didn't seem to work, but she kept trying. "We must be the only two people who know about this bathroom. We always have it to ourselves."

Erica walked over and pulled some paper towels out of the dispenser. "It's a staff toilet. You shouldn't be using it."

"Oh." That made sense. There was never anybody in it. "Are you going to tell on me?"

Erica fisted the paper towels into a ball and threw them in the bin. "No, it's fine. I need to get back to work." She still didn't look at Charlie as she went to leave.

"What's wrong?" Charlie asked her.

"Nothing." Erica still wouldn't look at her.

"There's clearly something," Charlie pressed.

"There's nothing wrong. Go back to that girl and enjoy your night."

"Is that what this is about? Because I've been hanging out with Hannah?"

Erica turned around to look at Charlie then, her face like thunder. "Hanging out with?"

"Well, I know she was touching me at the bar. And yes, she seems interested, but—"

Erica raised her voice even louder. "Touching you? You were fucking kissing her a few minutes ago!"

That answered that question—Erica *had* seen them. But that didn't give her any right to speak to Charlie like that. Charlie felt her own temper rising then too. "And? What the hell do you care, Erica? You're the one playing me hot and cold every time you see me. You talk to me when you want. Ignore me when you want."

Erica lowered her voice again. But it held a cold tone. "That's not true." She folded her arms. "You have to *be* something to play hot and cold, and me and you, we aren't anything."

Charlie stuck her hands on her hips. "Yeah? Why are you jealous then? If me and you are nothing. Why do you care about who touches me, or who I kiss?"

Erica let out a sarcastic laugh. "I don't care. And I am certainly not jealous."

"Oh. You're jealous. I'm not stupid, Erica. I know what jealousy looks like. I thought you weren't interested. Isn't that what you've told me time and time again? So, what right do you have to be jealous, or get pissed at me for what I choose to do?"

Erica paused. "I'm not," she said quietly.

"Then what is it that you want from me?" Charlie asked.

"Nothing. I don't want anything from you. I don't even know why I'm standing in this bathroom arguing with you. Just go, Charlie. I'm sure that girl is waiting for you to take her home anyway. Why don't you piss off back to her."

Charlie swallowed. "Why are you acting like this? I thought we were supposed to be friends?"

"Friends?" Erica's voice was raised again. She closed the gap between them in three swift steps. "Can you not tell by now that I don't want to be your fucking friend, Charlie?"

And then Erica's hands were pulling Charlie to her, and her lips crushed against Charlie's. For all the hesitating Charlie had been doing that night, she didn't hesitate with this. Not for a second. She wrapped her arms around Erica's shoulders, pulling her as close as possible. There was nothing gentle about the kiss, their lips moving in furious rhythm, and Charlie poured every ounce of want, frustration, anger, and longing into it. She nipped at Erica's bottom lip, pulling it between her teeth. She grinned when Erica whimpered.

Charlie walked Erica backward, never breaking the kiss, until Erica's back hit the wall, and she pressed her body firmly against her. They fit together perfectly. Every part of her body was crying out to touch Erica. Their breathing was ragged, and Charlie found it incredibly hot. All of this was hot. Her hands were in Erica's dark hair now, grabbing and tugging. When she ran her tongue along Erica's lip, Erica moaned and met it with her own. Charlie didn't know how long they were like that, an entanglement of hands, lips, and tongues. She didn't care. She could kiss Erica forever. They could just stay, in this bathroom that no one else knew about, and kiss. Why couldn't they? Nothing else felt as good as this did.

However, not even the best things lasted forever, and eventually Erica pulled away. They kept their arms wrapped around each other, their chests heaving up and down. Erica pressed her forehead against Charlie's. The only sound in the room was their ragged breathing, which neither one of them seemed able to control.

"I can't, Charlie," Erica whispered. She closed her eyes but made no attempt to move away.

"Why not?" Charlie risked going in for another kiss. She leaned in slowly and paused just before their lips touched, waiting for permission. Erica gave it—she pressed her lips to Charlie's again. This kiss started gentler, Erica's soft lips massaging hers, but it wasn't long before they found the same passion as they had found in their first kiss. It hadn't been a fluke. When Erica's hands slid down Charlie's back to her bum it was Charlie's turn to moan. That only made Erica squeeze tighter. Charlie yanked her lips away and started to kiss Erica's neck. Erica was still taller than her, even without the heels, so Charlie had to lift her head slightly to reach. She kissed up to the sensitive spot below Erica's ear, before biting gently on her earlobe. Erica groaned again and turned her head to catch Charlie's mouth with hers again, kissing her hungrily. This time, the kiss slowed naturally, and they both eased apart. They stared at each other for a few seconds.

Charlie took a small step back and licked her lips. "Um."

Erica pushed herself off the wall. "Yeah." She cleared her throat. She turned toward the mirror and started to fix her hair.

Charlie did the same. They didn't speak while they fixed themselves. "Um," Charlie said again when they finished. *Seriously, Charlie?*

Erica spoke softly. "I really do have to get back to work."

Charlie nodded. "Yeah. Of course. I know." She was still nodding.

"I'll see you later." And Erica was gone.

Charlie pressed her fingers to her swollen lips. She couldn't help but smile. "So…not friends, then," she said out loud to no one.

Whatever Erica did next, there was no way that she could deny the chemistry that they had. Not after that kiss.

Kisses. Plural. Hot, sexy, unbelievable kisses. Charlie had imagined kissing Erica. Pictured it in her head. Fantasized about what it would be like. But she could never have imagined *that*. Charlie didn't even know that kissing like that existed, and she had kissed plenty of women before. None of them came close to this one.

All the questions Charlie had before disappeared, and she was left with just one. When could she kiss Erica again?

She reapplied her lip gloss in the mirror. She didn't want it to be too obvious that she'd been kissed into next week in the bathroom when she went back out to face everyone. First things first, she needed to tell Hannah that nothing was going to happen between them. She had pretty much come to that conclusion already, even before the kiss. But post-kiss that decision was cemented. Hannah would have to find another knee to grab. There was only one woman whose hands Charlie wanted on her.

Charlie was ready to call it a night. She had some processing to do. Ice cream would need to be involved.

CHAPTER TWELVE

It was after midday when Erica opened her eyes. She hadn't stayed in bed that late since she was a teenager. There were two reasons why it had been a good idea. One, she had a day off, and she needed to catch up on her sleep. She had been so tired lately, and it was making her act impulsively and irrationally. And two, the longer she slept, the longer she could avoid thinking about those very same impulsive and irrational acts.

It didn't work. As soon as she woke up her brain was flooded with images of making out with Charlie like her life depended on it, in the Oasis bathroom, no less. She groaned out loud. She kicked off her sheets and got up. If she was going to have to face up to what she had done, she was going to need to be caffeinated. And it was what *she* had done. Not Charlie. It was Erica who had instigated the kiss. Made her own fantasy a reality. Well, part of her fantasy. Erica shook off any thoughts of more—she wasn't going there. Not right now. She had enough to think about.

After Erica fixed herself some coffee and toast, she mulled it over. She went back to that night, before the kiss, when Charlie had complimented her eyes. Her own reaction had overwhelmed her. That simple comment had made her heart almost burst out of her chest. How was Charlie to know that, though? It wasn't like Erica had smiled or said thank you for the compliment like a normal person would have. No, Erica had made some snippy remark and run away. And why? Because of some preconceived idea she had that Charlie wasn't right for her. Even though Charlie had done nothing the past few days but show Erica how wrong her preconceived idea really was.

All Erica had done since she met Charlie was push her away. And even after Charlie had been there for her, and been so kind, Erica continued to push. So, it was hardly a shock when she saw her with another woman. Charlie wasn't doing anything wrong. She was single and free to flirt with, and dance with, and kiss whoever she wanted. It was to be expected. What was unexpected, however, was Erica's reaction to seeing someone else's lips on Charlie's. Erica had never been a jealous person, but in that moment, she felt so green with envy that she half expected to morph into the Incredible Hulk.

Erica had known that she needed to tamp down the annoyance and the jealousy. And that had been her intention. She had slipped away and taken a few minutes to cool off and to find some sense and rationality again. Then Charlie was there. And she was beautiful in her tight blue dress and flowing blond hair. And all Erica could picture was that other girl's lips on Charlie's, and any sense she had found quickly disappeared again.

She hadn't planned to kiss Charlie, until she couldn't not kiss her. It was like everything that had happened between them had been building up to that moment. All restraint went out the window—along with her doubts, her worries, her self-control. All that was left was the two of them and their feelings for each other, all poured into a magical, life-changing, earth-shattering kiss. The feelings weren't one-sided. Charlie had wanted that kiss every bit as much as Erica had. She could almost feel Charlie's lips on her neck still. Erica reached her hand up and touched it.

What would happen next? She and Charlie couldn't work, could they? Erica was only in London for a short time. Erica would go home again, and when she did, the expectation was that she would pair up with Victoria. And if not her, then someone similar. Certainly not Charlie, the sexy animal nurse from London. Besides, it was unlikely that Charlie had suddenly become the settling type. Erica knew Charlie's reputation. And although she knew and believed that Charlie was truly interested in her, she also knew that Charlie's feelings wouldn't last. That was just who Charlie was. She had never pretended to be anything different.

Erica grabbed her phone and typed out a message. She wasn't emotionally equipped to handle this whole Charlie situation on her own. Zachary or Tess? Tess, she decided. Zachary was much too idealistic. Tess would give her the kick up the arse that she badly needed.

Kissed Charlie. Now having a meltdown.

Ten seconds hadn't passed before Tess's name lit up Erica's phone. "Voice of reason, is that you?"

"I don't know about reason, but it's the voice of a very excited, surprised-yet-strangely-not-surprised, can't wait to hear every dirty detail friend. Will that do?"

"It's going to have to. I need you."

"Wait," Tess said. "I need to see you for this."

Erica's phone beeped to tell her that Tess was requesting a video call. Erica swiped to accept. Her best friend's smiling face appeared on the screen, and Erica was so happy to see her. "Hey. You look great."

"So do you. Tired, but great. I miss you even more now that I can see your face," Tess said.

She propped her phone up against the sugar cannister and jumped up on the stool. "I miss you too. We should be at brunch right now."

Tess propped her phone against something as well. "Hopefully, we will be brunching again soon. Unless...are you staying in London now?"

"What? No. Why would I be staying in London?"

Tess's eyes went wide. "The kiss. Charlie. Do we call her Charlie now? You were all pissy about that before. And how did we go from hating her to kissing her? I have so much to learn." She opened a bag of something. "Start talking. I brought snacks."

"Where do I start?" Erica blew out a breath. "My head's all over the place."

"Okay, okay. Start by telling me this. Do you like this woman?" Tess asked. "Don't overthink it. I can literally hear the thoughts whirling around in your brain. Yes or no?"

Was it that simple? "Yes," she said. Out loud. For the first time. And the world didn't end.

Tess smiled at her. "Okay. Tell me about her."

Erica told Tess everything from the beginning. She had glazed over the details the last time they had talked but she needed to go over everything properly so that she could understand herself how they got there. She went over it all again. Then she told Tess all about how good Charlie had been with Hera, and with her.

"Wait a second? Even after you being a complete..."

Erica pretended to glare at her through the camera.

"...not...nice...person."

"Good save. Kind of."

"I thought so. Anyway. After all of that, she did everything she could to help you, when there was nothing in it for her?"

"Maybe she had her reasons."

Tess glared at her though the camera this time. "Erica. She didn't care about the consequences with her boss, she put you first. She took care of your cat for two nights—given, Hera is the cutest. Tell her I love her." Tess put her hand on her heart and pouted. "Then she gave you shoes so your feet didn't hurt anymore. Come on, that's a lot of work, and thought, just to get into your pants."

"I know. She has been so sweet."

"Sounds like she has. It's totally understandable that you kissed her. Hell, I want to kiss her."

Erica gritted her teeth.

Tess pointed. "What? What's that face?"

"That wasn't when I kissed her."

Tess sighed and ran her hands through her hair. "What did you do?"

"Who said I did anything? Maybe it was Charlie who did something."

"Was it?" Tess asked.

"No. It was me. Well, I suppose she did something too. But it was probably my fault."

"What happened?"

That was the downside to being on a video call. Erica had nowhere to hide. "She said something nice to me when I went to pick Hera up from her place, and I brushed her off. Again. So, she moved on."

"Moved on. What do you mean moved on?"

"Kissed someone else. At Oasis. The girl who she had been dancing with a few nights ago. I don't know the details, if they arranged to meet up or whatever, but she was there. She was all over Charlie. And then they kissed."

"And you didn't like that."

An understatement. "No, I didn't like it! I felt sick to my stomach."

"Little Miss Jealous."

Erica nodded. "I admit it. I was."

"When was this?" Tess asked.

"Last night."

Tess waved her hand in the air. "Hold up. Last night? Then how the hell did Charlie go from kissing that girl to kissing you?" Tess squinted at the phone. "Are you blushing? You're blushing."

Erica put her hands to her cheeks. She glanced at the little square in the corner of her phone where she could see herself. "I was fuming. Mostly at myself, but also at the whole situation in general. And at Charlie for kissing her, I guess. Which isn't fair but it's true. I wanted to hop the bar and tear them apart. Instead, I went to the bathroom—took a breath. Then Charlie was there, in the bathroom. We ended up arguing."

Tess closed her eyes. "Oh, tell me there was hot, angry kissing."

"There was hot, angry kissing."

"Yes," Tess shouted. She punched her fist in the air. "I love hot, angry kissing. Tell me all about it. All the details."

"A lady doesn't kiss and tell."

"Oh, don't give me that. Who instigated the kiss? You can at least tell me that."

"I did. Okay? I kissed her. And she kissed me back. And it was *un*believable, Tess. Hands down the best kiss I've ever had in my entire life. It was hot, and messy, and wild. So good."

Tess fanned herself with a magazine. "Damn. I think I need a cold shower, so I can only imagine how you feel. What happened after all the sexy kissing?" Tess gasped. She lowered her voice to a whisper. "Is she there?"

Erica snorted. "No, she's not here. You can stop whispering."

"That's disappointing. What happened then?"

"Nothing happened. I went back to work. I saw Charlie leave about five minutes after, and I haven't seen or spoken to her since."

"And I hope the end of this story was that Charlie left alone, and not with that woman? Because if she left with that other woman, I'm coming up there. And then she'll know what rude looks like."

Erica laughed. "Well, not alone, she left with her friend—but not with that woman. Thanks for the moral support, though. I know where to go if I need some muscle."

"Anytime." Tess flexed her arms. It wasn't all that frightening. "Didn't I tell you that London was going to be an adventure?"

"Now is not the time to be smug. Did you not see the part of my message where I said I'm now having a meltdown." She put her elbows on the breakfast bar and held her head in her hands. "Argh. Tess. What am I going to do?"

Erica couldn't see her from her position, but she heard Tess laugh.

"It's not funny, Tess. I'm serious." She rhymed off all the reasons why Charlie and she were such a terrible idea. Tess understood them. Tess might tease Erica about her mummy issues and her privilege—but she did know the pressures that Erica faced and was sympathetic. Tess agreed that all of Erica's worries were valid. "So, what do I do?"

"Listen. Yes, there are issues, geographical and otherwise. As for this Charlie, you can only judge her on the way she's been with you, and face it, Erica. She's been pretty fantastic. Maybe she does only enjoy the chase and she'll fuck off again as quickly as she appeared, but honestly, the evidence says otherwise so far. Some things last and some things don't. There's no crystal ball to tell you what's going to happen. Sometimes you need to give it a chance and see what happens."

"And what about Mother?"

"What about her? You've got every right to go out with whoever you want. I think you need to switch your brain off a little bit and go with the flow here. There are loads of maybes. Maybe it won't last long enough to worry about your mother going off on one. Maybe you'll be the one who loses interest. You won't know until you find out."

Erica sighed. "That's your big advice. Try it and see." Tess was right, though. Erica did have the right to see whomever she pleased. And whom she pleased was not any of the women in her mother's stuffy circle. She was beginning to realize that.

"My big advice is, do whatever makes you happy. You don't know what will make you happy in six months. But I think we both know what will make you happy right now."

Erica considered that. She was a planner. She liked to know outcomes. Her life was safe, and predictable. None of this, however, had been predictable. Not coming to London, not working in a bar, not her attraction to Charlie, and not her bathroom make-out session.

Maybe a little unpredictable would do Erica good.

❖

Four hours and twenty-seven minutes. That was how long it took Erica to work up the courage to go next door and knock on Charlie's door. She had been counting. Erica had to work that night, but she had still put extra effort into her appearance. She wanted to see Charlie before she left, and she wanted to look good when she did. She would tie her hair back when she got to work, but she chose to wear it down. She applied her make-up carefully. She didn't want to look like she was trying too hard, but at the same time she wanted to look her best and feel as confident as she could under the circumstances.

With Hera's carrier in hand, she rapped the door.

It swung open, but it wasn't Charlie. It was the roommate. Erica couldn't remember her name.

She went for friendly. "Hi. I'm Erica. I'm staying in the apartment next door."

"Yeah, I know who you are." She narrowed her eyes at Erica, as if she was trying to work her out. Erica wondered how much she knew. Probably everything if this was Charlie's best friend. "Val."

Valerie, Erica said in her head. She really needed to stop doing that. "Good to meet you. I've seen you with Charlie, but I hadn't had a chance to introduce myself yet." She smiled. "Is she here? Charlie?"

"Yeah. She's here." She turned her head back into the apartment and called Charlie, then looked back at Erica. She kept her voice down. "If you aren't serious about her, then don't fuck with her. She seems... vulnerable when it comes to you. I don't want to see her get hurt."

The don't mess with my best friend talk. Erica had never had one of those before. She couldn't say she was thrilled to be on the receiving end of it. Then again, Tess would probably do something similar if things were reversed. So, with that in mind, she gave Val a nod. "Understood."

Charlie appeared from a room behind Val. Probably her bedroom. From the look on her face, she hadn't been expecting Erica. She looked down at her own outfit when she got to the door.

Val shifted inside. "Good to meet you." She gave Erica a nod and a look that said *remember what I said.*

"You too," Erica replied as she disappeared back into the apartment. She turned her attention to Charlie, who looked as shy and awkward as Erica felt. Erica refused to show it, though. She had spent all day gathering her confidence, and she was going to use it. "Hi. How are you?"

Charlie looked down at herself again and then back to Erica. "Surprised. If I'd known you were coming, I wouldn't look like, well, this."

Erica looked at Charlie with her messy bun, oversized hoodie, and leggings. She had fluffy socks over the top of the leggings. She looked adorable. "I think you look great."

"And I think you're an excellent liar." Charlie looked down at the carrier in Erica's hand. She leaned down. "Hello, Hera." She made some kissy noises and put her hand against the mesh cover. Hera rubbed her head against it.

"We were wondering, Hera and I, if you wanted a companion for the evening?" Erica asked.

"And who would the companion be, Hera or you?"

"As much as I wish it could be me, I'm sure you can tell by the uniform I'm wearing that I have to work. Hera's evening is wide open, though."

"That's okay, I was hoping it would be Hera anyway."

Erica laughed. "Oh, were you now?"

"Of course. She's my movie buddy."

"Ah. That's why she begged me to bring her here. It all makes sense now." Erica paused. "You don't have to. I mean, she's back to herself again so she doesn't need to be looked after." She looked Charlie in the eye. "To be honest, I was looking for an excuse to come and talk to you."

"I told you—I like hanging out with her. What's the point of her sitting in an empty apartment by herself when I'm right here." Charlie took the carrier from Erica. "And you don't need any excuses to talk to me, Erica." She pointed into the apartment. "Do you want to come in?"

Erica shook her head. "I've got to get to work. But I was thinking...I wanted to ask you if you wanted to have dinner with me? Tomorrow night, if you're free? We could talk then. It's my night off, so we would have all night."

Charlie gave her trademark cocky smile. "*All* night?"

Erica had walked into that one. "You know what I mean."

Charlie chuckled. "Yeah. Dinner sounds good."

"Good. That's settled then." Erica's confidence started to waver. That was all she had planned. Wangle her way in with Hera and ask Charlie to dinner. Now she had to wing it. Should she hug Charlie before she left? Should she mention anything about last night? They were going to talk tomorrow, but maybe something needed to be said there and then.

"And we have our four a.m. rendezvous too, don't forget," Charlie said.

Erica frowned. "I keep forgetting that part. That's not really fair on you, is it? You have to get up for work in the morning."

"It's fine. I go right back to sleep after."

"Still. I can leave a key—"

Charlie stopped her. "I like it when you come to pick her up."

Erica looked at her. She felt bad for waking Charlie in the middle of the night, but the truth was she liked it too. She spent her whole shift looking forward to those few minutes she spent with Charlie while the rest of the world slept. There was something intimate about it. So, she was only slightly reluctant when she agreed. "Okay. I'll see you later, then."

"You kissed me," Charlie said, as Erica stepped away.

She stopped. "I did."

"Why did you?" Charlie stepped out into the hall after her. "It's been on my mind ever since."

She nodded. "That's part of what we need to talk about."

"Okay. Only, can I ask you one thing now? Because I'm going out of my mind here."

Erica cocked her head to the side. "Ask away."

"Do you regret it? Kissing me. Is that what you're going to tell me tomorrow? Because if it is, Erica, I would rather you just told me right now, out here, in this hallway. I don't want to spend another night guessing and doubting what's going on between us. If you regret it, it's ok. You can tell me. I know that it happened in the heat of the moment and—"

Erica closed the gap and pressed her lips softly against Charlie's, silencing her in the process. She cupped Charlie's face in her hands as her lips caressed Charlie's in the softest of kisses. Erica lingered for a few seconds before she pulled away. "I don't regret it," she said quietly. She ran her thumb gently over Charlie's lips. Then she walked away, leaving Charlie gaping after her.

Erica couldn't help but feel a little bit satisfied with herself as she did.

CHAPTER THIRTEEN

Erica had been put to work at the quieter bar at Oasis—not that it was much of a slower pace, but it was further away from the dance floor and was more geared to serving the customers in the seating area of the club rather than the dancers and livelier crowd.

Both she and Zachary had spoken to Brandon about working all the different areas of Oasis. She hoped it would give her a wider scope for her search and maybe she would gain some new suspects. Strangely, her conversation with Brandon had lasted a minute at most before he disappeared back into his office and out of sight again. Brandon didn't seem comfortable talking to Erica. Whether that was because of his history with her brother, or because he had something to hide—like money stealing—was still unclear. There was the possibility that he was awkward in general, but whatever the reason was, he wasn't helping his own case. Zachary might have been happy to rule Brandon out, but as far as Erica was concerned, he was right after Tom on her list of suspects.

Erica's new location gave her a better viewpoint of the main door, yet she was far enough away that it wouldn't be obvious to Tom that she was keeping an eye on him. She was stuck working with a couple of students who spent more time complaining about their jobs than actually doing them, which put even more pressure on Erica. She never thought she would be so relieved to see clumsy Damien, but she was. He came to the rescue when the queue kept getting longer instead of shorter. At least he knew what he was doing, even if he made a mess while he did it.

Erica was making cocktails, and she had no idea what concoctions she was giving people. She tried to follow the menu, but it was slowing her down, so she ended up doing a lot of improvising. She hoped that people were drunk enough that they couldn't tell whether they were drinking a martini or a Manhattan, or more likely, drinking something in between that was neither. Unfortunately, from some of the looks Erica was getting, her mistakes were entirely obvious and weren't going unnoticed.

Try it, you'll love it or *it's one of my secret recipes* were sentences she came out with on more than one occasion. She was surprised at how well that seemed to work, so she went with it. At one point she started getting orders for the secret cocktail. Talk about pulling off a bluff.

As for gaining new suspects—she didn't. Her new colleagues were both terrible at their jobs, but they hadn't done anything that Erica would call dodgy. Damien was still, well, Damien, but the most helpful and reliable of the bunch.

Erica looked over to the other bar. She strangely missed it, which she never thought would be the case. Ash had a long queue of folks waiting for cocktails—probably made longer by the customers that weren't happy with their Erica Specials. She snickered at that. Kelly-Ann looked like she was under pressure too. There was another guy working that Erica didn't recognize. Perhaps she would get a chance to sus him out later that night, or another time.

Another time. A couple of days ago Erica had been totally frustrated at how long it was taking to get round all the staff at Oasis. Another new face would only have annoyed her by making her task more difficult, dragging it out. But after recent developments, she was no longer in as big a rush to leave London. She didn't even hate bartending as much as she had a week ago. She wouldn't go as far as calling it fun, but it wasn't as terrible as it had been. Admittedly she wasn't the best at it, but she noticed a few small improvements every day. She was learning. Despite that, she was still more than happy to leave the cocktails to Ash.

Tom was watching Kelly-Ann like a hawk, as usual. He did his job, Erica noticed that. He broke up a fight at one point in the night. He controlled the crowd. She saw him turn some people away who had clearly already had too much to drink elsewhere. So, he was keeping an eye on the floor. But the rest of the time he watched Kelly-Ann.

Wait.

Every time Tom looked at Kelly-Ann, she was using the till. A lightbulb went off in Erica's head. Maybe the reason he was watching Kelly-Ann wasn't because he fancied her. Maybe Tom was keeping an eye on how much money was going through the till. It made sense. He watched the money that was being handled at the bar, so he would know which nights were raking in the most cash. And then, if he knew it would be worth his while, he would swoop in and help himself to a share of it. Or maybe he thought if there was more money there, any that he took for himself would go under the radar.

These were only theories, of course. But Erica felt like she had made a breakthrough. She could feel it in her bones. Tom was the key to cracking this case. It was him. She knew it was. She just needed to prove it.

It was near the end of the shift when Erica noticed Tom leave his station. That was her chance. The bar had quietened down, and Erica was able to slip away, so she followed him. She felt like she was in some kind of spy movie, the way she was sneaking around—peering around corners, shuffling with her back against the wall. But as much as that amused her, she had to keep her focus. She had missed her opportunity to see where Tom had disappeared to the last time, she couldn't make that mistake again.

Tom left the main bar through the door in the back. Erica gave him a few seconds' head start before she went through the same door herself. She didn't want Tom to catch her following him, so she made sure to keep a safe distance. Thank God for Charlie and her sensible shoes. Heels would have blown her cover by now.

She peeked through the doorway just as Tom reached the end of the corridor. He slowly went through another door at the end. His movements looked sneaky too. When Erica heard the door close, she rushed up the corridor after him. There was a small window beside the handle, and she risked a look through it. Inside was a large function room. Although it was dark, Erica could tell that the room was cluttered. Probably being used for storage. Judging from the covers over the tables and chairs, the room hadn't been used in a while. Erica noticed a door on the far side of the room was closing slowly. Tom must have gone through there.

She pulled open the door to the function room. Her palms were so sweaty, her hand almost slipped off the handle, but she managed to keep a grasp on it. She didn't want to make any noise or draw attention to herself. It wasn't like she was going to confront tough-guy Tom. She wanted to watch him from afar and remain unnoticed. If she saw anything suspicious at all, then she would report back to Zachary, and they could deal with it together.

She was sure that the thudding of her heart could probably be heard over the blasting beat of the club's sound system at that point.

She had never pretended to herself or anyone else to be overly brave, yet there she was playing James Bond.

Erica glanced around. She had to squint to make anything out. There were no windows, and Erica couldn't turn the light on for obvious reasons. She could make out some chairs stacked up, some tables, and maybe a pool table, she thought.

She crept to the door that Tom had gone through. It wasn't like she could just push it open and look—she had no idea where or what she would be walking into. She pressed her ear against it and listened. It was hard to hear anything. She thought that she could hear cars passing in the distance, so she guessed that the door probably led to outside.

Then Erica heard something else. Something that made her heart drop. Because this noise didn't come from the other side of door that she had her ear pressed against. No, this noise came from inside. Inside the same dark, creepy room that Erica was in. A room where she apparently wasn't alone.

She turned around quickly. "Who's there?" she called out, attempting to sound braver than she felt. Her eyes darted around the room as she tried to work out where the noise had come from. She needed some light. She reached for her phone in her back pocket, but before she could grab it, she was knocked from her feet. She flew sideways with force, crashing into whatever furniture was piled up nearby, which all fell down around her—and on top of her. She covered her head with her arms to try and protect herself, but it was already throbbing. She must have banged it as she initially went down. Everything happened so fast.

When the crashing and commotion stopped after several seconds, Erica scrambled to her feet. She pushed the fallen chairs to the side and climbed through the debris. The pain in her head was getting sharper, and the room was spinning as she tried to walk. She reached up and touched her forehead. It felt wet. She rubbed her fingers together and looked at them, but everything was blurry. She blinked to try to regain her focus, which made her head hurt even more. When her vision returned to normal a few seconds later, she confirmed her fear that it was blood on her fingertips. *Isn't that just great.* She put her hand up to her shoulder, which was hurting as well.

She rushed out of the room on shaky legs and staggered back out to the corridor. She looked around, but there was no one to be seen. She wasn't surprised. They had made sure they got a good head start by knocking Erica over so she couldn't follow them. None of that had been by accident. Whoever was in that room was ensuring that they got away unseen. It had to have been Tom. Erica had been sure that he had gone through that other door. Clearly, she was mistaken.

She made her way up the corridor toward the bathroom. She needed to get herself cleaned up quickly before she went back to work. She had been away long enough, and everyone would start wondering where she had disappeared to. *Ugh.* Work was going to be highly unpleasant with a headache.

"What the hell happened to you?" Kelly-Ann was already in the bathroom when Erica entered.

Erica had hoped to avoid making a scene. She just wanted to clean her face and hopefully hide any marks so no one would notice. She definitely didn't want to discuss what had happened. But no such luck.

"I fell," she said, looking at her head in the mirror. There wasn't as much blood as she had feared. She grabbed a handful of paper towels and held them under the tap before dabbing them against her forehead. "It's not as bad as it looks."

Kelly-Ann was staring at her with wide eyes. "It looks nasty. You might need to go get that looked at."

Erica smiled at her despite the pain. "I'll be fine." She dried the spot she had wiped and took a closer look in the mirror. There was a gash, but with all the blood wiped away it didn't look anywhere near as frightening as it had before. She turned to Kelly-Ann and pointed at it. "See. Not so bad."

"Where did you fall? How did you fall?" Kelly-Ann really was a sweet girl. She looked so shocked and concerned.

"I tripped over some boxes," Erica lied. "I went to the stock room to refill some drinks. I didn't see the boxes sitting right in front of me. I hit my head on one of the shelves on my way down." She laughed at herself. "I'm such an idiot."

Kelly-Ann was still looking at her with that same shocked look. She pushed herself onto her tiptoes to look at Erica's head. "I don't think it's bleeding anymore." She winced. "That must have really hurt."

Erica gave herself another once-over. There was no way to make the cut on her head unnoticeable. At least her shift was nearly finished. She hoped she wouldn't be asked too many questions about it before then. "I better get back," she said to Kelly-Ann.

"I'll walk out with you." She pouted. "Poor you. I wish there was something I could do."

"I'll be okay. It will teach me to be more careful." Like not trying to be a hero and follow muscle men into dark rooms where no one else was around.

The more Erica thought about it, she deduced that Tom wouldn't have had time to go out that door and get back again. She was only seconds behind him. Which meant that he had never left the room at all. Opening that back door might have been a diversion, a ploy to put Erica off. And she had fallen for it. Tom must have known that Erica was following him. It was the only explanation. And he hid in the room waiting for her to arrive. It wouldn't have been hard. There would have been at least fifty good places to hide. Then he shoved her out of the way so that he could make his escape.

Tom still hadn't returned to his station by the time Erica arrived back on the main floor. It was at least another fifteen minutes until he did. Erica hated that she felt her legs go wobbly when she looked at him, but she assured herself that it was a reasonable reaction after what had happened.

Tom didn't look anywhere near Erica for the rest of the night. That surprised her. Maybe he was ignoring her on purpose. Guilt. Avoidance. Deniability. Who knew? But it seemed strange to her that he didn't show any sign of recognition at all. He had to realize that Erica would *know* that it was him who had pushed her. She had followed him into that room, after all. Yet his scowling gaze remained on Kelly-Ann. Maybe Erica should say something to her. Warn her that she might want to stay away from Tom. But how could she explain why?

As for how to proceed with Tom—she wasn't sure. She hadn't caught him in the act, not exactly. She didn't see him with any money. And there were no witnesses, so she couldn't prove anything. Only she and Tom knew what happened in that room. Her word against his.

She needed to talk to Zachary. She was sure that he would give her a lecture for putting herself in danger like she had. But he had asked her to find the thief. She wasn't going to do that by playing it safe all the time. It wasn't like someone was going to come up to her one day and be like, "Hi. I'm making a fortune from pocketing the takings. Want some?" Besides, it wasn't that bad. It was just a bump on the head. She rolled her shoulder because it was still stiff, but it was nothing Erica couldn't handle. She would go home and pop a couple of painkillers and feel good as new.

On the upside, maybe Charlie would kiss it better for her. Was it home time yet?

Chapter Fourteen

Charlie checked her appearance in the mirror to see if it was as bad as she feared. She wasn't rocking her best look, that's for sure. One of her fuzzy socks had a hole in the toe, and she had owned the hoodie that she was wearing for the best part of a decade. She couldn't believe Erica had seen her looking like that. Erica, who had turned up at her door, looking all put together, and fresh, and sexy.

"This is why us ladies should always be prepared," she said to Hera, who blinked at Charlie, then looked away. "Yeah, yeah. You take her side, why don't you." She gave her some love anyway.

Even though it was going to be the wee hours of the morning, she needed to do something with herself. Especially now that Erica and she were kissing, in a very unexpected change of events. Charlie's entire body went on fire when she thought about that kiss. That first one. Who wouldn't want to be grabbed like that and kissed so fucking expertly? She could have exploded right there and then.

The second kiss was every bit as hot. Charlie hadn't been able to resist running her tongue along Erica's soft looking skin. It had tasted even better than she had imagined it would. Those little noises that Erica made—the moans and the whimpers—they did things to Charlie. If that's how it was when they were kissing, she couldn't begin to imagine what it would be like when she took Erica to bed. Charlie felt like she could spontaneously combust just thinking about it.

Then there was that third kiss tonight. The confident, sweet kiss that put all of Charlie's worries and doubts to rest—maybe the most important of all the kisses. Because she had been worrying. All night and all day. Recent history wasn't in Charlie's favour. She knew that there was a possibility that the kiss at Oasis was the start of something, but there was also a chance that it could have made Erica pull away from her for good. Now that Charlie knew that it wasn't going to be the latter, she felt like she was free to enjoy her memories of all those kisses for exactly what they were. Absolute perfection.

She showered and spent some time blow-drying her hair. She opted for some black sleep shorts and a tight-fitting black tank top to match. Did she want Erica to be affected by the fact that she was showing a little skin? Yes, that's exactly what Charlie wanted.

Then it was a waiting game.

Hera spent half the night curled up on Charlie's lap. She seemed to be getting used to Charlie now. Val found the whole thing odd, and she hadn't been afraid to say so. She wasn't exactly Erica's number one fan after everything that had happened, even though Charlie had explained to her that Erica was different now.

"I don't trust her, Charlie. What if she's using you? Have you even considered that? You've started doing all these things to help her, and now she's going to milk it for all it's worth," Val had said to her earlier.

Charlie didn't feel like Erica was using her. Erica had never asked her for anything. Charlie had offered. Or she just *did*. And Erica had been genuinely grateful when Charlie had helped her out.

"Well, if she is, then you can give me a big *I told you so*. But until then I need my best friend to support me," Charlie had said to her. "I've never felt like this before. I need you."

They had hugged it out after that.

Charlie loved Val, she was her best friend, but she couldn't keep living the same frivolous lifestyle just because it suited Val. It had suited Charlie too, for a long time, but now Charlie was ready for something more. Maybe if she hadn't met Erica, she would still be the same old Charlie, but she had met her, and she felt happy with the new direction that her life seemed to be taking. Excited even.

Charlie's alarm went off at three fifty-five. Most people probably didn't bounce out of bed in the middle of the night like they had a spring in their step, but that's exactly what Charlie did.

It was only a few minutes later when she heard the rap, rap, rap at the door.

When Charlie pulled the door open she was shocked at the sight. Erica stood before her, looking exhausted and hurt—literally. There was an actual, visible gash on her forehead. "What happened?" She reached out, took Erica's hand, and led her inside the apartment.

"It's nothing. I'm fine. Just a bump to the head," Erica said.

Charlie led her straight to the sofa and sat her down. She stepped right into Erica's space and leaned down to get a proper look at the wound. There was a big enough cut, and it looked deep. The skin around it was swollen and starting to bruise. "That's a bit more than a bump, Erica. How did it happen?" She kept her voice low so they wouldn't wake Val.

"That's not the same top as you were wearing earlier."

Charlie looked down and realized that Erica was eye-level with her chest, and her tank top didn't offer the best coverage, especially not in the position she was in. She straightened up and stuck her hands on her hips. "Don't change the subject. Your head. What happened?" Secretly, she enjoyed the attention—but this was more important.

Erica tried to brush it off. "It's really a very long story. I can't get into it now—you need to get some sleep."

"Why don't you let me clean that cut out properly, and you can give me the short version while I do?"

Erica hesitated, but Charlie gave her a look, and she nodded. "All right. I give in."

"Give me two seconds to grab some stuff from the bathroom." Charlie headed for supplies and returned with gauze, surgical tape, antiseptic cream, and a cloth that she had ran under some warm water. She stopped in the kitchen to fill a bowl with some salt and hot water.

"Are these the perks to knowing a nurse?" Erica asked when she returned.

Charlie grinned as she took a seat beside her. "I'm an animal nurse, remember. But I'm pretty sure there isn't much of a difference between cleaning a dog wound and cleaning a human one."

"Hopefully a little less hair."

Erica was funny. Charlie hadn't seen that side of her yet. She liked it. "I mean, it depends on the human." She dabbed the wet cloth on Erica's forehead as gently as she could. She felt terrible when she felt Erica flinch, and she hadn't even used the salt water yet. "I'm sorry. Are you okay?"

"I'm fine. It's a bit sore to touch is all. I can handle it," Erica said.

Charlie kept her touch as light as she could. "Anyway. You're meant to be telling me what happened."

Erica sighed. "Someone pushed me. I fell into some chairs that were stacked up. Banged my head. My shoulder doesn't feel too hot either."

Hold up. Charlie stopped and leaned back to look at her in the eye. "What do you mean someone pushed you? Like a customer?"

"No. That's why it's a long story." Erica pointed to her head. "Keep dabbing. You need to get some sleep tonight."

Charlie didn't care about that, but she continued cleaning. "This is going to sting when I put the salt water on it, but it will keep it from getting infected and help it heal faster."

"Yes, nurse."

"Why would someone push you?" Charlie asked. She dipped the cloth in the salt water and pressed it to Erica's wound.

Erica took a sharp intake of breath through her teeth.

"Sorry."

"Stop apologising." Erica took a couple of deep breaths. "You can keep a secret, I assume?"

Charlie nodded.

"There's money going missing from Oasis. There's been quite a substantial amount taken, and no one has been caught doing it." Erica flinched again as Charlie dabbed some more. "I have my own suspicions about who's been taking the money. And when there was an opportunity to follow them tonight, I did."

"Erica, why would you do that? Anything could have happened. If this person is prepared to steal from their workplace, from a nightclub, who knows what they're capable of." Charlie knew that it wasn't her place to scold Erica, but she couldn't help but worry if Erica was putting herself in danger. She hated that Erica had got hurt, and she hated the thought that something worse could have happened.

Erica held a hand up. "I know. But I was being careful. I kept my distance, and I didn't think there was any chance that he could have spotted me. Then I followed him into an old function room, and it was so dark in there. The next thing I knew I was tackled, sent flying, and ended up lying amongst a load of furniture with the room spinning round and round."

That made Charlie worry even more. "You could have a bloody concussion. Do you know that? Did you black out? How many fingers?" She held up three.

"That's a bit forward." Erica grinned.

"How many?" Charlie said, narrowing her eyes. As much as Charlie enjoyed this playful version of Erica with the wit and innuendos, making sure that she was okay was more important right now.

"Three," Erica replied like it was obvious. "And no, I didn't black out. I was just a little bit dizzy when I stood up. I've been fine ever since—no lasting damage."

Charlie finished cleaning Erica's wound and dried it off. "I don't think it needs any stitches. It's going to be a big bump, though. And it will be bruised." She reached for a piece of gauze and placed it on the wound. She secured it with the surgical tape. "All done."

"Do I have to wear one of those cones on my head?"

"That could be arranged." She smiled, then regarded Erica. "Seriously, it's not your responsibility. Let the bosses, or the security, or the police find out who's stealing that money. It's hardly in a bartender's job description." She paused. "You have told your boss what happened, right? They're going to deal with the person who did this?"

Erica lowered her gaze to the ground. "Yeah, you're right. And I'm going to call the owner first thing in the morning. That's a promise." Then she looked up at Charlie and pointed to her own head. "How does it look, nurse?"

Charlie felt like there was something that Erica wasn't saying, but she looked so tired, and weary. She was clearly still in some pain. The last thing that she needed was Charlie giving her the third degree. It was another Erica mystery. Charlie had a lot to learn, she knew that much. But not tonight. She leaned in and touched Erica's cheek. "You look beautiful."

To Charlie's delight, Erica leaned into her touch. "I highly doubt that's true, but thank you."

"Do you want to stay here tonight? I don't think you should be alone after a head injury." Charlie held her hands up. "I mean to sleep. I can take the sofa and you can have my bed. Or I can come over and sleep on your sofa if that's better?"

"You know, you keep surprising me with how sweet you are. I have to admit, I never expected that when we first met."

"To be honest, I never expected it when we first met either." They both laughed at that. "You must bring it out in me somehow."

"I'll be fine tonight. You have to get some sleep for work in a few hours, and all I'm going to do is take a painkiller and climb into bed myself."

"I'm going to worry about you." Charlie couldn't help it, she already cared about Erica. And what if Erica passed out in that apartment all on her own? How would she even know?

"How about you give me your phone number, and I'll text you as soon as I wake up? Will that make you feel any better?" Erica held her phone out to her.

"If this has been some kind of elaborate scheme to get my number, you really took it a bit too far. I would have just given it to you if you asked, you know." Charlie took the phone and keyed her number in. "It won't make me feel *much* better, but I'll take what I can get."

"Oh no, you worked it out. That's exactly what I was doing." Erica stood up. "Thank you for taking care of me. You really didn't have to." She walked toward Hera, who had already climbed into her cat carrier and was curled up fast asleep. "It seems like we're getting into a bit of a routine here. Even Hera's getting used to it."

"She's not the only one. Is it weird that I look forward to your middle of the night visits?" Charlie said. For some reason it felt easier to make those kinds of admissions during those visits too. Like they were in some sort of dream and Charlie could say anything she wanted. Things that she maybe wouldn't have the confidence to say in the light of day.

"If it is weird, then I'm weird too." Erica reached in and moved a piece of Charlie's hair that had fallen across her face.

Charlie seized the opportunity and pulled Erica in closer and kissed her, like it was now the natural thing to do so. Their lips moved gently against each other, and their tongues tangled softly and slowly. The kiss wasn't hurried, with neither of them in a rush to break it. Charlie immediately felt the loss when they eventually did. She didn't want to let Erica out of her sight after what had happened, but she was a grown woman, and who was Charlie to argue? She reluctantly said goodnight, and Erica disappeared into her own apartment. Well, Olly's apartment.

Charlie had so many questions. What was Erica not telling her about tonight? Why was she in London, staying in Olly's place? How long would she be in London? Where did Charlie know Zachary from, and why hadn't they seemed to want her to know?

She could text Olly. Ask him what was going on. Maybe he would tell her and maybe he wouldn't. But she didn't want to find out from Olly. She wanted to hear it from Erica herself.

Tomorrow night, Charlie was going to get some answers.

❖

"You've checked that phone about fifty times, and it isn't even ten o'clock yet," Liz said to her when they were between patients.

Charlie looked up from the screen, which still hadn't gone off with the text message that she was on tenterhooks waiting for. She sighed and set the phone down. She hadn't told Liz anything about Erica and her yet. She had to start at the beginning, and they had a busy day lined up, so Charlie was only able to tell Liz bits and bobs in their scarce free minutes. Liz was unsurprisingly delighted that Charlie and Erica were pursuing...something. Charlie didn't have a label to put on it yet.

"You *have* had a busy weekend. Wait until I tell Nancy about the kiss against the bathroom tiles. She is going to lose her mind."

Charlie covered her head with her hands. "I think *I've* lost my mind, Liz. I don't even know what I'm doing. I'm like a completely different person with her. She's so..." She tried to think of the right word, but she couldn't so she shook her head. "It's like I'm powerless against this. I get up in the middle of the night just so that I can speak to her for a few minutes. Like, who does that?"

Liz let out a soft laugh. "Someone who's falling hard."

"Oh, come on. I like her, but let's not get ahead of ourselves here."

"Okay, fine. But I will say, it's amazing the things that we'll do when we get feelings for someone."

"I don't even know her all that well. How can I possibly have feelings for someone that I know next-to-nothing about?"

Liz lifted her shoulder. "It happens. You'll get to know her. And your feelings will either fade if you don't like what you learn, or else they'll get stronger. For what it's worth, I really liked her," Liz said.

"Val doesn't. She thinks I should stay away from her."

Charlie watched Liz as she tried to think of what to say about that. That was the thing about Liz. Her words were always measured and thought out. She never said things that she didn't mean. And she had her head screwed on. Charlie valued her opinion. Trusted it.

"I'm sure Val is trying to protect you, but I'm not sure that I agree with her." She crossed her legs and leaned forward. "Look. I'm not surprised that Erica got the wrong impression of you when you first met. All she saw was this fun-loving, pretty girl, who was trouble, in her eyes."

"Trouble?"

Liz put her hand up. "Hear me out. I just mean that I think that's why she didn't entertain you. Erica is mature. Put together. She needed to see the real Charlie, the Charlie who I know and love. You don't let many people see that side of you. I'm proud of you for showing her. I always knew you would one day when you met the right person. Hell, I told you that not so long ago."

"So, you think that Erica's the right person then?"

"I can't say that. Nobody knows. But I will be here for you while you find out. Okay?"

"More than okay." Liz really was the best.

The rest of their morning went by quickly. Before lunch they saw a rabbit, four dogs, and three cats—none of which were as well-behaved as Hera. Not that Charlie was biased or anything.

It was after midday, and cat number three, when Charlie's phone buzzed. She nearly jumped across the room to grab it.

Made it through the night. Probably down to your nursing skills. Looking forward to dinner later. xx

"I don't need to ask who that is," Liz said with a knowing smile.

"She's making me dinner tonight." She typed back a quick reply so that Erica knew that she got her message.

So good to hear from you. I can't wait. Let me know if you need me to bring anything. C xx

Charlie hadn't got round to telling Liz about Erica's injury yet. Erica had asked her to keep it a secret, so Charlie didn't want to say too much, but she did feel like she had to explain that something was wrong. Liz was still her boss, and Charlie had spent half the morning checking her phone. She told her that Erica had hurt her head at work and that she had been worried about her. Kept it simple.

Their afternoon was spent performing surgeries that thankfully all went well. Some days working in a vet surgery were harder than others, but this was one of the good ones that made everything worthwhile. By the time all the surgeries were finished, Liz and Charlie had planned out her outfit for dinner and Liz had recommended a good bottle of wine to bring.

She wondered if Erica was as nervous as she was.

CHAPTER FIFTEEN

"Yes, I know it was stupid, Zachary. You don't have to go on and on about it." Erica's patience had started to wear thin. They needed to decide on their next move, and Zachary was obsessing over the fact that Erica had got hurt. She appreciated the sympathy, and it was nice that Zachary cared, but she needed him to be practical. He was still uttering something about how dangerous it was, and Erica had to raise her voice to be heard. "Okay, Zachary. I hear you! Now, what are we going to do about it?"

Her brother must have sighed three times before he spoke again. Erica tapped her foot while she waited. "We have no proof, Erica. There isn't even CCTV in that part of the building."

"Well, there bloody well should be. Then this whole mess could be over." She was prepared to take one for the team. A few bumps and bruises would have been worth it if it had led to the truth. That's what Erica was there for. But for it to count for nothing—Erica pinched the bridge of her nose—it was frustrating, to say the least. "Are you telling me there aren't any cameras at all, anywhere near that corridor? *One* camera that could have spotted *something?*"

"Nope. That area never gets used."

Erica closed her eyes. "You don't think, Zachary, that someone who is so good at stealing from us, and so good at getting away with it, might be smart enough to know that area never gets used?" She paused but Zachary didn't respond. "Why wouldn't you have CCTV everywhere?" She felt like tearing her hair out.

"Okay, point taken. I will look into it. But the fact still remains, we don't have any evidence. You didn't really see anything."

"I was attacked." Zachary wasn't making her temper any better.

"I know that. But as much as we know who attacked you, or we think we do, we can't prove that either."

Erica scoffed. "*Think* we do? There was only me and Tom there."

"Did you see Tom attack you? Did you look at his face?" Zachary asked.

"I told you, it was too dark, and it happened too fast. But I had watched him go into that room and he didn't come back out again. Not until after he knocked me over, and he was long gone by the time I was able to follow."

"How can you be sure he didn't go out the back door? You said you saw it close. Perhaps someone else could have followed you into that room."

"Are you saying now that you don't believe me? That you don't think it's Tom?"

"I'm not saying that. I'm just explaining why we can't prove it was him. And giving you other options, as unlikely as they may be."

They were both silent for a while. Erica was going over everything again in her head, and Zachary was probably doing the same.

Zachary spoke first. "I don't think you should go back. I really appreciate everything you've done to help. And you *have* helped. But it's too dangerous now."

Erica felt strange about that. Not so long ago she was arguing with Zachary about working at Oasis in the first place. Now she wanted to argue to stay. "Look. I came here to do a job. And I want to see it through."

"But, Erica—"

She spoke over him again. "I won't put myself in any danger. I won't follow people into dark rooms. I'll just keep my eyes open like I was doing before. In the meantime, I think it's time to confront Tom. We do know that he went into that room. That's confirmed. We can ask him what he was doing in there."

"I'll have to fill Brandon in then and let him speak to him. I know you don't trust Brandon, but we have no choice. We can't have people linking us together if you insist on staying there. Which is madness, in my opinion. A fortnight ago, I could hardly drag you near the place," Zachary said.

"You know if I start something I have to finish it." And the longer she worked there, the longer she needed to be in London—and Charlie was in London. She kept that part to herself.

Zachary was making some noises that showed he wasn't happy with the situation, but he knew better than to argue with Erica once she had her mind set on something. "Promise me you'll be more careful. Bide your time. Wait and see if you overhear anything. That's it, Erica."

"I promise." It wasn't like she wanted to put herself in a position where she could get hurt again. Erica didn't feel like she was in danger, though. Maybe she was being naïve, but she didn't think whoever attacked her—Tom—was really out to get her. They had just tried to slow her down so that they could get away, and yeah, she got hurt in the process.

"I will try and address this whole Tom situation before your next shift. And hey, if we find out it is him, you don't have to go back at all. Job done. Wouldn't that be great?"

No. "Even better," she said instead.

Typical. Just when she was starting to like London.

Erica decided that she was going to come clean with Charlie about the real reason she was in London. She doubted that Charlie would tell anyone. Erica hadn't gone out of her way to deceive her, but Charlie had met Erica the bartender. Erica just never made any attempt to correct her on that. Why would she? They had only just met. It wasn't the worst lie in the world. She was sure that Charlie would understand once she explained the situation.

When it was almost time for Charlie to arrive, Erica's phone buzzed. She wasted no time in picking it up. It was probably Charlie texting to say that she was on her way. Anticipation turned to annoyance very quickly.

I have put our names down to attend the Prescotts' annual charity dinner together. They're auctioning off some fabulous items this year, including one of their yachts. Very exciting. It's not until next month, so your mother tells me you'll be back. Maybe it will be our coming out as a couple appearance.

Victoria.

Erica growled and threw the phone onto the sofa. "We are not a couple," she said out loud to the room. Her mother was clearly still interfering back home, even without Erica's presence. Erica had never said to anyone when she was planning to return. The prospect currently wasn't appealing to her all that much. She took a few deep breaths. *Don't let it get to you, Erica.*

She pushed all thoughts of Victoria and her controlling mother to the back of her mind when Charlie arrived. She had been looking forward to seeing her all day, and she wasn't going to let anything spoil their first official date. At least she thought it was a date. That's what she had meant when she had asked Charlie to dinner. Charlie would have known that, wouldn't she?

That was the thought on her mind when Charlie walked in and passed her a bottle of wine. "This is a date, right?" she asked.

Charlie looked amused. "Hello to you too. And yes, at least I thought it was." She scrunched her nose. "It is, right?" Now she looked confused.

Erica nodded quickly. "Yes. It is. Sorry. Hi." She held up the bottle of wine. "This is one of my favourites, thank you." She leaned in and gave Charlie a soft kiss on the lips because, despite it only being their first date, they had already crossed that line and she could. "Hey."

Charlie didn't seem to mind. In fact, she looked pretty happy about it. "Hey."

"Will you take a glass?" she asked over her shoulder as she walked into the kitchen to open the bottle. Charlie said she would, so she poured two. She passed one to Charlie, who had already taken a seat in the living room, and she set the rest of the bottle on the coffee table. Erica was nervous for some reason. She never usually got nervous before she went on a date.

"How was life in the veterinary world today?" she asked when she took a seat next to Charlie. They were at opposite ends of the sofa. Then again, it wasn't the biggest sofa in the world. Shuffling closer wouldn't be too difficult.

Charlie was so…different from what she was used to. In a great, refreshing way.

First off, there was no bragging. Charlie wasn't trying to show off or make herself sound important. When she told Erica about the different animals that she and Dr Ashbourne had seen that day, she was so warm in the way she spoke about her furry patients. She truly cared about them all—Erica could hear that in her voice. It wasn't only about the paycheck for Charlie. It wasn't about getting recognition or praise. She had a genuine love for what she did. And she was good at it—Erica had seen that first-hand. When Erica told her so, Charlie's reaction was modest. Shy even.

If this had been anything like one of Erica's usual dates, there would have been a bunch of boasting and *look at me* comments, and any compliment Erica gave would only have resulted in massaging her date's already huge ego.

Charlie was the opposite.

Then the conversation flipped to Erica. *Again, hello?* That didn't usually happen. But Charlie seemed truly interested in Erica and what she had to say.

"Let me look at your head," Charlie said to her. She set her glass on the coffee table and made the short shuffle across the sofa to Erica. "It looks sore. It's more bruised now." She went into her bag and pulled out some more gauze. "I was going to change the dressing if that's okay?" She looked embarrassed when she said it. Erica didn't know what was embarrassing about that. She was just being the sweetest yet again.

Erica kissed her because she had to. Once. Twice. A third that lasted a little longer. "Thank you for thinking to do that."

Charlie smiled. She was gentle as she used a wipe to clean the wound again, and then she replaced the gauze with some fresh tape. It stung a little, but Erica tried not to flinch. She knew that it only made Charlie feel guilty when she did. "All done." Charlie leaned back and crossed her legs. She lifted her glass again. She hadn't shuffled away too far, which Erica was pleased about. Their legs touched now. "Now, how about your day? Did you get in touch with your boss about last night?" Charlie asked.

Erica took a large sip of her wine and licked her lips. She had hoped to wait until after dinner to get into that conversation, but that would mean lying again now that Charlie had outright asked—and she couldn't do that. A quick glance at the clock told her that dinner wouldn't be ready for a while, so there was no way that she could stall any longer. "Okay. I didn't give you the full story last night." She hoped this wouldn't make the evening take a nosedive before it had really started. She knew that it wasn't a big deal, but she hadn't been one hundred percent honest and that wasn't great.

"I got that feeling," Charlie said. She looked nervous about what Erica was going to tell her. "You're not the thief, are you? That's not what you're going to say?"

That's what Charlie was nervous about? Erica laughed. "If that's where you're setting the bar, this might not sound too awful. No, I've never stolen anything in my life. My friend stole a bar of chocolate one time when we were little, and I didn't sleep for two nights. I went back and gave the shopkeeper some money. And it wasn't even me."

That seemed to make Charlie relax. "Then what is it?"

"First of all, I've been lying to you, and I'm sorry. Let me get that part out of the way." She thought about her words. "Well, not exactly lying. More like hiding the truth. But the point is I apologize."

"Okay," Charlie said, dragging the word out. *In other words, spit it out, Erica.*

"You said last night that it wasn't my responsibility to find out who's stealing the money from the club. That isn't completely true." She took another sip of wine. "It is my responsibility because it's my money that's being taken. I own Oasis. Zachary and I do."

Charlie's eyebrows shot up. "Oh?" They came back down again. She nodded. "Oh." Her mouth stayed in that O-shape.

"Yeah."

It took Charlie a few seconds to let that sink in. When it did, she didn't look annoyed about it. "I wasn't expecting that. I thought it was going to be something terrible for a second there." She put her hand on her heart. "Phew. Why didn't you just tell me that?"

"Because nobody knows, apart from Zachary, obviously. And the bar manager. But none of the other staff know. It's like I'm undercover, in a way, so I felt like I needed to keep it to myself. Basically, to cut a long story short, our father passed away and left Oasis to us, and a few other bars too, but that's beside the point." She wasn't flaunting the fact that she owned several bars, but it felt important to get the whole truth out there while they were already on the subject.

"I'm sorry to hear that," Charlie said. "About your dad."

"Thank you. We weren't close, but yeah. That's a whole other story." She looked down and fidgeted with something imaginary on her fingernail. She didn't talk about her father much. She never knew what to say. Erica didn't really know him. But that didn't mean that she wasn't sad that he was gone, and she had never got the chance to know him. She had a lot of mixed feelings when it came to her father. "Anyway, my point is…Zachary does all the running of things here in London, for all of the bars, including Oasis. Meaning no one knows who I am, or probably that I even exist, so when it came to light that the money was going missing, it seemed like a good idea to take advantage of that."

Charlie nodded slowly like it was all clicking into place. "And that *is* where I recognized Zachary from. I thought I could picture his face from Oasis."

"Yes. And again, I'm sorry we didn't tell you the other day. I've been working there as a bartender—that part you do know. Which I'm awful at, by the way." She chuckled because it was true. "But I'm only doing that so that I'm able to do a bit of investigating on the sly. For obvious reasons, I didn't want anyone to find out, and when we first met in the bar, I didn't know you, so there was no reason to tell you. And after that I haven't been able to find the right time. But there it is."

"Wow." Charlie gave a little laugh. "Well, okay." She got a smug look on her face. "I told you that you were too fancy."

"You did. You saw through me right away."

"I didn't think that you owned the bloody nightclub, to be fair." Charlie scratched her head. "And you're staying in Olly's place because…"

"That part is true, what we told you. He's staying with Zachary, and he lent me his place because it's close to the club, which is beyond kind of him. Zachary lives way on the other side of London, which wouldn't have been practical." She smirked. "I don't think Zachary was too unhappy about sharing his place with Olly, so it was a win-win for both of us. And it's not like Olly won't get his place back. I'm only here to do a job…" She stopped herself from saying it.

"And then you'll be leaving London?" Charlie finished the sentence for her.

"I will have to go home at some point. Yes."

Silence hung between them for what felt like several minutes, even though it probably wasn't that long.

"How far away is home?" Charlie asked.

"Seven or eight hours on the train. Ten on the longer route."

"That's preposterous. You would think they could move it closer to London," Charlie said.

Erica laughed. "What, the entire town? They should move the entire town closer, should they?"

Charlie grinned. "Well, it would be a lot more convenient, yes."

Erica playfully nudged her. "You might get bored of me long before I have to leave again."

"I doubt that." Charlie cleared her throat and looked at her with a smile. "What's home like? Tell me about it."

Erica hadn't expected that. All kinds of responses had gone through her mind. *What's the point of this? Why didn't you tell me that in the first place? So, you're just going to leave? Fuck you then, Erica.* But Charlie surprised her once again.

She told Charlie all about her cottage—her own little clifftop paradise. Talking about it made her miss it. Charlie asked to see photos, and Erica scrolled through her phone showing her whatever she had of the cottage itself, and several of the sunsets and sunrises she had taken. Erica never stopped taking pictures of the view—she saw new beauty in it every single day.

"I see why you love it there," Charlie said. "It's breathtaking."

Erica agreed. "I never get tired of it. I love sitting out in the quiet, watching the sky change colour, or the waves crashing below." Erica kept scrolling and stopped at one of Tess and her. "That's my best friend, Tess." The picture of Tess and her laughing at something that she couldn't remember made her happy. It was clearly hilarious at the time.

The next photo was of Erica and a horse. "That's Roxie. She's a very sweet girl. I rescued her a couple of years ago. She was found abandoned in a tiny field." Erica frowned. "She was in very bad shape by the time she was discovered. But she's in an amazing sanctuary now and she's great. I visit her as often as I can."

"I love that. She is beautiful. Look at that colouring." Charlie studied the photo. "Some people shouldn't be allowed near animals. Who could abandon something so precious?"

"I'm sure you see things like that a lot."

"You have no idea. Too much." She shook her head. "It would never happen if I had my way. Animal cruelty would come to an end if I was able to make a world change."

"At least you help, though, right?" Erica said. "You make a difference."

"I try. As do you, it seems," Charlie replied. She sounded impressed and Erica couldn't help but feel a little pleased at that. She wanted to impress Charlie. And to impress her by being herself—it felt nice. She didn't have to pretend she was someone she wasn't or act a certain way just because that's what was expected.

She lifted her shoulder. "I do what I can. My mother runs a foundation and I do some work there—organize fundraisers and the likes. I try to support as many animal charities as I can in my current role, but there's a board who have the final say on where the money goes. I can only make suggestions on who to help and hope that they decide to support some of those. And as much as the foundation does help to fund some charities, there are a lot of rich people who continue to get richer too. That's what I don't like about it—putting extra lining into already wealthy pockets. I pay for everything Roxie needs out of my own money, though. And I make personal donations to the sanctuary that takes care of her. I just wish I could do more sometimes."

"That's amazing. It sounds like you already do loads. If your mum oversees this foundation, can she not just put you in charge of where the money goes? Then you would be able to help all the organisations you want to," Charlie suggested.

"There's no chance of that happening. Unfortunately, Mother is more interested in impressing the board than supporting me. And she cares more about the optics of the foundation, rather than the actual work that it does. As far as she's concerned if she gives a few large, well-publicized donations to popular causes then that's her job done." At Charlie's frown she explained further. "Mother is more interested in being seen at the most prestigious social events and photographed for magazines for the rich and glamourous than the charity work, and she wants me to follow in her footsteps. Frosts don't get their hands dirty, you see. She does give sizable donations, but it doesn't hurt that it makes her and the foundation look good. And the causes are carefully chosen by the board. I'm lucky if any of my suggestions make the cut."

Charlie was kind enough to look sympathetic. "So, she does do nice things but it's for the wrong reasons." She nodded her understanding. "It sounds like there's a lot of unwanted pressure on you."

Erica sighed. "You have no idea." She reached over for the wine bottle and refilled both their glasses. "But I don't want to dwell on that tonight." They needed a subject change. Erica didn't need to be offloading her baggage on Charlie. She held up her glass and smiled. "To first dates. I probably should have started with that. I'm glad you're here."

"To first dates." Charlie clinked her glass against Erica's. "I have to say, I'm surprised that we got here."

"I might have been a little bit wrong about you at the start," Erica admitted. An understatement. Charlie had proved her wrong, and then some.

Charlie looked down. "I didn't exactly make a very good first impression."

"Well, no. I *did* see you that first night, if I'm being honest. And I came to my own conclusions based on that. Which probably wasn't fair of me to do."

Charlie nodded but didn't look up. "I knew you had seen me. I wish I could say that behaviour wasn't normal from me, but I'd be lying. I'd gone out, I'd pulled—that's normal. I shouldn't have been looking at you when I had already hooked up with someone else, I know that. But you grabbed my attention. I couldn't not look."

Erica was surprised to hear Charlie admitting that, but she didn't interrupt. She wanted to see where Charlie was going with it. Maybe this really was all a bit of fun to Charlie, and that's what she was going to tell her. Erica didn't know how to feel about that. On one hand they were both single and free to do what they wanted. Who said everything had to come with commitments? Also, Erica would be leaving. Surely, something casual made more sense. Then again, Erica was Erica, and casual was not one of her attributes—so Erica hoped that wasn't the point that Charlie was going to make.

Charlie narrowed her eyes at the spot on the floor she was staring at, like she was trying to find the right words to say. "I don't date, Erica. Or at least, I haven't previously dated. If a woman asked me to go on an actual date, I would probably run a mile."

"Yet here you are."

"Yet here I am. And what I'm trying to say, in a pretty awkward way, because I suck at explaining stuff like this…is that it's different with you. I don't feel like running a mile when I'm with you. And you have my full undivided attention. You have since we met. Which never happens to me, but you have." Charlie shrugged. "And I want to be on this date with you. And I want to see what happens. I hope that's good enough."

Charlie had grabbed Erica's attention too. As much as she had tried to deny that to herself on multiple occasions, Erica was drawn to Charlie. She respected the fact that Charlie wasn't trying to hide who she was. There was no pretence there. Charlie wasn't making any promises, but she was trying. She remembered Tess's words to *go with the flow*. That seemed like good advice in that moment.

"Well…" Erica looked at Charlie from behind her glass. "You are growing on me a little bit too, I suppose."

Charlie laughed. "A little bit?"

Erica put her thumb and forefinger together. "Tiny bit." She smiled. "I'm happy to see what happens too. It's not like we need to plan everything out, is it?" That was exactly what Erica's life was usually like, but she was going, she was flowing.

"That's true." Charlie set her glass down on the table. She reached for Erica's and set it down too. "So, fancy nightclub owner, glamourous high society princess, and secret heiress—now that we have all the serious stuff out of the way and we're decidedly going with the flow, is there any chance I can kiss you again?"

Erica already found herself leaning in. "I think we can arrange that." Why had dating never felt this easy before? This comfortable?

Charlie was a *really* good kisser. Erica wasn't sure if she had ever dated such a good kisser before. Some kisses had been all right, some had even been nice. But kissing Charlie made her toes curl. Erica didn't even know that her toes *could* curl.

When the timer went off to tell Erica to take dinner out of the oven, she almost growled out loud. Did they really need dinner? They did. That's what she had offered, so that's what she would provide. Though the look on Charlie's face told her that she probably would have been happy to forego the whole eating thing too. She dragged herself into the kitchen before either of them suggested it. Yes, they had entered the whole kissing zone rather quickly—that was probably Erica's fault. But they didn't need to rush into anything else. And kissing, the way they kissed, could easily lead right to that somewhere else.

"I've never made this before, so I hope it tastes okay," Erica said to Charlie, who had followed her into the kitchen and was leaning against the breakfast bar. The pose was sexy, even though Erica was sure that was unintentional.

"It smells good, whatever it is. Can I do anything to help?"

She thought of stuff for her to do, because Charlie hanging around looking fantastic was way too distracting. Erica had already set the table before Charlie had got there, but she gave her a few condiments to set out. It wasn't long before Erica followed Charlie to the table with the plates. She'd made a vegetable risotto that she had found a recipe for online earlier that day. It did resemble the picture that they had shown on the website. That was a good sign. Hopefully the taste test went as well.

Charlie hummed her approval. She pointed at it with her fork. "This is great."

Erica had to admit herself, it wasn't half bad. *Thank you, internet.* "I'm glad you like it."

After a few moments of comfortable silence while they ate, Charlie asked, "Am I allowed to ask anything about your undercover op?"

"Sure. It will stay between us, though, right?"

"Of course. I won't tell a soul."

"Okay, shoot. What do you want to know?" Erica asked. She ate a small mouthful of risotto.

"Anything. How's it going? Do you have suspects? Do I need to worry about you? You already got hurt."

"I did, but I learned my lesson. I won't do anything careless, like follow people into dark rooms."

"Maybe don't follow people, full stop?" Charlie suggested.

She pointed at Charlie. "And that. I won't do that again. Like I said, lesson learned. So, no. You don't need to worry. And as for suspects, I'm pretty sure I know who's doing it. I don't have proof, but I have a strong suspicion."

"Oh? Who is it?"

Erica took a sip from her wine glass. She didn't see any harm in telling Charlie, after all, she had promised not to say anything. "Do you know the doorman? The one with the permanent angry expression on his face who looks like he lifts cars in his spare time for fun?"

"Tom?" Charlie asked.

She did know him then. "Yeah, Tom."

Charlie frowned while she took another forkful of rice. "Huh." She tilted her head. "I wouldn't have expected that."

That was Erica's cue to be surprised. "Really? He's so intense. And the way he watches Kelly-Ann. It's creepy. He's obsessed."

Charlie laughed. "I don't know which one Kelly-Ann is, but judging from the name she's hardly Tom's type."

"What makes you say that?" Erica asked.

"You don't know? Tom's gay. I've met him loads of times on nights out. He's actually a lot more fun than he looks at Oasis. I think he has a work scowl."

Erica did not know that. She always assumed that he was into Kelly-Ann. Then again, she had already come up with the theory that he was more interested in Kelly-Ann putting money in the till than the woman herself. And just because he was fun outside of work didn't mean that he wasn't stealing that money.

"Are you sure it's him?" Charlie asked.

"I'm not sure of anything." She was even starting to doubt herself, if she was honest. Charlie clearly didn't think that Tom could be guilty, and she hadn't exactly managed to convince Zachary either. "But he's the person I suspect most. And it was him I was following—there was no one else there."

"Hey, I'm not saying it isn't him. If it is, then shame on that guy. I'm surprised is all. I always thought he was like a big teddy bear. But we aren't like close or anything, so who knows," Charlie said.

"You won't say anything, will you?"

"Of course not. I won't say a word to anyone."

Erica believed her. It would be interesting to speak to Zachary and find out what happened with Tom. If he or Brandon had spoken with him. And if it wasn't Tom, then she would be back to square one again.

After dinner Charlie helped Erica clear up a little bit. They did the basics. Erica could finish after Charlie had left. It seemed like a waste of their time together. They returned to the sofa, and by unspoken agreement they sat closer to each other than they had before. They chatted some more. Charlie's arm rested on top of the sofa. Then Erica's did. It felt completely natural when Charlie took Erica's hand in hers, lacing their fingers together while they talked.

Erica hadn't noticed an hour had passed. It was so easy to chat to Charlie, about anything and everything. Erica told Charlie stories about the antics that she and Zachary used to get up to when they were younger—likely the reason that they had been sent to separate boarding schools. Erica an all-girls school, and Zachary, an all-boys.

Charlie spoke about her own childhood, which had been tainted by her parent's very volatile and messy relationship. After listening about the constant arguments, and how Charlie had been used as a pawn by her parents against one another, it was little wonder that Charlie had never rushed into a relationship herself. It was obvious that their relationship had tainted Charlie's view enough for her to stay clear all these years. At least Erica hadn't been around anything like that—one of her parents had just been non-existent.

They talked about their friends, their taste in cinema and TV, their favourite foods, their favourite books. There weren't any awkward silences, or disagreements. Then Erica gave a yawn that she couldn't stifle. Working all those late nights had been a shock to her system. She wished Charlie hadn't seen it because it resulted in her looking at the clock.

"It's getting late, I should let you get some rest," she said to Erica.

"Right now?" Erica asked. She looked down at Charlie's lips that she was dying to taste again.

The look didn't go unnoticed, as Charlie leaned in and touched those lips to hers. It didn't take long for them to find that heat again— the heat of the first kiss. Charlie's tongue found hers and she felt

Charlie's hands all over her—one ended up on her waist and the other behind her neck pulling her closer. Charlie eased Erica down onto the sofa and lay on top of her, slowly pressing their bodies together. Erica immediately felt her body react. She ran her hands down Charlie's back as they kissed and slid them back up underneath her top. She needed to touch Charlie's soft skin, to feel any part of her that she could. She felt Charlie smile against her lips, so she clearly didn't mind. Charlie ran her hand down the side of Erica's body, down the outside of her thigh. Erica wrapped her leg around her, and Charlie ran her hand back up again.

Erica wasn't sure how long they stayed like that. Kissing, touching, exploring—but never taking it too far. Though at that moment Erica didn't think that it seemed like a terrible idea to let it go further. She would have happily let Charlie rip off all of her clothes and have her way with her. Their bodies fit together perfectly. Erica was taller than Charlie, and it felt like Charlie's body was made for hers. Erica couldn't ignore the throbbing between her legs as they pressed together, and they both pushed against each other for more friction. Each of them moaned at the contact when they did. It was like the most beautiful form of torture.

When they wrenched their mouths apart, Charlie rested her head on Erica's chest while they both caught their breath again. It felt so good lying there with Charlie in her arms, and Charlie must have thought so too. Neither of them made any attempt to move. Charlie ran her fingers softly up and down Erica's arm.

"We're so good at that," Charlie said eventually.

"Hmm. I think so too." She still wasn't totally sure why they had to stop, but at the same time, she knew exactly why. Somewhere deep in her cautious and sensible brain she knew that they shouldn't rush into anything. They had already accelerated things at a speed that Erica wasn't used to. In Erica's experience, making out like that only happened after several dates. But with Charlie it had all started with a kiss, so there was no point in going backward—at least, that's how she justified it. However, they should press on the brakes a little bit.

"I should go," Charlie said as if she was reading Erica's mind. She pushed herself up onto her elbow and looked down at her. "It's not that I want to. I really don't. But I think we both know I should."

They were on the same page. She looked up into Charlie's dark brown eyes and reached out to touch her cheek. "Trust me, I don't want you to go either, but you're right."

Charlie leaned down and kissed her softly before pushing herself up. "Walk me out?"

Erica reluctantly pushed herself up too. She smoothed her clothes and patted her hair down—it was probably everywhere. Charlie didn't look dishevelled in the slightest. How was that even possible?

They said good-bye with one final kiss at the door. Followed by a long hug to stall some more, and a final-final kiss. It seemed ridiculous that Charlie was going to be right on the other side of the wall when all Erica wanted was to be in her company. Whether kissing, or talking, or doing other things that Erica tried to push from her thoughts—she was in no way successful. But Erica needed boundaries in her life. She wasn't spontaneous. She needed to be sure before she rushed into anything. Although she was getting more and more sure about Charlie, she should still play it safe.

And Charlie clearly felt like she had something to prove, especially after what she had told Erica about her previous track record. Maybe she was proving herself to Erica, or maybe it was to herself. Probably a bit of both. Erica knew now that Charlie wasn't just in it for the chase, as she had first suspected. Maybe she had been at first, but Erica trusted her when she said that things were different with her. The truth was that things were different for Erica too.

She might have finally been discovering what this whole dating thing was really all about. The next date couldn't happen soon enough.

CHAPTER SIXTEEN

C harlie took charge of their next date.

"Bowling? Are we going in here?" Erica asked as they stopped outside the building.

Charlie wasn't sure how Erica would feel about bowling—nothing about her screamed that she was the bowling type. But she didn't look horrified—more like intrigued. "We are."

"I've never done it before," Erica said.

"You've never been bowling?"

"No." Erica looked down at her feet. "Do I have to wear those funny shoes?"

Charlie looked down too. "I think those heels might be considered a safety risk. I don't even know how you walk in them, let alone do anything else." She laughed at Erica's horrified face. "I have to wear the funny shoes too. Don't be such a snob."

"I am a snob, self-admittedly. It's bred into me, I'm powerless against it. You already know this."

"I do. But you're my snob, so it's fine." *Oops.* That had just slipped out. "Come on. Let's go get you fitted for your funny shoes," she added quickly in an attempt to glaze over the comment.

Erica's amused look told Charlie that her glazing hadn't worked. "Am I now?"

Of course, Erica pulled her on her slip. At least she hadn't argued with the statement because the truth was, she already knew that she wanted Erica to be hers, even if she hadn't meant to come right out and say it. Charlie dragged her by the hand through the front door. "Don't distract me. Shoes. Let's go. I hadn't even thought about it, but now I'm dying to see your snobby little expression when you have to put them on."

Charlie paid at the desk and was handed two pairs of bowling shoes. She and Erica wore the same size, which made it easier.

She held them up. "Black with fluorescent pink swirls, or white with purple and green stripes?"

Erica glared at her. "How many strange, sweaty feet have been in those already?"

"They wash them, I'm sure." Charlie looked between the two pairs and then looked at Erica. "I feel like you're pink and swirly."

Erica still glared but the corner of her mouth quirked up. She reached out and took the pair from Charlie, holding them out with the tip of her finger and her thumb like they might jump and bite her at any second. "One snobby expression, coming right up."

They sat side by side on the bench as they put on their rented footwear. It took Charlie twice as long because she kept pausing to laugh at the disgusted faces that Erica was pulling—but to her credit, she put them on anyway. Charlie didn't believe her protests for a second. Erica was more excited than she let on.

To further prove that point, Erica stood up and gave a *ta da* motion as she twirled her foot round and round. "I think you're right. I am pink and swirly."

"I told you." She stood up too. "How about me? Am I green and stripey?"

Erica looked her up and down. "You're gorgeous." She leaned in and kissed her cheek. "Now, teach me how to bowl."

The reason that Charlie had planned bowling for the date was because she knew that she was good at it, and she wanted to show off in front of Erica. Impress her. She entered their names into the computer, and they flashed up onto the screen above the empty lane that was waiting for them.

"You're up first," Charlie said. She swirled a few of the bowling balls round until she found the one she wanted, and she passed it to Erica. "Just knock as many down as you can."

"I know the concept." Erica took the ball from Charlie and put her fingers and thumbs in the holes. "I'm just not sure how good I'll be at carrying it out." She frowned and took a step toward the lane. She threw the ball, but she didn't get a lot on it, and it rolled slowly down the lane before dropping down the gutter. She turned round and grimaced at Charlie.

"Don't worry, you have another go. Put a bit more force on it this time." Charlie gave her a thumbs up.

Erica took another ball and threw it again. This time she did use a lot more force. It went into the gutter much quicker than the time before. "This might be a very long game."

When it was Charlie's turn, she did a bad throw on purpose to try and make Erica feel better. She knocked down four pins.

"At least yours stayed on the lane," Erica said.

Charlie laughed as she stepped up to take her second turn. She knocked down another four. Erica was narrowing her eyes as Charlie walked back. "What?"

"Are you holding back?"

"What? Of course not," Charlie said. She turned her head away to hide her grin.

Erica picked up the ball and walked to the lane with purpose. She had clearly been watching Charlie, because she bent her knee this time, and swung her arm much more than she had done on her first try. She knocked down seven pins. On her second ball she knocked over another two.

That was a fast improvement. Charlie couldn't help but gape at her when she walked back.

"I'm a quick learner." Erica held her arms out by her sides.

"So I can see. Nine for you." Charlie was going to have more of a competition on her hands than she had thought she would. It was time to unleash her true game. She didn't hold back on her next turn.

"I knew you were good." Erica put her hands on her hips.

"I might be okay." Charlie winked at her.

"Oh, I think you're more than just okay," Erica said.

"At bowling, or...?"

Erica chuckled. "At bowling *and* or." She knocked down a respectable eight on her next turn. "If you hit a strike, I'll make out with you later."

"I'll look forward to it." Charlie stepped up with confidence and knocked down all ten pins with ease.

By the end of the game Charlie had a lot of kissing to look forward to after hitting five more strikes. Erica hadn't found the gutter again, which was good, and she gave Charlie a much harder match than either of them expected. Charlie won the game, of course, but the points difference wasn't miles apart, and Erica even hit a strike at the end herself. Watching her celebrate it was the most adorable thing that Charlie had ever seen in her life.

"I really thought that they would let you keep the shoes," Erica said to her as they walked home. "I thought that was the point of going through the challenge of daring to put your feet in them in the first place."

Charlie paused her step and pointed behind her. "I can go ask if you want. I'm sure I can convince them to let you have them."

Erica laughed and pulled her along toward home. "That was fun. Thank you for taking me. I've had a great evening."

"Me too," Charlie said. "And it's not over yet. I believe you owe me quite a few prizes."

"I do. It seems that losing worked out pretty good for me too."

By unspoken agreement they both quickened their step.

❖

"Mrs Peterson has brought Julio back in again," Charlie said as she looked down at their schedule for the day.

Liz was tapping away on the computer. "I wonder what's wrong with him." She pushed the enter key with extra enthusiasm before she turned in her chair and pushed back from the desk. "It's only a few weeks since he's been in."

Charlie flipped through the chart. "He's swallowed five things that he shouldn't have in the past two years." She looked at Liz. "My money's on number six."

"And if that's the case, then what do we do?" Liz asked her.

It wasn't a strange question for Liz to ask. She quizzed Charlie often to determine how far her veterinary knowledge went. "We determine what he's swallowed first. Maybe the owner will know. Depending on what it is, or the symptoms the dog is showing, we may need to X-ray. If it's passable, we give him meds to either throw it up or to help speed that process along and wait for it to reappear. If not, it could lead to a bowel obstruction so we would need to put him under and operate to remove the object." She looked at Liz for her reaction.

She seemed happy with Charlie's answer. "Have you thought any more about getting your vet qualification? You do know you could do it in your sleep."

Liz didn't ask often. She never pushed Charlie or told Charlie what she thought that she should do. She simply encouraged sometimes. Made her aware that she was capable. "Yeah, maybe. It's in there." She pointed to her head. "When the time's right."

"Well, it's time now to see what Julio has been up to." Liz pulled on a pair of disposable gloves and Charlie left the exam room to bring in the patient.

Charlie's guess had been spot on. Julio had swallowed a golf ball this time. It wasn't impossible for the ball to pass on its own, but it also wasn't impossible for it to get stuck. They needed to keep him in to give him an X-ray and they would go from there. Poor Julio. He really needed to start watching what he ate.

Hilary poked her head into the exam room. "Charlie, there's someone here to see you."

"Who is it?" Charlie asked. She wasn't expecting any visitors. No one ever came to see her while she was working.

"That woman from last week." She looked at Charlie over her glasses. "The pushy one."

Charlie tried not to laugh at that. She turned to Liz. "Do you mind if I step out for a second?"

Liz wasn't hiding her grin. "I don't mind at all." They had already discussed all things Erica that morning. To say that Liz was pleased about it was an understatement. It was nice to have someone rooting for them.

Charlie was hooked already. She wasn't afraid to say so. There was zero sign of the old Charlie. She didn't know how it was possible to change overnight, but that's how she felt—like a changed woman. Meaning that she wasn't remotely freaked out at the fluttering in her stomach, or the fact that her heart rate had doubled the second she laid eyes on Erica. Actually, she kind of liked it.

Charlie was right in her initial assessment of Erica—the one she had made that first night at Oasis before they had even spoken. There was something about the way Erica carried herself. Confident and elegant. She turned heads whenever she walked into a room. Just like there were a few heads turned in the waiting room, as she stood studying one of the posters on the wall while she waited for Charlie. When she noticed Charlie, she turned and beamed at her. Charlie felt like pinching herself—a woman so sure of herself, and so sophisticated, was smiling at her like she was the best thing that she had ever seen. Charlie's heart didn't stand a chance with this woman.

"Hey. This is a surprise," Charlie said as they met in front of the reception desk.

Erica set a box down and leaned her elbows on the counter. "That was exactly the point. I was out for a walk, and I was passing, so I thought I would pop in and say hi." She smiled. "So, hi."

"I'm glad you did." Charlie pointed at Erica's head. "It's starting to look a little better. You can hardly notice it." Erica had ditched the gauze and wore a small plaster instead.

Erica lifted her hand to it. "The wonders of foundation," she said. She pushed the box on the counter toward Charlie. "I thought these would make your day better."

Charlie opened the box, which was filled with all different types of doughnuts. "I mean, that would make anyone's day better. Although now I don't totally believe the whole *I was in the neighbourhood* story. You're a woman prepared."

"I might have made a point of passing. After I picked these up... with the intention of giving them to you."

Charlie laughed at that. "Thank you so much. There's a chance that I may now survive this day."

"Oh no. Bad?"

"No, just busy. It always is, but some days can be slightly more hectic, and the difference is beyond noticeable when it goes that little bit too far."

"Well, you can share those out and then you'll at least be tired and popular," Erica said. "Speaking of, I don't think I'm too popular with the lady on reception." Erica didn't seem annoyed by it—amused more like. And it wasn't as if she was wrong.

"It's because you're pushy, but you didn't hear that from me," Charlie whispered.

Erica waved her off. "A fact that I do not deny. I own my pushiness."

Charlie kept her voice down low. "I personally enjoy when you're pushy with me. Like when you pushed me down onto the sofa after bowling last night and demanded kisses. That is my favourite type of pushy."

Erica lowered her voice too. "Do you think that's how to win Hilary over?"

"I don't think she would be as receptive as me, but you can try, by all means."

"Nah, I like your receptiveness. I think I'll stick to you."

They were smiling at each other, like a pair of smitten teenagers, when Liz exited the exam room and joined them. "Good to see you again, Erica," she said as she took a spot next to Charlie.

"And you, Liz. I hope you're keeping well. Charlie tells me you're very busy today, so I won't keep her back any longer."

Charlie held the box of doughnuts up. "Erica was delivering treats for us."

"In that case, I can happily spare Charlie for five minutes." She winked. "You know, my wife Nancy told me to invite Charlie for dinner this weekend. I was thinking that maybe you could both come?" Liz looked between the two of them. "It might be nice to all get together. And Charlie will tell you, Nancy is an excellent cook, so I can at least promise a good meal. The company may be questionable." She nudged Charlie.

Charlie threw a mock glare at her. She looked at Erica. "Nancy is a chef. And she is amazing. I never miss an opportunity to go there for food. I've cancelled major plans to do so. There have even been occasions where I have begged to join them. I'm not ashamed of it."

"Hey, I was sold at dinner," Erica said.

"Great. Saturday?" Liz asked. "You don't have to work, do you? Just thinking, that's probably your busy night."

Charlie hadn't told Liz about Erica owning Oasis. She had promised to keep it a secret, and as far as she was concerned, that meant tell no one. Therefore, Liz was totally unaware that Erica could pick and choose whether she was going to work or not.

Unsurprisingly, Erica said, "I think I'm free Saturday, as it happens. Do you mind me crashing?" She looked at Charlie then.

"Of course not. I would have suggested it myself if Liz hadn't beat me to it." As if she would mind. She would walk over hot coals sixteen times if it meant another date with Erica.

Liz clapped her hands together. "That's settled, then. Charlie knows where to find us so she can show you. She arrives like a sniffer-dog anytime Nancy experiments with her new menus. Seriously, I'm sure her nose leads her straight to our front door."

They all chuckled at that.

"Sometimes, I wonder why I bother with the amount of stick I have to take. Then I remember you're right," Charlie said.

Liz raised an eyebrow at Erica. "See?"

"I look forward to it. Both the meal and Charlie getting some stick. I have to admit I've missed doing that since I decided to like her." Erica nudged her this time.

Charlie could take it. Also, Erica saying out loud that she liked her, to Liz. Yeah, Charlie felt things. Warm, fuzzy things. Apparently, even the smallest compliments resonated when you were really into someone.

"Well, I need to get back. I'll see you Saturday, Erica," Liz said.

"I'll be right there," Charlie said to Liz as she left. She pointed to the room behind her with her thumb. "I better get back too. Thank you so much for this." She held up the box. "And for coming to see me. Made my day."

"The doughnuts or me coming to see you?" Erica asked.

"You're okay, but it has to be the doughnuts. I'll give you a close second."

Erica sighed. "I knew I should have gone with cookies. I might have come out on top then."

"Oh, you can definitely be on top," Charlie deadpanned.

After a few more seconds of smiling and looking into each other's eyes, Erica left, and Charlie went back into the exam room.

Liz looked sheepish when Charlie walked in. "I hope you didn't mind me doing that."

"You aren't normally a meddler." She was glad Liz invited Erica, but it was pretty un-Liz-like.

"I know. But opportunities aren't normally served up to me on a platter smack bang in the middle of the waiting room. Plus, Nancy *had* suggested inviting you. That wasn't a lie. I just added in the Erica part—which Nancy will be delighted about. I'm pretty sure she wants you to get fixed up even more than I do."

She laughed. "I don't mind. And it's great because it means you and Nancy can tell me what you think. You know that both of your opinions matter to me."

"The only person you need to be listening to is yourself," Liz told her. "But for the record, I do like Erica. I told you that. She's a lot more mature and put together than most of those other girls you tell me about."

Charlie couldn't exactly argue with that. She did tend to have a type, and that type tended to be very different from Erica. Not that Charlie had dated any of them as such.

"Nancy on the other hand will probably analyse every single thing about her, and about the two of you together. You know what she's like. Be ready for it," Liz said.

"What have I gone and got myself into?" Charlie asked.

"What? With dinner or dating?" Liz asked.

"Both."

"A delicious mess and complete reorganisation of your life as you know it. You're going to love it," Liz said. She gave Charlie a pat on the back.

"Which one? The dinner or the dating?"

"Both," Liz said, mimicking Charlie's answer.

Charlie chuckled. She opened the doughnut box and lifted a caramel one before pushing the box in Liz's direction. Liz opted for the same kind.

"Hey, Hilary," Charlie called when the receptionist re-entered the room. "Doughnut?"

"Ooh, don't mind if I do." She reached in and picked up a strawberry flavoured one. "Where did we get these?"

"Erica got them for us. She said to make sure you got one." Charlie bit into her doughnut to hide her grin.

Hilary frowned. "See? She's even pushing sugar onto us now. And me meant to be watching my figure." She reached into the box and took another one. She had a ghost of a smile on her face that told Charlie that she wasn't annoyed in the slightest. Maybe Erica could win Hilary over after all. She left the room stocked up with sweet treats and perhaps a slightly more favourable opinion of Erica. Hilary could be a tough nut to crack. She took no nonsense at that reception desk.

"Erica must be pretty taken with you as well to be doing workplace visits," Liz said to her as they readied the room for their next patient of the day. Charlie sterilized everything and Liz assembled her instruments the way in which she liked them.

"I hadn't expected her to do that. She's so different than pre-bathroom-kiss-Erica was."

"What do you mean?" Liz asked.

"She just seemed like this unobtainable woman. I know I tried, but I always felt like she was a bit out of my league—not only because of how she looks, but she's so put together and well spoken. I thought it was going to be really hard to impress her," Charlie said.

"But it isn't?"

"Not at all. It feels so…easy when we're together. There's no games or pretence—not since we've both admitted that we like each other."

Even though it was early days, Charlie was finding it all very smooth sailing. The only obstacle that could really get in the way was

Charlie herself—but for all of her worrying about being unable to commit, she was discovering that she was entirely capable. More than capable—she wanted to.

Maybe she wasn't anything like her parents after all. She had always been so worried that their horrible relationship had rubbed off on her so badly, that she wouldn't know how to be in a normal relationship. She had witnessed the misery for too many years to ever want to repeat it. She never wanted to put herself or anyone else through that. Her parents constant arguing had been her only example of a relationship for a long time, but she had hidden behind that excuse for long enough. She had let it define her entire twenties. She knew plenty of happy couples now—she didn't need to look any further than Liz and Nancy. Maybe that could be her and Erica.

Okay, the whole distance thing wasn't great. She knew that. But she wasn't going to worry about it until the time came that she had to, and even then, there were solutions and ways to make it work.

Other than that, she couldn't imagine anything else getting in their way.

Chapter Seventeen

When Erica's phone buzzed on the breakfast bar, she nearly leapt for it. She hadn't heard from Zachary about the whole Tom thing. And she still wasn't going to, apparently. She sighed. She couldn't dodge her mother's calls forever.

"Hello, Mother," she said when she swiped to answer. "How are you?"

"I would be better if my daughter would return my calls." She sounded annoyed, which wasn't all that surprising. Her mother was used to having Erica at her beck and call.

"Sorry. I've told you that I'm working, and the rest of the time I try to catch up on some sleep. I'm not here on holiday, you know." She found herself pacing back and forth in the kitchen. Calls from her mother didn't tend to be pleasant whenever she wasn't getting her own way—which would be the case for as long as Erica remained in London.

"There's no need to take a tone, Erica. It doesn't suit you." A pause. "Zachary tells me that he joined you for dinner a few nights ago." It sounded more like an accusation.

Her mother always had an angle, but she wasn't sure what this one was. Erica was just going to have to go with it. "Yes, we spent the day together. It was lovely to catch up."

"Maybe the next time you *catch up*, you can tell him to sell those unseemly businesses and come back home to help with the real family business." Ah. There it was.

Erica snorted. "It's hardly a family business, there's a board of fourteen stakeholders who make all of the decisions." Apparently, London had made Erica braver.

"And who is head of that board?" her mother asked sharply. "Zachary would be much better taking up a position in the foundation like you. Those…those *bars*!" Gloria almost spat the word out. "They are unbefitting of a gentleman like Zachary."

"You do know that I own half too," Erica said.

"Yes, I've been made acutely aware, highlighted by the fact that you've swanned off to London on some sort of a crusade because you seem to want to prove yourself in some way. Neither of you should be involved in any of it."

"I'm not proving myself—I'm helping my brother. And he loves it here in London. He does a fantastic job at running several successful businesses, which are a lot classier than the picture you paint in your head." Her mother had painted that picture in Erica's head too, but unlike her mother, Erica was happy to have been proved wrong.

"Hmm. I'm sure." She sounded unconvinced. "Listen, darling. I'm just saying that it would be nice to have your brother home. Would you not agree?" Her mother clearly thought using a different approach would help her to get her own way, hence the tone change.

"I do. But it doesn't mean that it's what is best for him. He's got a life here. A home, a career. And he has Olly now. He wouldn't be happy if he came home."

She heard her mother scoff. "Your brother falls in love every other month." It wasn't like she was wrong about that.

"Things seem to be going well with this one. I only met him briefly, but he seems like a lovely fellow. And he's very sought after in the fashion world. Works with some of the biggest names." It was best to appeal to that side of things with her mother—success and money. Fame didn't hurt either.

"Hmm. He could do worse, I suppose," she said. "I hear that you have an admirer of your own."

Fucking Zachary. He couldn't hold his own hand. "Do I?"

"Zachary said that some girl dined with the pair of you. Sounded very cosy the way that he described it."

Erica closed her eyes. "She's Olly's neighbour. It wasn't cosy at all." There was no way she could tell her about Charlie and her.

"Zachary said she was looking after that cat of yours."

Wait until she got her hands on him. "Yes, Hera wasn't well, and Charlie works at the veterinary clinic that I took her to. She was very helpful."

"What sort of a name is Charlie?"

Erica immediately felt guilty that she had initially had the same opinion. That's how she had been brought up to think, but still. That needed to change. "It's just a name, Mother. And she's just a neighbour. It doesn't matter what her name is." She also felt guilty for denying Charlie, but she had to. Her mother was an exceptional case.

"I'm glad to hear that. I admit, I had been concerned after I spoke with Zachary. What about Victoria and you?"

"Victoria and I have only been on one date. I think it's a little premature to think of us as a pairing," Erica said. Her pacing took her into the living room where she started to straighten up some cushions. Anything to give her something else to focus on other than the uncomfortable conversation she was having.

"Do you know how lucky you are to be dating Victoria Barrett? For our families to merge together? Don't even think about throwing away this opportunity, Erica. I won't allow you to." *Here we go.*

"Yes. I know, Mother. And we have been in contact while I've been away. And she informs me that we'll be attending the Prescotts' annual dinner together." Erica left out how she truly felt about those kinds of decisions being made for her.

"Indeed. And you will be back. Do you hear me? Long before then, I would hope." It wasn't a request.

Erica's phoned buzzed and she pulled it away to look at it. A text from Zachary. She put the phone back to her ear. "Zachary is on the other line—I need to take it." It was almost the truth.

"Hopefully he's calling to tell you that he has caught that thief and this little charade of yours can be over."

"Maybe he is. I'll speak to you soon."

"Fine." Her mother ended the call. She wasn't one for loving good-byes.

Erica rubbed her temples. She felt like she was getting a headache—conversations like that one had that effect on her.

She didn't argue with her mother often. Her usual go-to was to neither agree nor disagree but to remain silent instead. It always seemed easier that way. The distance seemed to have given Erica a courage that she didn't normally possess. A courage to speak her own mind rather than allowing her mother to dictate what should and should not be. The distance had also given Erica a taste of the freedom that Zachary had found for himself, and she now understood his need for it. Could she too follow her own path? She had to admit, her time in London had given her the opportunity to reflect, and she dared to picture what it would be like to break free from the pressures and restrictions that her mother put upon her. Now that she had been able to take a step back and look at the life she had left behind—albeit temporarily—she realized how unfair and unreasonable her mother's expectations were. Despite all these realizations, Erica still hadn't mustered up the bravery to tell her mother about Charlie. She should have. She should have come out and said that she didn't want Victoria and she had met an incredible woman in London. But instead, she clammed up. Her newfound courage faltered. It was like Erica couldn't shake that last bit of desperation for her mother's approval—and she knew that the approval lay with Victoria. But the approval also came at the price of Erica's happiness. And now that Erica had finally discovered what her happiness looked like, she wasn't sure that she was willing to give it up.

Sighing, she turned her attention to her phone and opened the message from Zachary.

Tom NOT guilty. I'll explain as soon as I can. Can't call atm.

Erica stared at the message. How was Tom not guilty? She was so sure that it was him.

She perched herself on the edge of the sofa and went over that night again—the one where she had followed Tom. The movement that she had heard had definitely came from inside that room. Someone must have been already in there. And if it wasn't Tom, then she had no idea who it could be.

Her phone buzzed again. Charlie this time. She found herself smiling at that, which was a miracle after a painful conversation with her mother and Zachary's latest development.

Your surprise went down a treat. Even Hilary is thawing. Thank you again xx

Erica had gone to bed thinking about Charlie, and when she had woken up with the urge to see her again, she decided she couldn't wait.

It was the opposite to how she felt after her first date with Victoria. She didn't have any urges to make a doughnut delivery to her office the next day, or any other day either. The two women couldn't have been any more different. It felt like Victoria was everything Erica had thought she *should* want—but in actual fact, Charlie could be what she had really been looking for all along. She just hadn't known it.

Erica pictured Charlie's beaming smile when she walked out of the exam room at Little Paws to see her earlier that day, and she needed more of that. More of her.

Zachary had been able to move to London so that he could live his life his own way, so Erica could at least do the same during her time there. After that, she would work it out. Maybe Charlie would be bored of her before then. Maybe they would discover that they weren't suited after all. And if none of that happened and things did go well, then Erica was going to have to deal with that whenever the time came. Deal with her mother, who would probably never approve—their phone call was a stark reminder of that. Unless Charlie was a debutante and had a large number of zeros in her net worth, she wasn't likely to get Gloria Frost's approval. But that was a future issue. She just hoped she had the courage to stand up to her mother if that's what it came down to. She never had before, but she never had so much to lose before either.

She looked down at Charlie's text again and typed a reply. They had dinner planned for that weekend, but she couldn't hold out until then.

You and Hilary are very welcome. Dinner later? I'll only have an hour or so before work xx

She walked to the kitchen and peeked in the fridge to see if there was anything simple that she could throw together. She had stuff for a salad. That would have to do. Her phone buzzed again and her stomach flip-flopped.

I'll take what I can get. See you then xx

Yeah, she was not giving Charlie up anytime soon.

❖

Dinner had been short and sweet. They both discussed how their days had gone over the salad that Erica had prepared. Charlie hadn't even stopped at her own place first—she was still in her scrubs. That had still only given them about an hour and fifteen minutes, which went by far too quickly. Then Charlie had taken Hera home for company. Erica thought that it was cute that she wanted to do it, and at least she didn't have to worry about Hera being alone. They had, however, agreed to Hera spending the night at Charlie's. The four a.m. visits needed to stop—they weren't fair on Charlie, who had put up a fight, but Erica had insisted. Now that they were dating, they could see each other anytime they wanted, when it wouldn't impact on Charlie's sleep. Erica would hide a key for Charlie to let Hera back into the apartment before she left for work the next morning. Charlie, being Charlie, had joked about climbing into bed beside Erica instead. As much as she had laughed it off, the idea was becoming both more appealing and much harder to resist. Especially during those hot and heavy kissing sessions, which they had managed to fit in for a few minutes before Erica had to leave.

"Tom's looking for you," Ash said to her as soon as she walked behind the bar. Erica was back on the main bar for her shift.

She still hadn't heard from Zachary—which wasn't odd, as Zachary worked to his own timeline—and although he had told her that Tom wasn't guilty, she still wasn't comfortable meeting up with him alone. Not until she had the full story. "He knows where to find me," she said to Ash.

Ash pointed to her neck and nodded her head toward Erica. "Lipstick."

Erica reached her hand up to the spot Ash was indicating. She had fixed herself and reapplied her own lipstick, but she had forgotten about her neck, which Charlie had decided to tease mercilessly before she left. That she had made it to work at all was an achievement.

Ash laughed and leaned down to a shelf and passed her a wipe. "Here."

Erica wiped the spot and Ash gave her a thumbs up to say she'd got it all. "Sorry about that," Erica said.

"Hey, no need to apologize to me. I just assumed you'd want to know," Ash said. She didn't mention it again or ask Erica anything about it. They weren't close enough for her to pry, though Ash was the person that she got along with best at Oasis. Kelly-Ann was nice enough too. She needed to make more effort with everyone else. She didn't know a lot about them, and if she was going back to square one, she needed to amend that. With that in mind she positioned herself beside Damien.

"I still haven't got the hang of making those," she said to Damien as he started to mix up some cocktails.

Damien smiled at her. "It just takes practice."

"Yeah? How long have you been doing this for?" she asked. It felt strange that every conversation she had at Oasis, private or otherwise, was with a raised voice to be heard over the music. Though, the more you got used to it, the easier it was to drown out the background noise and focus on whoever was talking. It helped that her lip-reading skills were getting better too—another bartending must.

"Here?" Damien looked at the ceiling. "Must be a year now. I've had a few other bar gigs too before that, so probably three or four years in this kind of work."

So, he was an experienced klutz. "Do you like working here?"

"I love it. It has such a good vibe, and everyone is so nice," Damien said. He scooped a load of ice into his shaker, dropping several bits on the floor in the process, and started pouring from all different bottles at lightning speed. Maybe if he'd slowed down a little, half of it wouldn't have ended up on the counter. Oblivious to his mess, he put the lid on and gave it a shake. "How about you? Are you liking it so far?"

Another nod. That was another thing about communicating over the noise—it was easier through body language and facial expressions. She leaned toward Damien. "I didn't know how I would find it. It's my first bar job." First job in general to be exact, but she didn't need to add that part. "But I really needed the money, so I thought I would give it a go. I'm enjoying it so far."

"Tell me about it. I've got student loans coming out of my ears. I'm starting to think I need to rob a bank instead of mixing cocktails every night of the week." He laughed.

Erica laughed with him. What an interesting comment—she noted it in her head. She knew to take it with a pinch of salt, but it wouldn't be so strange. If Damien had debts that needed paid, perhaps he would go to desperate measures.

Going down the money route seemed like a good approach. When she went back to join Ash again, she decided to try it again.

"God, I can't wait until payday," she said to Ash when there was no one waiting for drinks. "I swear, I need to find a side hustle."

Ash smiled. "If you come up with one, let me know. Try and keep it legal, though, yeah?"

That didn't sound like the answer of a nightclub thief to Erica. "I absolutely will. We can go in on it together." Her gut had told her that Ash was innocent from the beginning. It didn't seem like that was about to change.

"I heard about your accident the other night," Ash said. She tapped her head. "How is it?"

Erica had forgotten about her head. She had managed to hide it quite well with make-up and she only needed a small plaster to cover the cut. "Much better now. Hurts to touch still, so I try not to do that."

"What happened to you? Kelly-Ann said you fell?"

"Yeah. It was silly of me. I should have been watching where I was going," Erica said.

"Not your fault. That stock room is like an obstacle course. I don't know how many times I've said to Brandon that we need more space for storage," Ash replied.

Of course, Erica knew that she hadn't really tripped in the stock room, but it was clear that Ash didn't know that—not unless she was a really good actress. Another reason to keep her off the guilty list. Obviously, Kelly-Ann had bought Erica's story too if she was passing it around. Brandon on the other hand knew that there were rooms not being used. What reason did he have for *not* storing some excess stock there? It wasn't like space was an issue. Maybe he wanted those rooms to remain empty for his own reasons. Erica still liked Brandon for the thief. Her theory for his motive was that he was trying to get back at Zachary somehow. That's all they were, though—theories. She still had no idea what was going on, and she could guess all she wanted, but until she had proof, all she had were her own suspicions. And suspicions weren't good enough.

"Erica, can I talk to you a second?" She looked across the bar to see Tom, arms folded, intimidating look firmly in place.

"A bit busy here at the minute, Tom. Can it wait?" *Forever maybe?* A one-on-one conversation with Tom wasn't exactly high up on her wish list of things she wanted to do.

"It won't take long. Please?" His scowl seemed to soften slightly.

Erica sighed and looked toward Ash, who nodded at her to say it was okay. At least Ash knew where she was going to be and who she was with if anything bad were to happen. She was sure Tom wouldn't be quite so obvious to have a witness if he was plotting her murder. "Make it quick," Erica said to him.

She followed Tom to one of the quieter booths. There were plenty of people around, and they were in plain view, which made things a lot less intimidating. That, and the guy who was making a fool of himself with a badly choreographed dance routine right out of the eighties to their left. He was going to be red faced at work the next day—and judging from the girl pointing her phone at him, there was going to be evidence.

"I didn't do that to your head." There was no beating around the bush. Tom came right out with it. "Brandon told me that you think I did."

Erica turned away from eighties guy to look at Tom. She regarded him. "If you didn't, then who did?"

He shrugged his big, burly shoulders. "I don't know. I would tell you if I did."

"What were you doing sneaking around those back rooms?" she asked.

"Why were you?" he threw back at her. He fixed her with a glare of his own.

She leaned back against the back of the booth. She might as well just say it. "I was following you."

The conversation would have been a lot easier if Zachary had told her the full story about Tom. She felt unprepared, and Erica hated that. Did Tom know what she was really doing working at Oasis? She had no clue. She had to be careful with her answers in case her secret had somehow remained intact. If he did know, she was sure that it would come out during their conversation.

Tom gave a laugh that sounded more like a grunt. "Why would you be following me?"

"I'll explain after you tell me what you were doing down that corridor. Specifically, in that function room at the end of it." She would be doing the interrogating, not Tom. Erica was no pushover, and she wasn't going to act like one now just because Tom made her a bit nervous.

"I can't tell you that," he said.

Erica put her hands on the table to push herself up to leave. "Then we have nothing to talk about."

"Wait, wait, wait," Tom said, and Erica sat back down again. He leaned forward and lowered his voice. "You know that someone's nicking money from the club. Brandon said you know. He didn't say how you know, or why, and I didn't ask. That's your business. All I know is that you aren't the one doing the nicking, because it started before you got here." It sounded more like *you aren't the one doin' the nickin'* in Tom-slang. Pronunciation didn't seem to be his strong point.

"I'm aware that there's money going missing, yes. How do you know about it?" She was suddenly overly aware of how posh her own accent seemed compared to Tom's. It would probably seem like an odd contrast to anyone listening in—although she hoped that no one was. It wasn't the type of conversation that she wanted to share.

Tom had obviously had the same thought. He looked right and left to see if anyone was listening. He leaned in even closer. "A few weeks back, Brandon came to me and asked me to keep an eye out. Said a load of cash had gone missing. Wanted me to be his eyes and ears on the floor."

Brandon had never mentioned that he had brought Tom in on it. Not to her, and not to Zachary—not the last time they had spoken, anyway. Maybe that's what Zachary had to tell her. If that was all it was, then it didn't necessarily mean that Tom was innocent. It just meant he had a good cover. Maybe Brandon and he were in on it together, for all they knew. She decided to go with it for now. "And have you found out who it is?"

Tom frowned. At least, Erica thought he did. It was hard to tell with Tom. "I've got my suspicions. I was following up a lead when you were following me."

"I didn't see anyone else," Erica said.

"Look…I hadn't noticed anything suspicious until two or three weeks ago. I was outside having a ciggy. This fella pulls up in some flashy looking car. Parks it across the road."

Flash cars weren't exactly uncommon in that part of London. Erica wondered where he was going with this. "Right."

"He gets out of the car and crosses the road, this bloke in a baseball cap. I thought he was coming in the club. Then he turns left and goes round to the back alley. I had to go back to work before I ever saw him come back."

"Could the alley be a shortcut to somewhere else? Maybe he was cutting through that way."

Tom shook his head. "Has a dead end. I checked it out the next day. Nothing there but bins, rats, and our back door."

She had to admit that *did* sound suspicious. "What did he look like?"

Tom scratched his beard. "Hard to say. Wore that cap and kept his head down. One thing I did notice was that his shoes were fancy. Gleaming too. Thought that was weird, given him hanging round an alleyway. Anyways, I kept an eye out then. Sure enough, this guy came back again a few nights later. This time I waited until he came back out from behind the club."

"Why didn't you follow him when he went down there?" Erica asked.

"He would have spotted me a mile off. I didn't want to scare him away."

That made sense. She hadn't wanted Tom to spot her when she was following him. "Go on."

"What I did see was that he went down the alley empty handed, and when he came back again, he was carrying a backpack. Weird, eh?" Tom raised one of his bushy eyebrows.

"Very. Why didn't you call the police?" Erica asked. That's what she would have done if she had seen something like that. If she had caught Tom in the act, she would have called the police right away.

"Said to Brandon that we should when I told him about it. He wanted to hold off. Said we need find who's giving the fella the bag from the inside. Brandon has some kind of point to prove with the big boss—guess he wants to be the hero."

So, Brandon wanted to impress Zachary. She refrained from rolling her eyes at that. Maybe that's why he didn't seem too welcoming toward her. "And have you? Found out who's giving him the bag? How can you be sure it's the money?"

Tom tapped his head. "I'm not thick. What else could it be?"

Erica had to admit, she would have thought the same thing. And it explained how the money was leaving the premises undetected. "So, when I was following you, you were going to the alley?"

Tom nodded. "Knew that car was outside. I went right out the door, but there wasn't anyone there. No one. I went and checked that the car was still there, and it was. So, I waited in that alley ages, I did. No one came out through the back door. When I gave up, went round the front again and the car was gone."

"You're saying you weren't in that function room?" Erica asked. She was starting to believe Tom's innocence herself. She had seen that door close before she went into the room.

"Door locks from the inside. I had to come back in the front way. And I'm betting whoever that guy is went out the front way too. Had to. Reckon it was him in that room with you, along with whoever he's working with. It wasn't the first night I'd checked down there. Probably clocked on that I was looking for them and hid in there till I was out of the way."

Erica gave a slow nod. "Then I came in, and they hadn't been expecting that. They knew you were at the back door, so they couldn't just wait for me to leave and then escape."

"That's what I was thinking. Seen them chairs and tables scattered. You took a right bad knock. Glad you're all right like."

Maybe Tom wasn't so bad after all. "Thanks."

"You didn't see nothing, then?" Tom asked.

"No. I was on the ground before I knew what was happening. They must have run right out. Couldn't Brandon check the cameras if we know this man exited through the front door?"

"Said it was a waste of time. He only wanted to know who was helping him and that we wouldn't be able to get a good look if the bloke was wearing that hat." Tom went quiet for a few seconds. "You need to keep all this to yourself, right? I maybe shouldn't be telling you. But Brandon said you already know about the missing money, and I didn't want you thinking I attacked you, so…" He shrugged.

Erica made a spur of the moment decision. "As it turns out, you should be telling me all of this, Tom. I'm your employer. Zachary and I are co-owners of Oasis. So, I want to be informed of everything you have found out so far, and I want to be the first to hear anything else you come up with."

His jaw dropped open. Brandon mustn't have divulged that much information. He blinked a few times. "I didn't know that. Er, I'm very sorry, boss."

Erica rolled her lips in to stop herself from laughing. Seemed like Tom was the one who was nervous now. "Obviously this stays between us. We have the same goal, you and I. The reason that I'm here is to find out who is stealing from us."

"Yes, ma'am. I won't say a word." He held his hand up. "I swear it."

"Erica is fine, Tom. Now, tell me who you suspect it is?"

Tom leaned in closer again. "How I figure it, must be one of the lasses. Reckon the geezer in the cap is the boyfriend. I've been keeping an eye on all of them."

That's why he had been staring at Kelly-Ann. She was one of his suspects. He must have been watching all the girls. That was probably why Ash thought there was something shifty about him too. Erica couldn't have got things any more backward. She felt like kicking herself. "I'm sorry I blamed you, Tom."

"It's okay. I get why you did, boss, er, Erica."

Erica understood then what Charlie had meant with her comment about him being like a big teddy bear. She couldn't wait to tell her all the latest developments. She hoped she would get to see her the next day so that she could fill her in. And she needed to speak to her brother about everything too. It didn't escape her notice that telling Charlie had come to mind first.

"Let me know the next time that car is outside. Is there anyone who is always working whenever it's there?" she asked.

"A few of the lasses. Haven't narrowed it down yet. Thought it was Kelly-Ann, but then she was flirting with me, so reckon she doesn't have a boyfriend after all. Still watching her, though."

Now Erica knew that Kelly-Ann was barking up the wrong tree. It was quite funny that Erica had got things so wrong. "Let me know if you do notice anything. And not a word of this, Tom. I mean it. I'm just Erica who works behind the bar. Got it?" Erica gave him a pointed look.

"Got it. And don't you go following folk alone. If you see something, tell me and I'll go or I'll come with you," Tom said.

Tom was protecting her now. Talk about things taking a one-eighty. "I will."

They returned to their separate stations. With Tom out of the frame, Erica turned her focus to the ladies working the bar. There were still a lot of possibilities floating around.

The mystery wasn't solved yet, but she was getting closer—thanks to Tom. She even felt like she had an ally in her search—the most unlikely ally she could have imagined. At one point of the night, when she glanced over toward Tom standing on the door out of habit, she could even have sworn that he smiled at her.

When she got a spare minute, she got her phone out and sent off a text to Charlie.

Fancy a quick breakfast when you drop Hera off in the morning? If you have time before work? Lots to tell xx

Three dots bounced on her screen within seconds.

Does that mean breakfast in bed? xx

Erica laughed and the dots started bouncing again before she could respond.

Only joking. Breakfast sounds good if you won't be too tired. I'll come round half an hour earlier than planned? xx

Erica typed a response. *Great. Don't worry about me. Want to see you and fill you in on tonight's excitement xx* She typed again before Charlie could reply. *I would have done breakfast in bed, but as you were joking, you'll have to settle for the kitchen xx* Erica added a wink to the end of the message.

Charlie wrote back straight away. *I take it back. Not a joke at all. Completely serious. xx*

Erica grinned. *Too late now xx*

Tease xx was all that Charlie wrote back.

Erica typed a quick reply before she put the phone back in her pocket and got back to work again. *Maybe next time. xx*

CHAPTER EIGHTEEN

"A re you guys like, fully domesticated or whatever now?" Val asked Charlie one evening, as she walked back into their apartment carrying Hera. She opened the cat flap and Hera skipped out and jumped onto the top of the sofa—a spot that she had seemed to claim as her own since becoming a regular visitor at their place. Val had already been sitting on the sofa, and she reached up and scratched under Hera's chin. Her issue seemed to be with Erica rather than Hera.

Charlie understood where Val was coming from—she did—but she didn't understand Val's obvious disapproval. Yes, she and Erica had been grabbing time together anytime they could. It wasn't easy when Charlie worked all day and Erica worked all night, so they had to take what they could get.

Maybe it wasn't dating in the traditional sense, but it was working for them.

"What do you mean by that?" Charlie asked, as she took up the chair opposite the sofa. She draped her legs over the edge of it.

Val was tapping on her phone, and she didn't look up. "It seems like a lot. I thought you were only dating. Getting to know each other."

"Yeah. We are."

"No, you aren't." Val snorted. "This isn't dating. It's skipping to *oh we spend every second we can together.*"

"And? So what if it is?"

Val looked at her then. "Nothing. I just never expected you to be like this. Like *at all.*"

"I'm not any different. This is all new to me too, V. I don't see why you're getting on my case about it."

"I just mean that I thought you would be a bit more cautious. It seems to be going really fast. You've gone from zero commitment ever, to this full-on relationship in no time at all. I know that you like her, but I don't want you to go all in and end up getting hurt."

"Why would I get hurt? What have you got against Erica?" Charlie asked.

Val looked down at her phone again, scrolling through whatever she was looking at. "I've just got a bad feeling. Look at how she treated you when you first met. That wasn't long ago, Charlie. I know you say she's different now, and I believe that she is different right now. But what if *that* version of Erica comes back?"

"She's not like that. I appreciate you looking out for me. I do. But things are good, and I'm happy. I'd be even happier if I had my best friend's support." Charlie pulled her cushion from underneath her and threw it at Val.

Val looked up from her phone to glare at Charlie, but the corners of her mouth twitched up. "You always have that." She set the phone down beside her. "I also miss my best friend which could be making me grouchy. I miss us going out together. I miss us going out together. Is that not going to be a thing anymore now that you're with her?"

"*Her* name is Erica, as you already know. And of course I can still go out with you. Make a plan with the girls and we can all go. Next week sometime."

"You'll probably want to go to Oasis."

"I mean, if that's where you all want to go, then I won't argue." She grinned.

"Fine. I'll organize it. But I'll continue to worry about you because that's what besties do. Know that."

"Things are going good, Val. Erica's great—nothing like before. I don't think you need to worry about me," Charlie said.

"Hmm. And how about you? Have you freaked out yet? Even on the inside?"

"Nope. Not for a second. Can you believe that?" Hera jumped down from the sofa and onto Charlie's lap. Probably her way of saying *thank you for being nice about my human.* She curled into a ball and Charlie ran her fingers through her fur.

"Maybe you're more capable of love than you thought," Val said.

Whoa. Love? "I wouldn't go that far. I like her, sure. We're still getting to know each other. Seeing where it goes."

"Okay. Keep telling yourself that."

"What do you mean?" Charlie asked.

"I mean that you are so falling for her." Val lifted a shoulder. "Just make sure that she's falling for you too."

"No." She waved Val off. "I don't think we're there yet. I'm not there yet."

"It'll probably be after you sleep with her," Val said matter-of-factly.

"When have I ever fallen in love after sleeping with someone?"

"When have you ever practically co-parented a cat, or done anything to spend a few minutes in someone's company, or pined for them when you couldn't?"

She did have feelings for Erica. She would even go as far to say that they were strong feelings. But honestly, Charlie wasn't sure if she would even know how it would feel to be falling in love. She couldn't be. It was too soon, wasn't it? They had only known each other for a few weeks. "I still think love's a bit much."

Val focused on her phone again. "If you say so." She became engrossed scrolling again.

Charlie sat petting Hera and staring absent-mindedly at the TV, which was showing some kind of cooking competition. She couldn't have told you what any of the contestants were making—her mind was too busy with one question.

Was she falling for Erica?

❖

Charlie and Erica had agreed that they wouldn't see each other until their dinner date with Liz and Nancy that evening. Erica was meeting up with her brother and Olly that afternoon. Zachary had told Erica that Olly needed to grab some things from his apartment, and Erica wanted to discuss Oasis business with Zachary. That gave Charlie plenty of time to prepare herself, both physically and mentally, for their date.

This date seemed important—like it made them more serious. Spending time with another very well-established couple, a couple whom Charlie both admired and respected, seemed like it meant something about the direction their relationship was headed.

Time had seemed to slow down for the day. Maybe she was checking the clock more often than she usually did, but the hands weren't moving quick enough. She thought a haircut and some shopping would pass the time, but when she got back home again it was still hours before date time. There was some texting back and forth, which helped.

All seems good between Zachary and Olly, so he says that I'm welcome to stay in his apartment for a bit longer xx

Charlie smiled when she read Erica's text message. Erica had told her about Zachary's track record with relationships, which had made her a little nervous about how long she would get to stay in Olly's apartment.

She sent off a reply. *That's a relief. Olly's a good neighbour and all, but he doesn't make me dinner. xx*

I knew that you were just in this for the food xx came Erica's reply.

There's a possibility that you're better to look at too. But don't tell Olly that, he's very vain. xx Charlie added a few laughing faces to show she was joking, though Olly would probably have agreed with her. He was a fantastic looking guy, and he knew it.

Funny, my view next door isn't so bad either. Looking forward to seeing it again later xx

I'm looking forward to it too. xx

And she would try to make that view as presentable as possible. She had struggled a little bit about what to wear. It wasn't like they were going to a restaurant, or on a night out—it was just Liz and Nancy's place. That meant that *too* dressy wouldn't look right. At the same time, this was a date, and this was Erica, who could probably make a bin-bag look glamourous. She tried to anticipate what Erica would wear, but she wasn't sure, and she didn't want to ask. Heels she already knew, which would make Erica much taller than Charlie, so Charlie picked out a high pair of heels for herself. She also decided on a navy dress—tight fitting, and it stopped just below the knee. It wasn't dressy-dressy, not glitzy like a lot of her other dresses, but it was nice enough that it showed that she was trying.

Outfit chosen, hair done, and make-up fixed. All she had left to do was wait until it was time to pick Erica up.

When that time finally arrived, she was not ready for it. She might have thought she was, but nothing could have prepared her for how good Erica looked when she answered the door.

"You're staring," Erica said to her. The smile on her face told Charlie that she didn't mind one bit.

How could Charlie not stare? Erica was wearing high-waisted black jeans with a fancy looking belt at the top. Unsurprisingly, she was wearing heels—long black boots that went great with those jeans and made her long legs look even longer. Charlie was sure that the dark green blouse she wore was pure silk—it was tucked in, and there were plenty of buttons left undone at the top to torture her. The colour brought out the green in Erica's eyes. Charlie wondered if that was intentional or a lucky coincidence. Erica's hair was worn down and layered with waves. Charlie couldn't decide what she wanted to do first—run her hands through that hair, kiss that collarbone, or stare into those green eyes. The last one seemed to be the safest option for the hallway they were standing in—hence the staring. She wouldn't even try to deny it. "I am. I might just do that for the whole night." Charlie smiled. "You look a-mazing."

Erica gave Charlie an appreciative once over as well. "Right back at you." Erica indicated the apartment behind her. "Should we stay in and look at each other?"

"If we stayed in, I would do a lot more than look at you." The response was out of Charlie's mouth before she even had time to think about it.

Erica didn't look like she was overly against the idea, judging by the look on her face. Charlie was sure that her green eyes had gone a shade darker. She quickly reached to the hook beside the door and grabbed her coat. "Let's go before I agree to that, and we miss dinner." She stepped out and pulled the door behind her.

Charlie laughed. "Are you sure you don't want me to come in? I didn't even get to say hi to Hera." She helped Erica put her on her coat.

"Don't you use that ploy to get me back in there with you. You can say hi to Hera when we get back," Erica said as they fell into step beside one another.

"Does that mean that you're going to invite me in afterward?"

"Maybe," Erica said.

"Just for looking, or…"

Erica laughed. "I forgot about that Charlie-charm of yours."

"And I forgot that the Charlie-charm doesn't work on you."

"What makes you say that?" Erica asked. She looked sideways at her.

"You know. Everything that happened when we first met."

"Ah, yes. Well, that was more because I wasn't the only woman getting the charm, rather than the charm itself," Erica said.

"And that's where you're wrong—because since we met, you are the only woman who I've wanted to charm." Charlie swallowed because what she was about to say was a big step for her. "You know that I'm only interested in you, right? There is no one else." Like anyone else could even come close to the beautiful woman walking next to her.

Erica reached down and laced their fingers together. "In that case, Charlie-charm me all you like. I might be more receptive to it now."

"Does that mean that I am invited in tonight?"

Erica made a show of thinking about it. "I haven't decided yet. I'll let you know." She squeezed Charlie's hand.

They took a taxi to Liz and Nancy's. As they sat side by side in the back of the black cab, Charlie could feel that the heat had gone up between them. They both snuck glances at each other when they thought the other wasn't looking—and they both got caught doing it too. At least Erica seemed to be just as affected as Charlie was.

The cab ride took a little longer than Charlie had bargained for, but that was London traffic for you. At least they were a few minutes early, because she had been too impatient and hadn't wanted to wait any longer to see Erica.

"Their place looks nice," Erica said as they got out of the car and walked up the remainder of the driveway.

"It is. It's like a home-home, you know. I love it when they invite me over. I've asked them multiple times to adopt me and let me live here, but apparently, I'm too old to be adopted."

They were both laughing when Liz answered the door with a wide smile. "Hi, ladies, come on in." She gave each of them a welcoming hug as they entered. Erica passed Liz a bottle of wine she had brought. *They* had brought, she amended in her head as Erica told Liz that it was from both of them. Very couple-y, Charlie thought. She wasn't complaining.

"You have a lovely home," Erica said to Liz, as she took their coats and hung them in the closet in the hall.

Liz looked around her. "Thank you, Erica. We like it here. It's nice and quiet."

"How long have you lived here?"

"We moved in here right after we got married, so that's over nine years now. Wow. Time flies when you think about it like that," Liz said.

"Big anniversary coming up next, then." Erica said with a smile.

Liz smiled and nodded. "We were discussing that the other day. Thinking about booking a trip away for it."

"I'm in shock that it's been so long. I remember your wedding like it was no time ago," Charlie said.

Erica looked surprised. "You two have known each other that long too?"

"Longer. I hired Charlie as an apprentice when she was just starting her veterinary nursing qualifications. She's been with me ever since." Liz put her arm around Charlie. "She's extremely loyal, this one."

Charlie knew that was Liz's subtle attempt to talk her up, and she appreciated her efforts. Erica seemed encouraged by the comment too. She had never really thought about it as loyalty, but she supposed it was. She enjoyed working with Liz, though, so it wasn't any hardship. And Liz was equally loyal to her. They were a team. That's why Charlie had never wanted to go off and get her veterinary training. She loved working side by side with Liz. She still learned a lot. Liz taught her things that were way beyond what she would be expected to know in her own job, so it wasn't like her skills weren't developing. Her knowledge was constantly growing. And maybe she would decide to take the next step in her career at some point, and maybe she wouldn't.

"Where's Nancy?" she asked as Liz led them into the living room and got them comfortable.

"She's been in the kitchen for the last three hours. I offered to help, but you can imagine the response I got."

"Stay the hell out of my kitchen?"

"To put it mildly." Liz looked at Erica. "You can tell that Charlie is used to the dynamics around here."

They all laughed. It was true, though. Charlie remembered that she used to offer to help out all the time—chop things, stir things, clean up—but Nancy liked to work alone and wasn't afraid to banish everyone from her kitchen by yelling at them or throwing them dirty looks. Charlie only agreed to stop offering if she was allowed to clean up after all of Nancy's culinary genius was complete. So, that had become her and Liz's role during these dinners.

The dinners were usually a lot more casual than this one, though. Liz was going all out—playing the hostess with the mostest that night—Charlie could tell. Usually, Charlie walked in, threw herself onto the sofa, and put her feet up, but it wasn't that kind of night. Liz had dressed up more than usual too.

"Can I get you both a glass of wine?" Liz asked them, and they both said yes.

"Are you sure you're allowed in there to get it?" Charlie asked, indicating the door to the kitchen.

"I'm hoping to be in and back out before she ever sees me." Liz disappeared behind the door.

Erica was chuckling. "Liz seems so lovely."

"She is. You'll love Nancy too. I know we're making her out to be a little scary, but that's only when she's in full blown chef mode, and only to us. She's really one of the nicest people you'll ever meet."

Laughter sounded from the kitchen.

"Yeah, it doesn't sound like such a hostile environment to me," Erica said with a smile.

"They adore each other. I've always admired them as a couple—the togetherness. They seem to have everything so figured out."

"Couples aren't really like that where I come from," Erica said. "Well, I'm sure some are. I just don't know that many."

"No?"

Erica shook her head. "There's a lot of one-upmanship, and so many relationships that are just for show. Someone will marry someone because they have the best job or the most money or they come from the best family. And the affairs that go on, don't even get me started."

Erica hadn't told her too much about her life back home. She knew the basics—complicated relationship with her mum, whereabouts she lived, and a few things about her best friend—but apart from that, she really didn't know anything. From her description, Charlie imagined Erica to be surrounded by a bunch of pretentious pricks and hoity-toity snobs. Charlie knew that she would never fit in there. She wouldn't want to, either. Thankfully, Erica was nothing like that. Yes, she was obviously well-spoken and well-educated, and from a few of their conversations Charlie surmised that Erica did come from money—but the Erica she knew wasn't anything like the people she described.

"That doesn't sound like happiness to me. Surely that's what relationships and marriage should be about? Happiness," Charlie said. "I know I don't have a lot of good experience there, but even I know that."

Erica had been staring off into space, but she looked at Charlie then. "It should be, yes."

Liz arrived then carrying three generous glasses of red like a pro. "I've been told to start with this wine, as it will ready your palate for your starter. Then there's a different wine for the main." She passed each of them a glass before taking a seat with her own.

"A food *and* wine expert. I'm starting to understand why Charlie wants to move in," Erica said with a grin.

"She told you that, huh? I'm convinced if I even said yes as a joke, she would arrive with all her worldly belongings before dawn," Liz said.

"Forget the belongings. I just wouldn't leave. You could change your mind and get the locks changed before I returned. I would never take that risk."

The door to the kitchen opened again and Nancy stepped in looking way too glam for someone who was in the midst of single-handedly preparing a three-course meal. She walked straight toward Erica, hand extended. "You must be Erica."

"Guilty. Lovely to meet you, Nancy."

"So good to meet you too. I'm sorry I've been stuck in the kitchen. I'll get to chat properly soon," Nancy said.

Erica waved her off. "Don't apologize. Thank you so much for having me over. I hear your food is the best, bar none."

"You two decided on putting minimal pressure on me tonight, then?" She glared between Liz and Charlie. She made a beeline for Charlie.

Charlie stood and threw her arms around her. "Hey, Nance. Missed you."

"Missed you too. It seems we have *a lot* to catch up on." Nancy jerked her head toward Erica in the most obvious way possible. "A lot."

Charlie looked toward Erica and sighed. "You may get used to this. They won't stop until they've thoroughly embarrassed me."

"You can't blame us, Charlie—you've never brought us an audience before." Nancy looked at Erica. "She's never brought a date over here. We've been waiting on this moment for years."

"I did warn you that she would be worse than me," Liz said. She held her hands up as if that would deem her somehow innocent. Charlie knew Liz could be as bad as her wife—she was just a little more subtle about it.

At least Erica seemed to be amused by the whole thing.

"Charlie's been talking about moving in again," Liz said as Nancy perched herself on the arm of her chair and slid her arm around her.

"Oh no, this again? Change the locks when she leaves," Nancy said.

Charlie feigned shock. She gasped. "See? I told you."

They all laughed at that.

Nancy lifted Liz's glass and took a sip before passing it back to her. "As much as we do love to tease her, and we will continue to do so, we are so glad Charlie brought you here tonight, Erica."

Erica glanced over toward Charlie. "I'm glad she did too."

"Well, the starters will be ready very soon." She checked her watch and quickly jumped off the arm of the chair. She leaned down and kissed Liz's cheek. "Even sooner than I expected. Got to run." She rushed back into the kitchen again.

"I like her," Erica said to Liz.

"Yeah, she's okay, I suppose." Liz smiled softly. "Charlie might not by the end of the night, but that's okay. She always comes round again."

"It's the food," Charlie explained to Erica. "They know how to lure me in."

"I'll remember that," Erica said.

They chatted for a few minutes while they waited for Nancy to call them into the dining room. It didn't surprise Charlie that Erica got on well with Liz. She had a feeling that the two of them would have a lot in common. Liz was well behaved when she was alone. Charlie was sure that when Nancy joined them, it would be a different case entirely.

She didn't mind the teasing. She knew how fond of her Liz and Nancy both were—if there was anyone in Charlie's life who genuinely wanted the best for her, it was them, for sure.

When the starters were good to go, they took their places at the table, Charlie beside Erica, and Liz and Nancy opposite them.

"It's only a simple starter. Beetroot, goat's cheese, and sweet-candied walnuts," Nancy said as she carried all four plates to the table. She had clearly perfected that trick over years—Charlie would have dropped the lot.

"Soup is a simple starter, Nance. This is posh nosh," Charlie said.

"Happy to give you an upgrade, Charlie." She took her seat next to Liz and smirked. "A bit like your taste in women, it seems. Thank God."

"Oh, here we go," Charlie said. "I haven't even taken a bite yet and you've already started." She could hear Erica laughing softly beside her.

Nancy was laughing too. "How did you two meet, anyway? I've had the short version from my lovely wife, but she always forgets the best parts."

Liz nodded as she cut into her food with her knife and fork. "It's true. I'm a dreadful storyteller."

Charlie looked at Erica and asked, "Do you want to tell it, or do you want me to?"

Erica smiled back at her and shrugged. "You go. I'll interrupt when you need corrected."

"We met in a bar," Charlie said.

"Where many of the best romances start," Nancy said. She raised her glass. "We had our first proper date in a bar," she said to Liz, who hummed her agreement.

"I work at Oasis, the bar where we met," Erica added.

"Yes." Charlie nodded. "Erica works in the bar. She couldn't take her eyes off me, and the rest is history." She tried to keep a straight face. "She kept asking me out and eventually I gave in."

"That is *not* what happened at all." Erica's jaw dropped open.

Liz pointed with her fork. "The worst storyteller in the world can second that, that is not what happened. Even I could tell it better than that." She threw Charlie a look.

"I'm joking, I'm joking. Erica couldn't stand me when we first met."

"Now *that* I find much more believable," Nancy said.

"Charlie was checking me out while she was already hooking up with some other girl," Erica explained. She turned to Charlie and raised an eyebrow. "Weren't you?"

"Let's skim over that part, shall we?"

"Skim over it all you want, we'll still be having words about it later," Nancy said with a pointed look.

"Can't wait for that." Charlie went on to tell the real story of how they met—how they kept running into each other, then about how they finally connected when Hera was sick, and how they continued to get closer after that.

"So, she told me that she wanted to be friends. Then she got all jealous when some girl was trying to chat me up at Oasis, so she threw me against the bathroom wall and kissed me until my lips were numb," Charlie said to finish it off.

"I never actually said to you that I just wanted to be friends. You assumed that," Erica said with a shrug.

"You did." Charlie frowned.

"No. You asked me if we were friends, and I said I would think about it."

"What I want to know is if you really threw her against the wall and kissed the lips off her?" Nancy asked.

Erica looked abashed. "Yeah. I kind of did."

"Amazing." Nancy looked at Liz and grinned. "See, not everyone gets along when they first meet."

Erica gave them a questioning look. "You mean, you two?"

Charlie had forgotten that Liz and Nancy hadn't got off to the best of starts. Wow. When the poster couple started off badly, there must be hope for everyone else. Maybe it wasn't a bad thing that she hadn't had the smoothest of starts with Erica. If they ended up anywhere near as happy together as Liz and Nance, they would be doing pretty damn well.

Liz nodded. "She hated me."

Erica leaned back in her chair. "Seriously?"

"Oh, I absolutely did. I had got my first gig as head chef in a top-end, reputable restaurant. It was my first week. I was young, and cocky, and I knew it all."

"Some things never change," Charlie said. She had to get her own digs in whenever she could.

"Young and knowledgeable? Thank you, Charlie," Nancy said.

Liz rolled her eyes at her. "You were incredibly cocky. I can still picture you walking out of that kitchen that first time."

"Liz here…" Nancy put her arm around Liz. "Sent her food back. Said it was inedible."

Erica winced. "Ooh. That's a recipe for a bruised ego."

Charlie chuckled. "I see what you did there." Erica grinned back at her.

"I was already having a bad week. I had got a terrible write-up in the newspaper. A couple of horrendous reviews. And I was good. At least, I thought I was. Then Liz did that, so she was the one who felt my wrath." Nancy looked at Liz. "Still fancied you, though."

"As it happened, I fancied her too. And I kept trying until I managed to wear her down," Liz explained to Erica.

"Thank God you did," Nancy said. She leaned over and gave Liz a kiss on the cheek. "Turned out, one of the other chefs had been sabotaging my dishes on purpose because I'd got the job he wanted. Adding salt and spices to the food and things like that."

"Technically, that asshole did you a favour," Charlie said. "If Liz hadn't got a bad meal and complained, you two might never have met."

"That's so true, you know," Liz agreed.

"And so romantic that I can barely believe that it came from Charlie," Nancy said.

Charlie felt the warmth on her cheeks, so she assumed everyone noticed her blush. The truth was, Charlie hadn't even known this side of herself existed. Meeting Erica had clearly unleashed her inner romantic that she had kept hidden even from herself. Before she had time to get self-conscious about this latest display of the *new* her, Charlie felt Erica's hand reach for hers under the table. She laced their fingers together.

"Charlie's full of surprises," Erica said. "She's certainly surprised me anyway."

Nancy and Liz both smiled. "To bad starts, meeting in bars, and good surprises," Nancy said as she lifted her glass.

All four of them clinked their glasses together.

"You do know that you're meant to toast before the food," Charlie said with a bit of cheek.

"Oh, shut up, you."

Laughter filled the room again.

CHAPTER NINETEEN

Charlie's friends were great. Erica felt like she had known Liz and Nancy for ages, rather than the couple of hours she really had. They made her feel like she had instantly become part of the group, welcoming her with open arms. And their love for Charlie was so obvious that it made Erica's heart swell.

Erica had never been on a double date before. She'd been out in groups and attended big events with dates—but never anything as relaxed and intimate as the dinner they were having with Liz and Nancy. She couldn't remember enjoying a date as much either. She couldn't imagine Charlie enjoying herself at one of those stuffy events that she had to attend so often. She didn't even enjoy them herself. This was so much better.

She chatted with Charlie and Liz, while Nancy went to put the final touches on their main course. The starter had been delicious—full of flavour, and far more complex than Nancy had made it out to be. Erica was used to fine dining, and she would be hard pushed to find anything as tasty as that in the restaurants that she went to back home. It wasn't long before the table was filled with more of the most mouth-watering looking food than Erica had ever seen in any of those restaurants.

"I don't even know where to start. All of this looks incredible," she said to Nancy.

Charlie turned to Erica. "Nancy makes a lot of vegetarian food for Liz and me."

"Oh, that's good actually. I'm an almost-vegetarian."

Charlie smiled at Erica. "I didn't know that about you. There I was giving you brownie points for making veggie stuff for me."

"I'll happily take the brownie points anyway," Erica said.

"I suppose it would be cruel to take them away now. You can earn them in other ways," Charlie whispered.

Going by Liz's amused look, she had overheard Charlie's flirting, despite her whisper. But she didn't tease her about it. That seemed to be Nancy's role, Erica was learning.

"How does being an *almost*-vegetarian work?" Liz asked instead.

"Basically, I'm a veggie most of the time—but I cheat the odd time and eat chicken," Erica explained. "So, I can't lie and give myself the title of being vegetarian. But—nearly." A fact that made most people she knew tut or roll their eyes at her, but luckily, she was in much more pleasant company.

"I like that." Nancy laughed. "Well, you can eat anything here. There are cauliflower steaks, blue cheese polenta fries, kale fried rice, refried cannellini beans with saffron, fresh spinach and paneer, and a new recipe for a chestnut mushroom stroganoff that I'm trying out for work—so you all have to try that and give me an honest opinion as long as it's positive."

"Wow. It's like I've walked in and ordered the entire menu, and every single thing looks amazing. I need to try it all." She started adding little bits of everything to her plate.

"I usually can't move for at least an hour after I eat here," Charlie said while she piled her plate high. "It's so good. Thanks Nancy."

Nancy shook her head. "I can't believe there's another veggie. I thought you would even the teams for me, Charlie."

"Almost veggie," Erica reminded her. "I can join you in all things chicken, but only now and again. And when the vegetarian options taste this good, then probably never."

"Don't worry about her, Erica. She eats whatever meat she wants when we go out, whether she has an ally or not. It's not like I've banned her," Liz said.

"We give her disapproving looks the entire time, though," Charlie said. She ate a mouthful of rice and winked at Nancy.

"I've learned to ignore them, Erica. You'll learn to do that too, if you're planning on sticking with Charlie, of course. Speaking of which, are you?" Nancy asked. She took a sip from her water glass and nearly spat it out when Liz elbowed her. "What?" she said when she had managed to swallow despite Liz's interruption. "I have to grill her a little bit. This is our Charlie we're talking about here. We have a responsibility."

Liz shook her head. "I'm sorry, Erica. You don't need to answer her."

Charlie glared at Nancy across the table too. Erica, on the other hand, had no issues with Nancy's habit of saying things right out, or direct questions. She reminded her a lot of Tess. And she also knew it was all good natured.

"I'd say that everything seems to be going well so far, Nancy, if that's a good enough answer?" Erica said. She smiled at Charlie.

"More than good enough. See, I've got your back, Charlie."

"Thanks. I think," Charlie said.

They laughed, teased, joked, and chatted as they polished off the majority of the food that Nancy had made. Even when Erica had felt full, she still found room for a bit more. First impressions had not been a let-down—everything tasted amazing. As for the stroganoff recipe that Nancy had been experimenting with for work—it was hands down the best meal that Erica had ever tasted. And judging from Charlie's and Liz's compliments and many moans of appreciation, that seemed to be a unanimous opinion. Maybe she would bring Zachary and Olly to Nancy's restaurant some night. Charlie too, of course. If she did, she was ordering the stroganoff, without a doubt.

They finished off with a passionfruit pavlova parfait which was decadence at its finest. She understood exactly what Charlie meant about being unable to move afterward. Erica felt like she might never be able to move again.

Erica had offered to help clean everything up, but all three ladies had told her there was no chance she would be allowed to clear nor wash dishes. When Liz and Charlie went in the kitchen, Nancy filled up their wine glasses and the two of them retreated to the living room.

"I know I like to wind Charlie up and all, but honestly I'm really glad that she brought you here to meet us tonight, Erica," Nancy said when they sat down. "At the risk of embarrassing her further—which seems like a waste of time when she isn't here to experience it—it is a big step for her doing something like this."

"I'm glad she brought me too. I'm having a lovely evening." Erica smiled. "Charlie did tell me that she doesn't date much."

"Never. She never does. And she really likes you. The fact that she's brought you here tells me that already, but I wasn't expecting her to be so...natural." Nancy sipped her wine.

"What do you mean?"

"She's so into you. It's obvious," Nancy said. "Relationships have always terrified Charlie, but she looks so relaxed and happy with you."

Erica sipped her own drink. Relationship. Was that what she was in with Charlie? They hadn't put a label on it, but she supposed it was a relationship. An image of her mother's furious reaction flashed through her mind, but she pushed it away again. It wasn't the time or place to worry about that.

Then the other worry, when it came to Charlie and her, was Charlie's history that Nancy was reminding her of now. She tried not to let it be an issue, but sometimes it was in the back of her mind. *Will she get bored? Will she move on to someone else? Is she really interested in me, or is it just the thrill of the chase for her? Is she only after one thing?* It wasn't fair that she thought any of it. Charlie's actions and her behaviour had been nothing but perfect since they started dating. She had given Erica zero cause for concern. But she couldn't pretend that it wasn't an insecurity that she had.

"What makes you say that she's into me?"

Nancy laughed quietly and looked at her. "You're joking, right? Haven't you seen the way she looks at you? Liz told me she was hooked, but I didn't realize exactly how much until I saw you guys together tonight. She can't keep her eyes off you."

"You think so?" Erica asked.

"I know so. Trust me." Nancy leaned back again and smiled at her. "And I know that I don't know you as well, but I don't think it seems like it's one-sided."

Erica bit her lip and looked at Nancy. This was one of those conversations—it had a protective, *how do you feel about our Charlie?* vibe. Not quite the same sort of threatening vibe that she had got from Charlie's roommate. Just a friend looking out for a friend. "No, it isn't one-sided. The whole thing is completely…unexpected for me too. But I admit, I've grown to care about Charlie very quickly."

"She has that effect. She's like family to us—always has been to Liz, since they first met. Then I got to know her a little later and I've always been fond of her. And the thing is with Charlie, she never wants to hurt anyone. She's always been very careful about that."

"What do you mean?" Erica asked.

"I mean, she wouldn't be pursuing something with you if she wasn't truly serious about you. If she's with you it's because she wants to be, and she isn't planning on going anywhere." Could Nancy read Erica's mind? "She'll have thought the whole thing through about fifty times, knowing Charlie," Nancy continued. She shook her head and took another drink. "Anyway. I'm blabbering. I'm just happy that Charlie has finally met someone she has feelings for. You've achieved something many women have tried and failed."

"What have many tried and failed?" came Charlie's voice from the doorway.

"Putting up with you for longer than five minutes." Nancy was quick with her comebacks. It was impressive really.

Charlie narrowed her eyes at Nancy. "I hope you're behaving yourself." She took a seat beside Erica and turned to her. "Feel free to ignore anything and everything she says."

"Shouldn't you be doing dishes with my beloved wife?" Nancy asked.

"She kicked me out—told me to tag you in. Think she wants to smooch with you by the kitchen sink," Charlie said.

"In that case…" Nancy stood up and took a sip of her wine before setting it on the coffee table. "Excuse me, ladies."

"She's fun," Erica said.

"She is. And she's a torture. I hope she wasn't giving you too much of a hard time?"

"Not at all. I think they both want to make sure that I have good intentions with you."

"I see. And have you?"

Erica made a show of tilting her head from side to side. "You'll have to wait and see." It was easy to forget all her doubts and worries when they were together. They quickly disappeared into a little locked box in the back of her mind. She reached forward and took Charlie's hand. "I have a lot of intentions when it comes to you." She pulled her closer and kissed her softly.

Charlie stared at her lips as they pulled away and then looked at her with hooded eyes. "Is that so?"

Normally, Erica wasn't the type of person to be forward, and never so early on when she was getting to know someone. But this thing with Charlie was different from any of her previous dating experiences. She felt brave and brazen, and she loved watching Charlie's reactions when she made the first moves, loved the effect it seemed to have on her. "Mm-hmm," she mumbled, before she leaned in for another kiss— deeper, slower, lingering. She leaned back in her seat again. Charlie looked as hot and bothered as Erica had hoped she would be.

Charlie blew out a loud breath. "You're trouble."

Erica laughed at that. She picked up her glass and took a sip. "Am I now?"

"Yes. You are." Charlie seemed to regain some of her composure. "Are you going to share any of these intentions with me?"

"I'm not sure." She was enjoying toying with Charlie. "I probably will at some point."

"I was wrong when I called Nancy a torture. You—you are definitely the torture." Charlie folded her arms.

"I am not," Erica said. She crossed her legs. "You haven't even seen me be a torture yet."

"Who wants coffee?" Liz poked her head into the living room.

"Coffee would be lovely, thank you, Liz," Erica replied. Charlie was gaping at her, and she had to try not to laugh.

"Charlie?" Liz asked.

"Yeah. We'll have a quick one, and then we need to get going, if that's okay, Liz?"

Liz had a knowing look. "No problem at all."

"Why do we need to get going?" Erica asked, as innocently as she could, as soon as Liz left.

Charlie gave her a heated look. "Because I think we need to have this discussion somewhere a bit more private. Don't you?"

"I think when we go somewhere more private, discussing is the last thing I'll want to do." Erica returned Charlie's look with a flirtatious one of her own.

"You better drink your coffee really fucking quickly."

❖

When they were finally on their journey home, they didn't speak much. Erica put that down to a mixture of nerves, want, and anticipation—on both sides.

Their date couldn't have gone any better. Erica felt like she had made two new friends, and she looked forward to all of them spending time together again. Meeting the friends could be such a dealbreaker, so the date had felt significant. It also was further proof to how good she and Charlie were together. Even though they were still only at the dating stage, it had felt like they were already a long-established couple tonight.

As much as they had been having a good time, Erica was also looking forward to the two of them spending some time alone together, even though that also made her nervous. Erica talked a good game and maybe she was good at acting like she was cool, calm, and collected—but it was all acting. Inside, the butterflies had been swirling around her stomach all night. Truth be told, she had known from the second that she opened the front door that she was going to invite Charlie back to hers after their date. She was powerless to do anything else. Not only did Charlie look exquisite tonight, because she absolutely did, but she was Charlie—and the mere sight of her made Erica's heart pound. She had feelings for Charlie that only got stronger every moment that they spent together.

Even though it was completely out of character for Erica to rush into something like this, there was no way she could send Charlie away. No part of her wanted to. Not her head, not her heart, and definitely not her body, which tingled with anticipation when Charlie looked anywhere in her direction.

They climbed the stairs together slowly and in silence. Charlie was setting the pace, and she wasn't rushing. Maybe she was nervous too. Or maybe she thought that Erica was going to call it a night when they reached the apartment door. Erica might have hinted at it, but she hadn't come out and told Charlie anything otherwise.

Eventually they reached their floor.

Charlie shifted on one foot to the other. "I would invite you in, but I'm pretty sure Val's at home tonight. I'm not even sure if it's just her or if she has company."

"We better go to mine, then. Well, you know what I mean." She indicated the door to Olly's apartment with her head. She was starting to think of it as her own.

Charlie grinned. "I did want to say hello to Hera."

As Erica unlocked the front door, her mind flashed back to the time that Charlie had shown her how to do it. Charlie's teasing had affected her then, even though she had pretended otherwise, but that was nothing compared to how affected as she was now. "She would expect nothing less." She held the door open for Charlie to step inside. All of their movements were slow, as if neither of them was quite sure what to do next. Hera made that decision for them as she came bounding out of her bed and rubbed around both of their ankles. There were a few meows of excitement because she had two people to get attention from. "I'll put some food out for her quickly," Erica said.

Charlie had already bent down to scratch Hera's head. "Hello you. Thanks for being my ticket in here tonight."

Erica laughed. She walked over and set Hera's refilled bowl onto the ground, and Hera scooted straight over to it. "For the record, I was asking you in anyway."

Charlie stood and straightened herself. "Is that so?"

Erica nodded. "Drink?"

Charlie took a step toward her. "No. I don't want a drink."

Erica leaned against the worktop and folded her arms. "Food?"

Charlie shook her head. "Not hungry." She came closer still.

"Oh yes. You wanted to discuss things." Her heart started to speed up.

Charlie had reached her then and she ran her hands up Erica's arms. She spoke quietly. "You said you didn't want to talk."

Erica swallowed. Charlie was close enough now that Erica could feel her warm breath against her lips. Charlie's hands found Erica's waist as she completely closed any gap between them, pushing her body firmly against Erica's. "No," she whispered. "I don't want to talk." Erica needed to regain the control. She leaned down and pressed her lips against Charlie's. With just that one touch, all of Erica's nerves evaporated. The kiss went from zero to a hundred within seconds, igniting the passion that had been simmering between them both all night. Erica devoured Charlie's lips. And when she pushed her tongue against those lips, Charlie didn't hesitate to meet it with her own. The kiss was rough and full of lust and want, but at the same time it felt soft and full of meaning. Erica didn't even know how a kiss could be all those things at the same time, but this one was. Even the sharp nip that Erica felt when Charlie bit and sucked on her lip felt tender somehow.

They must have been kissing for several minutes before they pulled their lips apart to catch their breath. They had been at this point before. The point when they could stop. Erica could call it a night and avoid complicating her life any further. Instead, she found herself saying, "Stay?"

Again, there was no hesitation from Charlie. "Yeah. If you're sure."

"A million percent sure." Uncomplicated was overrated. Erica took Charlie by the hand and led her to the bedroom, stepping over their coats that she hadn't previously noticed had somehow jumped from their bodies onto a heap on the kitchen floor.

Erica found Charlie's lips again the second they entered the room, and they kissed like they had been starved from each other for years, rather than the few seconds since they had kissed before. Charlie tugged up her shirt where it had been tucked in and then started to undo the buttons.

"I would rip this off, but it looks far too good on you," Charlie said with a grin as she reached the bottom button. She eased the top down Erica's shoulders and dropped it on the floor. Charlie's gaze felt like a caress over Erica's upper body. Charlie leaned in and pressed her lips to Erica's neck, trailing kisses down her shoulders, and when her lips reached Erica's collarbone, she ran her tongue along it gently while her fingers unclasped Erica's bra from behind her back. Erica closed her eyes as she felt the straps slide slowly down her arms. She was only exposed to the cool air for a few seconds before she felt Charlie's warm mouth close around her nipple. She moaned at the contact and felt Charlie smile against her before she added more pressure, alternating between sucking and biting softly. She repeated the same on the other side, eliciting the same moan from Erica once again. When Charlie straightened, she reached down and undid Erica's belt, followed by the button on her jeans.

Erica reached for Charlie and pulled her back in for a searing kiss. She needed more. She reached around Charlie's back and felt for the zipper on her dress. When she found it, she eased it down and pushed the dress down Charlie's body and dropped it onto the floor, not breaking their kiss for a second. She ran her hands over Charlie's smooth skin on her back and reached up and undid her bra with one hand in a swift move—which was all luck, because when did that ever happen on the first try? It seemed like the universe was on Erica's side and allowing her to be completely smooth tonight.

Erica guided Charlie backward toward the bed and eased her down on top of it. She stood for a few seconds and took in the sight of Charlie lying in just her underwear.

Who was she to keep such a beautiful woman waiting? She climbed on top of Charlie and kissed her softly before she moved her lips downward. She took her time as she kissed her way down Charlie's neck. When she heard Charlie take a sharp breath, she knew that she had found a sensitive spot, so she kept her focus there, and kissed and sucked on the soft skin. Charlie groaned and writhed beneath her. Erica laughed softly and moved further down. As she moved her lips down Charlie's chest, she reached and took Charlie's generous breasts in her hands. She squeezed softly, and ran her thumbs over her nipples, feeling them harden at the contact. Charlie's breath was becoming more and more ragged, which only spurred Erica on.

Just like Charlie had done, she took each nipple in her mouth and sucked, gently at first, then harder and harder until she made Charlie cry out.

Erica continued her exploration as she kissed down Charlie's toned, smooth stomach. She could feel Charlie's hands in her hair, grasping and pulling gently. When she reached the band of Charlie's black underwear she continued her trail south, pushing her lips against the silky fabric. She ran her tongue between Charlie's legs, pressing down on the spot where she knew Charlie's clit was right beneath the material. She could feel the wetness even through the underwear.

"God, Erica," Charlie breathed. She bucked her hips upward.

Erica looked up and grinned at her as she hooked her fingers into the top of the underwear and eased them down Charlie's legs. She threw them onto the floor beside the bed and pushed herself up on her elbows to look at Charlie's naked body. "You're really fucking beautiful. Do you know that?" She eased herself back down again and ran her hands up Charlie's legs, pushing them open to reveal her glistening centre.

On one hand Erica wanted to take her time with Charlie—to take in every single part of her body and tease her until she begged for more. But on the other hand, she wanted to lavish all her attention on Charlie right there and then. She chose the latter. After all, they had all night. She could ravish Charlie first and take the time to memorize her entire body after.

She kissed her way up the inside of Charlie's thigh. When she reached the top, she couldn't resist tasting Charlie straight away, so she ran her tongue along her clit. Charlie immediately moved her hips upward at the contact, and Erica pushed her tongue harder against her. They quickly found a rhythm as Charlie moved her hips and Erica licked her faster and harder.

Erica pushed inside Charlie with one finger at first, slow and deep, while she kept circling Charlie's clit with her tongue. When Charlie moaned, she added another finger and pushed deeper, making her cry out even more.

"Don't stop," Charlie said in a breathy voice as they both picked up the pace and pressure, matching each other's rhythm like they had been doing this together for years.

It wasn't long before Erica felt Charlie tense up beneath her and she heard her breath get faster. Then Charlie cried out as her body arched upward. Erica moved with her, wanting to drag out the orgasm for as long as possible, and she kept moving her fingers and tongue right until the waves stopped.

When Erica felt Charlie's body relax, she placed a final kiss on her thigh and eased her fingers out slowly. She grinned when she felt Charlie's body jerk again. She climbed back up and lay down beside her, drawing circles on her shoulder with her fingertips.

"I need a minute." Charlie's eyes were closed, and her chest was still moving up and down quickly.

Erica laughed softly. "Take your time. I'll enjoy the view." She leaned in and placed a kiss on Charlie's cheek.

After a couple of minutes Charlie rolled over to face her, pulling Erica into her arms. "That was amazing."

Erica lifted the shoulder she wasn't leaning on. "That was just a warm-up."

"You may kill me tonight, if that's what your warm-ups are like." Charlie laughed and leaned in to kiss her. This one was slow. Gentle. She leaned back again and looked down Erica's body. "How is it that I'm naked, but you still have jeans on?"

"I was more impatient than you were," Erica said.

"I feel very impatient right now." She rolled Erica onto her back and climbed on top of her. She eased herself down and removed Erica's jeans and underwear in one swoop before she covered Erica's body with her own. "That's better."

Erica hooked her arms around Charlie's neck and pulled her down closer, capturing her lips with her own once again. Charlie, having the better position, deepened the kiss as she ground her body against Erica's. Erica couldn't remember ever feeling so incredibly turned on. She reached her hand down between Charlie's legs and rubbed her clit, while Charlie ground against her. It was only seconds before Charlie pulled away from their kiss and cried out again as another orgasm pulsed through her. They both lay panting for a few moments.

"That was meant to be your turn," Charlie said when she got her breath back.

"Are you complaining?"

"No." She kissed Erica slowly. "But I still want to give you your turn. Right now," she said before she kissed her way down Erica's chin, down her neck, down her body. She gave her a cheeky smile before her head dipped between Erica's legs.

Oh, God. They wouldn't be sleeping much tonight.

❖

Erica wasn't sure what time it was when she woke up, but she knew that she couldn't have been asleep for very long. She could see through the gap in the curtain that the sun was already out. She put her arms above her head and stretched her body out. That's when she realized that every one of her muscles ached in the most glorious of ways. She smiled and rolled onto her side and felt for Charlie, but the rest of the bed was empty. She opened her eyes then and looked around the room. There were clothes scattered all over the floor—*her* clothes— but Charlie's dress was gone. Erica listened for signs of anyone moving around in the apartment but there was nothing.

Erica got a sickening feeling in the pit of her stomach when she realized that Charlie must have left while she was asleep. She checked her phone then to see if she had a message from her. Nope. She checked the time—it was early, before eight—and Erica knew that they had still been awake at three-thirty. That's when she had got up to get them both a glass of water. They had been in desperate need after hours of strenuous activity. And they hadn't even gone straight to sleep after their water break. Charlie couldn't have left long ago.

Spending the night together had only intensified Erica's feelings for Charlie. It had meant something. At least, it had to Erica. She had been so sure that Charlie felt it too, but the evidence said otherwise. Charlie had given Erica the best night of her life, and then disappeared. Why would she do that?

The only conclusion that Erica could come to was that Charlie had freaked out and run. She had always feared that it would happen, and now it had. Despite the fact that Charlie had assured her that she wouldn't pull those kinds of stunts—not with her.

Erica didn't know whether to cry or be pissed off. She felt like both. She threw the covers off and grabbed her robe from the back of the door and went out to the kitchen to check if there was a note or anything. She looked around for a piece of paper that wasn't there. Hera was asleep in her bed, which was odd. Usually, she circled Erica's feet in the morning and demanded food and didn't give in until she got it. Erica checked and saw that the food had already been filled. Strange. Charlie must have fed her cat before abandoning her.

Then she heard keys in the door. Instinctively, she made sure her robe was covering her and tightened the tie.

Charlie walked back into the apartment carrying a bag and two coffee cups. She had changed as well. Gone was the dress, replaced with navy jogging bottoms and a white T-shirt. "Oh no. You're already up. I was hoping to be back before you woke up."

Erica frowned. "I thought you'd done a runner."

"The only place I ran to was the bakery to grab us some breakfast. I was going to bring it to you in bed." Charlie looked down at her clothes. "I stopped by my place to change quickly. Wearing the dress gave too many dirty stop-out vibes."

Erica felt her whole body relax. Charlie hadn't abandoned her or freaked out. She was bringing her breakfast in bed. Her cold panic was quickly replaced with a warm feeling. "You know, technically, you are a dirty stop-out."

"I seem to remember—a lot of those dirty things were initiated by yourself as well." Charlie walked toward her and kissed her softly. "Good morning. Sorry I worried you."

"You did a bit," Erica admitted. "I thought you freaked out and left, never to be seen again. Went straight to the airport and left the country was the scenario that entered my head."

Charlie looked bewildered by that. She shook her head. "Quite the opposite. I'm staying until you kick me out." She passed Erica one of the cups. Then she set the bag on the counter and lifted out a selection of sweet and savoury pastries. There was enough to feed about six people.

Erica gave Charlie a questioning look.

"I didn't know what you'd want, so I bought everything they had. Hungry?"

She smiled then because Charlie was just too sweet. "Starving."

"Eat here? Or do you want breakfast in bed?" Charlie asked.

Erica took a seat on one of the stools. "Eat here and then we can go back to bed."

"That sounds good to me. I don't know about you, but I am knackered." She yawned on cue as she took a seat on the stool opposite. Charlie obviously had a sweet-tooth—she had opted for a cinnamon roll and some other Danish with custard in it.

Erica went for a sweet and a savoury as she always did, because why would she choose if she didn't have to. "I am pretty tired." She sipped her coffee, fiddled with her pastry, and took a small bite. "But we don't have to go to sleep right away, do we?"

Charlie started to smile. "I'm sure I can manage to stay awake for a little while longer."

They both looked at each other at the same time. "Eat later?" Erica asked.

Charlie nearly fell off her stool as she jumped up. She grabbed Erica's hand and led her back to the bedroom. She had pulled her robe open before they even got through the door.

They ended up having cold coffee and pastries for lunch. They still hadn't slept.

Chapter Twenty

Charlie snuck into her apartment as quietly as possible. She opened the door slowly, pressed it shut as gently as she could, and tiptoed across the living room toward her own bedroom. She was floating in a big bubble of happiness, and she didn't want Val's negativity bursting it.

She had almost made it to her bedroom door when the door to Val's room flew open.

"Why are you sneaking round the place? It's creepy."

Charlie sighed and stood up straight. "I wasn't sneaking. I was being quiet in case you were asleep."

"It's six-thirty in the evening." Val folded her arms.

"Okay, fine. I was sneaking."

Val studied her. "This is you only getting home now from your date with Erica, isn't it?"

At least Val used Erica's name this time. Progress. "Yes."

"You stayed there? All night? And all day?"

Charlie nodded. "I did. And I don't want you to start giving me a hard time about it."

"I'm not going to. Just because I'm apprehensive doesn't mean that I don't want you to be happy."

They stood in silence for a few moments, then Val looked at her expectantly. "Well, come on then. How did it go?"

"Oh." Charlie couldn't have kept the smile off her face even if she tried. "So good." That was an understatement, but she was sure that Val didn't want all the details. Not when she was in a constant mood about Erica and her. "So, so, so good."

It had been so hard to tear herself away from Erica, but Erica had to go to the club, so Charlie had no choice. The more time she spent with Erica, the more she wanted.

Dinner with Liz and Nancy had been great. Being there with Erica had felt like finding the missing piece of a puzzle that slotted in perfectly to finish it off. Charlie hadn't even realized that her puzzle had been incomplete until last night.

Then there was the sex. Charlie was hardly a stranger to spending the night with a woman, but she had never had a night like that. Not ever.

They couldn't get enough of each other. Charlie had wanted to explore every inch of Erica's body again, and again, and again. She wanted to memorize all of it. The moans that Erica made when Charlie slid her fingers through her wetness. The way Erica gasped when Charlie pushed her fingers deep inside. How Erica's breath sped up as Charlie thrust in and out of her. The sound of Erica crying out when her orgasm hit. The addictive taste that coated Charlie's tongue when she licked Erica over and over again because she didn't want to stop.

She felt the spot between her legs throbbing and flooding again with the flashbacks of their first night together. It had been *that* hot that the sheer memories turned her right back on again. But it was more than that too. As much as Charlie couldn't get the sex out of her head, she also couldn't stop thinking about the other intimate moments that happened in between. The soft touches and caresses, the long looks into each other's eyes, the gentle kisses that they both poured all their feelings into, and the way they held each other close.

Val's clicking fingers snapped her out of it. "Oh my God. You are like, completely dazed right now."

"Hmm? What did you say?" Charlie was sure she looked guilty. She felt very warm all of a sudden.

Judging from Val's knowing expression, she'd noticed. "I asked you when you're seeing her again."

"I don't want to say because your face is scaring me."

Val laughed at that. "That means it's sooner than I would approve of."

"I'm only home to get a shower and hang out here for a little while and then I'm going to sleep there so that I'll be there when Erica gets back from work."

"But you aren't moving fast, no?" Val said. She was teasing this time.

"Who cares. Life is short."

"Just—"

Charlie cut her off. "Be careful. I know."

"That's all I'm saying." Val walked over to the kitchen and flicked the kettle on. "I got chatting to that girl Hannah last night when I went out. You know, the one you were with."

Charlie followed her to the kitchen and sat down. "I'll take a coffee if you're making one." She gave Val her sweetest smile.

Val pointed to the two cups in front of her. "Already on it. Save your sucking up."

Charlie laughed. "Thanks. So, Hannah then. What were you talking to her about?"

Val didn't turn round. "This and that." She paused for a few beats. "She's nice, you know."

What was Val getting at? Surely, she knew that Charlie wasn't interested in Hannah. Especially not now that she was with Erica. "Yeah. She's nice enough," Charlie said. "Wait. Do you like her?"

Val paused again before she spoke. "I'm not *un*-interested. You wouldn't mind, would you? I know you saw her first and all that, and I know you guys slept together, but you're practically shacked up with Erica now. I figured you wouldn't care." Val poured boiling water into two cups and stirred. "We were only talking last night, but I wouldn't mind if it went further if I were to run into her again." She turned around and passed Charlie a cup before lifting her own. "By further, I mean back to her place," Val added with a bravado that Charlie used to share.

"Thanks." Charlie sipped and aahed. "I don't mind at all. Go for it." Who knew? Maybe Hannah would end up being Val's Erica, and they would all live happily ever after.

❖

Erica was running late, but she couldn't resist firing off a quick text to Tess before she went into Oasis for her shift.

How did that strange robot salsa dance of yours go? She put a wink at the end of it. Tess would know exactly what she meant.

Erica wasn't usually the type to kiss and tell, but she was too excited about Charlie. She needed to tell her best friend about it. She also knew that Tess was going to lose her mind when she read it. She laughed to herself as she pocketed her phone.

She was beyond tired. Way too tired to work. But after taking Saturday night off she needed to be there for that next shift. Zachary had texted to inform her of that week's cash loss, and it was a sizeable amount. Someone was getting away with stealing from them right under her nose, and although she wasn't in a rush to solve it and get home again, she needed to get her head in the game before more money went missing. Whoever this was couldn't be allowed to get away with it any longer.

Besides, maybe Erica could stay in London for a while, even when she was finished up at Oasis. It wasn't like she was missing much back home. And technically she wasn't required to be there for anything. She could stall a little longer. Spend more time with Charlie. And with Zachary. And as a happy consequence, she could put off the inevitable complications that were going to arise when it was time to go back home. Eventually, she would have to face the music and make some difficult decisions. Choose whether to upset her old life or her new one. In the perfect world, Erica wouldn't have to make that choice, but Erica didn't live in a perfect world. She couldn't have it all. She could, however, delay giving up a part of herself for a little while longer.

She checked the schedule in the staff room when she arrived at Oasis. She was on the main bar with Ash, Damien, and Kelly-Ann.

When she went behind the bar, Damien and Kelly-Ann seemed to be having a heated conversation about something. She tried to be discreet while she hovered nearby to hear what they were saying.

"It's me who has to pick up your slack," she heard Damien say.

It was harder to make out Kelly-Ann, who seemed to be trying to keep her voice down. Between that, the crowd, and the blaring music, Erica could hardly make out a thing. She thought she heard the mention of Tom's name, but without the rest of the sentence Erica had no idea of the context.

"Yeah? Who can blame him? I'd love to know myself." Damien stormed off to the other end of the bar. Kelly-Ann blew out a breath and turned to look in Erica's direction.

"Oh. Hey," she said to Erica. She smiled, but it didn't quite reach her eyes.

"Hey. Everything okay?" Erica asked.

"All good. Just a difference of opinion between me and Damien. We'll be fine."

Erica nodded.

"Hey. You can hardly notice your head now," Kelly-Ann said. She put her hand over her chest. "Thank goodness. I was so worried when I saw you covered in blood that night."

"Yeah. It's fine. No need for worrying."

It was clear that Erica wasn't going to get any more information about the argument from Kelly-Ann, but it had piqued her interest. After they got over the initial influx of people that always came at the start of the shift, Erica made her way toward Damien to do some further snooping.

"How are you?" she asked with a smile.

Damien smiled back. "Good. I'm good. How are you, Erica?"

"Yeah, I'm fine." She fiddled with some of the bottles, turning them so all the labels faced the same way. "I heard you and Kelly-Ann having a bit of a tiff earlier. Everything okay?" She held her hands up. "Not being nosey or anything. Just making sure you're okay." *But if you tell me everything that would be great, thanks.*

Damien scowled. "I had words with her because she keeps going MIA. She disappeared last night for ages, and we were swamped behind this bar. Could really have done with the extra pair of hands."

"Where did she go?"

Damien lifted his shoulders and dropped them again. "Said she went to use the bathroom. But it didn't only happen last night. It's almost every shift."

Alarm bells started to go off in Erica's head. No way. It couldn't be sweet little Kelly-Ann. Could it?

"Anyway," Damien continued. "Apparently, I wasn't the first person to ask her where she was going to. Tom asked her about it as well. So, she's got her knickers into a right twist and gone on the defensive."

Erica needed to speak to Tom. Fast.

"Who knows? Maybe she gets overwhelmed when things get too busy," Erica suggested. In reality, Erica knew that Kelly-Ann's disappearances could be down to a lot more. But she wasn't going to jump to conclusions. She had jumped to them with Tom, and look how wrong she had been there.

Damien considered that. "I've worked with plenty of them types. Can't handle the pressure. You could be right."

Erica looked toward the door, but Tom was dealing with a queue, so she couldn't catch his eye. Then Erica got swamped with orders. Talking to Tom had to wait.

"You're getting so much quicker," Ash said to her with a grin. She stepped beside Erica and grabbed one of the measuring cups. "You're even getting most of the orders right."

"And I haven't smashed anything tonight. Check me out."

Ash laughed. "Keep it up, Erica. There's a great bartender in you yet. I knew there would be."

"I wouldn't go that far." Erica was able to bluff her way through a shift, but she wasn't anywhere near as good as any of the others behind the bar. Still, Ash was trying to be encouraging, and she appreciated it. "I heard you guys were busy last night?"

"Saturdays always are, but it was something else last night. Seems like all of London came out to Oasis," Ash said.

"Damien was complaining because Kelly-Ann spent too long in the bathroom or something." She wondered what Ash knew about it.

Ash passed a couple of beers to a guy at the bar and took a note from him. "Yeah, Kelly-Ann does that. I reckon she has a man she sneaks off to meet, you know." She punched the order into the till and grabbed the guy's change.

"You think?"

"Just guessing. I hadn't really noticed until Damien mentioned it to me a few days ago, but she does disappear quite a lot. Probably getting hot and heavy in the corner of the club somewhere." Ash chuckled. "You'd be surprised how often it happens."

A couple of girls across the bar shouted their order to Erica, so she got started on making two gin and tonics.

"What about you?" Ash asked. At Erica's questioning look, Ash grinned. "No lipstick marks tonight." She was teasing her. Maybe they were becoming work friends. She'd never had one of those.

"I'm surprised there aren't," Erica said without thinking. Talk about giving yourself away.

"Ooh. Is it anyone we know?" Ash asked. "I haven't been single in years, so I wouldn't know, but apparently in here is a great place to meet women."

Erica couldn't argue with that. Everything between Charlie and her had started right there at Oasis. "Maybe."

Ash's mouth dropped open. "Oh, now you have to tell."

"Remember the girl who was chatting to me a while ago? Charlie?"

Her mouth dropped open even further. "No way? I knew she asked for you the other night, but I thought she was just trying her luck again. I didn't think there was anything going on."

"There wasn't at first, but things have changed. Turns out she's my neighbour. We've got to know each other a bit since then."

"A bit? I know my postman a bit, but he doesn't leave lipstick marks on my neck."

Ash was funny. "I take your point. We've got to know each other a lot. She's different from how she comes across when she comes in here."

"I've always liked Charlie. I don't know her that well, but she's friendly. It's just…I always heard that she was a little promiscuous too." Ash grimaced. "Sorry, that's the last thing you want to hear. Maybe it's all bullshit."

Erica was well aware of Charlie's past, right up until they had got together. She didn't particularly like it, but she was focusing on the present-Charlie. She was even beginning to think that she was falling for present-Charlie, but she wasn't ready to fully acknowledge those feelings. It was too soon. But after their night together, it was getting harder to ignore it. "I get that. But things have been going good between us. We're seeing where it goes. Nothing too deep," she said, downplaying it to both Ash and herself.

"I really hope it goes well. I mean that. For both of you," Ash said. "You guys would look so good together. I can see it."

"We'll see."

The next couple of hours flew by. At least when the bar was busy, Erica didn't notice the time going by. The closer she got to the end of her shift, the more she allowed herself to think about what was waiting for her when she got home. Charlie had asked if she could sleep over again, and Erica had never heard a better idea in her life. She was starting to yearn for the feeling of Charlie's arms wrapping round her when she climbed into bed beside her later. Even though she had got very little sleep other than the odd snooze here and there, she wasn't thinking about sleeping when she got home. Not right away anyway. She hoped that Charlie was having the same idea.

"Erica," Tom said. He tilted his head for her to follow him, which she did. "That car just went past. It didn't park up, but I reckon he'll be being more careful. Maybe he'll park further away and walk round."

"Do you think he'll go to the alley?" Erica asked.

Tom shook his head. "Doubt it. Haven't seen him there again. Cocky prick will probably walk right through the front door. I wouldn't know what he looks like without his hat."

"What about the shoes? Look for the shiny shoes you saw, Tom."

He pointed at her. "Good idea. You keep your eyes peeled behind the bar. See if anyone starts acting funny."

"We'll work together, Tom. We've got this."

Tom nodded. "Any funny business tonight, and we'll get them."

"We better not be seen talking for too long. Find me again if you see anyone you think could be him."

They separated and went back to their own stations.

"What did he want?" Ash asked her when she walked behind the bar.

"He was just telling me that he moved some things in the storeroom. That's what he wanted the other day when he asked to speak to me—to check that I was okay because he heard that I fell. Said he would stack some of the crates whenever he got a chance."

"That's good of him."

"He's not actually so bad once you get to know him a little better. I know you think he's shady," Erica said.

"He just looks so angry all of the time," Ash said. "I guess that's his job. But that was nice of him to ask if you were okay." After a few seconds she said, "I *knew* it was the storeroom that you fell in."

Erica squinted at her. "Yeah, sure I already told you that."

"I know, and that's what Kelly-Ann told me too after it happened. Then last night she said something about a load of broken furniture still lying on the ground in one of the function rooms after your fall."

"What function room?" How would Kelly-Ann know about the furniture, or that she was in that room? Unless...

Ash shook her head. "I have no idea. Down that creepy corridor, I think. I don't go down there. Gives me the heebie-jeebies." She shuddered.

Erica frowned. "But I told her that I tripped over some boxes when I was grabbing drinks from the store. Why would she say that I fell over furniture in the function room?" It was like a bad game of Cluedo. Could it be Kelly-Ann, in the function room, with some chairs?

"I don't know. When I corrected her last night, she looked kind of panicky at first, then she just laughed it off. Said she must be losing it. We were so busy, I hadn't paid much attention to it, but now that I think about it, it was weird."

Erica looked around her. "Where is Kelly-Ann?"

Ash made a point of looking too. "I have no idea. Maybe she's getting jiggy down in that function room she was talking about." She laughed. "Probably her and her fancy man who broke the furniture and she wanted you to take the blame."

Erica attempted a laugh too, but she wasn't sure how convincing she was. "I'll be back in a second." She gave Tom a wave to get his attention. She tried to be discreet about it, and luckily, he was looking in her direction when she signalled him. He rushed over to her.

She leaned in to talk into his ear. "Kelly-Ann's not here. And she knows the truth about where I fell," Erica told him as quietly as she could.

His eyes widened. "I fucking knew it. I knew it was her. She tried to throw me off her scent by chatting me up." He crossed his big, burly arms.

"Never mind about that right now. What about Shiny-Shoes? Have you seen anything?" Erica asked.

Tom shook his head. "No, nothing. What should we do?"

Erica thought about it. They didn't know what this guy looked like, but they knew Kelly-Ann. "I think we look for Kelly-Ann. If that guy's not using the alley anymore, then she could be meeting him anywhere in the club."

"She'd have to stash that bag somewhere if she was passing it off to him."

Erica racked her brain. "The bathroom. The one in the back. She was in that bathroom right after I was pushed over that night. How about I check there, and you check that corridor to be on the safe side? If they're stupid enough to keep stealing money, maybe they'll be stupid enough to keep going to the same place."

"Nuh-uh. I'm not letting you go in there on your own. The bathroom's on the way—we can check there and then check the corridor together," Tom said.

She didn't have time to argue. "Okay. Give me a second." She went back behind the bar and told Ash that she was helping Tom, and she would be back soon. Ash looked sceptical, but she didn't ask questions.

Erica met Tom at the corner of the bar, just before the double doors that led to the staff area and bathroom.

"Go quietly," she said to Tom. "We need to catch her in the act. If we don't have proof, then it doesn't matter what we know or what we think."

Tom nodded and pushed the door open slowly. He held it open for Erica to walk through. He pointed to the staff room, and Erica waited against the wall while he eased the door open and had a look around. He turned back to her and shook his head. There was no one in there.

As they continued up the corridor toward the bathroom, the thud of the music faded some, which made their footsteps sound way too loud to Erica's ears. She put her arm out and touched Tom's arm to get his attention. When he looked at her, she pointed to their feet and put her finger to her mouth. They both eased up on their steps.

When they got outside the bathroom door, Tom counted to three on his fingers before he pushed the door open and rushed in, Erica hot on his heels.

"There's no one here," Tom said after checking the stalls.

Erica frowned. "The lights were already on, though."

"So?"

"They're automatic. Someone was in here before us. I'm not sure how long it takes for them to go off again," Erica said.

Tom pointed to the locked stall with the handwritten *out of order* sign on it. "How long has that been here?"

Erica looked at it. She lifted her shoulder. "It's been like that since I got here."

"You don't think it's strange that it hasn't been fixed yet?"

Erica hadn't really considered it. It was only a staff bathroom— well, staff and Charlie's, as she had somehow stumbled upon it too—a fact that Erica wholly appreciated. She found her gaze drifting to the spot where she had pinned Charlie against the wall. *Focus, Erica.* She looked back at the sign. There were still another four cubicles available, so it had never come under her notice that one wasn't working. Plus, the time Brandon took to get things done around Oasis, the toilet would never get repaired. If he couldn't move a few boxes to an empty room, what hope was there for a leaky toilet?

Tom seemed to have his own ideas. He went into the stall beside it and climbed on top of the toilet. He leaned over the top and peeked over. "No one there."

"Thank God for that or you would literally be a peeping Tom."

He grunted a laugh. "That's funny, boss." He reached down and opened the lock from the inside, before jumping down again and going to investigate. He pulled the flush on the toilet. "Doesn't seem too broke to me. Bet in here's where she's been stashing the money."

Erica nodded. "Makes sense. It's quiet down here. Right beside the staff room."

Tom scratched his stubbled chin. "And right by Brandon's office where the safe is. Bet anytime she's been sent to do money drops she's been keeping the lot in here."

"Which is precisely why there should be CCTV cameras down here," Erica said quietly, mainly to herself. It was ludicrous to her that there were none, especially given the amount of money that was stored along that corridor. Now that she was involved with Oasis, she would be speaking to Zachary about making upgrades to their security systems.

Tom made a grunting noise which Erica took as his agreement. "There's no one here anyway. Do you think we're too late?" he asked.

Erica pushed her hands into her pockets. "I don't know, we might be."

"If the exchange is done in here, then we are."

Erica thought about that. "I don't think it would be done in here. Someone could walk in here at any time. Feels like a big risk to take."

"You think she stashes it here, and takes it somewhere else?"

"Ash said that Kelly-Ann said something last night about the broken furniture still being scattered everywhere in that unused function room in the back," Erica said. "What if they are still using that room?"

Tom was already opening the door for them. "Let's check it out. Stay right behind me. Kelly-Ann might be harmless enough, but it was probably that bloke that shoved you before. He could do anything if we catch him in the act."

Maybe Ash wasn't wrong about Kelly-Ann sneaking around the back rooms with some guy—her reasons were just a little bit more criminal than what Ash imagined. They hurried around the corner to the corridor leading to the function room. It felt a little ironic that the last time Erica had been there she had been following Tom, and this time she was teamed up with him following someone else.

They crept along the corridor until they reached the end. Tom put out a hand to stop Erica from going any further. He pointed to his ear.

Sure enough, when Erica stopped and listened, she could hear muffled voices. They both got as close to the door as they could, without going near the window.

"Literally everyone is on to me. We can't do this anymore. Not right now. I need to lie low for a while before I get caught." That voice definitely belonged to Kelly-Ann. She sounded like she was crying.

The other voice sounded male. It was raised so it was easier to hear him. "Do you know how much we're lifting from this joint? And you think I'm just going to let you stop? I don't fucking think so, baby."

"But everyone has noticed that I've been disappearing. Tom's been on my case for weeks now—he knows something's going on."

"So, do better. Be quicker. Don't get caught. They can think whatever they want, but they can't do anything if they can't catch you."

"I can't. Please don't make me do this," Kelly-Ann pleaded. "Maybe we can start up again when the heat is off me. But it's too dangerous right now."

"You'll fucking do it if I say so, do you hear me?" the guy yelled.

"Stop. You're hurting me."

"Say you'll get me my fucking money. I want to hear you say it. Say it!"

Kelly-Ann sounded frantic. "Let go of me."

Tom looked at Erica with raised eyebrows and she nodded. He didn't waste any time before he burst through the doors. The room was in the same darkness that it had been when Erica had been there before. She stayed close to Tom as she followed him through the door, and she quickly felt for a light switch. She flipped it on and revealed Kelly-Ann with a man holding her by the throat at the opposite end of the room.

Tom rushed toward them. The room was like an obstacle course, but Tom threw chairs and tables out of his path. "Leave her alone."

The guy pushed Kelly-Ann into the wall, and she collapsed to the ground holding her neck. He threw a rucksack over his shoulders and started swerving and hopping between the tables that separated him from the door where Erica was standing. Tom changed course to try to get to him, but the guy was quick and obviously knew the maze much better than Tom did. By the time Tom even got to the route he had taken, the guy already inches away from Erica.

"Stop," Erica shouted. She positioned herself in front of the door.

"Not you again, lady," the guy said as he ran toward her and pushed her out of the way. Erica didn't fall this time—she was ready for him—but he was stronger than she was, and she stumbled away from the door. She turned back and tried to grab hold of him, but he shoved her off as he flung the door open and ran out. Erica went to follow him, but Tom appeared then and grabbed her arm.

"I'll go after him. You deal with her." He took off, sprinting down the corridor. If that room hadn't been packed with so much stuff, Tom would have caught him no problem. Erica was sure that it was no accident that they used that room and had an escape route already sussed out.

She wove her way through the tables until she got to Kelly-Ann, who was still sitting on the floor. Tears were flooding down her cheeks. "It's not what you think."

"No?" Erica said. "Because I think you've been stealing money and giving it to your boyfriend. I'm wrong about that, am I?"

Kelly-Ann sobbed some more. "It was only meant to be once. Please, Erica. You can't tell anyone. I'm begging you. Keep this between us and I'll never do it again. I swear."

"I can't do that, Kelly-Ann."

"You can. Just turn a blind eye—you and Tom. I'll do anything. They'll arrest me if you tell." She sobbed again. "I can't go to prison, Erica. Oh fuck, what have I done?"

Erica stared at her. She looked so lost sitting on the floor with her head in her hands. "Why did you do it?"

Kelly-Ann sniffed. "My boyfriend came up with a plan for some quick cash. There are some nights that they make so much money in here…a little going missing wouldn't even get noticed. All I had to do was take one of the money drops and pass it to him out the back. Then I'd go straight back to work again. It sounded pretty low risk."

"But you didn't stop there," Erica reminded her. "You kept going."

She shook her head slowly and closed her eyes. More tears ran down her cheeks. "He told me it was only a couple more times. And then it became something we did. He wanted me to grab some cash more and more often, and things started to get risky. The bosses obviously discovered the money was disappearing. People noticed things. Tom was snooping around. Then you came in here the other night and almost caught us."

"But you made sure that didn't happen. Didn't you?"

"I'm so sorry about that. I felt so, so terrible. You weren't supposed to get hurt. He was only meant to knock you off balance while I snuck out and then he was going to make a run for it."

Erica snorted. "I saw you in the bathroom right after. You're certainly a good liar, I'll give you that."

"I'm sorry. That shouldn't have happened. And I should have stopped. But he told me how much we were making, and he wanted me to keep going. Things just got so out of control."

"You didn't really expect to get away with it forever, did you?"

"Of course not. I just hoped no one would think to pin it on me." Kelly-Ann took a breath. "I was telling him tonight that I wanted out. That's why he got angry with me."

Erica almost felt sorry for her, but she knew she was only sorry because she got caught. If Kelly-Ann and her shitty boyfriend could have continued to get away with it, they would have kept going. "Yeah, well. It's over now anyway."

"It's over. I promise it is." Kelly-Ann stood up and wiped her eyes and cheeks with her hands. She ran a hand through her hair. "Look, Erica. Me and you, we're friendly, right? Is there no way we can keep this between us? And Tom. If Brandon or the big boss find out, I'm finished." She lowered her voice. "I can even cut you in on what we've taken, if that helps?"

Enough was enough. "There will be no need for that." She looked her in the eye. "I am the big boss, Kelly-Ann—and I've been here looking for you. It's over."

❖

The rest of the night felt like a blur. Kelly-Ann's boyfriend, whose name she refused to give up—Erica had no idea why she would protect that piece of shit, but she did—had managed to get away from Tom. It didn't really matter. It wasn't like they expected to get any of their money back. They just wanted to catch the inside man—or woman—and they'd done that. Erica was sure it was only a matter of time before the police caught the boyfriend too. They would probably be able to get a name from Kelly-Ann or do whatever investigations that police officers do to find out those kinds of things.

It had been quite a spectacle as the whole club witnessed Kelly-Ann being escorted out in handcuffs and put into the back of a police car. Erica did feel bad for her. She couldn't help it. She had even asked Zachary if it was really necessary to call the police—but he insisted that even if they sacked her and let it go, that she would only go and do the same thing to somebody else. He was right, but it still made her feel sad. Erica had liked Kelly-Ann. She was too sweet a girl to be wrapped up in something like this because of some scumbag boyfriend.

Zachary had been her first call, and he had arrived within an hour of her and Tom's discovery to help Erica get everything tied up. They contacted the police together. Brandon stayed in his office most of the time—Tom told her that Brandon wasn't happy that he had gone to Erica rather than straight to him. She would have to discuss Brandon with Zachary. He might not have been the guilty party in this—but she didn't see him as manager of her club either. Damien had been shocked that Kelly-Ann's disappearing acts had been down to criminal activity. Erica was just as surprised that clumsy Damien had turned out to be a big help in cracking the case by highlighting Kelly-Ann going missing in the first place.

"How the hell did I not see this?" Ash said, waving her finger between Erica and Zachary. "You two are so obviously related."

"Twins actually," Zachary said. "Though I'm clearly the better looking one."

Erica scoffed. That was only the fifteen-hundredth time that she had heard Zachary come off with that.

Ash put her hand on her head. "Oh shit. I told my employer that she's a bad bartender."

Erica laughed at that. "I am a bad bartender. And you told me tonight that I was improving. It's all good."

"I didn't even know there were two owners. How did I not know?"

"That's how she wanted it," Zachary replied, pointing to Erica. "The secret's out now, Sis."

Ash put her hand on her head again and groaned.

"What?" Erica asked.

"I told my boss she had lipstick on her neck. Teased her about it even." Ash covered her face. "Shit. I am so sorry."

Erica put her hand on Ash's shoulder. "Since I've been here you've been nothing but helpful, patient, and welcoming. Stop worrying. You haven't done anything wrong. And I was glad you told me."

Zachary stayed silent for a few seconds. It must have killed him. Eventually he caved. "You had lipstick on your neck?"

"I think we can leave that story until tomorrow, Zachary. Tonight's been a lot."

He blinked a few times. "Fine." He went to walk away but he turned back again holding a finger up. "But please tell me it was Charlie's?"

Erica tutted. "Yes, it was Charlie's. Okay?"

"Yes!" Zachary clapped his hands. "I knew it. I even told Olly that you two were going to get it on. I just knew it."

"Zachary…" she said with a warning tone.

"What? I'm allowed to be happy. But seriously, you two make so much sense. I don't know how, or why. But you do."

Erica didn't know how or why either, but she knew that Charlie made her happier than she had ever been before. She looked at her brother. "I know I've done my job here. But is Olly in a rush to get his apartment back?"

Zachary's look was knowing. "No one's rushing anything, Sis. You take all the time you want with that girl."

That was the problem. Erica was starting to think that having all the time in the world still wouldn't be enough—and now she had limited time to work out what to do about it.

CHAPTER TWENTY-ONE

Charlie was going to be late for work. She knew it—let it happen anyway. She should have been up for at least twenty minutes already, but since she'd started waking up tangled in Erica's naked body every morning, she lacked any and all motivation to move. More than once, she'd questioned if she really needed a job. She always came to the unfortunate conclusion that she did, but that didn't mean that she was happy about it. Okay, that wasn't true—Charlie loved her job—but the leaving Erica part, not so much.

It had been almost two weeks since Erica had climbed into bed beside her in the middle of the night and told her that she had caught Kelly-Ann. Initially, Charlie's heart had sunk, because that meant that Erica would be leaving.

But then Erica had surprised her and said, "I think I'm going to hang around for a little while longer. Make sure everything starts moving in the right direction at the club before I leave. Security needs upgraded for starters. Staff roles need to change."

It was the best idea Charlie had ever heard. They hadn't spent a night apart since.

She felt Erica shift, and strong arms tightened around her at the same time as warm lips kissed her neck. "You should be up already."

"I know," Charlie said.

"You still aren't moving."

"I know," she repeated.

Erica laughed softly. "I'm going to make you coffee, and you're going to get in the shower and get ready, before I have Liz knocking down my door yelling at me for being a bad influence on her star employee."

"That's just ridiculous. Liz never raises her voice." She moaned when Erica rolled away and started to pull the sheets aside. Instant loss.

Begrudgingly, she threw her legs off the side of the bed and got up. "Do you want to join me in the shower?"

Erica threw on an oversized T-shirt that Charlie had left there a few days ago. She looked amazing in it—leaving plenty of her long legs on show for Charlie to stare at, which she openly did.

Erica stuck her hands on her hips. "The last time we showered together you missed your first patient."

"I can be very quick this time."

Erica looked like she was considering it. Then she narrowed her eyes at Charlie. "No. I'm making coffee, temptress. Meet me in the kitchen in ten."

Less than thirty minutes later, Charlie was ready, caffeinated, kissed, and on her way to work. She could get used to that morning routine. It made her question what she had been wasting her time doing throughout her entire adult life—but then she realized she had been waiting for Erica. The morning routine only worked with her.

Charlie arrived at Little Paws with five minutes to spare and she shot off a text to Erica to tell her what they could have done in those five minutes.

Her phone buzzed with a reply within seconds. *Hurry home after work please.*

Charlie laughed. Her message obviously had the desired effect.

"What are you grinning about this morning?" Liz breezed past her and went to her desk. "Or do I even need to ask?"

"Let's just say, you can thank Erica for me being on time for work, much to my dismay—but don't expect me to hang around after."

Liz sat in her chair and swung from side to side. "God, I miss that new part of the relationship."

"Oh please. One day last week you got here twenty minutes late, and you couldn't get your hair to sit right the entire day."

Liz attempted to look surprised, but she wasn't fooling anyone. "Maybe I was having a bad hair day."

"Yeah, if bad hair days are caused by Nancy's firm grasp."

"Fine. Busted. My relationship is fantastic."

Charlie laughed. As if Liz and Nancy's relationship would ever die. That didn't seem possible. "I'm taking Erica out tonight. And then I think it's time we had a conversation about us. It's not like she's going to stay in London forever."

Liz hummed her agreement. "Probably wise to talk about it. Do you know what you're going to say?"

Charlie shook her head. "I haven't got it planned out or anything. I just want to make it clear that I want to be with her and see if she feels the same way. Then we can figure out how we could make that work."

"That's big, Charlie. For anyone. For you, it's massive."

Charlie held her arms out. "What's the worst than can happen? Either she wants me or she doesn't. And let's face it…" Charlie grinned. "Why wouldn't she?" Complete bravado. Inside, she was petrified.

Liz could see right through her. "It'll be fine. Don't overthink it."

Charlie blew out a breath. "Any other advice?" She hadn't been nervous before she started talking about it.

"Be yourself."

"That's probably the worst advice you've ever given me in my life." She lifted the clipboard. "Let's get our first patient in here before I throw up. What are we starting with today?"

"Squeezing Bandit's anal glands."

Charlie grimaced. "I'm not sure that's going to help."

❖

"You were awfully quiet during dinner," Erica said to Charlie, as they left the restaurant hand in hand. "Everything okay?"

"Was I?" Charlie knew that she had been. It wasn't intentional. Ever since she had decided that tonight was the night that she was going to tell Erica how she felt about her, she had struggled to think of any words that weren't *I love you*. Because that was how she felt every second she was with Erica. She just needed the right moment to say it. She turned to Erica and smiled to reassure her. "Everything is more than okay." She squeezed her hand. "If I had talked more, I wouldn't have been able to finish my pizza."

Erica laughed. "That makes perfect sense."

It was a mild evening, and they weren't too far from their apartment building, so by unspoken agreement they walked back rather than getting a taxi. Charlie tried to make up for her lack of conversation by telling Erica about her day as they walked home.

When they reached their apartment building, Erica opened the door for Charlie. "Why do we always walk up the thousand stairs it takes to get to our floor when there's a perfectly good lift right there?"

"I don't think it's quite a thousand."

"It feels like it," Erica said as they bypassed the lift as usual and started the climb.

"Stairs don't get stuck. Lifts do."

"Ah. I get it now. But if you were in a lift with me and it got stuck, I'm sure we could find some creative ways to pass the time."

They rounded the corner to the next flight. "Oh really? What did you have in mind?"

"If you beat me to the top, I'll show you." She took off up the stairs, heels clicking on the tiles, before Charlie even had a chance to react.

When Erica's words sank in a second or two later, Charlie scrambled up the stairs after her. "Seriously?"

She heard Erica's laughter up ahead of her. Erica might have had a head start, but Charlie was quick. They both burst through the door to their floor at the same time. They laughed breathlessly and wrapped their arms around each other. Charlie pressed her lips against Erica's. "What do I get for a draw?" she asked as she pulled away.

Erica leaned forward and kissed her again quickly. "I've got a few ideas. Follow me." She took Charlie's hand and hurried her around the corner and along the hallway.

As much as it had been nice for them to go out together, Charlie was looking forward to getting home again. Back to their bubble. She hadn't been able to kiss Erica the way she had wanted to all night—to touch her. They could spare a little time for that before they got to the serious stuff. They had all night, after all. Charlie would show Erica how much she loved her, then she would work up the courage to tell her with words.

Suddenly, she felt Erica let go of her hand, and it dropped to her side. Charlie felt the loss immediately.

"Mother," Erica said in a higher voice than usual.

Charlie looked ahead and saw a woman standing in front of Erica's front door. Erica's mum, so it would seem. Erica had told Charlie snippets here and there about her mum, none of them overly positive.

As they got closer Charlie observed Mrs Frost further. It was strange because her face didn't move at all—it bore no expression— yet it still turned cold. Sure, the older woman was very beautiful. Her clothes looked seamless and expensive. Her posture perfection. But something about her presence made Charlie feel uneasy.

"What are you doing here?" Erica asked as they approached her.

Charlie noticed how much Erica had stiffened beside her as well. Apart from dropping her hand, Erica put some distance between them too. She adjusted her already straight posture and walked even taller, if that was possible. And unlike the mum's, Charlie could read Erica's face. She looked like a deer caught in the headlights, even though she was trying to play it down.

"I came to see you, darling. You've been gone so long that I missed you. Your brother gave me this address." Erica's mum looked at the apartment door like it was diseased. Her face didn't adjust much as she shifted her attention to Charlie. "And who have we here?" She gave a smile that Charlie knew was as fake as the woman's lips.

Before Charlie could introduce herself, Erica said, "This is Charlie. A neighbour."

Neighbour. Ouch. Charlie tried not to show that the impersonal introduction had stung. She attempted a smile of her own. "Nice to meet you, Mrs Frost."

"Yes." Her gaze darted between Charlie and Erica. It settled on Erica. "This is why you live in the middle of nowhere on your own. It isn't common practice to hold hands with your neighbours, Erica."

Erica sighed. "Mother…"

Mrs Frost's eyebrows shifted upward as much as her face would allow, which was only very slightly. "I'm just saying it looked rather snug to me."

"We were just messing around," Erica said. She set her jaw in a way that Charlie had only seen her do back when they had first met— when Erica hadn't wanted anything to do with her.

Erica's mother laughed humourlessly. "Messing around? Imagine what Victoria would think if she saw what you were up to."

Charlie felt her unease intensifying. Suddenly, she felt nauseous. Who the hell was Victoria? Erica had never mentioned a Victoria before. She was sure that they couldn't be talking about a girlfriend, yet that's exactly what it sounded like. Charlie had never thought to ask Erica if she was involved with anyone back home, but given their recent relationship, it had been safe to assume that she was not. What was Charlie to Erica, then? Her London fling? A secret affair? *What the hell?*

"Don't start about Victoria right now, please, Mother," Erica said in a low voice. As if that was going to stop Charlie from hearing everything.

"What do you expect me to do when I see you hand in hand with some other woman. Victoria has been very patient waiting for you while you've come here on your little crusade to prove yourself. Then Zachary tells me you're done with that—yet you still haven't returned home." She eyed Charlie again. "I didn't realize this was the reason."

The reason, Charlie repeated in her head. The reason that Erica hasn't returned home to Victoria.

"The reason I haven't returned home is because I'm getting things sorted at the club before I return. Nothing else," Erica said in a cool voice.

Charlie knew she should say something. Anything. But she felt like she was frozen to the spot being stabbed through the heart by Erica's repeated dismissals and the revelation of Erica's secret girlfriend.

Erica and her mum were staring each other down. Mrs Frost spoke first. "So, there's nothing going on here?"

Charlie watched Erica swallow. It was the first chink in her armour that Charlie had noticed since this whole interaction had begun. "Of course there isn't. I told you, she's just a neighbour." Erica let out a cold laugh of her own. "As if there would be something going on between me and Charlie. Goodness—you think the most ridiculous things at times. It's nothing like that at all. Sure, it isn't, Charlie?"

The final blow.

Charlie looked at Erica then. Erica didn't look in her direction, which seemed pretty fucking rude considering she was basically putting a blade through Charlie's heart and twisting it round and round before ripping the heart out and stomping on it in her six-inch heels. She cleared her throat and hoped that when she spoke, she would be able to get the words past the growing lump in her throat. "Exactly. Nothing like that, Mrs Frost. We're nothing at all." She paused for a few seconds. "I'm going to go in now."

Erica's mum stared at her while she fumbled in her bag for her key.

Her hands were shaking, but Charlie held it up when she found it. "Goodnight to you both."

Mrs Frost gave her a simple nod.

Erica cleared her throat then but still didn't look at her. "Yes. Thank you for your help tonight. Goodnight." She got her own key out and opened her door at the same time.

Charlie didn't wait to watch them go in. She got her door open as quickly as she could and leaned her body against it as it closed.

That's when the sobbing started. The uncontrollable sobbing. It started silently, then got louder without Charlie even realizing it. She sank onto the floor as the tears started falling down her cheeks.

Val came out of her room then and rushed over to her. "What the hell?" She got on the ground beside her and hugged her. "What's wrong?"

Charlie sniffed and tried to take a breath to steady herself, but the tears kept on coming. "I think you were right all along."

"Oh no. Charlie." Val hugged Charlie while she cried. After a few minutes she got up and held her hand out. "Come on and sit down and you can tell me everything."

Charlie took her hand and allowed herself to be dragged off the floor. "You're not going to say told you so?"

Val shook her head. "No, of course I'm not." She sat Charlie on the sofa and then went to the kitchen to put the kettle on. "I'll make us tea. Tea makes everything better."

Charlie nodded because she agreed that was true. She wasn't sure if it would work with this, though. She felt pretty shitty. And pretty stupid.

A couple of minutes later, Val passed her a cup. "Now, tell me what happened."

Charlie took a few sips of the hot tea. It didn't make her feel much better, but it did help to stop the crying, which was something. She told Val about everything that had happened out in the hallway.

"Do you think I'm overreacting?" Charlie said when she was done.

"What? That she just dismissed you like you were absolutely nothing and treated you like you were a piece of shit on the bottom of her shoe?" Val's eyes widened. "No. I think you've got every right to be upset."

"You should have seen how cold she was, V." Charlie sighed. "I mean, if she didn't want her mum to know about us, then fine. Fair enough. Whatever, you know? I would have gone along with that. But this was brutal."

"Can I go in there?" Val went to stand up. "I'm going in there."

Charlie reached over and kept her on the seat. "No one's going in there. I could have said something at the time if I'd wanted to, but I didn't. There's no point. Even if she has some kind of excuse or explanation—it still won't change the way she acted."

Val leaned back in the seat again. "I wonder who the fuck this Victoria is," she said after a minute or two.

Charlie had been thinking the same thing. "No idea. She never mentioned anyone to me." She looked at Val. "I was going to tell her that I love her tonight." She felt the tears starting up again.

"Oh shit." Val gave her a sympathetic look. She got up and went back into the kitchen. She opened the freezer and pulled out the honeycomb ice cream and two spoons and returned to the sofa. "We needed something stronger than the tea."

"Do we have more?" It felt like more than a one tub kind of night.

"I stocked up earlier in the week," Val said. "We can eat ourselves into an ice cream coma if that's what you need."

That sounded exactly like what Charlie needed right then. She felt her phone buzz.

I'm sorry.

She held it up to show Val, who read it and snatched the phone off her.

"What are you doing?" Charlie shifted to try and look at the phone screen. "Don't reply to that."

"Relax, I'm not replying," she said as she tapped the screen. She passed Charlie the phone back.

"What did you do?" Charlie unlocked her phone and went back into Erica's message. Val hadn't written anything.

"Made sure you won't get any more messages."

"You blocked her? Don't you think that's a little bit extreme?"

"No. You need a break to get your head together without bullshit excuses and apologies. You can unblock her later if you want to—just give yourself some space first, Charlie. Trust me."

"You're right, I suppose. I don't even know what I'd say back anyway. She knows where I am if she's so desperate to speak to me."

"Exactly," Val said.

Charlie looked back at the message again before she put her phone down. *I'm sorry.*

Not as sorry as Charlie was.

CHAPTER TWENTY-TWO

E rica constantly lifted her phone to check it, but Charlie didn't send any reply to her message—not that she could blame her. Erica wouldn't want to speak to a disloyal, spineless coward either. She resisted the urge to message her again. She didn't even know how to begin to explain her behaviour anyway, and a text didn't really seem like an appropriate way to do so. She needed to see Charlie. Try to explain face to face. But she couldn't do that while her mother was there.

"It's not as bad on the inside," her mother said as she moved around the apartment inspecting everything.

Erica looked up from her phone. "The apartment's fine. It's been more than comfortable. It was very kind of Olly to let me use it." She looked back down at the phone screen again and opened her previous text conversation with her brother.

You could have warned me she was coming! Why did you tell her where I was?

She did get a quick reply from Zachary.

She's there? Shit. She asked me where you were staying but I never thought she would show up unannounced!!! Sorry, Sis.

Erica sighed and set the phone on the table face down so that she would stop torturing herself. Charlie wasn't going to reply. Erica knew that in her gut. She tapped her fingernails on the table and stared at her mother. "What are you really doing here?"

Her mother, who had still been carrying out her investigation of Olly's living room, turned to look at her. "I'm here to bring you home." Hera brushed herself around her ankles and her mother stepped out of the way. She wasn't exactly a cat lover. Hera got the hint and retreated to the sofa.

Erica ran her hands through her hair. She didn't like having confrontations with her mother. That's why it was much easier to agree with everything she said and go along with whatever she wanted. But sometimes, she needed to say *something.* "You do know that I'm almost thirty-six years old, Mother. Don't you think that's a little bit much?"

Gloria shook her head. "Well, I wasn't getting through to you on the phone, so I don't see what other options you left me with."

Erica kept her cool. "It wasn't that you weren't getting through to me. I wasn't ready to come home. I'm still not. We're upgrading the security at the club, and I want to make sure all the loose ends are tied up before I leave."

"And loose ends with your neighbour, no doubt." Her mother fixed her with a piercing glare.

Erica shied away from the scrutiny, which was probably telling. "It's got nothing to do with Charlie. I told you, she's just a friend." She felt terrible even saying those words, but nothing compared to the guilt she felt for saying them right in front of Charlie. She hadn't even given her the courtesy of referring to her as a friend then, instead referring to her as being the lowly neighbour and nothing else.

"Seriously, Erica. You must think I was born yesterday. I'm glad I didn't ask Victoria to accompany me like I was going to."

"Victoria and I have been on one date. *One.* Again, don't you think that's a bit much?" Once her mother decided that something was happening, it was impossible to change her mind. And she had decided with no uncertainty that Erica was going to be with Victoria.

Her mother approached her. "I'm not going to let you mess this up, Erica. Can you even imagine how that would look? What people would say?"

Oh yes. Because that's what was important. Erica's free will and happiness, not so much. She sighed. "Listen. When I get home, I will see what is happening between me and Victoria. We might not even be compatible."

Gloria laughed. "What does that matter?"

Erica blinked at her. Surely, she couldn't be being serious.

Gloria continued, "Financial security. Status. Connections. Perceptions. Those are the things that are truly important. That's the true reason for marriage—self-preservation. Victoria can provide you with all those things."

Erica pushed her chair out and stood up. "Funny. I can't imagine any of those being the reasons that you were with my father."

The next thing Erica felt was a sharp slap across her face. She immediately put her hand to the stinging pain in her cheek where her mother had struck her.

"Don't you dare speak to me about your excuse for a father," Gloria spat. "I wish I'd had the sense to listen to my own mother. But I learned, Erica, and I listened eventually—before it was too late. I won't allow you to make the same mistakes as I did. Do you understand me?"

"You're saying that I don't have a choice, then?" Erica said in a quiet voice. There was nothing quite like a slap in the face to put the fight out of a person.

"Oh. You always have a choice. But don't expect me to stand by you if you make the wrong one. I've given you quite the life, Erica. I think you would be very foolish to throw all of that away."

Erica nodded her understanding. She did have a choice. She could live her life however she chose, with whoever she chose, but she would lose her mother—or she could do what her mother asked. She always knew that was the position that she was in, but she had never known any alternatives to her life as it was. Not until she met Charlie.

Even thinking about the way that she had treated Charlie made her feel sick to her stomach. Her mother had a very strange effect on her—one she felt powerless to fight against—but that was no excuse. They had been having the perfect night—more than that—the perfect relationship over the past weeks. Erica had even had full intentions of coming up with a way that they could stay together after she had to go home again. She had been planning to talk to Charlie about it tonight, after their dinner.

But who was she fooling? That had only felt like a possibility in the absence of reality—because Erica hadn't been living her real life. The whole reason she was in London was to pretend to be someone she wasn't—so in those circumstances, it was easy to pretend that she and Charlie could work. Her mother arriving was a harsh reminder of what her life really entailed—and it wasn't Charlie. It couldn't be Charlie.

It would be the kind thing to do to let Charlie go now. Yes, she could probably buy herself a couple more weeks in London, apologize, and hope that Charlie could forgive her for tossing her aside and pretending she meant nothing to her. Maybe Erica could live her happy lie for a little bit longer. However, that wouldn't be fair to Charlie. There was no point in stringing her along when Erica now admitted to herself that their relationship couldn't go anywhere. She had thought it could. She had convinced herself that she could make it work with Charlie. But the moment she was faced with her mother she had crumbled on the spot—a stark indication of how weak she really was. She wasn't brave enough to choose happiness. And after tonight, she knew that she didn't deserve it. She wasn't worthy of Charlie. She had already indulged more than she should have. She had enjoyed Charlie. She even loved her. She had suspected that she had done for a while. But wasn't loving someone about wanting what was best for them? And walking away was the best thing.

"What about the club?" she asked. "I am in the middle of some upgrades." She didn't even know why she was still putting up a fight. She was well and truly defeated.

"Your brother will handle the businesses like he always has. I'm sure he can manage without you."

Erica nodded slowly in reluctant acceptance. She knew Zachary would be fine. It wasn't like he had needed her before.

"We'll leave in the morning. I've already booked us onto the ten o'clock train," Gloria said. She smiled genuinely for the first time since her arrival—she liked getting her own way.

"Fine." Erica tilted her head toward the door of the spare room. "You can sleep in there. I made it up with fresh sheets when I arrived. No one's been in it."

Her mother put her hand on her shoulder. "You know I only want the best for you, darling."

The stinging sensation in her cheek wasn't exactly proof of that. Still, she didn't argue any further. "I know that, Mother. Sleep well."

Erica on the other hand did not sleep well at all. She wasn't sure if she even got any sleep at all. For half of the night, she played back her behaviour out in the hallway on repeat and hated herself for it, and for the other half she just felt numb—as if her heart hurt so much that her body didn't know how to cope with the amount of pain it was going through, so it blocked everything out. If she hadn't already realized that she had fallen in love with Charlie, she was no longer in any doubt at all. It didn't matter and it didn't change anything, but it did make her decision hurt a hell of a lot more.

She watched the clock. She knew that Charlie left for work at 8:30. She hoped that her mother stayed in the spare room later than that to give her the chance to go next door. The least Erica could do was apologize in person and tell Charlie to her face that she was leaving, rather than just disappear. She knew that she owed her a lot more—but that was all that she could offer.

At 7:40 she swung her legs out of bed and took a few minutes to make herself look half presentable. At 8:02 she paced the bedroom trying to think of what she should say. At 8:15 she worked up the nerve to go next door and knock.

The roommate opened the door. From the look on her face, she knew everything. Erica knew that Val didn't like her anyway, but this morning there was a whole new level of hate. It was obvious.

"Hi. Can I grab a minute with Charlie before she goes to work?" Erica asked.

"She already left." Val went to close the door, but Erica stopped it with her foot.

"She doesn't usually leave until half."

Val looked down at Erica's foot, then back up to her face. She opened the door again. "She went for a run, then she went in early. Not that it's any of your business."

Erica hadn't factored in Charlie going for a run. She had got out of the habit in the mornings that they had spent together. "Look. Can you give her a message for me? She's not answering my texts."

Val snorted. "Can you blame her? After what you pulled last night? I don't think I will give her a message for you. In fact, I don't think Charlie wants anything more to do with you. So, why don't you go away and leave her alone."

Erica deserved that. But it didn't make it any easier to hear it. She cleared her throat. "I am, actually. I'm leaving this morning. She won't have to see me again, but I do want a chance to talk to her. Can you tell her that I'll call her tonight once I get back home? Please?"

Val stared at her. "Fine." She slammed the door shut in Erica's face.

Erica stood there for a few seconds. Maybe it was minutes, she wasn't sure. She wasn't going to see Charlie again. Possibly ever. She no longer felt numb, but she wished she still did. She felt like her heart was being squeezed in a vice that kept getting tighter and tighter. Tears burned the back of her eyes, but she refused to let them fall. What would her mother say if she knew that Erica had been crying?

She took a few deep breaths to steady herself and went back into her apartment. But it wasn't her apartment. It had felt like hers for a while—but it was Olly's place. Nothing in it was hers.

When she went to pack her bag, she was surprised by the number of Charlie reminders there were. A hair bobble and a half glass of water on Charlie's side of the bed. A pair of socks bunched up on the floor.

A jacket hanging on the wardrobe door. Charlie's oversized T-shirt that Erica liked to wear when she got up in the mornings was lying on top of the bed. She lifted it up and held it close, then she packed it into her suitcase. She had to. She needed to keep *something* of Charlie's. She packed the shoes that Charlie had given her for work too, in that sweet gesture that Erica hadn't deserved back then. She certainly didn't deserve any kindness now either.

She gathered up the rest of Charlie's things and put them into a bag. She was sure that Olly could return them to her. She didn't feel like facing Val the roommate's wrath again.

It didn't take Erica long to pack up her things. She stripped the bed and put on some fresh sheets. When she looked around, everything looked exactly like it had when she had arrived. She made sure that the rest of the apartment was left the same way. Then she gathered Hera's things and packed them and zipped up her case. Hera strolled into her cat carrier with no coaxing required—she probably thought she was going to Charlie's.

"I wish we were, Hera. We're going home."

When they arrived at the train station, Erica realized that the last time she had been there she had been dreading coming to London. Now, she was dreading leaving it.

The worst thing about realizing that she was making a terrible mistake was that she knew that she was, and yet she went ahead and did it anyway.

After a very long journey home, laced with constant snide comments from her mother, she made it back to her cottage. She went to her usual chair outside and she looked at the view that she had been missing so much. It didn't have the same appeal as it had before—not that night anyway. Not with how she was feeling. That was when she let the tears that she had been holding back all day finally fall. She let herself fall apart for a while and then she picked up the phone.

She almost hated the thought of hearing Charlie's voice—it would only make her feel ten times worse—but she had told Val to tell Charlie that she would call.

She tapped on Charlie's name before she could chicken out. Straight to answerphone. She tried again twice, but the same happened both times.

She didn't try a fourth time. She got the hint loud and clear. Charlie didn't want to hear from her again.

She typed out a text message to Tess. She could hardly see the screen because her eyes had filled up again.

I'm home.

After no time at all Tess replied.

Shit. I'm coming over

CHAPTER TWENTY-THREE

W hy do we never sit out here?" Charlie looked around the garden with its perfectly sculpted trees and flowers blooming in every colour. There was a small pond with a trickling water fountain that looked like wooden buckets pouring water into one another. It really was quite picturesque.

"That's what we were thinking," Nancy said as she took the seat beside Charlie. "Liz works her ass off out here and no one gets to appreciate it but us. Hence, the outdoor dinner party this evening." She put her feet up on the chair in front of her.

"I forget about Liz and her green thumb sometimes," Charlie said. She copied Nancy and put her feet up too.

Nancy lazily turned her head to look at her. "She's obsessed. I've been dragged round every garden centre in the city in recent weeks. Even some outside of the city too. I don't even know the difference between a shrub and a tree."

Liz approached them with a tray and set it on the glass table in the middle. Charlie leaned forward to peek at the selection of cheese and crackers on display. She didn't know how she would manage to fit anything else in after the meal that they had just finished, but she would give it her best shot.

"A shrub is smaller than a tree and you were not dragged anywhere. You moan if I don't take you with me. Listen to nothing that she says, Charlie," Liz said as she topped up all three of their glasses. She took the seat across from them and put one leg on top of the other.

"I never do. I'm not listening to either one of you ever again." Charlie didn't miss the look that passed between Liz and Nancy. They knew that she was referring to Erica. None of them had brought the subject up all night, so Charlie thought it was time to address the elephant in the room. Although Charlie didn't want to think about

Erica, it was proving impossible to forget about her. They might as well discuss it.

"I can't believe I got it so wrong," Liz said. She shook her head slowly. Charlie and Liz had already discussed Erica at work, of course. At length. Every day. No matter how much they talked it out, analysed it—neither Charlie nor Liz could make any sense of what had happened. To say Liz had been shocked would be an understatement. That was the first time Charlie had seen Nancy since, so Charlie was interested in her input.

"How long has it been since she left?" Nancy asked Charlie quietly.

"Two weeks? Nearly three? I'm not counting." Actually, it was two weeks and four days since she last saw Erica, and she absolutely was counting. She just refused to admit it. Charlie wasn't sure exactly when Erica had left, but it couldn't have been long after that night.

"And you haven't heard from her at all?"

Charlie shook her head. "Not since that last text message she sent. Val had her blocked on my phone, but I unblocked her after a couple of days in case she did call or text again. Alas, she did not."

"And Charlie doesn't want to reach out to her," Liz told Nancy.

"No?" Nancy said.

"Why should I? You should have seen her that night, Nance. She was so ashamed to be seen with me. She was able to just dismiss me out of hand and she didn't even blink an eye when she did it. And then she just leaves?" Charlie took a gulp from her glass. "No. I've got nothing to say to her."

They all remained quiet for a few minutes.

"The mother must be a piece of work," Nancy said.

An understatement. "You know like those rich and glamourous women you see on the TV? They look great, but they have no soul and can wither you with a single look? That's the mother."

"It doesn't excuse what Erica did by any means," Liz said, "but that must be tough. It's clearly a complicated relationship."

Charlie reached for a cracker and some cranberry cheese. Liz and Nancy followed suit as if they had been waiting to see who would cave first. It usually was Charlie. "I did get that impression from a few things that Erica had said to me before."

"Like I said, it's still not an excuse to snub you," Liz said. "Maybe a pathetic explanation for why she did, but it doesn't make it okay by any means."

"She obviously didn't have any real feelings for me, guys. Complicated relationship or not—Erica was ashamed of me. It didn't mean anything to her, our relationship. She would never have acted like that if it did."

Nancy frowned. "I really felt like she did care about you when I saw you two together. I don't believe that was faked."

"I think she did too, Charlie. I don't think that was the issue," Liz said.

"This woman Victoria, on the other hand, could very well have been the issue," Nancy suggested. She led the charge for the next round of cheese and crackers. Charlie and Liz followed her lead like sheep.

"Now you're talking sense." Charlie popped a cracker into her mouth.

"Do we know anything about her? Was there ever any mention of anybody at all?" Nancy asked.

"Never. That was the first time I ever heard the woman's name. Erica never gave me any indication that she was involved with anyone else." Charlie had racked her brain over and over, but she was sure of that.

Liz hummed her agreement. "Nance has a point. If Erica was already with someone and the mum came along and caught you together, that could explain her behaviour too."

"Still, not okay," Charlie said. "Possibly, worse."

"At least it would mean she wasn't really ashamed of you," Liz said.

"It would also mean that she was a liar and a cheater," Charlie said. "And a hypocrite. Don't forget how she treated me at first—and that was all because I looked at her when I was with that girl who I'd known for all of an hour."

Nancy snickered. "Still not great behaviour."

"No. But you get my point."

"Whatever the reason, if I ever see that woman again, she'll be getting a piece of my mind. No one fucks with our Charlie," Nancy said.

"Absolutely. We're always on your side, you know that," Liz added.

"Thanks guys." She was lucky to have such great friends. That's what was getting her through this whole heartbreak. "Anyway, you can understand why I never want to speak to her again."

"Couldn't agree more," Nancy said. "Forget about her."

Liz held her hands up. "I'd need the answers if it was me, but I understand what you mean, and I stand by your choice."

"What's next, Charlie? Back to breaking hearts all over London's nightlife?" Nancy asked with a grin.

Charlie blew out a loud breath. "I think I'm going to lie low for a little while. Take some time for me."

Nancy smiled knowingly. "Did my lovely wife suggest that?"

Liz raised her eyebrows and sipped from her wine glass.

Charlie laughed. "What can I say? You married a smart woman."

Nancy reached forward to hold Liz's hand. "Yes, I did."

As much as Charlie always admired Liz and Nancy's loving relationship, and still did, it stung a little to watch it now. She had been so close to having something similar herself, and now it felt like she was watching what could have been.

She swallowed back the lump in her throat that had become a daily occurrence since Erica had vanished. "You guys are coming out for my birthday next week, aren't you?"

"As if we would miss our Charlie joining the thirties club," Liz said.

"We are there," Nancy agreed.

Erica wasn't mentioned again for the rest of the night, but it didn't mean that she wasn't on Charlie's mind. She always was. Erica was like an unwanted squatter who had pitched a tent in Charlie's brain, and no matter what Charlie did, she couldn't get her to leave. On top of that, Charlie did silly things that only made herself feel worse. She read over their entire text conversation every night before she went to sleep. She looked at the three photographs that they had taken together and cursed herself for not getting more. She knew that she should delete the lot, but she could never bring herself to do it. Anytime she was in the hallway, she stared at Olly's apartment door as if Erica was going to walk out of it at any moment.

"Do you want to stay here tonight?" Liz asked her.

Charlie nodded. It would be a welcome change from her new routine of torturing herself. "Does that mean I can move in?"

"No," Liz and Nancy both replied at the same time.

"It was worth a try."

❖

Val was lying on the sofa scrolling through her phone when Charlie arrived home from work the following night.

"Hey. How was Liz and Nancy's?" she asked when Charlie dropped her keys on the kitchen table.

"Yeah. It was good." Charlie walked to the fridge and pulled out a drink. "Want anything?"

When Val didn't answer, Charlie looked round to see that she was staring at her. "What's up?"

"What do you mean?" Val said.

"You're watching me. I can barely pry your phone out of your hand to have a conversation at the best of times, and you've abandoned it. Look at it, lying there, all lonely, on the sofa. Something's up."

Val was a self-confessed phone addict. She only left it down when she had to. Charlie laughed when Val pouted and looked down at the forsaken object.

Val snapped her gaze back to Charlie. "Okay. There might be a couple of things I want to run by you."

Charlie walked toward the sofa and took a seat beside Val. "Okay, shoot."

"Well…" Val stalled again for a few more seconds. "You remember how I said that I was talking to Hannah?"

"Yeah?"

"And you said you didn't mind because you were with…*her*."

"If that's what this is about, I still don't mind, Val. Go for it."

Val put her hands over her eyes. "I have spent a couple of nights with her already." She looked at Charlie then. "Full nights. And days."

"Wow. That's not like you."

"It wasn't like you either, but you did it," Val said.

"No, I know. But I really liked…oh…." The penny dropped. She smiled at Val. "You like her."

Val screwed her face up. "I feel terrible."

Surely Val knew that Charlie would never stand in the way of her happiness. She was her best friend. She was gobsmacked that Val would think that she would be annoyed. "Why would you feel bad? It's great news."

Val lifted a shoulder. "But you saw her first. You guys hooked up already."

"You know that was just a bit of fun. If anyone understands that, it's you," Charlie said.

"I know, but still. Would it not be weird for you?"

"Not at all. And it shouldn't be for you either. There's literally no reason for you not to get with Hannah. I'm excited that you want to. That is *big*."

"It's not only that. It's the timing of it too. Here you are moping around with a broken heart, and I feel like if I pursue this, I'll be like… flaunting it in your face or something."

Charlie put her hand on Val's arm. "You know that I'm not that selfish, right? Just because I'm a bit down at the minute doesn't mean that I don't want to see you be happy. In fact, it would cheer me up to see you find your happiness."

"I don't even know if it will go anywhere, but we click, you know. I wasn't expecting it to happen—it just did," Val said.

"That seems to be how it works. Except we managed to avoid the clicking for a decade."

"We did, didn't we. For good reason. Though, thankfully so far, Hannah seems nothing like my toxic ex, so that's something." She gave Charlie a sad smile. "Speaking of toxic exes, how are you about Erica now?"

She took a deep breath and let it out again. "Sad. Upset. Annoyed at myself for being those things. I miss her, which annoys me even more, because I don't want to miss her."

Val lifted her phone and looked down at it. "I've been doing some digging trying to find her on socials. And I've stumbled across something that you'll either really want to see, or you really won't want to see. I don't know which."

Charlie sat in silence for a few moments. She let the possibilities roll around her head. She hadn't looked Erica up herself. It wasn't that she hadn't wanted to. She had almost been tempted a few times, but she reckoned that she was torturing herself enough and she didn't need to add any fuel to the fire.

She wasn't surprised that Val looked for her—social media accounts were usually the best way of finding information about someone, and Val was never off hers. As much as she knew that it would probably be better to remain oblivious, her curiosity won out.

"What did you find out?"

"You sure you want to know?" Val asked.

"Just show me before I change my mind."

Val lifted her phone. "Okay. It was actually pretty easy to find her." She tapped a few things on her phone. She turned the screen toward Charlie and sure enough, there was Erica's smiling face looking back at her. She looked amazing in her profile picture. Erica was dressed in an evening gown and at some sort of event. Her hair and make-up were perfect. The picture wasn't filtered, but then again, why would it be? Erica didn't need a filter. "The rest of her profile is private—but I dug a little deeper."

Tap, tap, tap. Val stared down at the screen. She winced.

"It's okay. You can tell me whatever it is."

"There was an article in one of the local magazines down there. It covers social events and things like that."

Charlie nodded. "Fancy people."

"Exactly." She scrolled on the screen. "I think I've found Victoria…well, I know I have." She hesitated for a few seconds and then reluctantly passed the phone to Charlie.

The title jumped out at her first. "Has There Ever Been a More Perfect Pair? We Don't Think So." When she scrolled down, there was a photograph of Erica with another woman. The woman's arm was possessively around Erica's waist giving out a clear message—*She's mine. Back off.*

The woman couldn't have looked more different from Charlie. She was older for starters—that wasn't a bad thing. She looked flawless. Distinguished. Her hair was dark and styled to perfection. She looked about the same height as Erica. And she looked expensive, if that was possible. She wore a perfectly fitted dress with a professional looking blazer. The outfit made her look chic, and like she could easily run the world single-handedly. They looked like a power couple.

Charlie studied Erica, who also looked amazing. She blew the other woman, Victoria, out of the water. Erica would blow anyone out of the water. Erica was smiling, but Charlie could tell that it was posed. When Erica smiled her whole face lit up, and this smile didn't reach her eyes. Charlie looked closer at the photo. She looked like Erica, but at the same time she looked nothing like Erica. She wasn't the Erica that Charlie knew. This Erica looked like she belonged nowhere else but in that superficial world of the rich and fabulous. She certainly didn't belong with Charlie, the veterinary nurse, in her leggings, in a shared two-bedroom apartment in London.

She skimmed the rest of the article. It was basically a journalist trying to decipher what labels they were wearing, who they were out with that night, and how hot their relationship was. Hot enough that the journalist had heard a rumour that wedding bells could soon be in the air, apparently. Charlie did learn that Victoria Barrett was some kind of high-flying barrister. Good for her. She was sure that Erica's mum didn't look at Victoria like she had crawled from beneath a stone.

She took one final look at the photograph, because she basked in heartache, apparently.

Why would she look like *her* Erica? This was Victoria's Erica, and probably always had been. Charlie had fallen in love with a woman that she could never have. She was crying over a woman that didn't care about her. Pining over someone who didn't want her back. Erica probably hadn't given Charlie a second thought since she had left.

Acknowledging that didn't make it hurt any less.

She passed the phone back to Val. "At least that's the Victoria mystery solved, then."

"I'm so sorry, Charlie," Val said. "I found that Victoria woman's profile and it isn't private, if you want to have a look. That's all I have on Erica, though."

Charlie shook her head and attempted a smile to put on a brave face for Val. "I think I've seen enough."

"I shouldn't have said anything. I thought it would give you some sort of closure—"

"Stop." Charlie put her arms around her friend. "I'm glad I saw it. You were right to tell me."

Val hugged her back. "You sure?"

Charlie nodded. It was a good thing that she knew. It hurt like hell, but maybe it was exactly what she needed in order to move on. She knew that's what she had to do. Erica was gone and had a fancy life and a Victoria. Charlie had nothing to hold on to anymore.

"Now, let's talk about more important things. Are you going to bring Hannah to my birthday?"

Val's face lit up even though Charlie knew that she was trying to hide it. "Maybe. If that's okay with you. Where are we going? We can't go to Oasis."

Charlie snorted. "Why not? It's not like she'll be there. I can go wherever I want." She smiled—her cocky Charlie smile this time. She had that one well-rehearsed. "And I can do whatever I want."

Val let out a cheer and clapped her hands. "Watch out, ladies. She's back."

At least Val was convinced. Maybe if she pretended to be her old self for long enough, Charlie could convince herself too.

CHAPTER TWENTY-FOUR

One of the things that Erica hadn't missed about home while she had been away in London was the multitude of boring events she had to attend. Erica had always hated going. Since she had returned home, she hated them even more, because her mother also insisted that she attended the events with Victoria by her side.

As she listened to Victoria bragging about purchasing her second holiday home for the fourth time that particular evening, Erica couldn't even pretend to look interested. Luckily, everyone was too wrapped up in themselves to notice.

"Maybe a good spot for a wedding," said Doug, the man sat across from them. He was a friend of Erica's mother.

As a man on his fourth wife, he would know, Erica thought to herself. "Whose wedding are you talking about, Doug?"

He let out a hearty laugh. "You don't have to be shy amongst friends, Erica. I saw the article saying that you two lovebirds weren't going to wait around." He waggled his finger between Victoria and her.

"Oh, Doug. You're such a gossip," Victoria said with a wave of her hand. She laughed quietly as she sipped her champagne.

Erica forced a smile. "What article is this?"

"Have you not seen it?" He lifted his phone from the table and tapped a few times. "Here." He turned the phone toward Erica.

She scrolled through it quickly. "I don't know where they got that idea."

Victoria, still smiling, turned to her. "You know that the reporter is good friends with Gloria."

Doug gave an over-exaggerated wink. "Mums know these things."

Erica passed the phone back. "Or think they do," she muttered.

Victoria shifted nervously beside her. "All in our own time, right, Erica?"

Erica sipped her champagne without answering.

As Victoria brought Erica home, she felt a whole new dread building up inside her. She dreaded going out with Victoria, then she dreaded returning home. Victoria always went in for a kiss. The thought of kissing Victoria, or anyone who wasn't Charlie, repulsed her. Not that Erica ever let it happen, but it was still awkward. Erica turned her head so that Victoria only got her cheek.

There wasn't any time of the day that Charlie wasn't on her mind. She had hoped that spending time with Victoria would help her move on. That ended up being a very naïve thought. Being with Victoria only made Erica yearn for Charlie even more. Now that she had seen what love was really about, she was painfully aware of what she was missing.

She had almost contacted Charlie so many times. Each time she stopped herself. What would contacting her achieve now? They still couldn't be together. Erica couldn't make any of her behaviour okay.

Charlie hadn't made any attempts to talk to her either, even though Erica had hoped that maybe she would. But there had been nothing. Charlie obviously didn't want to speak to her. Who could blame her?

But Erica still never stopped thinking about her. She spent most of her nights, which were once so peaceful, in a state of regret. Even Hera hadn't been the same since they had got back. Erica was convinced that it was because she was missing Charlie too. Maybe she was projecting her own feelings onto Hera, but she and Charlie had got close. Who knew what went through a cat's mind?

Instead of enjoying her view, which somehow seemed to remind her of Charlie—which was weird because it had nothing to do with Charlie—she climbed into bed. Hera jumped in beside her and cuddled in close, as if she could sense that's what Erica needed.

When she closed her eyes, she tried to picture what Charlie was doing. Was she in her apartment? Was she at Oasis moving on with some other girl on the dance floor? Maybe she was at Liz and Nancy's?

It didn't really matter—the only thing that mattered was that Charlie wasn't with her. She let her heart hurt for a little while longer before she closed her eyes, because she deserved to feel the pain of that reality. Then she did what she did every night. She closed her eyes and pretended that she was back in London, and Charlie had just got up for work. She imagined Charlie kissing her good-bye before she left her in bed, and when she tried really hard, she could almost feel

Charlie's lips on hers. None of it was real—not anymore—but living in her own fantasy helped her fall to sleep.

She would deal with the disappointment again in the morning.

❖

Erica chose to meet Tess at a restaurant a bit further from town. If they met at any of their usual spots, she ran too big a risk of running into her mother, or Victoria, or at least someone who would bug her about her *hot new relationship.*

Tess was already there waiting for her by the time Erica arrived. She stood and waved Erica over to the table.

"It looks nice in here," Erica said as she leaned in and gave her best friend a hug in greeting.

"It does, doesn't it?" They both went to sit down. "Don't worry, I've already scoped the place out and I haven't seen anyone we would want to avoid."

Erica had a quick look around herself. She whipped back round to look at Tess. "That's Audrey over there. Table by the window," she whispered.

Tess checked it out discreetly. "I didn't see her. Who's that she's with?"

Erica risked another quick look over her shoulder, but Audrey was staring right back at her this time. Erica raised her hand and waved. Audrey waved back, but she looked like she had seen a ghost. She said something to the woman she was with before standing up and heading toward her and Tess.

Erica had always liked Audrey. She wondered if she had got over the worst of being the gossip mill's latest topic. She was probably about to find out.

"Hello, Audrey. How are you?" She stood and air-kissed the woman on each cheek. Tess did the same.

"Hello, ladies. I wasn't expecting to see you all the way out here." Her smile didn't falter but her eyes gave her away. She looked back over her shoulder at the woman she was with. That's when Erica realized why Audrey looked like she had been caught in the act. Erica thought back to Victoria's indignant tirade about Audrey and the waitress she was dating weeks ago. Erica was in little doubt that Audrey's woman friend was the waitress in question.

Erica tried to put Audrey at ease. "We were in no mood for wagging tongues or judgemental opinions today."

Audrey noticeably relaxed. "It seems like we are here for the same reasons, then. It's a shame that we have to travel so far to have some lunch in peace."

"Tell me about it." Erica indicated to the other woman with her head. "A nicer atmosphere for your friend too, I'm sure."

Audrey let out an exasperated breath. "An understatement, Erica."

"You remember my friend Tess? She's attended some charity dinners with me as my plus one."

"I do. It's lovely to see you again, Tess," Audrey said.

"And you, Audrey."

"Erica, could I ask you not to mention to your girlfriend that you ran into me here with Jane? You know what people can be like. We're keeping a low profile for now."

The waitress did have a name, then. It was nice to finally learn it. "I'll not say a word to anyone. And for the record—Victoria is not my girlfriend, if that's who you mean." It felt good to say that out loud.

"Oh?" Audrey sounded surprised. "Sorry. I just assumed." She held her hands up. "Wrong of me to do so. But, well...you know what it's like."

Erica put a hand on her arm. "Of course I do. I'm guilty of it too. Victoria told me that you were still with Lydia."

She shook her head. "I ended that, despite what everyone else thought about it. Everyone kept telling me who I should or shouldn't be with. I'm ashamed to say that I almost gave in to it too, in a moment of weakness." She smiled at Jane and waved her over. "Thank goodness I saw sense." Jane approached them looking a little bit sceptical, but she gave them a warm smile nonetheless. Audrey put her arm around her. "Jane, these are friends of mine—Erica and Tess. And this is my girlfriend, Jane," she said proudly. Audrey looked at Jane with what could only be described as pure adoration.

Jane beamed. Erica thought they might be witnessing an important step in their relationship. She was sure that there weren't many of their friends that Audrey could introduce Jane to as her significant other. "Great to meet you guys," Jane said.

"It's so good to finally meet you," Erica said. She meant it too. Good for Audrey for having the nerve to go against everyone in her life to be with the person she loved. If only Erica had her courage. She turned to Audrey. "I envy you."

"What do you mean?" Audrey asked.

"Let's just say that recently I *was* too weak, and I did give in." Erica gave her a sad smile. "It's a long story. For another time"

Audrey looked sympathetic. "It can be so much easier to go along with expectations. I've done it myself too many times, Erica. You know as well as I do how strange our world can be. But I'm glad that I stood up for what I wanted this time. Maybe the next time you get a chance, you'll stand up for yourself too."

"That's what I keep telling her," Tess said in agreement. She turned to Erica. "And it's never too late to try and fix things."

Erica didn't see any way back. She had already done irreparable damage to her relationship with Charlie. She had chosen her path, even if she knew it was the wrong one.

They said their good-byes to Audrey and Jane and took their seats again.

Erica picked up her menu and studied it intently to avoid Tess's inevitable stare. "What should we order?"

Tess cleared her throat. "Just because you've chosen not to look at me doesn't mean that you can pretend that you don't know what I'm thinking. Did you see how happy they are?"

"I saw." Erica kept her eyes on the menu. "Everything looks so good. I don't know what to pick."

"You know that you can be happy too. It's okay to choose happiness. Even Audrey just said it was the best decision she'd ever made."

Erica looked at Tess then. "Audrey doesn't have my mother breathing down her neck."

"Is pleasing Gloria *really* worth it? You're miserable! You have been from the second you got back," Tess said.

Tess was right, Erica *was* miserable.

There wasn't one second of any day that she didn't regret what she had done. If she could go back in time and do everything differently, she would. And it hadn't been worth it. She had thrown everything away, and it still wasn't good enough for her mother. But the damage had already been done with Charlie. "I know I made a mistake, but there's nothing I can do about it now."

Tess frowned at her. "Of course there is. You've just admitted that it was a mistake. So change it. The only thing getting in your way is you."

"It's too late. Charlie must hate me—*I* would." Every time Erica replayed that night in the hallway in her head, she was overwhelmed with shame. How could she ever come back from that? She deserved to be miserable. "At the very least, I know she doesn't want to speak to me. She could have called or something if she wanted to."

Tess reached over and covered Erica's hand with her own. "Maybe she doesn't. But why don't you try anyway? You'll only wonder *what if* otherwise."

"There's no point. I messed it up, and now I have to live with that." She glanced down at her menu again before she lost the battle with her tears. "Can we talk about something else?"

She heard Tess sigh. "Okay, okay."

Tess didn't mention Charlie again during their lunch. Erica was both glad and disappointed about that. She couldn't help but glance round every so often to look at Audrey and Jane. They looked so happy, so in love. Watching them together felt like torture. Erica could have had that. She did have it. She'd thrown it away for a shell of a life and an ungrateful mother, whom she should have outgrown trying to impress years ago.

As she finally watched Audrey and Jane leave the restaurant hand in hand, her heart ached for what could have been. *It's never too late to try and fix things.* Tess's words from earlier echoed in her head. But she couldn't have another chance, could she?

Maybe she should at least apologize. She had never got to do that, other than one pathetic, unanswered text message. Surely, she at least owed Charlie a proper *sorry*, even if Charlie ended up slamming the door in her face. At least then Erica would know for sure that there was no chance. But if Charlie didn't slam the door, and Erica could tell her how she felt and show Charlie that she was truly sorry, then maybe— just maybe—could she dare hope to get another chance?

"Oh, sod it." Erica quickly stood and pushed her chair back. "I have to go."

"What? Where?" Tess looked bewildered.

"London."

Tess grinned. "It's about time."

❖

She rushed home from the restaurant and checked the train times. Not wanting to wait any longer than she had to, she booked the train leaving in three hours. She gave her cottage a quick clean, cleared out her fridge, sorted Hera's things, and she was almost finished packing when she realized that she might not have a place to stay. How did people live this impulsively?

She texted Zachary. *Is Olly's place still available? Tell him I'll pay him whatever he wants if I can move back in right away.* Erica hoped Olly hadn't rented it to someone else yet. This was why she wasn't usually spontaneous. There were things to sort out.

She grabbed her phone the second it beeped. *It's all yours. Oh yay! Does this mean that you've finally seen sense?* She laughed to herself and threw the phone on the bed. She could fill Zachary in on the train. She needed to finish packing.

There was a bang at her front door. She checked the clock. She didn't have time for whoever it was, but they banged again. She rushed to get rid of them, but when she pulled open the door, her mother came storming in.

"You haven't been answering my calls," her mother said as she walked past her. Erica pushed the door shut and followed her into the living room. "What are these?" She pointed at the two bags that Erica had already packed.

Erica tried not to sound as annoyed as she felt. "They are my bags, Mother. I'm going back to London."

Her mother's shrill laugh sounded in the quiet room. "Whatever would you be going back to London for? Your little business escapade is over."

There was no point in making excuses or trying to hide anything. Not anymore. "I'm going back to see Charlie."

Her mother looked disgusted. "The neighbour?"

"She was never just a neighbour. I think you know that."

"Then what exactly was she, Erica? Spit it out." Her tone indicated that she already knew.

Erica sighed. "She was everything. She *is* everything. She's a fantastic veterinary nurse, and she's a kind, loyal, sweet person. I should never have hurt her."

Her mother glared at her for what felt like an eternity. Erica felt like squirming under the scrutiny, but she kept her head held high. Finally, Gloria spoke. "I will not let you throw your life away because of some fling. I was almost stupid once, like you are now. My mother made sure that I didn't settle for some silly man who was never going to amount to anything. We are better than that, Erica."

"You mean my father?"

Her mother scoffed. "Rick was never a father. The best thing I ever did was send him away and protect you from him. Full of romantic ideas and nonsensical dreams. My mother was right, he was never going anywhere. He would only have dragged me down. Dragged you and your brother down. You marry up, Erica, not down."

Erica had always known there was more to the story when it came to her father, but never once did she think that her mother would have kept him away from them. She had always believed that was his choice. "He tried to see us?"

"Oh, for a while. Then he gave up, didn't he? He could have contacted you when you were grown, but he didn't. He was away playing in those silly bars of his. He didn't care about you."

For the first time in her life Erica felt defensive about her father. "Those *silly bars* are very successful. He *did* make something of himself. He proved you wrong. He built his own little empire, and he left it to us. So, no, he never forgot us, even though it seems that you tried to make sure that he did." Erica stormed back to her bedroom to finish packing. If she hadn't already decided to distance herself from her mother, she did now. Her mother was worse than she had ever realized.

Her mother followed her. "What about you and Victoria?"

"There is no *me and Victoria*. She knows it, I know it, you know it." She lifted two sets of heels to choose from, looked at them, then threw them both in her bag. "I'll call her and explain. Besides, I hear Lydia is available again. Victoria always thought she was quite the catch." She was half joking, but she wouldn't be surprised if they did get together. That's how things worked around here.

Her mother's expression was incredulous. "You are so ungrateful. So selfish. And so very stupid if you throw away a successful woman like Victoria. I won't let you do it. After all I've done for you. You're not going to humiliate me like this."

Erica folded a coat into her bag and zipped it up. "It's not about you. I never wanted to disappoint you. In fact, I almost destroyed myself in the process of trying to please you. But it's gone on too long, and enough is enough. It's my choice and I'm going."

"Then you and I are done," her mother replied coldly. She turned and left Erica's room.

As much as Erica expected her mother to react exactly this way, it still hurt. She followed her and stopped her just as she opened the front door to leave. "You're my mother and I love you, so I really hope that's not true. I would love it if you could support me and understand why I need to do things my own way. I hope, when you aren't as angry with me, that you will be able to do that. But if you can't, then always remember that's your choice. I would and will never turn you away."

Erica jumped as the door slammed closed with a bang.

CHAPTER TWENTY-FIVE

I am not wearing the badge," Charlie said.
"It's compulsory. You're wearing it." Val ignored her protests and clipped it onto her dress. "There. Don't touch it."

Charlie glared at her. "I don't need to advertise my birthday."

"Why not? Maybe you'll get a birthday kiss from a hot stranger." Val wiggled her eyebrows up and down.

"Who's kissing hot strangers?" Nancy asked, as she and Liz returned from the dance floor and slid into the booth beside them.

"No one is kissing hot strangers. I'm definitely not," Charlie said. "Look how it turned out the last time I kissed someone here."

"She has a point. Maybe Charlie should steer clear of Oasis women for now," Liz said. Always the level-headed one. Charlie gave her a grateful look.

"Spoilsports." Nancy turned to Val. "What about your girl? Hannah, was it? Are you inviting her to join us?"

Charlie laughed when Val's cheeks reddened. Val had been seeing Hannah exclusively for weeks, but she still refused to call it dating. Charlie knew that Val would come round in her own time, so she didn't push the subject. However, Nancy was Nancy.

"She might come after she finishes work," Val said. "And she's not my girl," she mumbled after.

"She's not? Why?" Nancy asked.

"It's a casual thing," Val said.

Nancy waved her off. "Nonsense. Charlie told me you guys have been dating for a while now. Didn't you, Charlie?"

"Leave me out of it." Charlie gave Val a grin. "It has been weeks, though."

Val glared at her, and Charlie laughed.

"See. You should just ask her out properly. What do you think, Charlie?" Nancy asked.

Charlie shrugged. "I think she should."

"Don't let these two pressure you, Val." Liz threw Charlie and Nancy both a look.

Val sat back with a smug look on her face. "Exactly. Pressurizers."

Everyone burst out laughing.

Ash approached their table with a tray of drinks. Charlie pointed to the tray. "We didn't order these." She hadn't noticed anyone go up to the bar. "Did any of you get a round in?"

They all shook their heads.

Ash smiled. "The boss sent these over. Says they're on the house." She unloaded the tray and looked at Charlie. "Oh, and the birthday girl gets free drinks for the rest of the night too."

Charlie hadn't expected that. "Wow. Thanks, Ash."

"No problem. Enjoy, everyone. Give me a shout if you need anything," Ash said.

When Charlie looked around the table, Val, Liz, and Nancy were all watching her. "Zachary must be here. Erica's brother," she explained.

Nancy gave her a sympathetic look. "Are you okay?"

"I'm fine." Charlie smiled to prove it. "Zachary is lovely." She looked around to see if she could spot him anywhere. "I'll have to thank him."

"Will it not be awkward seeing the brother?" Val asked her.

"I mean, I was always going to run in to him at some point, wasn't I? Either here or if he was at Olly's place. Might as well enjoy some free drinks while I do." She didn't feel quite as cool as she was playing it, but it would be fine.

Nancy looked at something behind Charlie, and she nudged Liz with her elbow. She leaned in and whispered something in Liz's ear, and Liz's gaze shifted to the same spot as Nancy's.

"What's wrong?" Charlie went to turn around to see what they were looking at, but Liz grabbed her arm. Charlie looked down at Liz's hand and then gave her a questioning look.

"I don't think the drinks were from Erica's brother," Liz said.

Charlie froze. If they weren't from Zachary, that could only mean one thing.

Val turned round to look. "Oh, for fuck's sake."

Charlie didn't need to look round to realize who they were looking at.

Erica.

Charlie had to remind herself to breathe. She was certain that her heart hadn't actually stopped, but it sure felt like it had. The worst thing was, that mixed with the shock and apprehension she was feeling, was excitement that Erica was there. Charlie hated that Erica still had that effect on her after everything.

"Let's go somewhere else," Val said.

Charlie made herself snap out of it. "No. Don't be silly, guys. I'll be fine." She fidgeted with the drink in front of her. The drink that Erica had sent.

"I'm going to speak to her," Nancy said. She started to slide out of the booth and Liz stopped her.

"What's that going to achieve?" Liz asked. "What do you want us to do, Charlie?"

She was still staring at the drink. "Hmm?"

"Will I have a word with Erica?" Nancy said.

Charlie looked at her then. "No. It's not worth it. Just pretend she isn't there." She took a long drink so she could collect herself, then she tried to act unfazed. "What were we talking about?"

The subject was quickly changed. Everyone acted a bit awkward, but they made an obvious effort to distract Charlie and take her mind off Erica. An impossible task, but Charlie appreciated their efforts. She tried to nod and laugh at the right parts of the conversation, but in truth, she only heard about every tenth word. Her mind was firmly on the woman behind her. She was dying to turn around, and it took everything in her power to stop herself from doing so.

Erica was back. Why was she back?

Oasis *was* Erica's club, so Charlie supposed that her being there had never been completely out of the realm of possibility. It had seemed pretty bloody unlikely, though.

She probably managed to stay in her seat for a full fifteen minutes before she caved.

"I'll be right back." At Val's cynical look she said, "I'm only going to the bathroom. Don't worry. I just need a minute." Charlie slipped out of the booth.

Don't look behind the bar. Don't look behind the bar.

She looked behind the bar—as if she could stop herself. And there she was. It was really her. Erica—who was looking unfairly beautiful— was talking to Ash. She hadn't seemed to notice Charlie looking at her. Charlie wasn't sure whether to be disappointed or relieved about that. She went with relieved because no part of her should want Erica noticing her.

She rushed toward the bathroom. Not the staff one, she wasn't that stupid. She went to the normal one with the queue of about fourteen women in front of her. After five or six minutes of waiting she got a cubicle. She locked herself in, put the lid down on the toilet, and sat down. "Okay, Charlie. Just breathe," she whispered to herself so no one would hear.

Erica could have been back for any number of reasons—none of them to do with her. Maybe she was as surprised to see Charlie, as Charlie was to see her. Maybe Erica had hoped not to run into her.

Charlie looked down at her chest—that stupid, big badge displaying the fact that it was her birthday for all to see. Erica had probably seen it and then felt obligated to send her a drink. It didn't mean anything.

She needed a game plan. Everyone was out to celebrate with her, so she couldn't ditch. Leaving and going elsewhere seemed unnecessary, and besides, why should she? She could see who else was out that night—see if there were any women she could dance her night away with. What would Erica think of that? But that seemed juvenile in the circumstances.

Her best option was to stay at the booth with her friends for another couple of hours, avoid the bar, ignore Erica's existence, and head home again. That's what she would do.

She left the cubicle and washed her hands before heading back out toward the main floor.

"You don't trespass in staff only areas anymore?" Erica's voice came from somewhere behind her.

Charlie turned around to see Erica leaning against the wall looking sinfully good in a fitted black dress and her signature heels. She swallowed. "Thought I better not. Only seems to get me into trouble."

Erica pushed herself off the wall and walked toward her. "Hi. Happy birthday."

Charlie tried to swallow again but her mouth had gone dry. "Thanks. And thank you for the drink. Drinks. You didn't have to do that."

"You're welcome." Erica didn't take her eyes off her. "We need to talk."

"We don't have anything to talk about, Erica. I need to get back to my friends. Excuse me." She turned to head back to her booth, but Erica's voice stopped her.

"Please, Charlie. I have things that I really need to say to you. Can we talk for a few minutes? Later even?"

Did Erica really think she could just waltz back to London after everything, and Charlie would just do whatever she asked? There was nothing that Erica had to say that Charlie wanted to hear.

"No. We can't. Why don't you go and talk to your girlfriend? Victoria, is it? Speak to her." Charlie stormed off back in the direction of the booth.

"Everything okay?" Nancy asked her when she sat down.

"Fine," Charlie said, sharper than she intended.

Val eyed her. "Take it you saw her, then?"

"Yeah. She wants to talk. I said no."

"We were talking while you were at the ladies'," Liz said. "It's your birthday, Charlie, and we refuse to allow Erica to spoil your night. We were thinking of drinking these, then heading back to yours and Val's place."

"Pick up a couple of bottles of wine on the way," Nancy added. "Or a few. Whatever you're in the mood for."

"What do you think? Party at ours?" Val asked.

She had never been so grateful for good friends. "Best idea ever."

Charlie rarely got drunk—but she only got to turn thirty once. She wasn't used to the hangovers, though, and the headache she woke up with the next morning made her feel like her brain was about to explode. She kept hearing banging. Three bangs, then silence, then three more. It made her flinch each time she heard it. Was that normal for hangovers? The banging? She blinked a few times, as if that would silence the hammers in her head, but the banging continued. It took her a minute or two to realize that it was someone knocking on the door. "Ugh." She lifted her head. She must have fallen asleep on the sofa. She had a quick look around. No one else had fallen asleep in the living room. She vaguely remembered Liz and Nancy getting a taxi home at one point.

She dragged herself up and rubbed her eyes until she reached the front door. It was only right before she pulled it open that she realized that her make-up was still on from the night before, so she probably looked like a panda after smearing mascara round her eyes.

Maybe she was still sleeping, and all the knocking *was* a dream, because sure as hell when she opened the door, Erica was standing there.

"Hi."

"You're not here." That didn't make any sense. Charlie knew that—but how was Erica Frost at her front door? Then she suddenly remembered Oasis. The free drinks. Erica in the black dress.

"No? I think I am." Erica seemed amused by her comment. She held a cup out toward her. Charlie looked down at it, then back at Erica. "Relax. It's just coffee. I thought you might need it. Sounded like a late one."

"How would you know?" Charlie was aware that she sounded grumpy. She was sure that would be the case with or without a hangover.

"Shared walls, remember. After the party last night, I thought coffee would be a welcome surprise." Erica held the cup out even further.

It pained her to accept anything from Erica, but what she was offering was possibly a requirement at that point. "Thanks," she mumbled as she took it. She took a few sips, and she had to admit it tasted like liquid gold.

Erica clasped her hands together, as if she didn't know what to do with them now that she wasn't holding anything. "I get that you weren't expecting to see me last night. Honestly, I didn't know you would be there either—I was planning to try and see you today. It was really good to see you at Oasis though."

"Was it?" She laughed, not because it was funny, but because it seemed ridiculous to her. "I find that hard to believe."

Erica looked at the ground. "Look—"

Charlie interrupted her. "You look. You left, Erica. No, first you treated me like shit, *then* you went back to your secret girlfriend."

"I get how it looks, but if you would just let me explain," Erica said calmly.

Charlie wasn't as calm. "Do I look like I want to stand here and listen to your excuses?"

"Maybe not right now, no. But if we could meet later? Or another day even. Just sometime. I really want to talk to you. And then afterward, if you never want to see or hear from me again, I'll leave you alone."

"You already did. Without a word, remember?" Charlie folded her arms.

"I texted you and you didn't reply." Erica held her hands up before Charlie could argue. "I understand why you didn't text me back. I wouldn't have either. But I came by to say good-bye before I left, only you had already left for work. I asked Val to tell you that I would call. And I did call, but when I kept getting your voicemail, I assumed you didn't want to speak to me. Again, I get it—but I wouldn't say I left without a word."

Okay, so Erica had tried to say good-bye. Not that it made any difference. Erica's damage had already been inflicted before she left. Charlie wasn't surprised Val hadn't told her. Val knew that Charlie never wanted to hear from Erica again.

"Well, you assumed correctly. Val didn't pass on your message, but I wouldn't have wanted to speak to you anyway. I still don't, Erica."

"Please, Charlie. I know I don't deserve your time or your forgiveness after the way I behaved, but if I could at least try to explain things—"

Charlie heard a door open inside the apartment and she turned around. It was her bedroom door, and Hannah was walking out of it. What was Hannah doing in her room?

Hannah walked sheepishly toward them as if she had hoped to slip out unnoticed. "Sorry to disturb you guys. I have to get home. See you soon, Charlie. And happy birthday again." She slipped past them and gave Erica a shy wave too before she scurried down the hall.

"Bye, Hannah," Charlie said as she left. She almost laughed at Hannah doing the obvious walk of shame.

Erica was doing that thing that she did where her jaw was set. Charlie was getting to know Erica's different mannerisms, not that it mattered now. And then suddenly Erica's expression softened, and she looked rueful instead of annoyed. "I should never have expected... well, I don't really know what I expected. But of course you've moved on. As you should have." Erica attempted a smile, but it wasn't very convincing. "You deserve to be happy, Charlie. I'm sorry for just showing up here making a nuisance of myself. I'll go."

Charlie frowned in confusion, and then she realized Erica's mistake. Erica assumed that Hannah had stayed with Charlie. She knew that she should probably correct her impression, even though she didn't owe Erica any explanations.

Erica had already started walking toward Olly's apartment. Charlie stepped out into the hallway after her. "Hannah's with Val. That's why she was here."

Erica stopped walking and turned to face her. "With Val?" she repeated.

"Yeah. I don't want you to get your wires crossed or whatever. I think it's important to be up front and honest about whether I'm with someone or not." Jab fully intended.

Erica's face fell, which told Charlie that she understood the implication. She nodded slowly. "I see." She looked like she got lost in her thoughts for a few moments, then she took a step toward Charlie. "Are you? With anyone?"

"That's not really any of your business anymore."

"I know," Erica said. "But are you?"

"No," Charlie said after a few beats. "But whether I'm single or not doesn't change anything between us."

She thought Erica was going to argue with her again, then she seemed to accept it. "If you change your mind and decide to hear me out, you know where to find me."

"Just for reference, when are you going home this time?" She didn't want to play the game of trying to avoid Erica in the hallway forever.

"Now," Erica said as she pointed to Olly's door. "How do you think I knew about your party? The noise kept me awake for half of the night."

Charlie rolled her eyes. "You know what I mean. Home, home."

"This is home, home. I'm renting it from Olly. See you later, Charlie. I hope so, anyway." Erica gave her a little wave and walked inside, closing the door behind her, leaving Charlie standing with her mouth open.

When she managed to pull her jaw off the floor, she went back inside and headed toward her bedroom. She peeked in. Sure enough, Val was in there too. She'd guessed as much after Hannah had walked out of there. Charlie knocked on her own bedroom door, which seemed ridiculous.

"What?" came a mumbled reply.

"I'm coming in." Charlie opened the door fully. "Why were you and Hannah in my bedroom?"

Val groaned and pulled the covers over her head. "She went to bed first and she got the wrong room."

Charlie gulped down the rest of the coffee that Erica had given her like her life depended on it. It might have at that point. She set the empty cup down. When she heard Val's breathing deepen again, she clapped her hands to make some noise. "Wake up. I need to speak to you."

"You're evil." Val pushed the covers down slightly and rubbed her eyes. "You were already asleep on the sofa. And she was asleep, I didn't want to disturb her, so I slept in here too."

Charlie screwed her face up. "You better not have done anything in my bed."

"I just said we were sleeping, didn't I? God, it's too early to have to think of words," Val said.

Charlie sat on the edge of the bed. "Erica was just here."

Val sat up then. "Okay, I'm awake. What did she say? Are you okay?"

"She wants to talk to me. To *explain*, she says." Charlie glanced at Val. "Did she stop by? Before she left?"

Val blanched. "Yeah. She did. I'm sorry I didn't tell you. I didn't want her upsetting you more than she already had done."

Charlie wasn't angry. She probably would have done the same thing if she had been in Val's position. "It wouldn't have changed anything anyway."

"I was just trying to protect you," Val said. "I knew you'd call her if you decided that you wanted to talk to her."

"It's okay. I know." Charlie lay down beside Val. "She's next door."

"Staying at Olly's again?"

"Oh no, not staying. Apparently, she lives there now. Or so she told me about five minutes ago."

"Like lives there, lives there?" Val asked.

Charlie shrugged. "That's what she said."

"She's got some nerve." Val shifted onto her back. "Does she really expect to show up here, apologize, and what? You'll forget it and get back together with her?"

"Dunno. I'm guessing that's part of the explaining that she wants to do."

"Are you going to hear her out?" Val asked.

Charlie thought about it. "I can't pretend I'm not curious about what she has to say, but I don't think it's a good idea. I think I'm just going to try to avoid her. Who knows, maybe she'll disappear again."

"I'll support whatever you decide to do."

"You don't think I should talk to her, though?" Charlie asked. She was well aware that Val didn't have a very high opinion of Erica. Especially now.

"I don't want you to get hurt again," Val said.

"Avoid?" Charlie asked.

Val nodded. "Avoid."

❖

Charlie's feet were rhythmic in the way that they beat against the rocky path. She loved running. For her, there was no better way to clear her head. Some people gathered their thoughts when they ran, made life decisions, mental shopping lists—Charlie, on the other hand, switched her brain off. Focused on nothing else but her breathing, and her feet pounding on the path in front of her. After Erica's unanticipated return, she needed to hit her off switch for a while—so she ran. She felt a trickle of sweat run down her forehead—the weather had been warmer lately. She needed to break out her lighter running gear before her next run.

She had gone on her longer route that morning, opting for an extra twenty minutes that her leg muscles would probably hate her for later. It had seemed like a good idea at the time, but as the weather got hotter, she was glad when she reached the home stretch. There was a cool shower waiting for her before she got ready for work.

A familiar figure was walking along the path toward her. Erica. She was tempted to run right past her, but she couldn't do that. She slowed her run to a walk as she reached her. "Okay. Now you're literally following me."

"What do you mean? Am I not allowed to go out for a walk? Look around you—it's a public park. Are all these other people following you as well?" Erica looked down at Charlie's legs and her eyes roamed up her body. When she reached her eyes, she beamed.

She was so obvious. *Don't forget what she did.* "Those other people aren't looking at me like that."

Erica waved her hand. "Their loss entirely."

"I'm not going to be able to avoid you, am I?"

"Ah." Erica gave an exaggerated nod. "Is that what you've decided to do?"

"It might be the option that I'm leaning toward, yes. Difficult, though, considering you've informed me that we are neighbours. And now here you are on my morning run." She squinted. "Are you sure you aren't following me?"

"No." Erica cocked her head. "I'm maybe…increasing my odds of running into you. But that's all."

"Decreasing my odds of avoidance, then. You'll be showing up at my work next."

"You're kidding, right? I'd have to get past Hilary first. She would never let me near you. You're safe there."

Charlie had let herself forget how easily she was charmed by Erica. With a simple look, she could become putty in Erica's hands— she had to be careful not to let that happen again.

Refusing to be charmed, she asked, "What are you doing here, Erica?"

"In truth, I had an idea I wanted to run past you."

"I see. Let's hear it then," Charlie said.

"How about you put this whole steering clear of me thing on hold—come for dinner tonight? See Hera. She misses you. Gives me the cold shoulder half the time now. Unless she's hungry or sacrificing her morals for attention. Come and hear what I have to say. If you want to give me a wide berth forever more, I'll do everything in my power to make it as easy as possible for you to do so."

Charlie stared at her. "You're persistent."

Erica lifted a shoulder. "So were you, if I remember things right."

"Ha. Yeah—I guess that's true." If she didn't listen to what Erica had to say, she knew that she would spend the rest of her life wondering what she had wanted to tell her. It didn't help that she was still undeniably in love with her, no matter how hard she tried not to be. But despite all her better judgement, she was, and she hated that she was. Unfortunately, that also meant was that Erica still had the power to hurt her. Charlie knew this, but still, she found herself agreeing. "I'll come for dinner."

Erica's entire face lit up. "Great. Tonight? After you finish work?"

That soon? "Yeah. Okay. But I'm only coming because I want to see Hera."

"I wouldn't dare to think otherwise." Erica was still beaming. "I'll see you tonight, then. I'm going to go before you change your mind."

"See you tonight." They looked at each other for another second and then awkwardly went in opposite directions. When Charlie looked behind her, she caught Erica doing the same thing.

❖

If there was someone who Charlie really trusted to give her good guidance and advice, it was Liz.

"She's back for you. You do realize that, don't you?" Liz said as she clicked through her emails.

"Not necessarily. She has businesses here." Charlie started to get their patient forms ready for that day.

Liz stopped typing and faced her. "I know. But that's not why she's back. She's back for you, Charlie. Just, please, be careful."

"What do you mean?" Charlie asked.

"She broke your heart. As your friend, I don't want to see that ever happen to you again," Liz said.

"Do you not think I should go?" Doubts had started to creep in ever since she agreed to dinner.

"If it were me, I'd want to hear what she has to say." Liz put the question back on her. "What do you think? You must have agreed to it for a reason."

"Curiosity, I guess." Charlie knew it was a lot more than that. "It doesn't really matter why. I'm not going to get back together with her or anything. No matter what she says, it's too late now."

"Is it?" Liz said. "Think about it. You've been miserable without her. And now she's back, for good it would seem—and by all indications, she at least wants to explain things to you."

"Go back to the part where she broke my heart. Remember the evil mum? The secret girlfriend?"

"That's why you need to hear her side of the story. Life's complicated sometimes. Families can be extremely complicated."

"I'm going to listen to her side of the story. But complicated or not, it won't make any difference. What's done is done."

"One chance and she's out, then?" Liz said.

"Whose side are you on here?" Charlie asked.

"Yours. Always. But if you have a chance at love and happiness, I don't want you to throw all of that away to make a point. I'm only telling you to keep an open mind."

"Maybe." It wasn't opening her mind that Charlie was afraid of, it was opening her heart.

Chapter Twenty-six

"Mother asked me if I'd seen you today. That's progress." Zachary loitered beside Erica while she chopped vegetables for dinner. She slapped his hand away when he tried to pinch. "Not fair."

Erica laughed and passed him a piece of carrot. "She hasn't contacted me since I left. I don't know whether I want to hear from her or not. Especially not after all that stuff about Father."

"Yeah. I'm still processing all of that. Even for dear old Mum, that's—"

Erica interjected. "Cold? Ruthless? Unforgiveable?"

Zachary pointed at her. "All of those. And you wondered why I moved away?"

"I never wondered why. I just always wished that I had your gumption."

"And finally, you have. How did it go when you called Victoria?"

"You know those unbearable women that we grew up with, who always get their own way, and will walk over anyone and everyone to do so?"

Zachary gritted his teeth. "Yeah?"

"Imagine telling one of those women *no*."

"I don't want to."

Erica laughed. "She was not a bit pleased. Needless to say, I don't think I'll hear from Victoria Barrett again."

"Good riddance." He crunched a bite off his carrot stick. "What are you going to do now? Are you selling your place back home?"

"No. I love that cottage." She sliced into a pepper. "I have commitments back home. And Tess is there. I don't have a plan yet."

"That's not like you." Zachary pushed himself up on the counter, ignoring Erica's dirty looks about him doing so.

"I know, but I have to wait and see what happens with Charlie.

I'm not going to stay here if it makes her uncomfortable. I don't want to upset her life if she doesn't want me here." She looked at the clock. "Speaking of Charlie…you need to go before she gets here."

Zachary put the rest of the carrot in his mouth and grinned at her. "You sure you don't want me to stay? Make sure you don't fuck it up this time?"

"Oh, look who's the expert now that he's found the love of his life." Erica threw another carrot at him, but he caught it.

"You know it, Sis." He jumped down off the counter. "Speaking of *mon amour*, he said he'll be over during the week to collect some more of his stuff. I'm having to clear out drawers and all sorts for him—I have to dispose of clothes, Erica. Me."

"Nightmare."

"Hmm. Okay. I'm off. Good luck for wooing or winning back your woman—whatever you want to call it." He leaned in and kissed her cheek. "I'm going to go and sack Brandon now."

They had made the decision together that it was time for Brandon to go. He had become less and less visible in the club, hiding away in his office and dodging any issues that arose. "Good luck with that. I'll speak to Ash tomorrow about stepping up." She heard the door click shut behind him.

When she had dinner prepped, she spent a few minutes perfecting her appearance. Erica couldn't remember ever feeling as nervous. She had no control over any of this. All she could do was tell Charlie the truth—a truth where she was far from blameless or innocent—and hope that Charlie could find it in her heart to forgive her.

She had just finished feeding Hera when Charlie knocked. When she came in, Charlie immediately went over to Hera, who stopped eating to greet her. Erica had never seen Hera stop eating for anyone before. "Hey, girl. I missed you," Charlie whispered to her, as she crouched down and petted her. Erica felt a twinge of guilt watching them together. After a minute or two, Charlie stood up and Hera went back to resume her dinner.

"Did you come straight from work?" she asked.

Charlie nodded. "I didn't want Val to lecture me, so I thought I'd come right over. Hope that's okay?"

"Of course. You're always welcome here." Erica turned the cooker on and waited for it to heat up. It was hardly a surprise that Charlie's friends weren't her biggest fans. Val never had been. "I suppose you already got lectured by Liz about coming over?"

"Not really, no." Charlie was walking around the apartment, as if she didn't know whether she should sit down or not. "Liz said I should hear what you've got to say."

Erica thanked Liz in her head.

Charlie leaned against the sofa and regarded her. "Are you and that Victoria woman together?"

Erica had been stirring the dinner and stopped. "No."

"But you were?"

"It's complicated."

Charlie snorted a laugh. "I knew you were going to say that. Everything is complicated, apparently. Were you with her when we were…whatever we were?"

She had hoped to discuss everything over dinner, but she couldn't blame Charlie for demanding answers there and then. She just hoped that after Charlie got her answers, that she still stuck around long enough to eat the dinner she'd made. She turned the heat down a little. "I had been on one date with Victoria before I came to London. Not a date that I would call successful—and we were by no means an item. It was one of the reasons I was happy to get away for a while." She approached Charlie and indicated for her to sit. She sat on the sofa beside her, but she kept a respectful distance. "My mother was very pushy with regards to Victoria and me."

"Ah yes. Your mother."

Erica went to take Charlie's hand, but she moved it out of the way. She swallowed. "I am so deeply sorry for how I behaved toward you the night that my mother came here."

Charlie looked away, like she couldn't stand to look in Erica's direction. "That was bad."

"It was vile. I'm not going to make excuses, because nothing would excuse the way that I treated you," Erica said softly.

"Were you really so ashamed of me?" Charlie asked.

"No," Erica said straight away. "Never, Charlie. Anyone would be lucky to be with you."

"But you acted like you were."

"For my mother's benefit only—which was terrible of me." Erica sighed. "My relationship with Mother is a difficult one to explain, but I'll try." She didn't even know where to start. "She has always had impossible expectations of me. Even when I was a child, she seemed to put more pressure on me than she did on Zachary—as if she was holding me to a higher standard. One that I never seemed able to achieve no matter how hard I tried. It's like she's trying to mould me into some perfect version of herself—and I suppose because I've always been seeking her approval in a way, I let her. I've always done exactly what she wanted. Mother has certain ideals about who she wants me to settle down with and what she wants me to do with my life. And it was easy to go along with it for a long time. I thought that I wanted the things that my mother wanted for me, so I wasn't unhappy. Annoyed and frustrated sometimes maybe, but I never knew that I wanted my life to be different. Not until I came here." She looked into Charlie's eyes. "Not until I met you."

Charlie looked at her for a moment, then broke the eye contact. "I would have understood if you didn't want to tell your mum about us. Okay, I might not have been thrilled that you wanted to keep me a secret, but you treated me like I was a disease, Erica. You didn't even have the decency to pretend I was as much as a friend."

Erica closed her eyes. "I know. I panicked. I told you, there's no excuse. I'm disgusted at myself. I regretted it immediately. Whether you decide to forgive me or not, I'll always regret it."

"And what about Victoria? I'm assuming you picked things up with her when you got back. I saw a photograph of you together. Looked cosy. Did I read correctly that wedding bells were in the air as well?"

Erica couldn't hide her surprise that Charlie had seen that article. "Don't believe everything you read," she said. "I did attend a few events with Victoria. I suppose you could call them dates. I didn't feel like I had any choice—Mother was very insistent about the whole thing. To be honest, after I messed things up so badly with you, I intended to go back home and get on with my life as planned. And Victoria was a part of that, though I never had feelings for her. I tried to make it work with her, because I was a coward, and I was terrified to defy my mother." It sounded even more pathetic when she said it out loud.

"You looked happy in the picture." Charlie frowned.

"I'm well-rehearsed in keeping up appearances. My life's been full of it. Everything looks flawless and perfect on the surface, but it's all fake. A lot of it is anyway."

"And it was all fake with Victoria?"

"From the very beginning, yes," Erica assured her.

"She's very beautiful," Charlie said quietly.

Erica nodded. "I'm sure a lot of people think so, sure. But for me…well, she's not you."

Hera jumped onto Charlie's knee. Talk about choosing sides. She purred as Charlie stroked her before curling up into a contented ball.

"Hera didn't like her either," Erica said, trying to lighten the mood. "Wouldn't go near her. She's firmly a Charlie fan."

It seemed to work. Charlie laughed as she petted Hera. "She has excellent taste." She turned toward the kitchen. "Speaking of taste—I think I smell burning."

Erica leapt off the chair and hurried toward it. "Shit." She flapped a tea towel in an attempt to get rid of the smoke, and she pulled the pan off the heat. "I mustn't have turned it down enough." It was charred—to say the least. "I think I can safely say it's ready. Burnt Mediterranean stir-fry okay for you?"

At least Charlie seemed to see the funny side of it. "Yeah. Sounds good."

Erica dished out two plates. She tried to give herself the bits that were burnt the most so Charlie's wasn't totally inedible. She carried Charlie's to the sofa and handed it to her. "Here. So, you don't have to disturb Hera. She missed you." Erica took the seat beside her again. They ate in silence for a bit, but not a comfortable silence like they used to. It was silence laced with unresolved issues and a hundred unsaid sentences.

"You know, this isn't all that bad," Charlie said when she was almost done.

"Thank you for lying and eating it anyway."

Charlie laughed and Erica joined in.

It was probably one of the most important dinners of Erica's life and she had ruined it. Just her luck. She grabbed the plates and left them in the kitchen. There was more silence when she returned to the sofa. "What do we do now?"

"I don't know, Erica." Hera jumped off Charlie's knee and went to lie in her bed. Charlie fidgeted with her hands instead.

"I want to be with you." This could be Erica's only chance—she might as well get everything out in the open. All her thoughts, her wants, her feelings. "I know it was me who messed everything up, and I am so sorry. I will never do anything like that again, I swear to you. And I need to say it again, because I don't feel like I can ever tell you enough—I am sorry for how I treated you in front of my mother. Just so you're under no doubt about where things stand now—I've now told her everything about us. She knows I want to be with you, and I no longer care what she thinks. I am a million percent unashamed of you, Charlie. Please know that."

Charlie stared off into the room. "I was going to tell you that I loved you that night. I wanted to tell you that I loved you, and I wanted to make our relationship official." She blinked quickly.

Charlie loved her. Past tense? Present tense? Erica didn't know whether to ask that or not. She thought it was safer not to. She didn't want to push things or scare Charlie off. "That's what I wanted."

Charlie looked at her then, her eyes glimmering with tears. "Did you really, Erica? Just think about that for a second. You still left. If you were truly as sorry as you say, if you instantly regretted it—how could you have left straight afterward? I understand that you needed to go home at some point, but there's no way I could have left things like that."

"I tried to speak to you."

"You didn't try hard enough. I know now that you came to say good-bye—but still. You could have tried harder. You could have found me. You could have kept calling. Something."

"I was scared, Charlie. My life was supposed to be a certain way, then I came here, and I met you, and none of it was planned."

"And you think that I planned any of it?" Charlie took a breath. "I can't trust that you have feelings for me. It seemed so easy for you to walk away—I don't see how you could have. Not if you felt anything like what I felt. You've basically admitted that you *wanted* to forget about me so that you could get back to your safe, mapped out life."

"That's not what I really wanted, Charlie. I made a mistake. I could never forget about you." It was now or never. Erica had to put all her cards on the table. "I love you. I've spent every moment that we've been apart wishing that I was back here with you. I should never have left. I should have been braver—but I came back because I'm totally in love with you and I couldn't stand being apart from you for another day. That's how I feel about you." These weren't the circumstances or the way in which she had wanted to tell Charlie, but there was no way she could hold it back. Erica reached forward for Charlie's hands. She felt her own eyes start to well up. "Say we can be together. Say we can start again. Please."

Charlie took her hands and looked at them. She ran her thumbs over them gently. "I'm afraid it would only happen again, Erica. It might be a different issue next time, but something will come between us. Your world is so different from mine. Your mother has so much sway over you. You would be giving up everything. If I say yes, I'll be the one to blame for putting myself back in that position. I don't want to give you a chance to hurt me again."

"I won't." How could she make Charlie understand that she would *never* do anything to hurt her?

"You might. Things happen. There are complications, like you said. Nothing is guaranteed." Charlie took her hands away and rubbed her cheek. "This is exactly why I've always avoided relationships. So many of them don't work. It's not worth the risk."

"So that's it, you'll never take a chance again? Is that what you're saying? You're just going to spend the rest of your life alone so no one can ever hurt you?" Erica knew that Charlie was running scared now— and there was nothing quite like fear to make someone pull away. Erica didn't know how to stop it.

"It was working out okay for me before I met you." Charlie shrugged. After a few seconds she said, "I think I should go."

Erica felt the panic bubble up inside her. She had thought they were getting somewhere, but now Charlie was pulling away from her completely. "I really do love you, Charlie." She said it again because there was nothing truer in this world, and Charlie needed to know. "Will you at least think about it? About us?"

Charlie stood up. "I don't know, Erica. I feel like I'll always be waiting for it to happen again—for you to decide I'm not good enough for you, and then you'll run back to your life again. Maybe it's best for both of us to leave it here. We can still be friendly when we inevitably bump into one another in the hall, or at the club. But I don't want to string you along if I won't be able to get past what happened."

"How can I make you see that I don't want that life anymore? I'm here to stay, Charlie. I want you. I want what we had and so much more. Please, at least say you'll think about it. And if you decide that there's a chance that we could start over, meet me at the bar on Friday night." Where it all began.

It seemed wise to give Charlie some space. Let her digest everything that Erica had told her. Maybe Charlie just needed some time.

She could tell that Charlie was mulling it over. "Okay. I'll think about it." She walked toward the door, stopping to say bye to Hera.

All hope wasn't lost yet. "I'll see you out."

Charlie hovered for a few seconds. "Thank you for dinner. And for explaining."

"I don't think that dinner deserves thanks, but you're welcome. I should thank you for eating it," Erica said. "Friday, then?"

"We'll see. I'll think about everything you've said. That's as much as I can promise."

"That's probably more than I deserve. You surprised me. I was never expecting us to happen, and maybe I wasn't as ready as I wanted to be before. But I'm ready now."

Charlie gave her a sad smile. "You surprised me too. And I worked hard to be ready for you. And now I'm not sure I am anymore."

Charlie disappeared down the hall, and Erica fought the urge to follow her. To call her back. Anything. She knew that she had to give her space, even though that left her feeling powerless.

Hera was staring at her from her bed when she went back in.

"Oh, stop judging me. You could have at least put a good word in for me. You know you want her back too." She went over and scratched her ears.

If only she could erase the past few weeks and go back to that night and do things entirely differently—a do-over. But she couldn't.

The next move was up to Charlie.

"It's going to be a long week until Friday, Hera."

❖

Would you just chill? She's going to show.

Erica stared at the message. She wished that she had Tess's confidence. She hadn't seen or heard from Charlie since their conversation several nights ago, and the waiting was torture. At least she would finally get her answer tonight, one way or the other.

"You're here early," Ash said as she walked past. She put a hand to her head. "Oh, tonight's the night, isn't it?"

Erica nodded. "I really don't think she's going to show." She pocketed her phone.

Ash waved her off. "She'll show."

"I appreciate you saying that, but it doesn't make me feel any less nervous." She looked at Ash's outfit. "You're looking very professional, manager."

"Boss is here tonight. Thought I'd better dress to impress."

Ash had been over the moon when she and Zachary had offered her Brandon's job. Erica was equally pleased that Oasis was left in competent hands whenever they weren't around—though Erica was becoming a lot more hands on since her return. Together, Ash and she had already resolved several issues and were working together on plans for expanding the bar, making use of the empty rooms.

Ash leaned down to check the stock in one of the fridges, noting what was needed on a notepad.

"You know you can delegate that sort of work out now, right?" Erica said.

Ash looked up at her. "I know, but I still like to do the things I always did, as well as my new role."

"I know what you mean. I never thought I would say this, but whenever I'm here I just want to jump behind the bar and help you guys." Erica leaned her elbow against the bar. "Imagine, *me* choosing to bartend."

Ash gritted her teeth. "I can maybe schedule you for one of the quieter nights."

"Ha. I take it all back. The power has clearly gone to your head."

Ash laughed. "I'm kidding. You are bar owner slash bartender extraordinaire—better?"

Erica hummed. "I'm not sure if I believe you now."

"What are we not believing?"

"If it isn't our big, fancy head of security," Ash said. "Evening, Tom."

"She's mocking my bartending skills," Erica said.

Tom grunted a laugh. Then another. Then it turned into a real laugh.

Erica glared at them. "I could fire both of you and hire new people who are nice to me."

"Liars, then?" Ash said, making Tom laugh even harder.

"Nah," Tom said between laughs. "We already had one of them, and it didn't work out so well."

"I'm officially in a huff with the pair of you."

Ash stood up from the fridges and started stock checking the spirit bottles. "You can't be in a huff with us. You need the moral support tonight."

That was true. She did. The nerves hit her again with a bang. She put her hand to her stomach.

"What's tonight?" Tom asked.

"Friday," Erica said dryly.

Tom looked confused and Ash stepped in. "Decision day for Charlie. If she shows, it's game on. If she doesn't, it's over."

"Ash!"

"As if you weren't going to tell him."

It was true. Erica had become closer with Tom after she had wrongly suspected him of being a thief.

He gave an enthusiastic nod. "That's tonight, huh? She's gonna show, you know that, right?"

"Oh, God." Erica groaned. She leaned down and put her head on the bar. "No, Tom. I definitely do not know that."

"If I see her coming, will I give some sort of signal or something?"

"If she shows, you can do somersaults for all I care," Erica said. She lifted her head and took a breath.

Tom scratched his beard. "I'm not sure I could pull that off."

"I'd pay to see it," Ash said.

"I doubt you'll have any reason to somersault. She all but told me no the other day. I blew it and she didn't want to give me the chance to blow it again—which she thoroughly seems to believe that I will."

"What's tonight about, then?" Tom asked.

Erica sighed. "Tonight is about me not wanting to take no for an answer, therefore holding on to the tiniest shred of hope that she may have changed her mind about everything somehow."

She caught him grimacing at Ash. It was fine. She knew the chances of Charlie showing were slim.

It wasn't long before things kicked off, and there was no more time for bantering with the staff. Everyone had a job to do, and they were good at getting on with it. Ash ran a tight ship, just like Erica had known she would.

Erica's phone had been buzzing in her pocket all night. She pulled it out and saw that she had texts from Tess, Zachary, and Tom, and an unwanted notification from Victoria, which she opened first. It was a selfie of Victoria cosied up with Lydia, Audrey's ex, a perfect match for Victoria. Erica snorted a laugh. *So predictable.* Was she supposed to be jealous or something? How childish. "A match made in heaven," she muttered before deleting it.

She opened Tom's text. *No sign of her yet. I'm watchin.* She glanced up at him. He caught her eye and shrugged his shoulders before taking on his usual stern look again while he checked a couple of guy's ID's. She opened Tess's texts next.

Anything yet?

How about now?

Now?

Anything?

Erica, don't you even think about ignoring me until tomorrow. I want to know if she shows.

I didn't mean if. When. When she shows. She's deffo going to.

Erica sent a quick *not yet* back to Tess so she wouldn't explode. She added the fingers crossed and the sweating emojis. She should have known that Tess had been the main cause of all the buzzing.

Zachary next. *Good luck, Sis. She better come or else she'll have your little brother to answer to.*

She sent him back a love heart.

She almost wished she had more texts to answer as a distraction. She had spent most of the evening stealing glances toward the door. Luckily, Tom knew what was happening or he would be getting a complex by now.

Erica wasn't sure if she was just more aware of it than usual, but the DJ seemed to be playing a lot more break-up songs than usual. When she heard "We Are Never Ever Getting Back Together," she really started to take it as a sign.

"How are you holding up?" Ash said into her ear as she leaned against the counter beside her.

"It's not looking good," she called back. She scanned the floor again, checking every girl with blond hair, but none of them were Charlie. She checked every other hair colour too just in case she had randomly decided on a hair dye that week. Now she was really grasping at straws.

"Blond woman coming through the door right now," Ash said with a hopeful look on her face. She stood on her tiptoes to look.

Erica's heart sped up as she turned her head to look too. There were people in front of the person in question. She waited until they moved. "Not her," she said. She was pretty sure her whole body deflated.

Ash pouted. "Sorry, Erica. Hang in there. There's still time." She patted her arm, then went to serve the newcomers, none of whom were Charlie.

Eventually, the slow songs started to play. Couples took to the dance floor to dance, and kiss, and flirt. Erica hated them all. And she realized it was growing late.

She checked the door and saw another group of girls coming in. She craned her neck to look. Tom glanced at her and shook his head. Not her.

Erica finally got the message. Her heart sank, and she had to fight back the tears that threatened. She couldn't cry at work. Erica reached for her phone and fired off a text to Tess.

She didn't show.

She looked around the bar, but everyone including Ash was busy serving. So, she slipped away into the bathroom. The lights flickered on when she entered, so she knew she was the only one there. She allowed a couple of tears to escape before she wiped them away and fixed herself.

She looked around, and she realized it was a stupid place to go and collect herself. She was only reminded of the stolen moments she and Charlie had shared. Their first kiss. She tried to think back to their last—but the only memories she had of that night were of how badly she had messed up. And now she was paying the ultimate price.

"Erica, I know I dissed your bar skills earlier, but any chance of a hand? We're under pressure here," Ash said to her when she returned.

She had been planning to call it a night—go home, sulk, and lick her wounds—but she couldn't leave the team to struggle. "Sure. Where do you need me?"

Ash pointed to the far end of the bar. "Some folks waiting down there. Thanks, Erica."

Erica walked in the direction Ash had pointed.

"Hey," a loud voice shouted, stopping her in her tracks.

Maybe her mind was playing tricks on her, or maybe it was wishful thinking, but Erica was sure that she knew the voice. She turned around slowly.

"Any chance of getting served around here?" Charlie was sitting at the bar, chin in hand, smiling at her.

Erica blinked a few times. "Hi." She glanced back toward Ash, who was leaning against the bar grinning at her. She gave her a thumbs up. *Under pressure, my ass.* She looked back at Charlie. She let out a relieved breath. "You're here," she said, stating the obvious. It hadn't been obvious to her. In fact, she couldn't quite believe it was happening. "I didn't think you were going to show."

"She was always going to show," Tom piped in as he appeared at the bar beside Charlie. He reached over and grabbed a water bottle, giving Erica a wink as he did. The water had clearly only been an excuse to come over. "She's a good one. You made the right choice," he said to Charlie before he walked away again.

Charlie laughed at Tom. Then she held out her hand to Erica. "I'm Charlie."

Erica glanced down at it and gave Charlie a puzzled look.

Charlie grinned at her. "Starting over, right?"

Erica felt the smile spread across her face when she caught on to what they were doing. She took Charlie's hand in hers, but she didn't let go. "Shall I call you Charlotte?"

"Not if you expect me to answer."

Erica laughed. "I prefer Charlie anyway. Suits you better."

"This is the part where you tell me your name. It is the reason I'm here, after all," Charlie said with a glint in her eye.

"That's very presumptuous of you." Erica leaned on the bar to get closer to Charlie. "Tell me, are you always so cocky?"

"Yes."

"I see. And why should I tell you my name?" Erica asked. "I don't often give my name out to random girls in bars. Even girls as attractive as you."

"Oh, so you think I'm attractive?"

"I think you're extremely attractive." Erica roamed her eyes over Charlie's body, just to prove her point. She smiled when her gaze met Charlie's. "That's beside the point."

"Interesting." Charlie tapped her chin. "Now you have to give me your name."

"Do I now?"

"I can't very well ask you out if I don't know your name, can I? That would just be weird."

Erica raised an eyebrow. "Well, that's true. In that case, I'm Erica. Now, hurry up and ask. In fact, I'll get straight to the answer—yes."

Charlie laughed, and it was the most beautiful thing that Erica had ever seen. When the laughter faded, they smiled at each other.

Erica looked down at their hands clasped together. "You know I'll never hurt you again, don't you?"

"I came, didn't I?" Charlie said.

"We can start over?" Erica asked.

Charlie made a show of thinking about it. "I was thinking about this whole starting over thing. Does it mean that we can't fast forward to the good parts?"

Erica had a better idea. "Maybe, instead of starting over…we can pick up where we left off?"

"In that case, can we get out of here? Because, if I'm remembering our last date correctly, there were a few things that you wanted to show me."

Erica hadn't forgotten. "Let's go."

When Erica rounded the bar to meet her, Charlie put her arms around her. "I have one more thing to say. Just one final response to our conversation the other day, and I need to get it out of the way right now."

Erica wrapped her arms around Charlie's waist. "Anything."

"I love you too."

As her heart exploded, Erica leaned down and kissed Charlie softly, slowly, not caring where they were or who was watching them. She was vaguely aware of whistling and cheering in the background— likely Ash and Tom—but she ignored all of it and lost herself in the kiss. In Charlie. *Her* Charlie.

When they pulled apart, Erica gazed right into Charlie's eyes and saw all of her own feelings being mirrored right back at her. There was no better feeling in the world.

"I thought you said you didn't pick up girls in bars," Charlie said.

Erica smiled at her. "I changed my mind." She kissed her again. "I hear that's where the best love stories begin."

EPILOGUE

"Charlie," Erica called out. "Are you nearly ready?"

Charlie walked out of their bedroom putting in her earrings. "I had to make sure I had everything packed. Do we really have to leave right after the wedding?" She stopped. "What are you staring at?"

"You." Erica walked forward. "Maybe we could spare a little bit of time *before* the wedding." She put her arms around Charlie and pulled her close.

Charlie gave her a quick kiss. "Nice try. But, as your brother's best man, you have to be there on time. And knowing Zachary, he's probably having a complete meltdown as we speak."

Erica held up her phone. "I've had seventeen calls already."

"It's not even nine a.m. yet," Charlie said with a surprised look on her face.

"It's Zachary. Like you said—meltdown." She gave an appreciative hum as she appraised Charlie's outfit. "You look amazing. What were you asking me again? I'm distracted."

"My eyes are here." Charlie pointed at them. "And I was asking if we have to leave straight away once the wedding is over?"

"Your eyes are amazing too." Erica grinned. "And yeah, pretty much. Just back here to collect our stuff and Hera. It's going to take a few hours to get there and he's already a day old. I don't want to miss any more days."

"Okay. Make sure you remember to pack the baby presents. And Tess's present too. We can't forget about mum," Charlie said. "Have they picked a name yet?"

Erica shook her head. "You should know what Tess is like by now—unless it's a wall colour or a rug, she's painfully indecisive."

Charlie laughed. "Maybe they will have by the time we get

there—I have to say, I'm looking forward to seeing our view again. As well as the little one, of course."

Since Erica had got Charlie back, they hadn't spent a lot of time apart. Charlie had unofficially moved in with her right away, refusing to sleep in her own bed any night, and Erica refusing to let her. They had spent enough time apart. They made it official, shortly after that. The same went for Erica's cottage—any time Erica had gone home, Charlie had gone with her, and they had made that their home too.

"Are you okay about seeing your mum?" Charlie asked her.

Erica had only seen her mother twice since their fall-out. Neither time had been warm and fuzzy, not that it ever was with them. They had spoken a few civil words to each other, which was more than Erica had expected. There was still bad feeling on both sides.

"Yeah. It's a public event with many watchful eyes. Mother will be on her best behaviour. She might even be happy—dare I say it? She always did say she looked forward to Zachary settling down." She hesitated. "Are you okay about seeing her? I know she's not exactly pleasant to you."

Charlie lifted a shoulder. "I'm fine. I'm working on it—using my charm to wear her down slowly. We'll get there. I did notice a slight facial movement the last time, when you told her I had started my training to become a vet. Maybe I'll be good enough for you once I qualify."

"Ah, yes. The way to Mother's heart. Prestige." They laughed. "Speaking of work…are Liz and Nancy meeting us there?"

"Yeah. Val and Hannah too." Erica had got to know Charlie's friends better after they had got back together, and Charlie in turn had grown closer to Zachary and Olly. They all hung out together as often as they could. Charlie's friends had remained wary of Erica for a while, but they came around when they realized how much Erica cared about Charlie. Even Val. "Liz is driving them—she offered to pick us up too, but I told her that you would probably need to get there hours before the ceremony to keep Zachary calm. Well, maybe not calm. Unhysterical is maybe a more realistic goal," Charlie said.

"I don't know why you're putting this all on me. You'll be helping," Erica said. She checked through her handbag to make sure she had everything. "Liz didn't mind giving you the time off for us to go away after the wedding?"

Charlie shook her head. "But she did say that I'll suffer for it afterward, because she'll be giving me intense prep for my exams."

Erica chuckled. Liz was trying to mould Charlie into a mini-me. They would continue working side by side, both during and after Charlie's studies. Erica knew that was one of the reasons Charlie had been holding back on her training—she didn't want to leave Little Paws—but there was no way Liz would let her go. She enjoyed working with Charlie as much as Charlie enjoyed working with her.

"I take it you got everything organized at Oasis for leaving?" Charlie asked her.

"Ash and Tom are prepared, instructed, and delighted to see the back of me for a few days." Erica had been spending a lot of time at work, and she was just as happy to get a break. Expansions were going well, and they were close to opening their new jazz bar—Rick's. The difference they had made in the old, dusty function rooms was amazing. Oasis also held a monthly charity night now, with all the takings going to charities of Erica's own choosing—no board or family approval required.

Charlie checked her phone. "Okay, now we really, *really* have to go. Olly says that Zachary has texted him nineteen times to make sure he's going to show up." She showed Erica.

Erica rolled her eyes. "He's such a bridezilla." She rushed over and put food out for Hera, which she didn't touch. "Have you been feeding her treats again?"

"She looks at me with big, hungry eyes. I can't resist. Besides, she deserves them." As if she could understand their conversation, Hera rubbed herself round Charlie's ankles, purring away.

"And what if I look at you with big, hungry eyes?" Erica asked.

Charlie covered her own eyes with her hand. "No. Wedding. Now. Let's go."

Erica laughed. "Fine. But you better make it up to me later."

"Don't I always? As if that'll be a chore…Do you know how difficult I'm finding it to resist you right now? Look at you." Charlie fanned herself with her hand.

"If that's true…one kiss for the road?"

Charlie leaned up and pressed her lips against Erica's.

Erica cheated slightly by deepening the kiss, sliding her tongue against Charlie's. Judging from Charlie's whimper, she didn't mind too much. She knew she could convince Charlie to be late if she really put her mind to it—but as much as it pained her, she behaved. "I love you," she said when Charlie eventually pulled away. "Have I told you that yet today?"

Charlie smiled. "You have. Please tell me lots." She checked her watch. "But later. Right now—get your sexy, fancy butt out the door."

"I love it when you're all bossy." Erica helped Charlie on with her coat before putting her own on. "Let's go get my brother married off."

Charlie leaned up and kissed her again. A bonus kiss that Erica hadn't expected.

"What was that for?"

"That one was because I love you too."

About the Author

Claire Forsythe lives just outside Belfast in Northern Ireland with her partner, Mary, and their pets, Charlie the dog, Midnight the cat, and Jazz the goldfish. Claire owns a coffee shop, which keeps her both busy and well-topped-up on caffeine—flat whites, specifically.

Apart from her love of coffee, Claire enjoys cooking and experimenting with new recipes in the kitchen, sipping red wine, traveling and exploring new places, reading a variety of novels—from romance to crime, playing poker even though she's a terrible bluffer, and binge-watching box sets. She's a big football fan and loves cheering on her beloved Liverpool FC. She loves to spend as much time as she can with her family and friends, who mean the world to her. She and her partner get beaten by two of their best friends in doubles badminton weekly, though they turn up every week in the hope that their luck will change. It hasn't yet…

Claire has loved words and books ever since she was little, and it has always been her ambition to write. After finding herself with some unexpected free time on her hands in lockdown during the pandemic, she decided to follow her dream and start writing. Now that she's started, she never wants to stop.

Books Available From Bold Strokes Books

Hands of the Morri by Heather K O'Malley. Discovering she is a Lost Sister and growing acquainted with her new body, Asche learns how to be a warrior and commune with the Goddess the Hands serve, the Morri. (978-1-63679-465-5)

I Know About You by Erin Kaste. With her stalker inching closer to the truth, Cary Smith is forced to face the past she's tried desperately to forget. (978-1-63679-513-3)

Mate of Her Own by Elena Abbott. When Heather McKenna finally confronts the family who cursed her, her werewolf is shocked to discover her one true mate, and that's only the beginning. (978-1-63679-481-5)

Pumpkin Spice by Tagan Shepard. For Nicki, new love is making this pumpkin spice season sweeter than expected. (978-1-63679-388-7)

Sweat Equity by Aurora Rey. When cheesemaker Sy Travino takes a job in rural Vermont and hires contractor Maddie Barrow to rehab a house she buys sight unseen, they both wind up with a lot more than they bargained for. (978-1-63679-487-7)

Taking the Plunge by Amanda Radley. When Regina Avery meets model Grace Holland—the most beautiful woman she's ever seen— she doesn't have a clue how to flirt, date, or hold on to a relationship. But Regina must take the plunge with Grace and hope she manages to swim. (978-1-63679-400-6)

We Met in a Bar by Claire Forsythe. Wealthy nightclub owner Erica turns undercover bartender on a mission to catch a thief where she meets no-strings, no-commitments Charlie, who couldn't be further from Erica's type. Right? (978-1-63679-521-8)

Western Blue by Suzie Clarke. Step back in time to this historic western filled with heroism, loyalty, friendship, and love. The odds are against this unlikely group—but never underestimate women who have nothing to lose. (978-1-63679-095-4)

Windswept by Patricia Evans. The windswept shores of the Scottish Highlands weave magic for two people convinced they'd never fall in love again. (978-1-63679-382-5)

A Calculated Risk by Cari Hunter. Detective Jo Shaw doesn't need complications, but the stabbing of a young woman brings plenty of those, and Jo will have to risk everything if she's going to make it through the case alive. (978-1-63679-477-8)

An Independent Woman by Kit Meredith. Alex and Rebecca's attraction won't stop smoldering, despite their reluctance to act on it and incompatible poly relationship styles. (978-1-63679-553-9)

Cherish by Kris Bryant. Josie and Olivia cherish the time spent together, but when the summer ends and their temporary romance melts into the real deal, reality gets complicated. (978-1-63679-567-6)

Cold Case Heat by Mary P. Burns. Sydney Hansen receives a threat in a very cold murder case that sends her to the police for help, where she finds more than justice with Detective Gale Sterling. (978-1-63679-374-0)

Proximity by Jordan Meadows. Joan really likes Ellie, but being alone with her could turn deadly unless she can keep her dangerous powers under control. (978-1-63679-476-1)

Sweet Spot by Kimberly Cooper Griffin. Pro surfer Shia Turning will have to take a chance if she wants to find the sweet spot. (978-1-63679-418-1)

The Haunting of Oak Springs by Crin Claxton. Ghosts and the past haunt the supernatural detective in a race to save the lesbians of Oak Springs farm. (978-1-63679-432-7)

Transitory by J.M. Redmann. The cops blow it off as a customer surprised by what was under the dress, but PI Micky Knight knows they're wrong—she either makes it her case or lets a murderer go free to kill again. (978-1-63679-251-4)

Unexpectedly Yours by Toni Logan. A private resort on a tropical island, a feisty old chief, and a kleptomaniac pet pig bring Suzanne and Allie together for unexpected love. (978-1-63679-160-9)

Crush by Ana Hartnett Reichardt. Josie Sanchez worked for years for the opportunity to create her own wine label, and nothing will stand in her way. Not even Mac, the owner's annoyingly beautiful niece Josie's forced to hire as her harvest intern. (978-1-63679-330-6)

Decadence by Ronica Black, Renee Roman & Piper Jordan. You are cordially invited to Decadence, Las Vegas's most talked about invitation-only Masquerade Ball. Come for the entertainment and stay for the erotic indulgence. We guarantee it'll be a party that lives up to its name. (978-1-63679-361-0)

Gimmicks and Glamour by Lauren Melissa Ellzey. Ashly has learned to hide her Sight, but as she speeds toward high school graduation she must protect the classmates she claims to hate from an evil that no one else sees. (978-1-63679-401-3)

Heart of Stone by Sam Ledel. Princess Keeva Glantor meets Maeve, a gorgon forced to live alone thanks to a decades-old lie, and together the two women battle forces they formerly thought to be good in the hopes of leading lives they can finally call their own. (978-1-63679-407-5)

Peaches and Cream by Georgia Beers. Adley Purcell is living her dreams owning Get the Scoop ice cream shop until national dessert chain Sweet Heaven opens less than two blocks away and Adley has to compete with the far too heavenly Sabrina James. (978-1-63679-412-9)

The Only Fish in the Sea by Angie Williams. Will love overcome years of bitter rivalry for the daughters of two crab fishing families in this queer modern-day spin on Romeo and Juliet? (978-1-63679-444-0)

Wildflower by Cathleen Collins. When a plane crash leaves eleven-year-old Lily Andrews stranded in the vast wilderness of Arkansas, will she be able to overcome the odds and make it back to civilization and the one person who holds the key to her future? (978-1-63679-621-5)

Witch Finder by Sheri Lewis Wohl. Tasmin, the Keeper of the Book of Darkness, is in terrible danger, and as a Witch Finder, Morrigan must protect her and the secrets she guards even if it costs Morrigan her life. (978-1-63679-335-1)

Here For You by D. Jackson Leigh. A horse trainer must make a difficult business decision that could save her father's ranch from foreclosure but destroy her chance to win the heart of a feisty barrel racer vying for a spot in the National Rodeo Finals. (978-1-63679-299-6)

Digging for Heaven by Jenna Jarvis. Litz lives for dragons. Kella lives to kill them. The last thing they expect is to find each other attractive. (978-1-63679-453-2)

Forever's Promise by Missouri Vaun. Wesley Holden migrated west disguised as a man for the hope of a better life and with no designs to take a wife, but Charlotte Rose has other ideas. (978-1-63679-221-7)

I Do, I Don't by Joy Argento. Creator of the romance algorithm, Nicole Hart doesn't expect to be starring in her own reality TV dating show, and falling for the show's executive producer Annie Jackson could ruin everything. (978-1-63679-420-4)

It's All in the Details by Dena Blake. Makeup artist Lane Donnelly and wedding planner Helen Trent can't stand each other, but they must set aside their differences to ensure Darcy gets the wedding of her dreams, and make a few of their own dreams come true. (978-1-63679-430-3)

Marigold by Melissa Brayden. Marigold Lavender vows to take down Alexis Wakefield, the harsh food critic who blasts her younger sister's restaurant. If only she wasn't as sexy as she is mean. (978-1-63679-436-5)

A Second Chance at Life by Genevieve McCluer. Vampires Dinah and Rachel reconnect, but a string of vampire killings begin and evidence seems to be pointing at Dinah. They must prove her innocence while finding out if the two of them are still compatible after all these years. (978-1-63679-459-4)